THE RISING GUARDIAN

ANTONIUS & THE CURSE OF SIRIUS

*To Dr. Grafe.
from Above*

AL MAIOS

GOLDLINE AND JACOBS PUBLISHING

GOLDLINE AND JACOBS PUBLISHING

Published in the United States
by Goldline and Jacobs Publishing
10 Franklin Road
P. O. Box 714, Glassboro,
New Jersey, 08028, USA
www.goldlineandjacobs.com

PUBLISHER'S NOTE
This is a work of fiction. Names, characters, places, and incidents either are products
of the author's imagination or are used fictitiously, and any resemblance to actual
persons. Living or dead, events, and locales is entirely coincidental.

Library of Congress Control Number: 2017934400

Printed in the United States of America
On acid-free paper

ISBN: 978-1-938598-29-6

Cover Image: Patrick Bredland

Chapter 1
Escape from Philonia

It was quiet and dark. This was nothing out of the ordinary for the prison cell that was used to hold one whom his accusers had deemed ruthless and vengeful. The cold winter wind blew in through the cell window. This man whom had been deemed ruthless and vengeful had been chained to the wall. The only thing that had kept him company was the silence of the cell. The silence had been his only companion up until that moment. He heard the door of his cell creak open. Someone had come in but he did not care who. He refused to recognize the stranger's presence. The stranger held a small candle that only revealed from his torso and downwards. The stranger approached him and came very close to the prisoner's face.

"Open your eyes."

The prisoner kept still not saying a word or moving.

"Talk to me brother, I know you're still alive." The stranger said.

"Why would you do this to me?" the prisoner asked.

"You were in my way brother. I could not have my plans fail," the stranger replied.

The prisoner felt something wrong with his brother. He felt as if he did not know the person who was speaking to him. He had never seen this side of his brother. He knew his brother had a temper but he never thought him to be vindictive or murderous.

The man with all his might struck the prisoner in the stomach. The prisoner spewed out blood that spilled over his brothers' garment.

"Look brother," the stranger said, "it's nothing personal. You already know how it works. I mean, I'm not the first in our family to overthrow his superior."

"I did not overthrow him, he left. Were you to blind to see it?"

"Blind you say." The stranger laughed.

"You are not worthy of that crown," the prisoner said.

The stranger smiled and walked closer to the prisoner and whispered in his ear. "You see it one way, the people see it another. You abandoned them, you betrayed them and I am the only one left they can trust. If there is anyone left who is worthy, it is me," the stranger said, then left the cell and thereafter transformed itself into a woman.

A few hours passed by. The cell door creaked open and a dim light was seen. The prisoner kept still again. As the light approached closer to him he acted as if he were dead. He peaked to see who it was and saw that the light was right in front of him. The light ascended to the individual's face. It was the prison guard. The prisoner still acted as if he were dead.

"I know you're still alive Antonius," the guard said.

Antonius smiled slightly.

"What do you want?" Antonius asked.

"I know you're innocent," the guard responded.

Antonius looked up at the guard.

"Do not test me," Antonius said.

"I have nothing to gain from this if I lie to you."

"Then why are you helping me?"

"Many years I have seen innocent men sentenced to death. I have been forced by my superiors to remain silent of all those executions. My conscience still speaks and by setting you free, I may relieve some of the weight of guilt on my heart."

"My worth is no more than those men you betrayed by keeping silent."

"But you are the true king."

"King?" Antonius said with distress in his voice. "Is anyone even still loyal to me after what my brother has made me out to be to the people?"

The guard unlocked Antonius's chains.

"I am" he said "My king, head south to the shores near Penthis. You must leave the kingdom, we need you alive."

"Are you going to come with me?"

"No, I will serve whatever punishment your brother has in store for me. Besides, I am old, my years are spent, of what use would I be to you."

The guard helped Antonius to his feet. Antonius was still a bit dazed so he leaned back against the wall. The guard gave Antonius his sword and removed his armor and put it on him.

The guard gave him the keys to the cells of the other prisoners. He told him to free them.

"You'll need all the help you can get. Some of these men are fierce fighters and very loyal to whomever they follow. Lead them well."

He collected the keys from the guard and went to the cells and let the prisoners free. Antonius gathered the men. They were a hundred and fifty in all. They climbed to a higher level in the dungeon, fought off and knocked out all the other guards. They locked them in the cells afterwards.

Antonius and the group left the prison camp, and headed south.

They fled towards a small city called Belvain. They came upon the city to find it in ruins. The men were puzzled as to how this could have happened. Antonius remembered that he had been told by one of his advisors of a mysterious calamity befalling one of the southern cities. The name of the city escaped him but he remembered the devastation that his advisor had described to him and it was eerily similar to the city they were walking through.

He gathered the men together at the entrance of the ruins of the hall of the city council. He climbed up the broken steps, looked down and picked up a sword that laid his feet. He pointed it to the sky and addressed them.

"It is said that the strength of a man is not measured in the weapons he carries but in his will. His will to fight, his will to overcome all obstacles against him. Today I ask you men, how willing are you to live? Many of you know my face and are aware of my statutes. I make no promises that I cannot fulfill. Join me and I promise you men a better life. If you help me, and we overcome, a great reward shall befall all of you. I promise you'll never be prisoners in this land again!"

The men went into uproar of excitement and many of their hearts were more eager to aid his cause. All but one man named Julian, the son of a war veteran. His mind was not on what Antonius said but on the city around them. The place was very familiar to him. His birthplace, streets he knew, houses he had been too, all devastated, discarded, and forgotten.

"For now, let us focus on surviving through the journey." Antonius continued "The woods around this city bear good fruits. Fifty of you will be involved in setting up a resting place for the rest of us; another fifty will set out to gather what we shall eat when night time falls upon us. The rest of you will keep guard to see if anyone is following us."

They divided themselves and did as he commanded. But a timid man from among them approached him and asked.

"Where exactly are we heading to?"

"You'll know in the morning, for now do what I say so we can survive long enough to get there."

The night came upon them and they regrouped. They sat around the fire they made and told stories. One among them told this.

"I heard of a story from my grandfather. He told of a kingdom much greater than any of the seven kingdoms that exist now. He told me that about five hundred years ago appeared a creature that blended among men. No one knew what it was or where it came from. Then it disappeared without a trace. He told me that a small tribal people known as the Erolichians were the last of its victims."

"A creature you say? What did this creature do?" someone asked in a skeptical tone.

"They say it sang, it sang till men went mad." The story-teller replied.

"Such nonsense, all just legends."

"No it's true. They also said it appeared because of it was time for a man to be chosen and transcend to become a Guardian. It was around the time the eleventh Guardian was chosen."

"Guardians." The man scoffed. "Men becoming Guardians? Your tales are even more absurd."

"My king you tell them, you know more than I."

Antonius stared into the fire for a while. He had a little twig in his hand. He fiddled with it for a little while, and then he took a deep breath, snapped the twig, and then began,

"Guardians and men are much alike." He said but his tone doubted his words. "I remember a story my father told me when I was much younger. He told me that over three millennia's ago the world was drenched in blood spilled by the sons of the fallen Guardians. A war humanity was about to lose. It was at this time a man was chosen to take the place of a fallen Guardian. It is said that the man chosen became the first Guardian...But that was a long time ago."

Some of the men had heard of the story Antonius told. But as the years past, stories such as those became legend and legend slowly became myth.

Julian thought for a moment. Then he said.

"My father told me that the Great King, the father of the pure Guardians has been choosing from among men, people to take the place of his fallen sons, is this true?"

"Only those who can read the prophecies know."

"Not many are capable of understanding..." Julian was still speaking but was interrupted by Antonius.

"Be quiet...I hear...horses."

Antonius rose up and looked north. He saw torches in the distance approaching towards where they were camping. He immediately threw sand over the fire they made and ordered all the men to divide themselves. They each headed to the ruins of the surrounding houses, hid and waited in the shadows.

The men approaching from the north entered the ruins of the city thinking the ex-convicts had already passed through the terrain. The men from the north got into the dense part of the ruins; they were twenty one in all. They stopped. The silence around them chilled their spines. The full moon shone bright in the sky but all the ex-convicts were well hidden. Then Antonius stepped out from the shadows and stood in front of the twenty one men. The leader among them got down from his horse and drew his sword. He kept keen eyes on the man who had just stepped out of the shadows. He started walking cautiously to the figure and when he saw that it was Antonius, he burst out in laughter and so did the other men once they realized who it was.

"Antonius is that you? Well then, look men, the men he escaped with have abandoned him. Now he has come out thinking he can contend against us." The man laughed again. "You dog, ever since you got kicked out of the palace you have become worthless. Your crime will always haunt you. You will never escape the guilt. So give yourself up to us and stop this foolish attempt to escape."

Antonius didn't respond.

"Why don't you respond, are you deaf now; did the king hit you so hard that he knocked the sense out of you?"

Antonius showed no emotion but stepped back into the shadows. The leader of the twenty ran into the shadows after Antonius. The others surprised by this waited. Then, there was a scream, the remaining twenty all got down from their horses, drew out their swords but before they could head out to rescue their leader, they were surrounded by all the ex-convicts. They were outnumbered.

Before the leader could attack Antonius, Antonius anticipated his movement and twisted his arm, almost dislocating it. He released his sword and let out a loud scream. Antonius punched him across the face. The punch knocked him out. Antonius lifted his body and took him outside. He saw that the prisoners that came with him had made sure the others who came after them from the north were kept in place. They took the ropes the men from the north had and used it to tie them in three groups of seven. Antonius stood in front of the leader of the twenty one, who was now regaining consciousness.

"Glad to see you're finally awake." he said.

"I swear you will pay for treating us this way."

"You threaten me when you are the one at my mercy." Antonius said

"I don't care, kill me now, slaughter me, what do I care? If you want, slit my throat!"

"That would be too easy."

"What?"

"Fire." Antonius said with a straight face. "Nothing is purer than fire. It shall cleanse this world of you. Men…"

"No please don't, I'll tell you anything you want to know."

"Now you beg for your life."

"I'm not a pitiful man. Promise to let us live, then I'll tell you everything I know."

"I will not make a promise I cannot deliver, but I promise you, none of these men will harm you. Now tell me, my brother, the one whom you call king, has instituted my arrest and retrieval back to the dungeon hasn't he, what does he plan to do to me?"

"We do not know, he only instructed us to capture you."

"That's it? He just wanted to retrieve me. There's more to this isn't there?"

"He says he is going to purify the kingdom," the leader said.

"Purify? How so?"

"I don't know."

"Tell me what else you have seen."

"It is not what has been seen but what has been heard."

Antonius folded his arms.

"Go on." He said.

"We have heard songs, songs that were mystifying."

"Songs?"

"Yes songs, they are heard every night by everyone in the city."

"The songs that you hear, what effect do they have on the people." Antonius had seen what effect the songs had on the people but he wanted to hear it from the leader of the twenty.

"The songs have a power over the people, it is frightening. Whenever the voice is heard, they begin dance insanely. Drunkenness and perversion fill the streets. It breaks my heart thinking about such things."

"But you and your men came from the city to capture us. So you to must have heard the songs and had your share in such pleasures as well."

"No, wait."

"Do you think that I'm gullible to your lies and tricks? If you don't stop playing games with me I promise you none of you will leave here alive."

"Please trust us."

"Trust you? You would have killed me the first chance you had. Now you expect me to turn a blind eye to that."

Antonius was growing impatient with the foolish antiques of the men who had come to take him. One from among those who he had fled the prison with came forth and said,

"My king, I have with me a letter sent to me by my brother. He lived in one of the cities that were destroyed by the mysterious plague. I don't think he still lives but here is the letter."

Antonius took the letter from him, and read it out loud to the group.

Dear Brother Phillip.

The days are growing darker, the nights are becoming longer. It would seem that these changes would be normal if we were in the winter months but summer has never been so grim. The smell of death lingers and has replaced the aroma of roses. The city broke into a riot yesterday and it has not died down. I feel it has even gotten worse. In haste I write this letter to you because I know this will be my last night. I thank you for being good to me. Beware brother; beware of the melodies of the night. Sang by voices that seem as that of the Guardians but breathes the fire from the bowels of Hades. If you hear any mysterious songs in the city that you are, leave immediately because the melodies imprisons men of weak hearts and betrays the daughters of the land. My wife has left the city with my children. They will be staying with you and your wife, take good care of them, when you get out of prison.

Thank you, Love Matthew.

"When did you receive this letter?" Antonius asked.

"Over five months ago."

"Then I guess my suspicions might have been right but it's worse than I thought. Men we must leave this place now."

"Antonius," the leader bellowed as he watched Antonius mount his horse about to leave. "Are you going to leave us bound here in the middle of nowhere?"

"Would you prefer I kill you now?" Antonius said and looked away from them. "Men let's leave this place."

The men did as he commanded and they left the search party bound in the middle of the city. Antonius mounted himself on the horse that belonged to the leader of the search party, and the rest of the horses were mounted by some of the ex-convicts. They left with great speed. Even those who were on foot did not lag behind.

At once the men who had come in search of Antonius attempted one last plea to him. But, it was too late. He and his men had vanished in the darkness of the night.

A few moments later a dark mist began to circulate around the twenty one men. Suddenly they began to hear singing. "No, not here." said one of them. The rest began to panic but then a voice from the mist said, "Be quiet and listen."

An unseen entity cut the ropes that bound them.

"Do not let him escape. Go after him, I give you my strength, go now and do not disappoint me."

The men with great fervor ran after Antonius and the ex-convicts.

Chapter 2
Battle at Sea. Old Bonds and Visions

Morning arrived as Antonius and the ex-convicts got to the shores near Penthis. There was a still morning breeze that calmed the scene. At the far end of the shore there were ships. There, sailors and fishermen went about their business. Antonius led the men to one of the sailors who he had placed as head of import and export for the resources needed and produced by the kingdom. Next to the sailor's ship was a bigger armed ship that belonged to the Commanding general in charge of the navy force of the kingdom.

"Philip" Antonius called out.

Philip, the sailor saw him and immediately got off his ship and ran to him. He was a mild mannered man.

"Your majesty, it's so good to see you. But what are you doing here?"

"No time to explain. Get your ship ready, we must set sail immediately."

"Why must we leave in such haste?" Philip asked.

"I said there is no time. We must set sail now."

"Yes, your majesty." Philip replied.

Some of the men got on the ship with Antonius. Others boarded smaller boats and rowed behind. Antonius had ordered the head of the navy to follow beside the ship and guard it. Philip captained a ship that was not armed. Antonius captained an armed ship. The men were still confused as to what Antonius was planning but they trusted him and followed him onto the ship.

"Why do we have to be so protected? No one is following us. The men are still tied up and they would have been devoured by wild beast by now." one of the ex-convicts said to Antonius.

After the ship had gone some distance from the shore. Antonius fixed his eyes on the shore. So did some of the men. After a matter of seconds they saw what had caught his attention. The men saw that the twenty one had made their way to the shore. They continued to observe and saw that some of the sailors that were still on land, up to sixty in number tried to stop the twenty one but they were overpowered by them. The twenty one got aboard a ship loaded with cannons and set sail. They began firing at the three ships and small boats that held Antonius and the ex-convicts.

The head of the navy was Felix, a tall man with a barrel chest and a full bearded face. He captained an armed ship that followed close behind Antonius's ship. He told his crew to aim and shoot at the ship of the twenty one. They did as he said. They fired ten cannon shots towards the ship but all missed.

"Don't stop firing until those bastards are dead," he bellowed.

The twenty one men shot at the ships again and hit the ship that Antonius was on. The men on board panicked but Antonius was not moved.

"Antonius, what do we do?" they asked him.

Antonius looked up at the sail of the ship. The wind had picked up and was beating against the main sail.

"Call Felix, tell him to sail closer to us." He said. "Leave the rest to me."

Antonius took a rope and began climbing the sail of the ship. He got to a high enough point and tied the rope on the log above him. When the ship of Felix had sailed close enough, he used the rope to swing unto the ship. Then he told the men to do as he did. He, in the meantime, got a plank long enough for some of them to cross. Some swung over and some crossed to the other ship on the plank.

A shot was fired from the ship of the twenty one men once more. The shot destroyed the plank. Another shot was fired that destroyed the sail of the ship that was sinking.

"How can this be?" Felix said, "Impossible!"

"Reload the cannons. Get them ready and don't stop shooting" Felix ordered the men. He turned to Antonius and said, "Why are these men after you, what did you do?"

"I have done nothing that they accuse me of." Antonius went to one of the cannons and said "I'll prove my innocence one way or another but I am not going back to jail."

He lit the fuse. The cannon fired and hit the main sail of the ship that the twenty one were in. The men began shouting. The ship of the twenty one was slowly sinking, but one more shot was fired from the ship. The shot hit one of the small boats that a few of the ex-convicts were on.

"Stop the ship!" Antonius ordered Felix.

"We cannot. We must keep going. It may be too late for them." Felix replied.

Antonius heard nothing of what Felix had to say. He jumped out of the ship into the waters. He swam towards the wreckage. He got to the wreckage and called out but got no response. It was almost noon at that time, but still no one could see a body. Suddenly Julian swam up, holding a fellow passenger who had been knocked unconscious by the blast.

"There is one more man down there," Julian said.

"Go after him. I'll take this man back to the ship," Antonius replied. Antonius took the man and began swimming towards the ship.

Felix made a line of rope tied end to end that was long and strong enough. He threw it to Antonius.

Antonius took the line and twirled it around his right hand.

"Pull me up," Antonius said after he had a firm grip of the rope.

They pulled him up. He laid the unconscious body down and jumped back in the water. The sailors attended to the man who Antonius just rescued.

Julian had not yet emerged from the water. They waited for almost a minute and then Julian came hurdling up, trying to catch his breath. He swam to Antonius and said.

"He is too far down. I could not reach him."

Antonius was saddened to hear that.

"Let's go back to the ship," he said to Julian.

They swam back and were both pulled up by the line, one after the other, Julian going first. All the ship crew had their eyes fixed on Antonius. Felix got a blanket and put it over him.

"Well done." he said and started clapping. The other men joined in, soon there were all applauding him.

Felix proposed a celebration. He sent some men down to the cellar of the ship to get a barrel of wine.

Felix filled his cup first and said.

"A toast to the humble king of Philonia, You have put your kingdom and your subjects before yourself. For that we thank you."

The men began celebrating they all drank and were merry for they had survived a fierce battle. They celebrated into the night.

Antonius took a cup but did not drink. He went downstairs to the cabins and sat alone. He was thinking of all that had happened. He thought that Felix and the sailors did not know of his arrest. Then his mind drifted to Titus, his brother, the man who had taken his crown. As he pondered the recent events, he heard footsteps coming down into the cabin where he was. It was Felix, he was holding a candle.

"Why are you here alone in the dark?" Felix asked Antonius.

"I just wanted a quiet place to think."

"About what exactly, the men are still celebrating, why not join us."

"The men above us don't know that my presence on the ship has put their lives in danger."

"Do you say that because of what happened earlier? Or are you hiding something from us?"

Antonius did not answer. Felix went and sat by his side.

"So tell me, how many days were you in prison?"

"You knew?" Antonius asked.

"We all knew. And we have all pledged our loyalty to you. Some soldiers from the main land sent a letter three days ago. I refused to believe that you killed the Elders."

"Thank you for having faith in me."

"You have always had my loyalty…besides; I am just returning a favor your father asked of me."

"What favor?"

"Your father was an exquisite man, fine in taste and valor. There was no man with a virtue as his. Maybe you're the only one of his sons that matches up to his standards."

"So you say, but I don't feel it. The Elders told me that many of my father's choices were not exactly the best."

"In the many years you've sailed with me I haven't told you of my past have I?"

"No I don't believe so."

"How many stories did your father tell you in the early days of your youth?"

"There are too many to remember."

"Did he speak of his adventures at sea?"

"Yes but not much."

"Almost every person your father met he changed in one way or another. I was not always the captain of the Navy you know. I was young once."

"How long ago was that?" Antonius said with a slight smile.

"Very funny," Felix remarked. "Your sense of humor is just like his." He paused then continued. "Back then I was a different man. I became what I hated the most but I could not stop myself, I loved taking what wasn't mine, terrorizing small villages close to the sea, I was of a sort, a pirate, a very wicked one. I had exceeded the fear that title had on my enemies. I was more than a pirate. Some called me a lord over the seas. I became a threat to the nations. My infamy was glorious. I loved the power and the recognition. With only a few hundred crew men I could take on an army of a thousand. I had a thousand mighty men and ten ships at my disposal. I conquered the Blue Sea, looted many trade ships, had so much gold I stopped counting. The six kings could not stop me. They didn't know how to instruct their forces well. But your father, he was the only king who had not made an attempt at coming after me. I attacked two villages close to the ship port near Penthis. I did this to test your father. Till this day, I have considered it a good thing that I provoked your father."

"Why do you say that?"

"If I hadn't something worse could have become of me. At the time I was unaware that your father had made a plan with the king of Konstuliana."

"Was the king before Mitis not a wicked king? I thought he hated my father."

"He was but it was his father that your father made a plan with."

"His father, you mean Hermes?"

"Hermes the first. After they had rallied their troops together, they headed to sea. From the distance, far off the shore of Venduria, I could see their ships coming. I laughed thinking they have to be foolish trying to fight me at sea. I looked through my telescope and saw a man standing on the figurehead of your father's ship. I thought it was your father at first then I looked closer."

"What did you see?" Antonius asked.

"A man dressed in the cloths of a shepherd. He had in his right hand a rod taller than he was. I was not prepared for what happened next. The man jumped into the air, he held the bottom end of his rod with both hands and struck the water once he landed. His feet hit the water as a man's feet would hit solid ground. The waters grew higher than I had ever seen in my life. Higher than any storm had lifted them. The waves were crashing fast, pursuing my ship. The waves toppled six of my ten ships. The ship I was on managed to stay afloat. The man who caused the waters to rise was nowhere in sight. When the crashing waves stopped, your father's ship was closer to ours. The battle was fierce, your father won, and I luckily survived. But it was not a thrill to me for I knew death was going to be the only punishment that could fit my crimes." He took a sip of wine, Then continued, "The seven kings met to discuss my punishment, I was the common enemy in their presence. They brought all the gold I had taken into the court. They laid them before me as I knelt there, some of the gold coins, inches from my grasp. My hands were chained behind my back. As much as they glistened before me, the gold could not gain back my affection. I bowed my head in shame. They discussed in lent as I knelt for what seemed like hours. I waited to hear how I would die."

A light breeze blew into the cabin through a small window.

"The kings decided to share the gold among their nations. I felt my execution was decided. I knew my end had come. That was when your father stood up and said that he'd give all his share of the retrieved treasures and more to buy my freedom. The other kings went into a fit and insulted your father. I remember the senators were there also. I looked back and saw them shaking their heads in disdain. He bought my freedom. Before the court, he took the keys and unlocked my chains. He helped me to my feet and look into my eyes. He saw something in me that I had denied was there. I asked him why he did this, he said he saw a potential for good in me. He gave me a second chance. He took me and gave me a small home. A short while later, he asked me to join his mighty fleet of sailors."

"What became of your crew?"

"Many abandoned me. They swam away or stirred their ships far away. The few that were caught were arrested. After I joined the navy of your father, he promoted me quickly. In a matter of two years I became the commander of his fleet. Your father was a young king at the time, yet very wise."

"When did all this happen?"

"Thirty years ago. Your father was the first man to win my full loyalty. The same loyalty I gave him, I give too you."

"That means a lot to me."

"I'll leave you. You need some time to rest. If you get thirsty there is plenty of wine upstairs."

Felix went upstairs to the main deck. It was just before sunset. Antonius lay down and slept.

Early the next morning, Antonius told Felix to set sail for an Island west of their current position. Felix looked at his compass and redirected their course. Felix got a map and looked at it keenly for a moment.

"Where exactly are we going?" Felix asked

"To this island here." Antonius replied as he pointed to the map.

"Isn't that too close to Konstuliana territory?"

"Yes but don't worry. We'll be safe"

"Is there something you need there?" Felix asked

"Not something, someone." Antonius replied

Felix looked at the map once more and recognized the island.

"This is it isn't it. The island you visited once every year."

"Yes I had to keep in touch with him and make sure that he was still okay."

"Do you think he'd want to help us?"

"I don't think he'll have much of a choice. He is part of the royal family so this involves him too."

"You are right but we must keep on our guard nonetheless."

The journey took about half a day. They reached the island by sunset. As they were approaching the island they saw that a fire had been built just on the beach. There were two dead antelopes lying next to it. Antonius was the first to get off the ship.

A man emerged from the dense forest in front of them carrying a third Antelope. The man looked young and well built in stature. He was tall, had a full bearded face and long hair to his shoulders.

"Greetings" the man said. "I saw your ships from afar and I thought I'd get some dinner enough for all of us," Felix whispered to Antonius. "This cannot be him."

"It is him."

Antonius walked up to the man and embraced him.

"Good to see you again Marcus."

"Likewise brother," Marcus replied with a chuckle. "Glad to see you too. You came early

this year, and with more company than usual."
The man replied.

The men formed ten groups. Fifty men
were in each group. They unloaded some of the
materials they needed from the ship. Felix took
a hand of twenty five men who assisted in unloading some of the wine. Another twenty five
assisted in unloading some of the food they had
brought along with them. At that moment, the
ship that Philip captained arrived at shore.

Antonius yelled to Felix from the shore.

"Don't unload everything we won't be
staying long."

"Okay then, when do you think we should
leave?"

"We'll leave as soon as repairs are made to
the ships."

"Agreed."

Marcus then asked Antonius.

"So why did you bring this many men
with you?"

Antonius still looking towards the sea kept
silent. Antonius sighed.

"I know something is wrong. So tell me,
what is it?"

Antonius took a breath and said.

"I was overthrown, Titus is the new king."

"Is that so?" Marcus replied. "To think
brother would have the guts to do something
like that?"

"I was charged with murder by the counsel
of senators."

"Well, who did you kill?" Marcus said, testing his brother.

"I killed no one. Somehow it was made to appear as if I killed the Elders."

"The Elders are dead? Do you think Titus is capable of such?"

"I don't know. That's what makes me afraid. It may not have been him. I heard strange songs days before the Elders died."

"Songs?"

"Yes and these songs are sung with bad intent."

"You mean like the songs of a siren."

"A siren?" Antonius said in a doubtful tone. "Let's not jump to conclusions just yet. We do not know what we are dealing with. It would be best now to wait it out a little and see what we can learn."

"Wait? Wait for what?" Marcus said.

"Your patience bores me brother."

"Don't worry; you will be entertained soon enough."

Antonius turned and started heading towards the forest from where Marcus emerged with the antelope.

"Where are you going?" Marcus asked.

"To the waterfalls" Antonius replied.

Marcus was astonished but did not say anything. He was worried about Antonius, because Antonius wanted to venture to the waterfall on his own.

Marcus wanted to go with him but respected his brother's wishes.

Felix approached Marcus. Marcus still had his eyes on his departing brother.

"Marcus…" Felix called out.

Marcus turned to him.

"What is it?" Marcus asked.

"Would you like to join the feast?" Felix asked.

Marcus looked at him for a moment. Then back at the forest. Antonius was gone.

"Join us I insist. We have more than enough to drink."

Marcus smiled.

"Fine."

Antonius walked alone through the thick forest. Being that it was night, it was almost impossible to tell where he was. But his strong desire to get to the river kept him going. He had once been to the river. Two years back, he had ventured to it with Marcus. Then he remembered that he felt something there, a peace he hadn't known in a while. He longed for the sound of the rushing waters. He thought more clearly whenever that sound graced his ears.

For a moment he felt a little faint because of the humidity of the area where he was. It got very hot in an instant. He took of the jailor's armor. He unclothed himself until he was only in his pants and his boots. He carried his sword by hand.

At a point in his journey, he felt tired and fell to his knees. He found it hard to catch his breath. He closed his eyes and thought of his kingdom. He also thought of the letter he had read and what his brother had said. 'Sirens?' he thought, 'Could it be?' 'Sirens' he thought once more. 'If the tales of father were correct then they should be vanquished, never to venture in the affairs of men ever again. Those children of fallen guardians have been defeated. Surely…I hope.' He struggled back to his feet and continued on his way.

'But then how did those men sent by my brother get so strong. I felt in my spirit that they were still after me. How could they have known where I was going?' He groaned. 'I can't worry about that now. I must get to the river.'

He got to the top of a hill and when he looked down he saw it. 'Yes there it is.' he said. In his field of vision he saw that there was a lion close to the river. He bent low, crawled and hid behind a tree. 'I don't have enough energy for this'. He thought. He waited a while and looked back towards the river. The lion was still there.

Through the night he waited behind the tree. He felt drowsy and feel into a deep sleep. As he slept, he dreamt. In his dream he awoke in the exact same place where he had fallen asleep. The environment was the same. He looked up towards the sky and thought, 'Morning already. I don't remember waking up. The lion!" He turned back toward the river to see if it was gone. It was not there. He was astonished to see that the river had turned red. He went down to the river.

When he got to the edge of the river bank he gazed into it. It appeared as red as wine. 'What is this' he thought. He knelt down and put his hand in. He could feel that the river was thicker than water and wine. The smell of it was also strong. 'Blood' he whispered. When he brought his hand out he fell back in terror for the flesh on his hand had disappeared and he saw his bones. He watched in bewilderment as his flesh grew back over his bones and he felt his blood rushing through his veins. 'What sought of apparition is this?' he thought.

He stood up and stared into the river. He looked around once more.

Then he heard a voice call his name from the other side of the river.

He looked but saw no one. He heard his name again.

"Who are you, show yourself!"

A man emerged from the trees on the other side of the river.

When Antonius saw the man, tears welled up in his eyes.

"Father"

"Shall you cry every time you see me?"

Antonius wiped his tears and smiled.

"It's been so long. It's good to see you again father". He wanted to join his father on the other side but the river was in his path.

"There is no way to cross over here my son."

"In all the times that you have visited me we have not been separated in such a way. Why is this happening?"

"I'm afraid I can't say my son. But I am here to encourage you."

"I must cross over to where you are father. I feel that this is a dream. If it is I cannot then be limited like this."

"No please my son, do not do it. This river flows with the blood of those who have lost their lives in the cause for good. If you come to where I am, then you will die."

"But how can that be?"

"I am sorry but that is the way it is. It is not my will. Please you must understand that I am here to let you know you are not alone."

"What is happening father? What is happening to the kingdom?"

"If I told you all at once, you will be overwhelmed. But I promise that I will guide you, I will be there when you need me. I will not leave your side."

"Thank you Father."

Antonius looked up upstream and saw that the waters flowed from the heart of a high mountain and by the time they reached the bottom to form the river, the waters turned red.

At the top of the mountain, there was a light which shone as bright as the sun. Antonius quickly averted his eyes from the top for the intensity of the light source was too much.

His father then said, "son, do what you can to never let your *will* be diminished by your circumstances, for the road ahead is rough. Be prepared son. I will see you soon."

Antonius nodded. He fixed his gaze on his father who was now vanishing slowly before his eyes. 'Goodbye father. I will not disappoint you.'

At once he woke up. He slowly got back to his feet and then turned his eyes back to the river. The lion was gone. He went down there and drank from it.

Far on the horizon, the sun had set its course for another day. Antonius replenished decided to head back to the beach. He was about leaving when the lion came from the bushes charging at him.

He reached for his sword but it was not by his waist. He had forgotten it by the tree where he fell asleep. With no time to do much, he jumped into the roaring rivers. The lion jumped straight after him. He swam with the current of river. The lion was swimming fast close behind him. He saw ahead the top of the waterfall. He looked back and saw the lion getting closer to him. He tried with all his might to swim towards the river bank. But to no avail.

He stopped for a few seconds and tried once more. The lion was getting closer. He managed to get a hold of a rock. As the lion passed him it clawed his back. Then it was swept away by the current down to the waterfall. The lion roared as it fell to its death.

Antonius started bleeding. He was in tremendous pain. He felt his grip of the rock slowly slipping. 'No' he said. He looked to the river bank. 'I only have one chance to do this or I'll get swept away with the current.' He let go of the rock and swan a few feet to land. He pulled himself out with the remaining strength he had. 'Every time I venture alone trouble always seems to follow me.' He said, smiled and then fainted.

Chapter 3
The Elders, the sons of Calix and the Senate

At that same moment at the shore, Felix arose from his sleep. He still felt dazed for he had drunk too much the night before. He looked at Marcus, who sat a few feet away. Marcus sat with his legs crossed and his eyes on the horizon, carefully watching the rising sun. Felix turned to Marcus and said,

"Did you not rest?"

Marcus did not respond.

"Marcus" Felix called out.

"I heard you. No I didn't sleep."

"Is Antonius back yet?"

"No I've been waiting through the night."

"Should we wait a little while?"

"I'm done waiting. I am going to find him."

Marcus got up and started heading towards the waterfalls. Felix called to him and tossed his sword. Marcus caught it and thanked him.

He ran off immediately heading for the waterfall. He had mastered the terrain of the island. As he got to the humid part of the forest he knew what to do to avoid the heat. He climbed up a tree he was familiar and walked across the thick branches. Many of the higher branches of different trees overlapped. It was cooler in the trees than it was on the ground. At a point in his journey he stopped because something odd caught his eye. He looked down and saw pieces of clothing and a metal object that reflected sunlight at him.

He climbed down and after he picked up the armor and shirt he thought, 'He's not far from here'. He continued on his way. He got to the hill and saw the river below. He turned to his left and saw a sword at the base of a tree. He went and picked it up. He turned to his right and looked downstream. Then he made his way downhill.

When he got to where Antonius was, he found him holding a long stick with a thin line made of leaves at the end of the stick that extended into the river. The bleeding had stopped but his wounds still hurt.

"You had me worried. Why are you still here?" Marcus asked.

"I haven't had anything to eat yet."

"There's much food at the ship"

"I know. I just want some fish at the moment. I should get a catch soon. Come, make a line and join me."

Marcus broke a branch from a tree close by and made a line from thin leaves. He sat by Antonius. They sat together and waited for the lines to move. They sat in silence together for a little while before Marcus asked.

"Why are we doing this brother?" "Doing what?" Antonius responded calmly.

"Don't act as a fool," Marcus said, "you know what I mean, you are aware of everything that is going on. Yet you act so calm. You want to wait it out?! Why can't you take action and do something. We must find a way to stop whatever is causing the strange things in the kingdom."

"It's not as easy as that…"

"I never said it was going to be easy. I said we must take action. You came to this island for a reason. You came seeking my help. And now you have found it. What will you do with it brother? What would you have me do to show you how important it is that we act fast before something worse happens?!"

Antonius's line began to move. He pulled it, and a fish flew out of the water. He caught it. Then he said to Marcus.

"Please Hand me your sword."

Marcus gave it to him. Antonius took it and cut the fish in half.

"Take and eat." He said. "Replenish your strength."

Marcus took it.

"When we're done eating, we head back to the ship," Marcus said.

"Indeed we must head out soon but repairs have to be made to the ship before we sail," Antonius replied.

"The men who Titus sent against you followed you to sea?"

"Yes, the battle was short but there were some casualties."

"I'm surprised Felix was willing to help you knowing that he would be rebelling against him."

"Felix had faith in me, in my innocence."

Antonius finished his part of the fish and threw the bones in the water. He got up and they headed back. They got to the shore and saw that the sailors and navy men had all arose and repairs on the ship had commenced. The repair operations were being led by Felix, and Philip joined to assist him.

Antonius went to Felix and asked.

"How soon will we be able to set sail?"

"The damages were worse that we thought. The men are working as fast as they can but supplies are low. There's not much we can do. It takes time to turn these trees into fine timber. It might take a few days to complete repairs."

"We must leave as soon as possible."

"I'm sorry but that's as soon as we can do, with the supplies and the pace at which the men are working."

Marcus set his eyes on the ships and observed the damages.

"These are not much at all. I have enough timber to fix this."

Antonius surprised by his statement turned and asked.

"Do you really have enough timber for two ships?"

"Yes. I'll need about thirty men to assist me."

Felix ordered Philip to assemble thirty strong men. In a few minutes they assembled themselves and stood before Felix. Felix motioned to Marcus to step forward. Marcus stood in front of the men and said.

"I am not going to repeat myself. So listen carefully. I will guide you to where to get more timber but you must follow closely at all times. When we get there and we get the timber we need we head back at once. Understood!"

The men responded in unison, "Understood!"

"Alright then there's no time to waste."

Marcus started running towards the forest and the men followed behind him.

Three days prior in Noble city, the capital of Philonia, the new king was about to be officially crowned by the council of senators. The council was made up of thirty men and five women, each person represented a province in the kingdom. Darius, the leader of the counsel was not especially pleased as to how power in the kingdom had changed hands. He called for a meeting of the council a night before the coronation.

They gathered in the senate house. A beautifully designed building with statues of battle heroes at the front of the building and a statue of Antonius's father, Calix Maximus, stood in the middle of the scene. The statues depicted a historical event.

The senators gathered together in a large oval room and took their seats. Some of the senators were rowdy before the meeting began. They were discussing among themselves as to why the meeting was called for.

Darius walked into the room and proceeded to the high seat. The council had their eyes fixed on him.

He began, "I am not here to make a speech on why I don't agree with the coronation about to commence tomorrow. I just want to make one thing clear; I don't think it should take place so soon."

The younger senators in the council did not agree with this and then began to bicker.

One of them said, "How can we suspend having a king? That puts our kingdom at risk if war were to break out. Who will lead the troops and who shall serve as the model to encourage them?"

"Quiet!" Darius said. "Titus is not prepared to become king. He doesn't know the duties he is about to assume. His inexperience in battle and his short temperedness make him inadequate to rule as of now. He needs to mature and show more potential before he is made king."

"Why don't we just bring back the murderous Antonius and give him back the crown because he sure had a lot of patience to spare?" A young senator said in mockery of Antonius. Some of his peers laughed but the older ones in the council were not amused.

A young beautiful female senator by the name of Cara spoke up.

"Darius, May I say something?"

"Yes what is it?"

"I think it is best we commence with the coronation but we will limit the power of the king."

"We are the council, we have always had that power but the people believe the king to be more powerful, so that is not going to be effective. By delaying the coronation we can organize the kingdom as we please. We can settle the doubts of the people." Darius replied.

"Shall we elect new Elders?" Cara asked.

"No, those of us who have had at least ten years as senators will serve as both new Elders and senators."

There were only seven among them who had had that much experience. Darius was one of them. The younger men were very displeased with Darius and there was a division in the senate.

❖

The Council of Elders was set up by Calix in his fifteenth year as king. He chose five of his closest friend, very respectable men and gave them the responsibility to oversee the policies of his sons whenever they were to ascend to power.

It so happened that when Marcus took power at the age of twenty one, the powers of the Elders came to be recognized. They stopped Marcus from making rash decision and as the years progressed, Marcus's contempt for the Elder's grew. Antonius was appointed at that time as the Global Ambassador of Philonia to the Nations. He spent about ten months in each year in other nations.

He was well liked by four of the five kings of the seven nations. The king of the fifth nation had passed away, so his wife took over the kingdom and she grew very fond of Antonius. She invited him very often to the kingdom. He rejected many of her invita-

tions because he felt she was crossing the boundaries of the relationship they had as leaders. Her son saw it but she didn't.

The king of the sixth nation, Konstuliana, was a well-known family friend of the house of Maximus. He had been appointed as king over the nation after a war between Konstuliana and Philonia took place. Calix led that war and won, thereafter he removed the old king who had become very blood thirsty. He exiled him to an island. He appointed a childhood friend of his, Mitis Miles, as king over the liberated nation. Foreign relations between the nations got better until after the death of Calix.

In the fifth year of his rule, Marcus had grown to hate the Elders. They had limited his power so much that he felt inadequate as king. He was only given the power to enforce legislations that had been made without his consent. Many of which he disagreed with.

He sent a letter to Antonius who was at sea with Felix at that time. In the letter he explained that he had had enough of the Elders and was willing to give the crown to Antonius but if Antonius did not get back to the kingdom in time he was going to lead a coalition of men who would see to it that the Elders will be "put in their proper place". He explained in the letter that he did not want to do away with what their father had established to make sure they ruled effectively but he felt the Elders had taken their powers to levels their father did not intend for.

Antonius upon receiving the letter agreed to his brother's demand. When he returned to Philonia, he headed straight to Noble city. Marcus and Antonius

came before the senate and the Elders. In their presence, Marcus handed his crown to Antonius and
said,

"There is no reason for me to keep being king if I
am going to be restrained in every decision I make. I
have had it with you bigots. You promised my father
that you would let his line continue but you have
slowly stolen the power from this crown. I'm done.
Antonius you are next in line, take It." he handed
him the crown and started to make his way out of the
room but Antonius held him by the arm and whispered in his ear, "Please brother reconsider what
you're doing. You are about to walk out on a people
who trust you. Give it time; we can restore power to
the crown." Marcus shrugged off Antonius's hand
and said, "I have made up my mind brother. I can't
stand this any longer. If I stay I might end up doing
something this senate will forever regret." Marcus
then left the room. The council of senators and Elders
had their eyes fixed on Antonius. Antonius looked
down at the crown and back at the council. He put it
on and said.

"Tomorrow we shall have a coronation; it will
not be good for the kingdom to be without a king."
He was twenty two at that time.

Antonius ruled for five years before the incident
with the Elders took place. In those five years he
managed to regain most of the power back to the
crown. He did this by getting on the good side of the
people and especially the military. He would even get
involved in building projects that took place in the
city. He would put on the clothes of a mason and
work in the company of common men. The people

grew to love him more because of this. Darius grew jealous of him and the Elders restrained from disrupting his rule but still possessed more power than him.

After he was accused of murdering the Elders, he was denied a fair trial and was immediately thrown in jail by order of the senate. The creature that took the form of his brother and went to see him in jail was responsible for the death of the Elders.

The creature's presence was always preceded by songs heard all around the city. They had begun six days before the Elders were killed. Each night the city would hear melodious humming that made the people ecstatic. They would drink very much and stagger in the streets. When the songs stopped they would awaken as if from a trance and not be aware of what had occurred. Many were affected by these songs except for Antonius, Titus, and anyone who was in the cathedral when the songs were heard in the city.

On the third evening, he was watching from the window in the palace what was unfolding in the streets below. This was the first time he saw the effects of the song. He ran to his study room and grabbed a book called the 'Libro Prophetiae'. He opened the big dusty book and flipped through the pages. The book told of many stories of ancient heroes and a great falling of half of the beings in a higher Order of creatures that looked like men and called themselves Guardians. The book also held keys to future events but the prophecies were written in a cryptic text. Calix and the queen of Konstuliana were the only ones, among a few, known to possess *the ability to read the prophecies. Antonius did not turn to the cryptic texts but to a section in the book that spoke about the union of Guardians and earthly women.*

He reread the story he had been told during the days of his youth by his father. As he read, he flipped to the next page to find some sections were not there. The pages had been ripped from the hem. In frustration he slammed the book shut and clenched his fist. He ran back to the window and looked outside. The songs had stopped and the people returned to normal. He was confused. It was late in the evening so he decided to retire to bed.

At the third hour after midnight, he heard loud screams outside the palace gates. Then after a few minutes, there was a loud pounding on the door of the king's chamber, his bedroom. He retrieved his sword that lay underneath the bed and sprung forth taking careful slow steps towards the door. At that moment the weather seemed to have changed abruptly. It began to pour heavily outside and thunderstorms hovered above the city.

He opened the door and saw no one. Then immediately there was a loud shriek, a strong wind blew into the room, the curtains blew up and the windows swung open violently. Suddenly an unseen force struck him so hard that he flew back a few feet and was almost knocked out. A darkish gray mist began to fill the room. He got back to his feet and started hearing the songs he had heard the previous evening. "Who are you, show yourself" he yelled out. A fiendish laughter was heard but no one was seen. He gripped his sword tightly.

"Fool" a voice spoke out from the mist, *"Your mortal weapons are useless. You cannot see me yet you want to come against me."*

"Show yourself you coward!" Antonius said even louder.

The wind in the room became stronger and the mist thicker. He found it harder to breathe. Suddenly the winds died down and the black mist slowly disappeared, then it was quiet. The storm clouds had passed and a cold gentle wind blew in from the opened windows.

Antonius dropped his sword and wondered. It seemed to him as if he had just awoken from a trance. Titus came running into the room.

"Antonius, are you alright?"

He turned to Titus and responded.

"I don't know"

"What do you mean?"

"Just...leave me. I'll be fine."

Titus left. Antonius could not sleep the rest of the night so he went to his study. There he wrote about his experience in a book only the eyes of the king was allowed to see.

So it came, the sixth day of the creature's presence in the city. The day went about normally. When evening came, things changed. The sky became a maroon color. The Elders were about to depart from their workplace. They had built for themselves a well-furnished and extravagant building they called, the house of the law. The building was even more furnished than the city cathedral. The cathedral was in need of some restoration. The Elders knew this but had always ignored the people's request to repair it.

They controlled the funds that went into city projects. These funds had come from the personal treasury of the king, which they slowly acquired access too during the reign of Marcus.

Then it happened, a loud explosion let loose from within the house of the law. The foundation of the building was rocked and shaken. The pillars gave way and the building came crashing down on everyone who was still inside. Fifty six people were killed, including the five Elders. The explosion was heard all around the city.

At that time Antonius was at the Market place having a discussion with a woman selling some fruits. When he heard the explosion he got on his horse and rode back to the palace. From the market place to the palace took him about fifteen minutes. When he got back to the palace he was welcomed by Darius and a group of soldiers.

"Antonius" Darius said, "You are hereby under arrest by order of the senate for the murder of the council of Elders." The soldiers seized Antonius.

"Wait let go of me." Antonius commanded. "What is the meaning of this? I did not do anything."

"Well then" said Darius "How do you explain this" Darius was holding shreds of one of Antonius's regal robes. It was distinct in its design, made only for him. "This was found beside the rubbles of the building".

"That's from my robe."

"I am aware of that. This is the reason we came here to arrest you."

At that moment Titus came out of the palace to see what was happening.

"Darius what is going on?" he asked.

"Your brother here is responsible for the explosion that occurred but a few moments ago."

"Yes I heard it, what happened?"

"The house of the law crumbled killing all the Elders"

Titus raised his eyebrow.

"Titus" Antonius said. "Tell them, I'm innocent, you know I can't do something like this. Tell them brother. I was nowhere near that building."

"I'm sorry brother, I can't do that."

"What?!"

"Only the king has that authority, and I am not the king." Titus replied then turned his back and went back into the palace.

The men took Antonius away and put him in jail.

Chapter 4
The Prince's Delight

Splendid! He thought. "To think that tomorrow I will be become king." He smiled. Titus was standing on a balcony just outside the throne room. The balcony overlooked the city because the palace was set at a high point in the city.

He walked back into the throne room and looked at a bust made in the likeness of his father. He walked to it and gazed at it for a while. Then he walked and sat on the throne. He crossed his legs and had a wider smile now. The throne room was spectacular in its design. A red carpet ran from the throne to the door. This throne room was one of two in the palace and it was the more splendid of the two. Portraits of previous kings were place all around the walls of the room.

"Antonius, I thank you for doing what Marcus was too scared to do. Those bothersome Elders are out of the way. My rule shall be unhindered. I will try to be a good king like father was. Hmm but first I want a monument built for myself. No, that might not be fitting at the moment. I can't decide what I want. It is all so exciting." All this ran through his head as he sat on the throne. He was nineteen years of age. He was ambitious and well known for his aggressive tendencies. Many considered him spoilt but he never gave a second thought to anyone's opinion of him.

Darius had just left the meeting with the senate and made his way to the palace at that late hour. He arrived at the palace and asked the guards if the prince was still awake. They confirmed that he was because they had spotted him on the balcony a few moments earlier.

Darius entered the throne room and saw the young prince clothed in his father's robes. Titus noticed him and walked to him.

"Just the man I wanted to see," he said. "Does this robe look too big on me? I was hoping to wear it tomorrow at my coronation as a way of saying to the people that I will try to be a good king as my father was."

"Young prince don't you think it is out of place to put on your father's robe. Not even your brothers did such at their coronation."

"That was because my brothers were not as brave as our father." He pulled out his sword and swung it as if he were fighting someone. "I heard stories from my mother about how my father fought off a hundred men on his own. And when he had overwhelmed them, he could not remove the sword from his hand. That is the kind of king I want to be, brave, determined and conquering."

"Young prince, the responsibilities of the throne may weigh too heavy on you," Darius said. "It may be best that you wait before assuming your kingship."

Titus stopped his play and turned to Darius. He put his sword away.

"What do you mean Darius?" he asked.

"I am saying that the coronation should commence at a later time, tomorrow is too sudden." Darius responded.

"I see what this is about." He said as he walked closer to Darius. "You are trying to do exactly what the Elders did to my brothers." He smiled. "You see Darius; I am next in line to the throne. The Elders, they are no more, there is none to limit my power." "I admire my father in many ways but I consider what he did by creating the council of Elders to be quite foolish."

"You see" he continued "I have been waiting for my turn to take the throne and see how the Elders would try to steal my power but oh how Antonius made my ascension so much more pleasant. Now Darius, you of all people want to take this joy away from me. The senators have not the power the Elders possessed. When Marcus ascended to the throne after the passing of my mother, the powers of the Elders came into effect. The power of that crown was split among five people and the king. Slowly but surely the Elders sank their claws deeper and deeper into the heart of the power of that crown and kept taking and taking until they drove Marcus insane and he left because he felt powerless. When Antonius ascended, he too felt the pressure but he was wise. He sided with the people and regained some power to the crown. I thought he might fully become unhindered but the Elders proved me wrong. But brother, oh brother had a side that I did not know existed. Within all that reserved patience and meek attitude he advertised, there was a clever criminal. Thanks to him the Elders are dead. Now it is my turn to rule and there are no Elders to stand in my way. Antonius has put enough power back in that crown that if I were to place it on my head, the people will believe me to be king and I will do as I please. So I advise you Darius not to interfere with my rule or you will suffer a fate so terrible that what happened to Elders would be considered merciful."

Titus then walked out of the room and back to his chamber.

Darius stood there shocked at the audacity the young prince had to say such to a man of his age. He was a man in his late sixties whose term in the senate had run for about thirty five years. He longed for the crown, for a chance to be king but he kept such desires to himself.

He had hoped that by delaying the coronation the senate might acquire more power, so that a new council of Elders would be created with him in charge.

After hearing what Titus had said, he knew that he would face great opposition from Titus if he tried to carry out such plans. So he held his peace and went home. He sent a messenger to inform the other senators that the coronation will commence as planned.

Titus was livid when he got back to his chamber. He could not sleep because he kept thinking of the many ways the senate might try to limit his power. He got up from his bed and went to the king's study room.

The room was of a sort was like a small library within the palace. It had a relatively small number of books sorted by their relevance in relation to the duties of the king. Some had information of the lineage of all the kings and the way they ruled. None spared detail nor did any show favor towards any king. The truth of each king's reign was plain.

Titus scanned the sections of books but could not find what he was looking for. He looked at a table in the middle of the room positioned just in front of the window. On the table there was a candle whose light had been blown out by the wind. Titus felt cold so he closed the window. He went to the table and found an open book next to the candle. He observed the book closely. "This is it" he thought. It was the book that only the eyes of the king could see; the king's diary. The diary belonged to Antonius. Beside it on top a stack of books was "Libro Prophetiae."

He glanced at the big book beside the open book but it did not pick his interest. He was more concerned with what Antonius had written in his diary. Every king had his own diary that they filled out if anything out of place occurred on a particular day or they used to outline battle strategies. He saw that Antonius's feather pen was still inside the book. He read what had been added by Antonius the night he heard singing and the mysterious force invaded his chamber. As he read through and was about to get to the part where the creature came into Antonius room, he began to hear singing. "How peculiar" he thought. "Two consecutive nights I have heard such splendid melodies; I

must go and find where they are coming from."
He left the study.

The songs did not affect him the way it did
the people. He did not know or understand
why this was so. It had been that when he was
a child, his father had anointed him and his
brothers with holy oil, so that their heart will
not be entrapped by evil unless they chose to let
it be.

Whenever he heard the songs he would
stop and listen but now his curiosity had
caught the best of him and he had to know
where such melodies came from.

Once he left the study room the songs
stopped. He walked a few steps into the hallway wondering why the songs had suddenly
stopped. A guard came running to him, "My
prince" he said. "There is a woman in the palace gardens."

"At this hour?"

"Yes, your majesty she is bathing in the
pool."

"Bring her to me at once." He said.

He made his way to the throne room and
waited. He approached the throne and gazed
upon the crown that lay on a small pillow beside the throne. He reached out to take it but he
restrained himself. "Not yet" he thought. "Just
a few more hours."

At that moment the guard brought the
woman in. The guard had put a thin robe over
her to cover her nakedness.

"That will be all," Titus said.

The guard left.

Titus watched her from where he stood. He felt uneasy for a moment. He admired how beautiful she was. Never had any woman's beauty captivated him. She stood with the thin robe covering her nakedness. He stared into her piercing eyes. He adorned the curve of her face, her flowing hair, the grand curiosity her presence evoked in his heart. He had seen many beautiful women on his many wonders around the city, and he had come to know some of them. She was different. He wondered why he had never seen her before, such a beautiful face, he thought, he could not have never missed.

He approached her slowly and walked around her then stopped in front of her. She was almost as tall as he was.

"Never have I seen a woman so beautiful. I demand to know who you are." he said.

"Does your majesty not know who I am?"

"If we had met sometime before, I promise you I would not have forgotten."

"We have met once."

"When?"

She smiled.

"You do not remember."

Titus was patient with her for though he did not know her, he already developed a liking for her. They stared at each other for a moment under the light of the multitude of candles set around the throne room.

"If I have known you before and forgotten grant me the pleasure of knowing your name."

"Elana"

After she had said her name, Titus began to hear the singing he heard when he was in the study room. His eyes were still locked on hers, he felt the singing coming from her, her lips did not move but he felt the songs coming out from her. Like rushing waters, they covered him. His face lit up. He took her hand.

"Stay with me." He said. "Nothing this world has offered me will ever compare to you."

"I have no intentions of leaving. Tomorrow you become king, so I am here to serve you."

"I will make you my queen." he said softly. "Let us rule, together."

"If my lord so wishes, so shall it be."

Hand in hand, he pulled her even closer and kissed her. He felt the songs once more, this time he felt them within himself. This made him happy.

This took place the same day Antonius was arrested.

Chapter 5
A Plot for Love: The Prince and the Noble's Daughter

It was high noon and the repairs on the ships were progressing well. Marcus and the men who accompanied him into the forest had returned with a lot of timber. Timber they had gotten from a cabin Marcus built for himself. He saw no need of it anymore so he helped them take it apart. They used the wood from it to fix up the holes on the exterior and interior of the ships.

When the men were dismantling Marcus cabin, he had gone a few distance from them to a tree whose leaves gave off white flakes when the leaves were shaken or dried and crumbled up. The white powdery substance had the power to knock a man unconscious for hours if ingested. He had learnt of this after he experienced it a few years back when he first encountered the tree. He had with him a small bag tied to his waist. He plucked some of its leaves and put them in the bag.

When repairs were done, the men got on the ships and set sail for Konstuliana. Marcus went with them. It was the first time in four years since he had left the island.

He had plans of his own, reasons why he chose to leave the island. He had boarded the same ship that Antonius and Felix were on.

The route leading to Konstuliana had been decided before they set sail. There were two routes to Konstuliana from the island. The first route would require they sail around an area sailors called the Cursed Fog. This route would make the trip a day longer. The second route would be that they go through the Cursed Fog and save themselves a day's journey but risk losing their lives. Antonius and Felix agreed upon the first way of travel but Marcus wanted to go through the Fog, he had his reasons and the main ones were love and vengeance.

Marcus went down to the ship's cellar. It was dark down there so he had taken with him a small candle. He went discretely, certain that no one had seen him, but Julian had noticed him and hid himself as he followed him.

Marcus got to the wine supplies, opened the barrels, took the bag tied around his waist, and sprinkled some of the white flakes of the crumpled leaves into the wine. Julian saw him do this. Immediately Julian went back to the main deck and acted as if he had not known what went on below. He told no one.

After Marcus returned to the main deck, he searched for Antonius. When he found him he asked.

"So when will we arrive at Konstuliana?"

"In three days."

"Three days. Why? It should take less than that."

"Felix and I decided we shall sail around the fog."

"Why not sail through it and save us a day's journeys?"

"I know you are aware of what's in the Fog and I am not willing to put these men's lives at risk. With all the stories and legends I've heard it's best to avoid that place at all cost."

"Time is precious brother; a day wasted could prove disastrous."

"And you think going through the fog won't be?" Antonius asked.

"I detest these disagreements we have. Maybe we should have some wine to ease the mood. If the men wish, they can drink as much as they please. Let us make this three days journey more pleasant."

"Fine but no wine for me."

"No problem brother, rest easy."

Marcus left and ordered one of the sailors to bring up a barrel of wine and made sure that everyone had some to drink. The sailor distributed the wine to Felix, all the sailors and the ex-convicts. When Julian was given a cup, he reluctantly took it. When the server had gone, he tossed the wine overboard. The men drank till they were drunk and began to sing until they fell unconscious.

Marcus saw the drowsiness in their eyes as they each fell into a slumber that would last a full day.

Marcus went to the captain's cabin where Felix was. He found Felix with his head on the Map and a glass half filled with wine in his right hand. He raised Felix head up and took the map. "Sorry old friend" he thought "But I have my reasons for doing this. I know you can understand for you have also lost loved ones in the Fog."

Felix was well familiar with the Fog and what was in it that made it infamous to sailors. In his days as a pirate, he had lost over a hundred men in a battle with a creature that dwelt in the shadows of the fog. He knew that the truth about the fog was scarier than the legends told.

Marcus had lost someone very close to him when he sailed through it four years back. He felt he could not get her back but seeing her would be pleasure enough for him.

Among those who Marcus had given the compromised wine, was the Helmsman. Marcus had taken Felix's compass. He went to the Helm of the ship, looked at the compass and redirected its course, setting the ship on a course straight through the Fog.

At this time Antonius was in a cabin below the main deck. He felt the ship turning for quite a while that he thought Felix had redirected their course. He wanted to go and check but didn't feel compelled enough. So he waited and listened a while and the silence above him caught his interest. "It's too quiet," he thought.

The second ship was captained by Philip and he had gone ahead of them but still saw them when he looked back through a telescope. He did this often to make sure that Felix ship was on the same course as his. He looked back and when he saw nothing this worried him a little. He looked and scanned again and saw Felix's ship west of where his ship was and a little ahead. He saw that the ship was heading straight for the Fog. This worried him but he kept his ship on course towards Konstuliana. "I hope he knows what he is doing," he said.

Antonius walked through the passage leading to the main deck. There he saw some sailors passed out on the walkway and stairs. He checked some of their pulse but felt nothing. It was part of the effect the powder had on them. "How did this happen?" he thought. He saw trails of spilled wine beside some of the bodies. He felt that the wine might have been compromised but he was clueless as to who could have done such.

Marcus saw the thick fog ahead. "At last" he whispered to himself. He could hear some growls coming from within the Fog but this did not faze him.

Once the ship entered the Fog it was impossible for him to see anything. He put his trust in the compass and kept the ship facing north.

Antonius saw they had entered the fog once he peaked into the main deck. He immediately ran back down to his cabin to collect his sword.

At that moment, something from the Fog made its way onto the ship. Marcus felt its presence.

"Why are you here?" The person said.

Marcus knew the voice and turned around. He held back his tears but his voice cracked as he said, "It has been four years. Are you not happy to see me?"

"You have put yourself in danger by coming here."

Marcus began walking closer to her but she said. When he saw who it was, his stomach sank and his heart almost burst. The fog made it hard to see but when he got a better view of her, he saw she was holding a bow in her left hand. A bag of arrows were on her back.

"Stop don't come any closer to me, he is watching us."

"It should have been me. I'm sorry I let him take you."

A tear escaped her eye as she readied her arrow and pointed it at Marcus.

The person Marcus was talking to was the love of his life, his wife. She was a brown-haired young maiden when Marcus met her on one of his journeys when he was twenty years of age. They had met rather unconventionally for a prince and a noble's daughter. Her name was Xaria. She was seventeen then.

He was riding his horse through the woods on the south side of Venduria, a nation that bordered Philonia on the west. She was the daughter of a noble in Venduria. She accompanied her father on a hunting session that day. She had with her some arrows and a bow. She was quite skilled with them and for this reason her father always took her on any hunting session he went.

On that day, Marcus was making his way through the forest. Xaria spotted his regalia and the two men on horses with him. She wondered who he was. She took notice of the seal on the back of his robe. It was the seal of the royal house of Maximus. She knew this, so she readied her arrow and fired. Not with the intent of killing him but to get his attention. The arrow caught his cape from the side and almost knocked him off his horse.

"Who dares?" he said.

She emerged from the bushes riding on her horse. The soldiers with him pulled out their swords but he motioned for them to put it away. He got off his horse and she got off her horse as well. They approached each other.

"I dare" she said with confidence.

"You have quite the courage to shoot at me. Do you know who I am?"

"I have heard so much about you." She said.

"Really what about me has graced your ears?" he asked.

"Many things" She said with a smile.

"Is that so?"

"So what brings you to these parts? You know that a prince should never travel these parts with only a few men. It's dangerous out here."

"Well the only dangerous thing that has happened since I got here was your arrow ruining my garment." He took her by the hand. "But I'm glad it happened." He kissed her hand. "Join me this Saturday; my mother shall be having a feast in my honor. I'd like you to come."

At that moment her father came from the bushes after her on his own horse. He saw her with Marcus.

"Your majesty, it is an honor." The man gave a bow. Marcus smiled and got back on his horse.

"I would like you and your daughter to join me for a feast this Saturday."

"We shall be there your majesty."

"Wonderful, till then, stay well." He rode off and the men accompanying him followed.

When Saturday came around, the feast progressed as planned. Annabelle, queen of Philonia, who was the widow of Calix, was happy to see her son had taken interest in courtship and had made up his mind to take Xaria as his wife. They wedded a month after the feast. The wedding was a splendor and of great prestige. Many royals and nobles from other nations attended the wedding even the Prince of Venduria, Yuvon, who was known to philander with women and detested the idea of a man giving himself to one woman, was at the wedding and it was there that he met his spouse, a Princess of Napel, Amera. Because of this he became very thankful to Marcus and relationship between Venduria and Philonia improved greatly.

A year passed and Annabelle passed away. Then Marcus ascended to the throne with Xaria as his queen. In the five years of his rule she comforted him whenever he felt frustrated by the Elders. He would come back to the Palace and lay on her bosoms. They would talk into the night. They had talked about having children but Marcus did not want any of his heirs to be subjected as he was so he did not take the idea of having children with delight.

When he had enough of the Elders and decided to leave the kingdom, she left with him. She felt he was capable and knew what he was doing. Marcus decided to command a portion of the navy. He always loved the sea so taking upon this task was a delight.

They sailed together through the high seas with a handful of crew men who only accompanied them to lend their services.

On one unfortunate day a storm caught their ship and blew them off course and straight into the Cursed Fog.

The Fog was known to be the dwelling place of a creature called Gammon. He was a very deceptive and sly creature. He called himself lord of the shadows. He was one of the six remaining higher children of fallen guardians that roamed the lands of men. He had done this for seven centuries. He would often create chaos in the presence of men. There was no place found in Pacifica, the home of the Guardians, for creatures of his kind. Their fathers who were once Guardians because of their deeds were also banished from Pacifica and cursed to roam the earth. When they found that they had been stripped of their state of being, they grew mad and wagged war against the world of men. They were no longer regarded as Guardians but as Ghouls or fallen guardians. There were thirteen of them, with their children collectively numbered over a thousand. They fought against the then small inhabitants of the earth. That age of war was forever marked in history as the War of the Fathers. The fathers of humanity fought against the fathers of this new class of beings whose form was *like the sea, forever changing. During that time the first Rising Guardian born, one blessed with powers. He saw to it that the monsters that terrorized the children of men were dealt with. The First Rising Guardian fought with honor and strength and after he defeated six of the thirteen Ghouls, he passed his responsibility of protecting the earth to his son before his transcending. He had dreamt and seen that there shall be others like him in the future, those who shall take the place of the fallen ones.*

Now three thousand years later some of the off-springs of the fallen ones still roamed the earth causing havoc and leaving before their presence is known. Gammon was one of these creatures.

Gammon had powers beyond the physical world because of his non-human half. After coming across a strong man who cloth himself in the attire of a shepherd three centuries ago, he never sought to disturb the lands of men again. So he left and terrorized the Blue Sea. He created the Fog and made it his dwelling place.

Gammon's true form was monstrous. He could change his shape to that of a handsome man but this made him extremely vulnerable. When he took his other form, two broken wings would come sticking out of his back. He could fly without them; they were a reminder of his fallen state. He stood ten feet in his monstrous state and six feet, seven inches in his human form. He was one of the products of the union of the fallen Guardians with earthly women. He hated his origin and hated humanity for being more perfect in form than he was. His hands were enormous, his torso broad and his head was twice the size of a nor-

mal human's head. His eyes were always ~~red in his~~
monstrous form. When he took the form of a man,
they turned green.

When Gammon got on the ship Marcus could
not see him but he heard the loud thump sound produced when Gammon landed on the ship, and he felt
the ship shake violently.

Marcus saw the red of Gammon's eye when he
came up to the main deck to investigate what had
landed on the ship. Gammon stared straight at him.
Gammon growled. The sailors who were on board on
the main deck took their swords and surrounded
Gammon. They were terrified at his form when they
saw him clearer. He looked at them and smiled. They
trembled because of the evil they felt emanating from
him.

Gammon made the fog dissipate from the main
deck so that Marcus could clearly see what he was
about to do to the sailors. Gammon viciously began
taking out the sailors as they charged at him, crushing their heads with his palms, and stepping on some
of them, crushing their chest with ease.

Marcus was frozen with fear. Xaria heard what
was going on above her, she was scared but that did
not stop her from taking action. She remembered that
they had taken some holy oil with them when they
left Philonia. The oil was believed to have been
blessed by the Guardians and so had powers to weak-
en dark forces such as Gammon. She dipped all her
arrows in the oil and took her bow with her and ran
to the main deck.

She stood tall and fired at Gammon; an arrow
struck him in his left shoulder, another on his neck

and a third on his right bicep. He fell to his knees and gave a loud cry. Marcus saw what happened and regained his confidence.

He readied his sword and charged at Gammon. He cut off one of Gammons wings. Gammon gave a louder cry and swung his hand back, knocking Marcus a few feet back. Marcus landed close to the Helm of the ship. He landed on his left arm.

Xaria kept shooting at Gammon. With every arrow he grew weaker. Gammon ran to the ledge of the ship and leaped out into the fog. Marcus saw him jump and expected to hear a splash. But Gammon had flown high above them but made it look like he had jumped into the sea.

Gammon swooped down and picked up Xaria.

Marcus heard her scream. He tried to get up but his left arm was hurting him badly. He picked himself up slowly and looked up. He saw Gammon in the air holding Xaria.

"Let her go."

"If you say so but I don't think she'll survive the fall."

"No wait." He begged

"I'll give you a choice. You let me take her and I promise not to kill her. Or you try to fight me and you both die."

"How can I trust that you'll keep your promise?"

"You humans do many foolish things and I know you'll be foolish enough to come back this way because your heart will be incomplete without her. So when you do, she will be the first one to welcome you."

Gammon then laughed and flew away.

At that moment the ship emerged from the Fog. Marcus fell to his knees and wept. He saw the carnage of the battle and his heart was filled with more sorrow. He vowed to himself that one day he'd return to the Fog and rescue Xaria. The ship sailed unguided and hit the shore of an island.

Five months later he was found by a trade ship heading from Sarbu to Philonia. The men on the ship asked him who he was and where he had journeyed from that caused him to land on the island alone. The men did not realize who he was because his beard had made him almost unrecognizable. He told them that his story was not important. Once he learnt of their destination. He asked the captain for a favor.

"Send a message to the king. Tell him his brother lives."

They left leaving him on the island because he requested it. After Antonius found out about the whereabouts of Marcus, he left the kingdom immediately to see him. He wanted to visit him as often as he could because he knew Marcus had chosen to stay on the island, but Marcus requested that he come only once a year. He obeyed his brother's request. He would come once a year and spend a week with him. This continued throughout Antonius's rule. Marcus kept what happened to him in the Fog to himself. When Antonius asked of his wife, he told her that she went back to Venduria to her father's house. Antonius did not believe Marcus but did not want to question Marcus for he knew this might anger him.

He had used the ship he arrived on the island with to build his cabin in the woods. The parts of the *ship he didn't use he buried. He also buried the bodies of the sailors that lost their lives.*

Chapter 6
Lord of the Shadows and the Twelfth

The Fog surrounded the ship and he saw her more clearly. He stood close to the helm of the ship. She stood on the main deck, a few feet from the main sail. Their eyes locked. He saw that she had remained unchanged by the years. He had grown a little more muscular and his facial hair was much more rugged than when they last saw each other.

"I'm sorry" she said. "I love you."

She readied the bow and arrow she had with her and aimed it at him. He stood still. He refused to raise his weapon against her. She fired. The arrow flew through the air towards him but was knocked off course by the lid of a wine barrel that was thrown in the way by someone.

Julian emerged from the shadows of the main-sail. He walked up to Marcus, and then set his eyes on Xaria. He looked back at Marcus and saw that Marcus's gaze was so firmly fixed on Xaria it was as If he did not notice him. He looked at Xaria, who was now prepared to fire another arrow.

"This does not involve you." She said.

"I don't know what quarrel you have with him but I will not let you kill him. Despite what he has done, he deserves a chance to redeem himself."

"Your face is familiar. What is your name?" she asked.

"I am Julian, son of Thanos."

"The illustrious fighter." she smiled.

"Julian step away this does not involve you" Marcus said

"Glad to see you have come out of your trance. If you want to battle against her you will have to wait your turn. I don't know where this witch of the sea appeared from…"

"Watch your tongue. Don't you dare raise your weapon against her. She is my wife. She is more skilled than you think but she's not my concern at the moment." Marcus felt an evil presence knowing where he was he expected Gammon to be close. He looked up and said. "He is."

Julian looked up and saw Gammon's red eyes glaring at them.

"Never in my life have I seen such an ugly creature!" Julian said.

"Who are you calling ugly?!" Gammon said and growled. Then he swooped down and landed hard on the main deck.

"I have heard of you. You are the creature of the Fog, the lord of the shadows, Gammon." Julian said in a trembling voice. Then he took a step back.

Gammon smiled. "Yes I am."

"Yes indeed you are but a name rings in my head that I remember that they call you." Julian said. He tried to appear unmoved by Gammon's size. "Ah yes the great ugly one."

"Watch your tongue little man."

"Julian, do not anger him." Marcus warned

"I know how powerful you are Gammon but the most powerful force on you is your face. Your ugliness has done more damage to my eyes than you ever could inflict on my body."

"What are you doing Julian?" Marcus asked rather confused.

"Trust me, I've heard about this creature and I know he has another side to him." Julian said.

"Even in my weakened state none of you can match me." Gammon said.

Marcus, Julian and Xaria witnessed him transform from his monstrous form into the form of a man of normal size. He knew this state made him weaker but he had been hurt by the remarks by Julian about the ugliness of his other form. When Gammon transformed into his human state he was clothed in a dark-red cloak.

"What is this?" Marcus asked.

"Keep on your guard. By doing this he is now weaker but he is still stronger than both of us." Julian said.

Gammon ordered Xaria to shoot at them. Gammons stood a few feet in front of her. She

readied her bow and arrow and shot. The arrow dashed past Gammon's right ear and
struck Julian in his left shoulder.

Julian yelled out in pain. Marcus unsheathed his sword and charged at Gammon.
Gammon smiled. With every swing Marcus
threw, Gammon dodged with ease. His movements were too fast for Marcus. Marcus grew
tired, fell to one knee and looked at Xaria. She
had her arrow pointed at him ready to fire. She
pulled the arrow back against the bow. Then
she quickly changed her aim, pointed it at
Gammon and released it. Gammon caught the
arrow and broke it.

"Love always makes them rebel," Gammon said, then he sighed.

Xaria ran to Marcus and helped him to his
feet.

"This is going to be fun for me...." Gammon said. "Knowing you three have no chance
against me." Gammon saw a few bodies of
some unconscious sailors. "Are those sailors
dead? You spared me quite the work by dispos-
ing of these sailors. I know you wouldn't have
wanted me to do it myself."

Gammon walked to one of the bodies.
There was a cup full of wine beside the body.
Gammon picked it up and sniffed it.

"They're not dead are they? No they are
just too drunk. This drink your kind indulges in
to drown your sorrows has always fascinated
me. When I cause great sorrows to a man, I

don't want a meager drink to make him forget it. I want it to haunt him for the rest of his life. Every waking moment and when he goes to sleep I want him to see my face in his nightmares."

Gammon drank the wine.

"Just as I thought, sour."

He threw the cup away. He turned to Marcus.

"I am tired of talking. It ends here."

He tried to transform back to his monstrous form but once a part of him changed it reverted back to his human form.

"What, how can this be?"

Marcus saw this as his chance to attack. He charged at Gammon but his attack was futile. Gammon struck him in the jaw causing Marcus to fall back down. Gammon looked at his hand and wondered why he could not transform. He felt his stomach rumble then he whispered to himself.

"The wine."

At that moment the clouds above began to gather. A few moments later lightning began to flash and thunders rolled.

Gammon looked up and smiled.

It so happened that when Gammon landed on the ship and it rocked violently, it caused Antonius to lose his footing and he hit his head on the side of the door of the cabin where his sword was. He was knocked out. The rolling of the thunder woke him up. Now he felt different

in himself. He sensed the presence of a great
evil on the ship. He could also feel a strength
growing inside of him. This was not the first
time he felt it but he knew that whenever that
feeling hit him, his body was preparing to fight
something beyond his normal strength. This
was a gift he had. Something that made him
different, something he did not understand yet
but utilized when the time needed it. This had
happened on only one other occasion when he
was young. Only two people had seen him in
this state, Calix and Mitis.

He remembered how he got knocked out.
He got up quickly and did not hesitate. He took
his sword and started for the main deck. As he
got closer to Gammon, he could feel the power
in him rising. When he got onto the main deck,
Gammon noticed him and said.

"Lovely, we have another who has volun-
teered to die."

He charged at Antonius with the full force
of a fist aimed Antonius's face. His speed was
incredible but Antonius caught Gammon's
blow. Gammon swung with his left but Antonius caught that hand as well and tightened his
grip on Gammon's arms. Gammon yelled out
in pain. He moved his head back as he prepared to hit Antonius with his head. Antonius
saw his attack and moved his head back. Then
he raised his leg up and kicked Gammon in the
chest. Gammon slid back across the floor. He
rolled and sprung to his feet quickly.

Gammon was struck with fear and anger at that moment. He leaped back and tried to transform into his monstrous form. The effects of the wine lingered no longer. His form began to change. His arms and head doubled in size. His broken wing protruded from his back, his claws came out and his eyes turned blood red.

"Glad to see you in your true form Gammon."

"Who are you and how do you know about me?"

"Don't flatter yourself Gammon. Your reputation is well known beyond the Fog. You hide here and wait for ships to wonder by so you could kill and devour some men. Then you let some survive so they can tell tales about you so you could become a legend in the eyes of men. Becoming more feared with every passing generation."

"It seems you've figured me out. Everyone has to leave a legacy somehow. Perhaps you know me more than I know myself."

"I also know something most men don't know."

"And what would that be."

"I know what you are."

Gammon scowled.

"Yes, I know that you are the son of a fallen guardian. As your father you also take many forms but this form your true form is the ugly beast that stands before us."

Gammon sighed, gnashed his teeth and said.

"Again, that word. I don't like that word. It's a shame that I have to kill you because you could spread my legend around the world. Tell me fool, what is your name?"

"I am Antonius, son of Calix."

Gammon eyes widened.

"You are the son of the twelfth Rising Guardian." Gammon said "But the prophecies were wrong. Your father never transcended. Even though it is believed a Rising Guardian cannot die, he is dead and rotting in the grave."

Antonius did not let himself be moved to anger by what Gammon had just said so replied with a steady voice.

"You will not speak of my father again. Because you insulted him I will make sure that you do in fact become legend. But the perfect legends are all dead, so I will insure to it that you take your place in death with them.

Gammon laughed.

"I'll be damned if I let the son of a failure overcome me. I am Gammon, Lord of the Shadows, and son of Sirius!"

"Today you shall join your father in the abyss."

"How are you sure that I can even die. I am a ghoul, and unlike my father, I am immortal."

"Men are mortal, you are half a man, and you dwell in the flesh right now. Everyone knows this truth, that which has flesh can bleed and that which bleeds can die."

Gammon charged at him. Antonius readied himself and was not moved by Gammon's size or speed. He stood in a stance ready to defend himself against a strike. He had his left hand in front ready to defend himself and with his right, he tightly gripped his sword.

Gammon attacked with a swift right punch but Antonius stopped it with left hand. The great difference in the sizes of their arms was stunning.

Marcus watched as his brother stood toe to toe with Gammon. He was amazed at his strength. "Where is he getting this strength from?" He thought

Gammon growled and tried to use his left hand to strike Antonius from overhead but Antonius leaped back and dodged it. Gammon's hand struck the floor. It broke through the floor and got stuck. Antonius saw this as his chance. He readied himself, charged at Gammon and cut off his left arm. Black blood began to spill out from the damaged limb. The detached arm soon turned to stone. Gammon fell to his knees. He tried to control the bleeding with his right arm. Even on his knees he still towered over Antonius. Antonius walked to him and pointed his sword upwards at his neck.

"Listen. Can you hear it Gammon, can you hear the cries of the souls you've taken. They cry for justice. Now I answer them and give them what they have longed for. Never again will you cause fear upon the sailors who shall venture this path, or anyone else."

"Wait" Gammon said. "Please, spare me. All I did was to defend myself. Everyone that came to the Fog made me their enemy."

"Liar! Your crimes will be paid for in full and all seamen shall rejoice at the news of your death."

Gammon growled. Antonius swung his sword and cut off Gammon's head. Gammon's body fell back. His head rolled and stopped at the feet of Marcus. Marcus looked at the head and then at Antonius.

"I have never seen this side of him." Marcus thought.

Marcus turned Xaria's gaze away from the stone head of Gammon and asked, "Are you alright?"

"Yes I'm fine." She said

"It's over." he embrace her and kissed her forehead. "Come with me." He walked her to a cabin below.

As Marcus passed his brother to proceed downstairs, he saw Antonius's skin was faintly glowing. Antonius did not acknowledge his brother. He did not want to reveal his true strength to his brother. It was a secret he had tried to hide from Marcus for a long time. Whenever he felt the presence of evil, his body would react in this way. He wondered why this had not happened when he heard the songs in the city or when the creature that spoke from the gray mist invaded his room. He remembered that he could not sense anything from them. They looked like apparitions, when he heard the voice he felt lost in a trance, for the thing that spoke to him was not in a physical body at that moment. That was why he felt he could not sense it.

He went to Julian, stretched out his hand and helped him back to his feet. The ship at that moment emerged from the Fog. The clouds above them cleared. They both looked at Gammon's stone body. The night sky was beautiful. The light of the full moon touched everything. Julian helped Antonius toss Gammon's stone form overboard. But Antonius took Gammon's head.

"That was impressive," Julian said as he yanked the arrow out of his left arm.

"Are you alright?" Antonius asked.

"I'll be fine, I've experienced worse."

Antonius turned and left to go back to his cabin downstairs. He put Gammon's head in one of the empty wine barrels. He stayed in his cabin for a while looking at the ceiling. After about five minutes he heard footsteps approaching. The door opened, Julian came in and sat on the other bed.

"What was that up there? Never has a man defeated a ghoul with such ease. Not just any ghoul, Gammon."

"He was proud. He was careless. His mistake was my advantage."

"It cannot be just that. Even without much effort he can desecrate an army of a hundred men. But you stood against him and you moved as quickly as he did, even quicker. What is your secret?"

"There is no secret to be told. Nothing you need concern yourself about."

Antonius got up to leave but Julian took his arm.

"I demand to know."

"Let go of me please."

Julian let go of his arm.

"I still do not understand why it happens but the presence of evil awakens a power in me that feels strange." Antonius said. "It feels like I carry the responsibility of many men on my shoulder when I feel the power rising. This is the third time it has happened."

He said and then left the room. He went to Marcus's room. He found him sitting on his bed. Xaria had fallen asleep. Marcus was watching her as she slept. He noticed something strange on her neck. He saw there was a mark on the left side of her neck. The mark looked like an 'x' with a snake twisted around it.

"Is she alright?" Antonius asked.

"Yes she'll be fine."

"I see why you wanted to go through the Fog. I'm glad to see that you got what you wanted."

Marcus looked at Antonius. Then calmly asked, "How did you do it?"

"Can we not talk about it?"

"No, tell me." He bellowed but then lowered his voice as not to wake up Xaria. He walked closer to Antonius. "All this while you have had the power to take down a ghoul like Gammon and you have hidden such from me."

"I don't understand it either."

"What Gammon said of our father and the prophecies being wrong, what did he mean?"

"I don't know."

Marcus looked at him intensely. Then he left. Marcus went back to the Main deck and saw that Julian was keeping the ship on the course he had set it on. Julian had treated his wound by tying a torn piece of clothing around it.

Marcus went to him.

"Some of the men have begun to regain consciousness. Go attend to them; I'll take over from here."

Julian then left to attend to the sailors.

He went and assisted the sailors who were regaining consciousness. Antonius had at that time made his way to Felix's cabin after he noticed some of the sailors regaining consciousness. He found Felix seated at his desk, his hand was on his head and his face looked a little pale.

"Are you alright Felix?" Antonius asked.

"I hope" Felix answered with his hand still on his head. He was a little bit shaken but was slowly regaining his composure. "What happened?"

"There was something in the wine."

"In the wine?" Felix looked at his cup, it had been knocked over and the wine spilled on the floor. He took the cup, looked inside and saw a little puddle of wine still in it. He wanted to drink it but he stopped himself. "Maybe I shouldn't."

Antonius laughed.

Marcus set the ship route towards Konstuliana and they arrived at the shore of Demoir, a small beach forty seven miles south west from Petra, the capital of Konstuliana.

Chapter 7
The Coronation

Is everything ready? Titus asked.

"Yes my lord." The guard replied. "The bishop, the scribes and the people await you."

"Splendid." He said as he put on the last piece of his regalia. He was wearing a white shirt, a red vest on top of that and his father's royal cape. The cape was dark purple. White fur was trimmed around the cape and it had the crest of the house of Maximus on it. The crest was a design of three pillars surrounding a white wing lion with a red mane. The winged lion many had assumed to be a creature called a Faracot. This crest Calix designed when he became king. He wore black leather boots that reached his shin. He put on his gloves and was set to leave the palace.

On this glorious day, the new king was to be crowned. Everything was going as he wanted except for one thing. The fair lady, Elana, who he had wanted to become his queen, was nowhere to be found that morning. He had asked the guards to search for her but they reported to him an hour after searching that they could not find her. He asked them if they saw anyone leave the palace at night. They told him they hadn't. He had spent the night with her and she sang him to sleep. He enjoyed her presence.

Now on this new morning, he thought that she had taken something valuable from the palace and escaped the city. He worried that she was just a spy. Then he thought to himself, "I cannot dwell on such now. When I become king I will handle this properly." He looked at the mirror one last time, fixed his hair and left.

The weather was beautiful. A horse carriage was set just outside the palace awaiting him. He walked out the palace with a bravado that revealed his readiness to assume the duties that awaited him as king. Darius was on a horse just beside the prince's carriage. He saw the prince walking towards him.

"Morning young prince."

"Today shall be the last day, you call me that."

"Well I am savoring these last times, Young Prince."

Titus got in the carriage and looked at Darius.

"It's a pity Darius. You're so old and yet you act so childish."

The smile on Darius's face disappeared.

"To the cathedral," Titus said to the man that controlled the horses that pulled his carriage.

"Yes my lord."

The carriage took him to the cathedral where the people were gathered. On the way they passed the rubbles of the house of the law, Titus looked at it and smiled. "Pity" he thought "If only I were given a chance to do that."

They arrived at the cathedral. Although it was in need of a few renovations, it was still a captivating structure to say the least. Inside the people were gathered, the priests, were in their place, soldiers had made two lines along the aisle of the cathedral. They had stationed themselves with their swords pointed high in the air, in a manner that soldiers facing each other made their swords touch right above their heads.

Titus arrived at the cathedral. The trumpeters stationed outside saw him and blew their trumpets. The people inside the cathedral stood up, the soldiers raised high their swords. They began to sing a hymn. He walked into the cathedral, through the aisle, underneath the swords of the soldiers and to the altar where the priest awaited his arrival. The scribes were at the first row of seats recording the event. The senators gathered themselves at a place prepared for them just opposite the choir. He climbed the steps of the altar and got on one knee before the bishop.

"Venerable," he said.

"Your majesty" the bishop replied and laid his right hand upon the prince's head. On his left hand he held a book of ceremonies that outlined how the coronation was to take place and the oaths the new king will have to swear to before he ascends to the throne.

The bishop then spoke to the congregation.

"As we have gathered here today before the Guardians, sons of the Great King, He who watches over us, we shall commence to crowning our new king. Let us pray."

"The Great King calls all people to righteousness, he calls all to do well to their neighbors, and live by his statutes. He has set an example for all kings of the earth to follow. Today we shall crown Titus ruler over our nation and we pray that the favor of the Great King be with you. Let his blessing forever flow upon you and guide you in all your ways, So that you shall rule with justice and integrity over Philonia, just as The Great King does over Pacifica and all the worlds beneath his feet."

"May it be so." responded the congregation.

"Now it is time for the blessing." The bishop said.

The priest stood a few feet from the bishop. He had in his hand a bowl filled with holy oil. The bishop motioned for the priest to bring the bowl forward. He came forward and stood beside the bishop. The bishop dipped two fingers in the oil. He then placed his hand in the air just above Titus's forehead. The oil drips flowed down his face, touched his lips, continued down his neck and into his garment. Then the bishop placed his two fingers on Titus's forehead and said the blessing.

"As this oil flows down your body, remember the Philonian kings and queens, whose blood flow through your veins. All from our beautiful mother, Philonia. Remember all the good and humble kings before you, following in their footsteps. Learn from the mistakes of the ruthless and damned kings. I pray blessing upon you Titus, son of Calix. As you ascend to assume your duties as king, remember the ways of your father. Rule to protect your people and your reign shall be long. Amen."

Following the blessing was the crowning and then the oaths the king would take before his rule began. Darius had in hand a small red pillow, on which rested the majestic crown. He came forwards and stood on the other side of the bishop. The bishop took the crown and placed it on Titus's head.

"Titus, are you ready to assume your duties as king?"

"I am."

The bishop then looked at the book of ceremonies and began the oaths. There were seven oaths the king was to take before his rule commenced. The bishop began,

"Do you Titus Maximus promise to lead with integrity the people of this kingdom?"

"Just as the Great King rules with integrity, so also shall I lead these people with integrity."

"Do you Titus Maximus promise to Judge fairly when disputes are brought before you by the people, not to show partiality towards anyone you favor?"

"Just as the Great King judges all people fairly, so shall I judge my people fairly."

"Do you Titus Maximus promise to protect the people of this kingdom from all threats whether they are from without or within the kingdom?"

"Just as the Great King protects mankind from the wiles of The Adversary and the children of the fallen ones, so also shall I protect these people from whatever threats that may arise in or outside this kingdom."

"Do you Titus Maximus promise to serve the people in a manner that shows that you care for their needs and are willing to show your love for them as their king, just as your father and brother, Antonius did?"

Titus looked up at the bishop then back down to the floor.

"Just as the Great King rules with love and humbles himself to show his love for humanity" he said now in a different tone, "so shall I show my love for these people by my service to them."

"Do you Titus Maximus promise to rule with kindness and mercy the people of this kingdom, to show mercy, exhibit temperance and patience towards them?"

"Just as the Great King is patient towards humanity, so shall I show mercy, exhibit temperance and be patient towards the people of this kingdom." Titus said with a slight scorn in his voice.

"Do you Titus Maximus promise not to dabble in the dark ways or abandon the faith of your fathers', so that your loyalty shall be to the Great King, as our loyalty is to you?"

"The Great King is to be honored, so to him shall I give my loyalty."

"Finally, do you Titus Maximus promise that if you chose to take a queen that she also shall abide to the oaths made here today?"

Titus looked up at the bishop but before he could speak, he began to hear songs. Not from the choir or congregation but the songs that gripped his heart and made him wonder. The people heard it too and were entranced by it. The priest quickly dipped his hand in holy oil so as to rub on his ears, but it was too late. The songs had enchanted him and he knew it. The songs at first seemed to be coming from all around them. Then soon they were heard from a central point, the entrance of the cathedral.

Elana stood at the entrance singing as she walked slowing down the aisle. The songs came out from the core of her essence and filled the room. Everyone beheld her radiant beauty. Titus looked back and saw her walking down the aisle. Her skin, hair and face were radiating just as it was when he first saw her sing. She was clothed in a flowing purple gown. She had in her hand a small purple pillow with the queen's crown on top of it. The last person to wear the crown was Annabelle, his mother. When Xaria became queen, a new crown was made and she wore the new crown. Marcus had wanted to honor his mother by making her crown special, attributing it only to her so that she would be remembered as the last queen to wear it.

The crown was magnificent in its design. It was a silver crown with a diamond the size of a thumb in the middle. Titus got up and went to her. He saw the crown took it and placed it on her head. Then he grabbed her waist, pulled her to himself and kissed her. The congregation was released from their trance and saw the king kissing this lady who they had never seen. The priest also came out from his trance.

Titus took her hand and led her to the bishop. They both knelt at the bishop's feet.

"Who is this?" the bishop asked in astonishment.

"She is my queen," Titus said.

The bishop was about to question him but he held his peace and continued with the ceremony.

The bishop said the final blessings over the new king and his queen. Titus stood to his feet and so did Elana. Then a young senator by the name of Crispin Gino came forward and handed Titus his scepter. Another young senator came forward and gave Titus a new book with his name ascribed on it. It was a diary attributed to him. Darius was given a sword by a soldier that stood close to the altar. The sword belonged originally to Calix. It was attributed to him also by Marcus and kept as a relic to remember him. Darius handed the sword to the bishop and the bishop gave it to Titus. Titus took it and raised it in the air. The people roared in excitement.

"Behold your king and queen." The bishop announced.

Titus turned to Elana. Her gaze was firmly fixed on him. He took her by the hand and they both walked out together. The soldiers on both aisles raised their swords as the new king and his queen walked out of the cathedral.

They left the cathedral and arrived in the palace. The guards were warm and welcoming towards the new woman who they saw with the king. The guard who had spotted Elana bathing was standing at the entrance of the palace. As Elana walked past him she glanced at him and smiled. A chill ran down his spine. He tried to keep a steady face but his lips quivered.

Titus took her hand and led her to the throne room. He had told a servant to bring up some wine for him them. Two gold chalices were brought for both of them. The servant filled both cups with wine from a silver wine jug.

"Leave us," Titus said to the servant. He took the jug from the servant and placed it on a table close by.

"I'm glad you decided to return," he said as he took his cup. "I was worried I would have had to hunt you down."

"And would you have found me?" she asked.

"Yes," he said and then drank some wine. "I'm very persistent."

She smiled. He walked to her and kissed her.

"You're the most beautiful thing I've ever set my eyes on."

He took her hand and kissed it. She kept silent as he gazed into her eyes.

At that moment Darius walked in on them. Titus looked at him with contempt. He instructed him to stop where he was. Titus whispered something to Elana. She left then he went and dropped his chalice on the table. He walked to the throne and sat down. It was right about sunset at the time.

Titus motioned for Darius to approach the throne.

"My king," Darius said as he bowed and knelt on one knee with his hand over his chest. "The soldiers have retrieved the bodies of the Elders from the rubbles. We wanted to know what you want us to do with them. Should we prepare a new tomb for them?"

"No." Titus said casually. "Burn the bodies…and burn them outside the city, those men are not worthy of honor."

"But…"

"Don't argue with me."

"As it pleases your majesty." Darius responded with a quiver in his voice.

"Do I have to think for you Darius?" Titus said. "If I have to be reminded of anything that limits or anyone that challenges my power, I will see to it that they are dealt with and they are dealt with publicly. Watch your steps Darius."

Darius got up and left. The crown had received all its power back now that the Elders were no more and this made Titus very happy. The last king to have ruled unhindered was his father Calix.

He got up, left the throne room and went to his chamber. He had instructed Elana to wait for him there. He went in and saw her. She was staring out the window looking at the city. She had a chalice in her hand half-filled with wine. She noticed him enter and smiled. He went to her and kissed her.

"Sing to me" he whispered.

She put down her wine, took his hand and led him to bed. He lay down slowly and she lay on top of him. Her songs began to flow from her as he kissed her lips, cheeks and neck. The songs flowed into him and he felt a peace inside himself he hadn't felt in a long time. This drew him closer to her. His kisses slowed and he began to feel himself grow tired. Elana laid one lasting kiss on his lips before he fell into a deep sleep. When he fell asleep she gazed at him. She then kissed his forehead. She looked out the window. Nightfall had come upon them.

She got up from the bed and went to the closest. While going through his garments, she found one she liked. It was a red robe, splendid in design and made distinct only for the king. She removed her robe. As she stood there bare, she sang a quiet song to herself. She turned to Titus who was now fast asleep. As she sang to herself, her form began to change and soon she resembled him in likeness. She walked and looked in the mirror that hung on the wall by the door. She smiled when she saw that she resembled him completely. She then put on the robe. She blew out the candles in the room and left.

This happened a day after Antonius was arrested.

Chapter 8
A Prisoner Once Again

Land Ho! a young sailor exclaimed as he looked through a telescope and saw the shore of Demoir. He was far up upon the main mast of the ship, holding onto it as he looked through the telescope at their set destination.

Antonius arose at the young sailor's shout and made his way from the cabin below to the main deck. He was happy and welcomed the morning with a smile. Marcus was still guiding the ship on its route but could not see the land the young sailor bellowed about. He looked ahead, squinted a little and saw an array of tiny trees on one part and a small hill. Antonius went to Marcus.

"How's Xaria?" he asked.

"She is still sleeping." Marcus replied. "Something about her bothers me."

"She seems the same. Is there a need to worry?"

Marcus was thinking about the mark he saw on her neck.

"No, it is of no use to worry."

Antonius looked ahead and saw the shore.

"There it is." He said.

"Indeed so." Marcus said.

Antonius saw that there was no one on the grassy shore. There were boats and big ships of war but not one soul. This made him a little bit concerned because Demoir, as he remembered used to be filled with activities. When they made their way onto shore, he told them not to offload anything yet. He had wanted to head inland but he thought of the many men that were with him and wondered if they were a hindrance or if they could help further his cause.

Felix made his way off the ship, so did Marcus, Julian, Xaria and most of the sailors. Felix took note of Xaria's presence and remembered that he had heard the story that Marcus's wife was lost in the fog. Her presence confirmed his suspicion that they had sailed through the fog while he was unconscious.

Antonius went to Felix and said.

"Thank you."

"It has been my pleasure."

"So will you be heading back soon?"

"The navy is yours, we have sworn our loyalty to you, wherever you go, we'll follow."

Antonius with his hand on Felix's shoulder said,

"I cannot thank you enough for helping me but I would like for you to take these sailors and go back home. They have families and I don't want to separate them from their loved ones. When Philip's ship arrives tell him to set course back for Philonia, I'll be heading on from here."

"No one will be going anywhere." A voice said resounding from the thick forest behind them. A man came forth on a horse out of the bushes. He wore a knight's armor with the crest of Konstuliana on the left breastplate. He removed his helmet. He was a young man, about the same age as Antonius. He had very broad shoulders and a well-trimmed beard. His hair was black, short and well kempt. His eyes were serious. He had a crooked nose, one of the most striking features of his years of battle.

There was an army of knights on horses that followed him from the thick bushes. Some of them were armed with bows and arrows, some with crossbow, others with swords and shields. They numbered about two hundred and fifty.

The pompous young knight who emerged first from the thick forest spoke in a stringent accent.

"So what is this, an invasion of some sort? How many men do you have with you?"

Antonius kept stern eyes on him. He recognized the man but the man did not seem to know at the moment it was Antonius who he was speaking to.

"We are not here for a fight." Antonius replied.

"Well then why do you bring a warship? Is an armada on its way also?"

The man came down from his horse.

"I heard you talk of another ship on its way, if this is not an invasion why did you bring two ships?"

Antonius did not answer him, so Marcus spoke up at once.

"Do you think if we were looking to start a war, we would have brought only one ship? Don't be daft man, as my brother said; we are not here for a fight."

The knight turned to Marcus and with a smug look said,

"Do you know who I am?"

"No, please enlighten us." Marcus said in a mocking tone. Marcus had never met the man before.

"I am Jeffery Miles, nephew of Mitis Miles and head of the Knights Order. The king, my Uncle has given me power over the affairs of the Order of his Knights and power over the seamen of the kingdom."

"So why should we care about your responsibilities. Our business is with the king not with you." Marcus said.

Jeffery turned to Marcus and walked to him. He looked at Xaria and then back at Marcus. Xaria was standing beside Marcus.

Jeffery took Xaria's hand and kissed it. Marcus tried to keep calm but his palms began to sweat, he felt his heart beat increase and he ground his teeth.

"Fine lady" Jeffery said. "What are you doing with such a savage man? Come with me and I will treat you well."

Marcus took Jeffery's hand twisted it. Jeffery got down on one knee because of the pain. Some of the knights who Jeffery had come with readied their arrows to fire.

"Let go of me" Jeffery said in a calm voice. "Or I order them to fire."

"I could kill you before those arrows strike me down." Marcus said staring down at Jeffery.

"And I could kill you before those arrows strike you down." Jeffery said. His stare was cold. "I may be the king's nephew but I assure you, my place as first Knight has nothing to do with my relation to him."

Xaria held Marcus hand, he looked at her and then let go of Jeffery.

"Wise choice" Jeffery said. "I've had enough, Men ransack the ship." Then he started making his way back to his horse.

The knights got off their horses and charged at Antonius and the company of men with him.

Felix pulled out his sword, and so did the sailors. Marcus and Julian also readied their swords.

"Enough!" Antonius bellowed. "No blood shall be shed here today!"

Everyone fixed their eyes on Antonius as he walked to Jeffery.

"Who do you think you are too…" Jeffery said but, silenced himself once Antonius took a hold of his armor.

"You've said enough" Antonius said. "We will do as you say if you respect yourself and respect us. We are not here for a fight!"

Antonius let go of Jeffery and went to Felix.

"Let them take what they want from the ship. We have to get to Petra. I have to see the king. If letting them ransack the ship for spoilt wine and stale bread will get us closer to Petra so be it."

Antonius turned to Jeffery.

"Do as you wish."

"I would have done what I wished without your permission," Jeffery said.

Jeffery gave the signal and a hand full of knights climbed on board unto the ship and searched everything. From the captain's cabin to the crew's cabins and the wine cellars, no room was left untouched. The men brought to land all the materials they found on the ship. They found fifteen barrels of wine. Nine of which were empty, five were filled with wine and the last was the barrel in which Antonius hid Gammon's head. They found a chest in the captain's cabin.

The men brought out everything and brought it before Jeffery. Jeffery shook all the wine barrels and ordered for those that were empty to be put back on the ship. The rest he ordered to be carried with them back to Petra. He opened the chest. He beheld precious stones and gold coins. He smiled. He closed the chest and got back on his horse.

"We will take everything with us, including these prisoners," Jeffery said.

Marcus looked at Antonius in a manner that gave Antonius the impression that he did not agree with them being treated in such a way. Antonius looked back at Marcus and motioned slightly in a manner that showed that he was ready as well to fight but that they should keep the peace for the moment.

"You two quadrants," Jeffery said. "Stay here till the next ship arrives, I'll take the prisoners to the city."

Before they were taken away, Antonius noticed an unusual creature leap off from one of the trees on the right side of his field of vision. He made it out to be some sort of bird but he thought it to be bigger than any bird he had ever seen.

Half of the knights Jeffery came with stayed at the grassy shore and waited till the ship of Philip arrived. Once it arrived, about seven hours later they sent it back.

In the meantime, Jeffery lead the group of knights that were taking Antonius and the company of people that came with him to Petra, the capital of Konstuliana. They walked the twenty-seven mile journey with the knights surrounding them. Half way through the journey, a knight gave up his horse to Xaria who had grown tired. Marcus thanked the knight.

After they had traveled eighteen miles, the forest was not as thick anymore. They came across a narrow road that lead straight to the south gate of Petra. They walked the remaining five miles along this road.

They arrived at Petra. The city was known for its buildings structures that were admired and treated as relics of a different age, a more ancient time. Mitis had wanted to remodel the city entirely when he was crowned king after the war but the buildings of the city caught his interest. Their stone structures were a marvel to behold. He admired the way in which each stone was laid upon the other in a fashion that created very magnificent structures as a whole. This made them appear awesome, especially the way in which they had been preserved. After the war was won, he made sure that the damaged buildings were restored.

In the years when Hermes Helms the second, the wicked king ruled Konstuliana, Petra had one city wall but after Mitis began his rule, one of the building projects he undertook was the building of a second city wall surrounding the original city wall, after the wall had been repaired. So seven years later the city now had two city walls, the outer and inner city wall. The space between both walls was twelve meter. The space was used as a training ground for young squires. The inner wall was four and a half meters high and a meter thick. The outer wall was six meters high and one and a half meters thick. The only way into the city was through one of the four gates, either through the North, west, east or south gate.

They walked in through the south gate and into the city. The knights led them to the castle. They got to the gate of the castle and the guards stopped them. Jeffery got down from his horse, went to the guards and spoke to them. The guards told him that so many people could not be let in to see the king. He could only have to take a hand full of them. They told him that they could keep the rest of them in the prison yard while the king addressed the important prisoners he got. The guards also saw the bounty that Jeffery had acquired from his prisoners.

Jeffery looked back at the lot of people he had brought. Antonius stood first in front of all of them. Jeffery looked at him with spite. "You will be the first to see the king." Then he ordered the guards to chain his hands. They did as he commanded. Then they led Antonius into the palace.

Jeffery got back on his horse, the castle gates opened and he strode right in with ten other knights who were well armed and ready against Antonius. They reached the entrance of the castle. There stood a guard, "Sir" the guard said as he bowed and ushered Jeffery in.

Jeffery got off his horse and took a hold of Antonius's chain and dragged him into the castle as if he were some beast of burden. Antonius did not struggle but humbly walked in. They led him through the corridors of the palace, as they walked he admired the statues and bust of honored men who were set up in the palace. In the middle of the foyer, there was a grand sculpture set there that drew all attention to itself. He had seen the statue twice before but now it looked even more remarkable. It was a statue of his father, standing tall, holding in his hand a crown. There was at the feet of this statue a man, on one knee, set as if ready to be crowned by his father. He knew who that man was, and he was about to meet him, once again, this time as a prisoner.

They reached the entrance of the throne room and the guards standing there stopped them. One of the guards noticed Antonius and recognized his face. He saw a bit of shock and doubt on the guard's face but this did not surprise him. The guards opened the tall doors and let them in. He walked in and his gaze touched everything; it was the same, as he remembered it four years ago.

He walked in with chained hands but a free mind. He remembered the words of his father 'do not let your circumstance overwhelm you'. Mitis stood up once he entered. The first time the king ever stood up in the presence of a prisoner. Jeffery walked to the king, got on one knee, took the king's hand and kissed it.

"Your Majesty," Jeffery said.

"Why have you brought him here?" Mitis asked.

Jeffery stood up, looked at Antonius and then back at Mitis.

"We found him with a crew of over five hundred sailors," Jeffery said. "They came in a warship, I thought it was an invasion of some sort but he said they weren't here for a fight."

Mitis fixed his eyes on Antonius. Antonius was not very pleased to be treated as a prisoner.

Mitis made his way down the marble steps that led up to his throne. Antonius stood a few feet from the base of the steep steps, the knights surrounding him. As the king walked down, the knights stepped back from Antonius.

Antonius would still not look at him. Mitis face was now the more serious. He stood in front of him.

"I am not pleased by your presence. Why have you come here?" Mitis asked

"As you can see by these chains, I have been brought here as your prisoner." Antonius replied and looked Mitis straight in his eyes. To do such was deplorable. He was the prisoner, standing before the king, yet he acted as if they were equals.

"Jeffery brought you here because he said you were in Demoir, with a crew of over five hundred men. Also I hear you had warships. What were you doing in Demoir?" Mitis asked

"Even If I had come here alone I would still have been treated this way. Your nephew does not recognize me because I wear the attire of a sailor. So he has treated me like a mere prisoner." Antonius replied.

"I did not inquire about how you were treated. You have not answered my question. What were you doing in Demoir?" Mitis said more strictly in a slightly higher tone.

Antonius stared straight at him, showing no fear whatsoever of Mitis's taller stature or the look of disdain he gave him. They stood there looking at each other but for a few moments then Antonius spoke.

"I" he started, "…was hoping to make my way here."

"I've told you…" Mitis started but then was interrupted by Antonius.

"I know that I am not welcome here and my presence displeases you but I did not leave my kingdom as a fugitive to come here to say 'hello'. I came here because I need your help." Antonius said.

"My help?" Mitis asked rather surprised. "Why me, Why not one of the other kings who actually take pleasure in your presence."

"Because none of the other kings is as close to my family as you are." Antonius answered

"Two days ago, I got news from a senator in Philonia that you had been arrested for the murder of the Elders. So I see that not even your patience could be tested for so long. Why did you kill them?" Mitis asked knowing his words were not true. He did this to test Antonius.

Antonius was silent. His stare now diverted away from Mitis. He looked at the men surrounding him and then at Jeffery who stood beside the throne. He bent his head low and took a deep, silent breath.

"You won't give me an answer." Mitis said then he paused a few seconds and waited for Antonius once more. "I have other matters to attend to, knights take him away."

The knights seized Antonius and were about to drag him out of the throne room. Mitis turned and shook his head as he walked back to his throne. But then he heard Antonius respond,

"Why do you treat me like a commoner, a stranger, worse as if I was an enemy? Would you have treated my father this way if he came to you seeking help?"

Mitis stopped where he stood. One of the knights close to Antonius punched him.

"How dare you speak to the king like that?" The knight said.

Mitis looked back at Antonius. He turned and walked back down to Antonius.

"I reign as king because of your father but that does not change anything. I owe you nothing."

"Yes you do…you owe me a reason," Antonius said.

"A reason?" Mitis asked.

"Ever since my father's death, you've hated me and treated me as if I were the cause of his death. Never once have I insulted you. I have always respected you. Yet you keep pushing me away…"

"Enough," Mitis said.

"No, you will let me speak. My father gave everything to protect those he loved, my brothers, my mother, the people of our kingdoms and his closest friends. My mother told me that he died to protect us. Till this day I do not understand what she meant but you were there, weren't you, beside my father before he died. Did he die because of me? Is that why you have hated me since then?"

Mitis was silent because Antonius's words struck a nerve in him. It kindled back memories that he had long tried to move from. Mitis was taken back to the night of Calix's death. The night was clear in his mind. At that moment guilt gripped his heart. He bowed his head in shame and felt that he had in a way betrayed his best friend by not treating his son kindly. He stretched out his hand and helped Antonius back to his feet. He then embraced him. Then he said softly,

"Your father was a kind man and treated everyone with mercy, even his enemies. He taught me to do the same but his death made me forget his lessons." Mitis paused and uttered words he never thought he would say. "You are welcome to stay with me."

"Thank you." Antonius said.

"The men that came with you, the five hundred they can stay also, not in the castle but in the communal houses." Mitis said then turned to Jeffery. "Loosen the chains of the men that came here with Antonius and make sure they are well accommodated."

Jeffery walked down the marble steps of the throne and out of the throne room. But before he left, he went to Antonius,

"I, I.." He started but couldn't organize his words.

"All is forgiven," Antonius said. "Please treat Marcus and the rest more respectably. I know he can be a little impatient but for my sake be patient with him."

Jeffery unlocked Antonius chains and left.

"Marcus is here with you?" Mitis asked.

"Yes, surprisingly it wasn't hard persuading him to leave the island. I didn't know that he had his intentions for doing so."

"There's an agenda behind most action he takes." Mitis said. "Your father was the same way."

"It seems so. Thanks again for your kindness."

Mitis smiled.

"Come with me," he said. Then they left the throne room.

It was about three o'clock in the afternoon at that time.

Mitis led Antonius to a guest room in the castle. As they walked through the hallway, he admired the tapestry that hung on the wall in one of the many hallways. A purple carpet ran under their feet from one end of the hallway to the other. He remembered a day he had walked along the hallway with his father when he was a child. They got to his room and Mitis showed him in.

He walked into the room and appreciated what for what he saw. Mitis was taken by surprise that the room was already set and prepared. As if someone had known that he would be there today.

"Well this was unexpected," Mitis said. "This room hasn't been used in a while. Yet it seems to have been prepared for you..." he stopped then he smiled.

Antonius was walking slowly, admiring the room when he noticed that Mitis had stopped mid-sentence. He looked at him.

"Eulalie knew you were coming," Mitis said.

"Send my thanks to her."

"I think she'll be here soon, so you'll have the chance to do that. In the meantime rest easy,

I'll get you a personal servant who will be at your service when you need him." Mitis said

"No, that is not necessary. I'll be fine." Antonius responded kindly.

Chapter 9
A Special Guest of the King

The others who had come with Antonius had been by order of Jeffery, gathered in the Prison yard. Among them were Marcus, Julian and Felix. Xaria was the only woman in their mist. Marcus sat beside her on a bench close to the walls of one of the cells. He held her very close to himself. He could tell that she was not feeling well. He could see that when she gazed at him and faintly smiled, her eyes were wonderfully glowing but her face flushed a light red color. She pressed closer to him, he kissed her head.

"It's so cold," she whispered.

He took off his shirt exposing his body to the cold winter wind. He put the shirt over her and wrapped his arms around her.

"Is that better?" he asked.

"Yes" she replied softly.

The clouds above began to gather, soon a light drizzle poured over them.

"Why do they make us wait outside in the cold?!" Julian asked loudly and obviously dissatisfied.

"We have willingly become their prisoners" Felix said. "Never have I been captured without a fight."

"Antonius made a wise choice," Marcus said. He had wished not to admit it, but now he understood his brother's decision more clearly. "It's better that we are alive and no lives were lost, besides if we had chosen to fight, nothing good would have come out of it."

"In my glorious days, with a crew of just fifty men I could have taken on those knights," Felix said.

"Well those days are done. Don't conjure up unnecessary memories," Marcus said. "What could've been or what should've happened cannot change the situation. Let's just hope Antonius finds favor with the king."

It was late in the afternoon, a few minutes before the seventeenth hour when the drizzle stopped and the cold winds died down. The gates of the prison yard swung open as Jeffery rode in on his white stallion. He was not clad in his armor but was adorned in a robe that signified those of noble standings. He wore a white shirt underneath the outer eloquently designed purple robe. His sword was appropriately placed at his waist. The men were a little bit rowdy so he called for silence. Once there was silence he addressed them.

"Men of Philonia, by order of the king you are free-men, to depart if you wish or stay and be guests of the king."

They murmured among themselves. The prisoners that had left with Antonius took this offer with delight.

"We'll stay" shouted one of them. Following his words were noises made by other ex-convicts in agreement with what he said.

"He does not speak for us," a sailor remarked.

Amidst the sea of voices, and different opinions, Felix got up and walked to Jeffery, Irate and frustrated. The voices slowly died down.

"I don't care to stay here not one more hour here but my loyalty is to Antonius. I must speak with him."

"Antonius is a special guest of the king," Jeffery said. "The king must invite you in before you can see him."

"See here…" Felix said in a louder tone as he took a hold of Jeffery's robe. "I personally know the king. I demand his presence now."

"The king is the one who demands your presence not you his. I too personally know the king, he is my uncle." Jeffery said back in anger. "Let go off my shirt, old man," Jeffery said as he knocked away Felix's hand.

Mitis at that moment arrived at the prison yard. He strode in on his dark-brown stallion. He was accompanied by a hand-full of guards. They had brought with them food supplies and blankets for the now 'king's guests'. Felix saw Mitis and Mitis gaze caught Felix. He got off his horse and with a smile on his face he embraced Felix.

"I cannot believe it. Old friend, you finally decided to visit. How goes things?" Mitis asked.

"Visit? Yes visit." They laughed. "We are here for more than friendly greetings," Felix replied. "But in all it is good to see you too."

"Since you are here why not join me this evening for supper. The night will soon fall upon us."

"As much as I would love to, I must discuss matters with Antonius before I decide if I wish to stay."

"Very well, He's in the castle. I will be heading back soon. You can join me on my journey back."

Mitis looked around at the men in the prison yard. His attention stopped on Marcus. He observed as one of the soldiers handed Marcus a blanket, which he immediately wrapped around Xaria to keep her warm. Mitis was not aware at that point that he was looking at Marcus but he felt that the man who caught his gaze looked familiar. When Marcus saw Mitis, he stared at him for a few seconds and turned his attention back to Xaria.

"Excuse me old friend," Mitis said to Felix. "I'll return in a moment, there is someone I must see."

Mitis made his way to Marcus.

"You're a good man," Mitis said.

"I don't think you know me very well," Marcus replied.

Mitis gave him a curious look.

"I feel I've seen you before, who are you?"

"I am Marcus, son of Calix."

Mitis's eyes widened.

"I almost did not recognize you. I heard of what happened to you at sea. Good to see you are alive. This must be your lady."

"Yes, she is my wife."

"Well it is a pleasure to meet you." Mitis said with a smile. "Antonius has spoken with me and he has gained my favor. I also extend my kindness to you, join me, and stay in the castle as my guests."

Marcus looked at Mitis intently.

"What of these men, how shall they be kept out of the cold?"

"The guards will accompany them to communal houses not far from here. They will be well accommodated."

Mitis kept his word. The soldiers soon after led the men who wanted to stay in the kingdom to communal houses. Most of the prisoners that escaped with Antonius embraced the invitation to stay, the sailors however consulted with Felix. Felix told them that they should stay in the houses in the mean time until he consults with Antonius on how he would want them to proceed.

Mitis got back on his horse and asked a soldier close by to bring forth a horse for Marcus. The horse was brought to Marcus by the soldier. Marcus helped Xaria unto the horse first. Then he mounted it. It struggled a little but he calmed it and rode slowly.

Jeffery mounted his horse too. Felix feeling a bit excluded, mounted a horse that belonged to a soldier.

"I hope the owner won't mind." Felix said. Then he readied it to ride. The horse lifted its front legs into the air, then quickly stomped them on the ground. It neighed and strode around.

Marcus sighed.

"This is why I don't like these wild creatures. She's almost as wild as the sea!" Felix said. Soon the horse calmed down and he controlled it better. He rode it to position itself beside the horse of Mitis.

Mitis rode off first. Xaria leaned closer to Marcus as he readied the horse to leave the prison yard. She rested her head on his back as the horse slowly began to stride out of the prison yard.

Meanwhile in the castle, Antonius was gazing out the window of the guest room, watching the setting winter sun. He felt the chill of the coming night through the open window. He thought deeply about everything that had happened. His mind then drifted towards the night he felt the presence of evil in his chamber, the day before the death of the Elders. He was still unsure if it was a very vivid nightmare or an apparition. He closed the window and the pulled curtains together. He lit some candles to illuminate the room. Upon lighting the last candle, there was a knock on the door.

He went and opened it. It was Eulalie, the queen.

"Your grace," he said politely, greeting her. She smiled. She had in her hand a well-tailored blanket, which was blue and had white stripes. She gave it to him.

"Keep warm," she said. "The winter here is very harsh."

He took the blanket from her and placed it on the bed. She still stood at the door.

"The king said you knew I would be coming."

"Yes, my visions grew stronger in the last few days. I felt your presence drawing closer."

He invited her in and when she entered she went to sit on the chair beside his bed. He sighed as he went to sit on the bed to talk with her. She noticed the distress on his face.

"Why do you let your circumstance bother you?" she asked. "Don't worry you'll be safe here."

"I want to go back. I know how foolish I sound, but I must know what I saw."

"It's not safe to go now. You're a wanted man. News about you is spreading to all kingdoms. You must remain here for the time being."

"You are right. I cannot go, I cannot go alone, nor can I take Felix and his crew with me. I have put their lives in danger, because they still remain loyal to me. But...I...don't want to be the spark that ignites war between our kingdoms."

"That is not going to happen."

"Titus is not a patient person. Just like Marcus, he hated the Elders. I did not even give a thought to their power because I knew if I considered them, I might have grown to hate them. I don't understand what my father was thinking splitting the power of the crown. I was one man against five men who together all had the same power as me, maybe even more." He smiled a bit. "I know that you are aware of my innocence."

"Yes," she said kindly.

"Help me then, help me prove my innocence."

"I can't do that. It would be worse for everyone if you were to go back. Your presence here is even a danger to all of us, Mitis knows this, yet he let you stay."

"I cannot stay in hiding forever."

"No, you can't, not even if you wanted to."

"What do you mean?" Antonius asked.

"I think you know. You keep denying your feelings about things you fear might be true."

"You sound like my father. His words always have a way of digging through my pretense."

She smiled.

"Your father as good as he was, was not a perfect man but his lessons are to be heeded at all times. Anything that bothers you, you can tell me."

He took a breath and paused for a moment. His eyes wondered around the room for a few seconds, and then he looked back at Eulalie. At that moment a servant, who had run around the castle looking for the queen, stood just outside the open door. He had heard her voice as he was coming down the hallway.

"The king has returned" the servant said. Eulalie stood up.

"It is almost suppertime, after we have eaten, we can continue this conversation. As of now, I must go welcome my husband." She said then left. But before she departed his presence, she looked back at him and said, "I expect to see you downstairs when supper is ready."

"I will be there," he replied.

Mitis, Felix, Marcus, Xaria and Jeffery entered through the castle gate. The guests of the king were welcomed kindly by the guards and servants. Since they had found favor with Mitis, they had also earned the trust of those who were not only loyal to Mitis but loved serving him. He treated the guards and servants as family.

Eulalie met Mitis at the castle door. She kissed him once he entered. She also welcomed the men and Xaria, who stood beside Marcus.

"These are my guests." Mitis said. "They'll be joining us for supper."

They continued conversing for a while, about Antonius and how he was settling down.

Xaria still by Marcus's side looked at him and asked,

"Do you know the king very well?"

"He was my father's closest friend. When I was young he was as an uncle to me. He may not have recognized me in the yard because of this dirty beard. It has been ten years since I last saw him."

"Felix," Mitis said. "There's no hurry, the weather does not permit you to depart even if you wished. Stay here for supper."

"Only one thing can make me stay and I know you are aware of what that is."

"Yes, there will be enough wine for you to drink until you are filled up and unable to stand from your chair."

"Oh I'll stand and I will fall but I'll stand again!"

They shared a laugh together.

An hour passed and the supper table was set. Eulalie sent a servant to summon Antonius down. Once Antonius was summoned he left his room and began walking down the hallway making his way downstairs. As he walked down the hallway, he heard the strumming of a stringed instrument, the tune sounded familiar. A smile came across his face as he remembered the first time he heard it. For a moment he was happy, then the smile disappeared from his face as he remembered everything that happened on the day he heard it.

A summer after his reign began; Antonius was in Konstuliana, as a guest of Mitis. He was there trying to mend foreign relations between Konstuliana and Philonia. But Mitis was hesitant at first to let Antonius into the kingdom but after talking with Eulalie, he changed his mind and let Antonius stay a while. But he limited his stay to only five days. Mitis had always had the suspicion that Antonius's presence always brought bad luck. In a sense he was right, but it wasn't bad luck that Antonius attracted. It was the physical presence of evil. Eulalie knew this and always kept an eye on Antonius from his youth until he was a young man. One day, she knew she would have to reveal to Antonius what Calix had told her to keep from him until when she felt was necessary.

Antonius loved the company of the queen and the people of Konstuliana. He had not yet won the approval of Mitis. On the second day of Antonius's stay, he arose early to accompany Mitis on a hunting trip. He took with him, his sword, a crossbow lent to him by the queen, and a quiver full of arrows. He readied everything and made sure that he had all he needed and that it was all in place. As he made his way through one of the hallways of the castle, he heard the strumming of a stringed instrument. He followed the sounds and they led him to the chamber of the princess. Astra was her name, given to her by her mother to symbolize her worth in the eyes of her mother. Astra, meaning from the stars, she was as a star to her mother, precious in every way, unique and radiating with beauty. Her hair was dark-brown and it flowed like the river, streams caught in smooth sailing. Her shape was like a pear, her breast, hips and legs all were in perfect harmony.

She was twenty then.

Once Antonius reached her chamber, he saw that the door was cracked open a bit. He did not want to be a bother or interrupt her while she played. He stood at the door and watched her play her golden harp for the next two minutes. Her back was facing the door. She was aware of his presence but did not react until she had finished playing. Once she had finished, he spoke first,

"I've never heard anything so beautiful."

"How long have you been listening?"

"Only but a few minutes. I hope I didn't interrupt you."

She turned and looked at him then softly replied.

"No."

She took note of what he was wearing and it caught her interest.

"You are clothed in my father's hunting gear. And you have my mother's crossbow. That is very strange."

"I convinced your father into letting me accompany him on his hunting trip."

"But you know he does not like you."

"I am aware, that's why I must accompany him on this trip. Maybe he can tell me why my presence bothers him."

"Knowing father, he does not like to reveal his feelings to anyone."

"I'm not interested in how he feels about me. I just want to know why he has treated me differently since my father's death." He looked out her window for a second and saw that the sun was about to rise. He remembered that Mitis had instructed him to be ready, waiting outside the castle before sun rise. "I must be going" he said. "Your father is waiting for me."

"Wait." She said. He stopped and turned to her.

"What is it?" he asked.

She went to him and kissed him on the cheek.

"Good luck" she said with a gentle smile.

He smiled. Then he continued on his way down the stairs and out the castle. He got outside and saw Mitis mounted, ready on his horse. Beside Mitis was another horse prepared for him. Mitis turned back and saw him coming out of the castle,

"Do you see that Antonius?" Mitis asked looking at the risen sun.

Antonius got on the horse prepared for him.

"See what?" Antonius asked.

"The sun, it has risen. Why don't you listen to simple instructions? Before sunrise, that is all I asked of you."

"I apologize for my lateness."

"Let's go." Mitis said. He readied his horse and rode off, Antonius followed behind him. They were accompanied by three soldiers.

They left Petra through the first gate (the gate on the north side of the city.), and headed north. They journeyed through the thick forest of Ashburn and came to a river that ran from the Northeast village of Kindlar to a village on the southwestern side of Venduria. When they had reached the stream, Mitis led his horse to drink from the river. Antonius did the same. When both horses had drunk, both men used a rope to tie their horses to a tree nearby. Mitis knelt by the stream and washed his face. Then he drank from it.

They began to converse about Marcus's disappearance and how power had changed hands in Philonia.

"So he just handed you the crown and walked away." Mitis said.

"Yes, I tried to convince him to reconsider but his mind was already made up."

"Why would you try to make him stay if he wanted to leave?"

"I thought I was doing right. I felt it may have seemed like I tried to overthrow him."

"Did you?"

"I would never turn against him. He is my own flesh and blood. He left because he had enough of the Elders."

"Brothers have killed each other to have the power you possess. Somehow your father has raised you not to thirst for power as he once did. It's too bad he did not teach you all his lessons before he died."

He paused for a moment. "So, does Marcus still reside in the palace with you?"

"No, he took on my former duties as Philonia's Ambassador to the nations. He began sailing to other nations for the first few months. He was supposed to return to Philonia at least once a year."

"When was the last time you saw him?"

"It has been almost two years now." Antonius replied with a depressed look on his face.

"Come now, no need to worry, I'm sure he's fine. The duties of an Ambassador are stressful. I was one for your father early on in his rule. I thought being a soldier was hard. Imagine traveling so often and dealing with stubborn nobles and kings." Mitis sighed. "…I don't need to tell you. You already know the stress that comes with the position. But you must not worry yourself. Come on, we must continue the hunt."

They got back on their horses and foraged through the forest until they saw a fawn with its mother and a huge buck a little ways from them. Mitis had with him a traditional bow and arrow. He readied aim at the buck and shot. The arrow hit, right on target, on the buck's neck. The buck immediately started to skip away from his sight but before it could get away, he took two more shots at it and struck it down. It fell somewhere in the shrubs.

"Look at that. Three shots, three hits. My aim is still good," Mitis said with a smile.

The overcast sky above them began to thicken. The clouds became grey and soon, the little portion of the noonday sun that was seen was blocked from view. Mitis got down from his horse and began to *search rigorously through the shrubs trying to find the deer.*

Antonius was still on his horse and he began to feel something strange. He felt his heart beat faster than usual. This perplexed him because nothing he was aware of had caused this arousal, at least nothing he saw. He felt different, for a moment more powerful. How powerful? That he was not sure off. He looked up at the sky. There was a flash of lightning across the sky, soon followed by a roll of thunder.

"Mitis have you seen where it fell?" Antonius asked.

"No, I could have sworn it fell right here."

"We must be heading back soon; I think a storm is coming."

Mitis examined the spot where the buck landed. He saw a trail of blood. His heart leaped. Something had dragged it away. Thoughts of the type of beast that may have done this began to occupy his mind. He thought it was a bear, but if it had been, he would have seen it. Sure enough not very clearly because of the thickness of the forest, but enough to know it was there.

Antonius looked around to see how they could make their way out of the thick forest. The soldiers that accompanied them stuck close behind Antonius. Antonius got down from his horse. After he had scanned the area, he looked back at Mitis. The feeling of power was slowly rising, so was his heartbeat. He walked a few steps and stepped on a lower ground than he was walking on. It almost made him stumble. He looked at his feet and saw that he had stepped in a print created by an unfamiliar creature. The footprint was bigger than his boots.

"Mitis, I think it best we leave this place now."

He looked forward at where Mitis was. He saw something creeping behind Mitis. It was huge, almost twice his size, with the head of a wolf and the body of a well-built man. The creature was hairy from head to foot. The creature growled and was about to attack Mitis.

"Watch out" Antonius bellowed as he quickly readied his crossbow and shot the creature in the mouth. It fell back. Antonius quickly ran towards it. As he ran he unsheathed his sword. The creature got back to its feet. Mitis also readied his sword. But before he could act, he saw Antonius leap over him from behind. Antonius plunged his sword into the chest of the creature. The creature fell down but clawed at Antonius's neck before it hit the ground. Antonius twisted his sword that was still impaled in the beast's chest and pulled it out swiftly. He turned back to Mitis.

"We must leave this place now before more of these things come."

"You're bleeding." Mitis said.

Antonius saw the blood flowing down his arm. He touched his neck and felt the wounds.

"It's only a little." He said trying to turn the situation from his wound and back to the possibility they might be attacked again. *"We must leave this place."*

"Alright, let's go," Mitis said.

They started for their horses. They heard rustling in the bushes from behind where the soldiers *waited. Another of the creature leaped on one of the soldiers and knocked him off his horse and to the ground. The horses neighed loudly. The soldiers readied their swords and got down from their horses. The creature bit one of the soldier's necks. He yelled in agony.*

Antonius set another arrow in place in the crossbow and fired at the creature. The arrow struck its neck. One of the soldiers thrust his sword into the creatures back side, while the other soldier attacked from the creature's front. The creature knocked back the soldier that impaled it with its back paw. It roared loudly in the face of the soldier that was coming to attack it. The soldier looked in the creature's eyes and was gripped by an unspeakable terror. His sword fell from his hand; he fell back and was cowering away in terror. The creature reached its hand to its back and pulled out the sword. The creature inched closer to the soldier that was crawling away. It raised the soldier's sword high and was about to use it to smite the soldier. Then Antonius fired and hit the creature with another arrow. The arrow pierced through the creature's wrist. The creature turned at once, looked at Antonius with its flaring yellow eyes and roared. In a moment of shock, the creature with what sounded like a growl and words at the same time attempted to speak. It said only one word, a name.

"Antonius." It said.

Then it charged at him.

Antonius readied himself. He unsheathed his sword. The creature leaped at him and he struck it down. It tried to get up but with a swift motion he thrust his sword into its shoulder. Mitis began to make haste for his horse but it had run away. So he leaped unto the horse of the soldier that was taken down by the creature. The horse had been tied to a tree. He took his sword and cut the rope. Antonius also followed and leaped back on his horse, cut the rope he used to hold it in place and they left. One of the soldiers, the one that was crawling away from the beast in terror, had already mounted his horse and left once the creature turned its Attention to Antonius. The second soldier that was knocked back by the beast was still unconscious and the third was dead.

As they rode together, Antonius remembered he had witnessed the creature knock one of the soldiers unconscious.

"Wait." He said. Then he heeled his horse.

"Why are you stopping?!" Mitis asked "One of your soldiers is still back there, we must go get him."

"No, we must keep going before more of those things show up."

"But…"

"Listen to me." Mitis interjected. "We do not have any time to waste. It is either them or us."

"My father thought me better. He thought me to care for the lives of those that serve me more than I care for my own. These men serve you."

"They ran away like cowards."

"One of them, the other fought knowing he was putting his life in danger. Is abandoning him how you want to reward him for his service to you? I'm going back."

Mitis felt the truth of Antonius's words and followed Antonius back to where the soldier laid. They found him lying against a tree. Antonius helped him back up as he slowly regained consciousness.

"It's alright. We're going to get you out of here," Antonius said.

"We must hurry. Take my hand. He'll ride with me" Mitis said as he took the soldier's hand and helped him unto his horse.

Antonius mounted his horse and they rode off. They got to a less thick part of the forest. They stopped at another stream.

"Are we lost?" Antonius asked.

"No, Petra is just a few miles from here. We must cross this river first."

They crossed the river and rode another five miles till they reached thicker woods again. The terrain became familiar to Mitis. They travelled for a few minutes then emerged from the thick forest unto a grassy terrain on top of a small hill. Ahead, Antonius saw the outer city wall.

"There it is," Mitis said.

From behind them they heard the familiar growl of the creature.

"What were those things?" Antonius asked.

"How would I know, they seemed to be familiar with you. Why did it say your name?"

"I don't know but we must keep going."

They began riding again. When they were a little ways from the first gate they saw the outer gate being opened. One of the guard's on the tower gate began shouting that something was coming from the *bushes far in the distance. Mitis quickly entered the city. He gave the soldier to one of the guards.*

"Take him to someone who can treat his wounds." Mitis said and looked back. He saw that Antonius was still a few feet outside the outer gate. "What are you doing? Get in here so they can close the gate."

"More of those things are coming."

"Just get in!"

Antonius half-heartedly conceded to Mitis's order. He rode into the city and the outer gate was closed. They rode from the northern part of the city to the castle which was in the south. Once they arrived, Eulalie was waiting at the castle door. She was worried about them for she had seen visions of the creatures that attacked them. Mitis saw her and got down from his horse.

"My love, are you okay?" she asked.

"I am."

There were loud yells heard from the northern part of the city.

"Eulalie, go inside now please." Mitis said. Then he turned to Antonius. "I don't know why those things are after you but we must go back and see to it that they don't get this far."

Antonius was surprised to see that one of those creatures had made their way past the city walls and was now looking directly at him from on top of the castle. Still with his gaze set on the creature, he said to Mitis.

"I think it's too late."

Mitis looked at where Antonius gaze was set and saw the creature. Antonius readied his bow and arrow and shot at it. The creature leaped from the roof of the castle and unto the castle wall. It ran across the wall. Antonius took several shots and missed. Astra heard the growls from her room. She stood up from her bed and ran to the window. From her window she saw the creature leap off the wall and attack Antonius.

"Antonius!" she yelled.

Antonius quickly caught the creature's jaw in place as it tried to gnaw at his face. Mitis pulled out his sword and plunged it into the creature's back. Antonius broke the creature's neck before it could let out a roar. The creature fell dead on top of Antonius. He pushed it off himself.

"What are these things?" Antonius said still looking at the creature. Its body now had become hairless, and it shrank in size and resembled the body of a naked man. Its skin became as dust and ashes, soon after the wind blew it away.

"Why were they after you?" Mitis asked with a bit of anger his voice.

"I told you before. I don't know." Antonius replied as he stood up.

Astra came running out of the castle and into her father's arm. Mitis embraced his daughter. Eulalie came back out soon after.

"Father, are you hurt?" she asked.

"No, I am fine."

She walked to Antonius and looked at him. She saw the wound on his neck. Her eyes welled up with tears as she threw her arms around him. He held her closer to himself.

"Antonius." Mitis said. "Letting you stay here has caused nothing but trouble for me. I fear that if you stay longer you'll also endanger the lives of my family."

It started raining.

"Tomorrow, return to your kingdom and go handle whatever affairs you have awaiting you."

"I understand."

Eulalie took Antonius in and treated his wounds. But as she began to tend his wounds she noted that some of them had already begun to heal. He asked her if she knew what those things were that attacked them. She explained to him that the creatures used to be a tribe of people who had aligned themselves with fallen guardians and soon were deceived by Rudraco Vetserpen, the one whom they called The Adversary.

"Why were they after me?" he asked

"They know your worth and they seek to destroy that which you are destined to become," she replied as she placed a hot towel over his wound.

"I don't know why but I felt as if I could sense something from them."

"Sense what?"

"An evil I've felt once before, whenever such creatures appear there is a feeling within my spirit I can't explain."

"You should not worry so much over it. It's late you should get some rest. I'll prepare your things for the trip back."

"Does my presence pose that much of a threat to you?"

"Mitis feels so, he is my husband and king, I must obey him."

He knew the answer to his question but did not want to face the reality that wherever he went he was a target, targeted by those who served the darkness. He did not understand yet why the presence of evil caused an inner power to rise in him. That was his way of knowing when something bad was about to happen. He used the towel to wipe his face. He got up.

"Well goodnight."

"Goodnight" she replied softly.

He retired to bed. He woke up early the next morning and departed before sunrise.

Chapter 10
The Siren's Nature

The pain she felt in her heart was terrible. The moment her brother Gammon was struck down by Antonius, she woke up screaming in the palace. Titus woke up at once. His heart was racing because of her bellowing voice. Shocked and a little out of place he regained his composure and inched closer to her. He saw the tears flowing from her eyes.

"What is it my love?" he asked.

She could not tell him what really happened. She still felt the pain of her fallen brother. Because of the nature of what they were, they had been closely connected on a higher level than normal human beings. She kept this secret about herself from him. A curse placed upon them by the Great King. He decreed because of the pain they had caused humanity, whenever one of them was struck down, each of those who still remained alive will feel the deep pain of that fallen one.

This was her burden for being one of the offspring of a fallen Guardian. Her father chained in the depths of the abyss, she, cursed to roam the earth until she would meet her end. However that would happen, she did not know. But she did not care. She did not care much about the affairs of mankind until they hurt one of her own. But she also had a human side, just as her brother did, and would on rare occasions show a small hint of compassion.

Her tears were real, and the pain was still burning inside of her. Titus got closer to her. The moonlight peaked in through the curtains.

"What is it my love?" he asked again as he wiped a tear from her cheek.

"It was only a nightmare," she whispered with tears flowing down her eyes.

They heard the clinkering of armors approaching their room; they slept together in the king's chamber. Titus got up and opened the door in haste. Five of his guards were standing outside the door.

"We rushed here once we heard the queen scream." The lead guard said. "May we be of any service to your majesty?"

"No, leave, your service is not needed," Titus said.

They dismissed and went back to their post of duty.

Titus closed the door and looked back at her. She still seemed a bit shaken. So he went back to bed and held her again. Her skin was as cold as the mid-night wind. This made him feel uneasy for a moment but he loved her and did not want her to feel alone. He had lit a candle and placed it on a stand beside their bed. On a small table beside a chair that was close to another nightstand, he saw his crown lying upon a small pillow. It was where he had placed it. The light from the candle made the gold of the crown glisten. "Once my father wore that crown," he thought.

He lay down and she lay with her head just below his right shoulder.

"As a child my mother would read to me from my father's dairy when I could not sleep. His many journeys always made me feel proud to be his son. Although I never knew him, I'm still proud him."

"What great things did your father do?"

"There are too many to start naming. And from what I've read and what I've heard, the life he lived makes him seem more of a myth or legend than just a mere man, like me."

"You're not a mere man, you are a king."

There was a long pause. He took in a deep breath and said slowly.

"But I am still a man."

Elana did not respond, he looked to her and saw that she had fallen asleep. He keep awake, "A king". The word was now becoming more apparent to him than before. He was awake till the morning sun arose. He had lain in that same position. He rose from bed, washed his face and dressed himself in his regalia. He went to the throne room and stood outside the balcony, scepter in hand, his crown on his head, and the cold chill of the morning winter wind on his skin. He saw the whole city. He walked back in to the throne room and closed the doors that led out to the balcony.

The sons of the Elders were furious at what had been done with the bodies of their fathers. They were wealthy men, seven in all. The eldest among them was in his late forties and the youngest was in his early thirties. Together, they stormed through the doors of the senate house and came before Darius who was seated at his table going over some documents that had been recovered from within the rubbles of the house of the law. Darius was alone in the senate house that morning.

"We demand an explanation of why we were denied the right to bury our fathers?!" The eldest of the seven men said.

Darius with his attention still fixed on the document he was reading responded.

"The king had an order and it was done."

"I will not stand for this injustice. It's not bad enough that Antonius killed our fathers now his brother, this new king decides to burn their bodies. Our fathers deserved better than that."

"Why not bring your case to the king." Darius suggested.

"I don't want to even see his face. If I stood before him now I would thrust my sword into his heart."

"Watch your tongue; it's a crime to say such about the king." Darius said.

The man slammed both hands on the table and responded.

"Do I look like I care?"

"Fine" Darius said as he stood up. "What would you have me do about it?"

"Take us to the king."

Darius looked at them keenly knowing what might happen if they approached with such attitudes before Titus. So he did not want to associate himself with men such as themselves because they carried themselves in a way that hinted at the possibility of them becoming rebels to the throne. They went outside, with

Darius leading them, got on their horses and rode to the Palace.

When they arrived the guards let them in because they were with Darius. Darius asked one of the guards of the whereabouts of Titus. The guard replied that Titus was in the throne room at that moment.

They went to the throne room to find Titus conversing with a high ranking navy official. The official told him about the sighting of Philip and the men who were with him. The official also told him that Philip aided in Antonius's escape from the kingdom. Titus asked about Felix, the official told him that Felix's ship was not sighted, so he had not returned. He told the official to take a thousand soldiers and seize Philip and his crew once the ship got to shore. The man bowed and left.

Titus then let in the men who were waiting at the door. Darius walked in first. He was followed in by the sons of the Elders. They came before Titus, Darius bowed but the sons did not.

"Who are these men?" Titus asked.

"They are the sons of the Elders. They have come…" Darius was saying but was interrupted by Titus.

"Why are you here?" Titus asked them as his gaze was fixed on Tiberius, the eldest among the sons.

"We want an answer to why you treated the bodies of our fathers in such a disrespectful way," Tiberius answered.

"I honored them the same way they honored the crown."

"How dare you." Tiberius said in anger. "After all the good our fathers did for this kingdom."

"What are you going to do about it? Your fathers are not here to protect you." Titus said with a slight smile on his face. He removed his crown and held it in his right hand.

"This crown" he began "has been restored to its former glory. I am now as powerful as my father was, unhindered by the Elders. First it was Darius who tried to take this joy from me, now you men have come against me…"

"You had no right!…" one of the sons began.

"I swear by the Guardians Transcended, if you interrupt me when I am speaking, you will be joining your fathers." He wore his crown.

One of the seven sons was pushed to the edge. He was filled with rage he could hold no longer. He pulled out his sword and began towards the throne. The two guards at the base of the throne attacked him but he quickly struck them and sprinted up the twenty steps to the throne. As the man reached the first step, he raised his sword to strike Titus. Titus anticipated his attack, pulled out his own sword at the moment he saw the man's exposed torso. Then it was, the sword of the king pierced through the man's stomach. The man's sword fell from his hand as he stared into the eyes of Titus. The man saw wickedness in Titus's eyes that griped him as he felt his blood gushing out of his wound. Titus swiftly removed his sword from the dying man. He put his hand on the man's face and pushed him back. He died before his body hit the last step.

The other six sons looked at Titus and were surprised at the strength he displayed. They knew one thing of him. He had never been in war but yet he fought as one who was well aware of his opponent's weaknesses. Titus was trained by Antonius. Antonius was trained by Marcus and Mitis. Marcus was trained by Calix and Mitis.

The unease that was initially felt in the room from the moment Darius entered with the sons of the Elders now intensified. Several guards stormed into the room and surrounded the sons of the Elders. Darius stepped away from them.

Titus took a breath.

"Disobedience will not be tolerated. Take them away."

Tiberius took out his sword.

"I'm not going anywhere until I get justice for my father," he said.

Tiberius was a gifted fighter. Many had now come to say that he was even as skilled as the famed Thanos of Belvain, the father of Julian. But this was far from the truth. Ten guards surrounded the six sons. Tiberius spared no time in attacking them before they could try to seize him. His blade struck down three guards. The remaining sons of the Elders fought fiercely but disarmed themselves when more guards poured into the room. The scene displeased Titus greatly. After Tiberius had struck down about four more guards, a guard was able to strike him in a manner that caused him to release his sword. He turned to the guard that struck him and punched him in the face. Immediately another guard knocked him over the head, he fell to the floor. The guard raised his sword to deliver the final blow but then Titus said.

"Stop! I want him alive. I will use him as an example to show the people what becomes of rebels. If the people realize what occurred here today they might begin to get ideas. I will not have anyone else oppose me at the birth of my reign. So I will make a spectacle of you, soon you shall meet with death. Pray that he meets you quickly because the remaining breaths you shall take from now till you die, shall be drawn in pain."

More guards with swords and dressed in well-equipped armor came into the room. The dead bodies were dragged out and a servant came and wiped the blood off the floor. Titus ordered the guards to take Tiberius to a place just outside the city that was called The Pit. The

area was known as the place where the most
gruesome of executions took place. During the
reign of Calix until Antonius, no one had been
taken to the Pit. Titus had read of an execution
his father witnessed used by King Iywan, the
King of Philonia before Calix. He found it intri-
guing and had on one occasion walked outside
the city on a summer's evening and looked
down the hole. He smelt something foul coming up from it. There was a wooden pole beside
the pit. Those who were going to be executed
there were tied to the pole a night before their
execution.

Tiberius was taken and by order of Titus,
was tied to the pole. Several guards were appointed to watch him till the next day. He was
stripped of all his cloths. The cold winter wind
bit his skin and he could not stop shivering till
morning. After Titus watched him being tied to
the pole, he said, "If you survive till tomorrow
consider yourself unfortunate."

Tiberius spat on Titus face. Titus wiped it
off and said, "I was going to have it done without the fire but you keep driving me to the
edge."

Titus ordered the guards to set the pit
ablaze. They gathered shrubs, twigs and logs
and threw them into the pit. Then they lit some
touches and threw them down. Soon the fire
started. Titus instructed the guards to keep the
fire going until it was time for the execution. It

was Thursday around noon. The execution was set for the following evening.

Titus left and returned to the palace.

Elana stood by a closed window in her chamber. Her room was splendid in its design. The curtains were made of purple linen. The ceiling tiles were a sea of white and amber mash with marvelous etchings on them. She opened the curtains and looked out the window. She did not care for the beauty of the city that was before her eyes. Her mind was far beyond the city. It was on the reason of the death of her brother. Her eyesight was shaper than that of an eagle but as far as she could see, she could not see all the way to where Antonius was. The distance was great.

So it was at that moment the hatred she harbored in her heart for Antonius swelled up to the brink. He was responsible for the death of one of her kind and he was going to pay for it. As she gazed out the window, her eyes set in the distance, she made her mind up on what transformation she was going to assume to investigate the whereabouts of Antonius. Like her father she could take many forms. She calmly began to sing to herself, softly underneath her breath. As she sang, feathers appeared on her arms, from her shoulders to the tip of her fingers. Soon her body was covered with feathers as she assumed a transformed state she used on rare occasions. She had transformed herself to a birdlike creature with wide wingspans. A force burst from her that pushed the windows open. She hopped onto the ledge and took to the skies. In this state she was still fully aware of whom she was.

She could sense Antonius. He was distinct from anyone she had focused her attention on. She knew what he was to become. She was one of those who were trying to see to it that he would falter before his time, so as to lose a special blessing bestowed upon him by the Great king.

Antonius's heartbeat was distinct. She could sense him from afar and so she followed the unusual rhythm of his heart. After hours of flight she saw him in the distance, at the shore of Demoir. She landed on top of one of the tall trees around the area. She observed what went on between Jeffery and the knights and Antonius and his crew. At a moment when the confrontation was coming to a close, just before Jeffery seized Antonius, she spotted that he had noticed her presence. At once she flew off back to Noble city.

Now that she was aware of where Antonius was her plan was set in her mind. She was keen on finding a way to convince Titus to journey with her to Konstuliana. She flew back the open window of her chamber and transformed back to her human form. She put on one of her finest dresses and made herself to look more beautiful than she already was. Then she began looking for Titus. She found him in his study. He was standing by the closed window looking out, observing the palace garden. It was just around evening at that time. The symphony of beauty in the majestic skies made the green array of the garden glisten. This caught his attention. He heard the creak of the door once she opened it. He could smell the sweet scent of her perfume. He had in his right hand a chalice half-filled with wine.

As she approached closer, he said in an indifferent tone, without even turning to her.

"Where have you been? The sun has set, the day is done, and since dawn until now I have been unaware of where you carried your presence."

"I have been here in the palace." She replied.

"Don't lie to me! When I need you most, I can't find you. The guards and servants looked everywhere for you. All came back confirming your absence."

She walked closer to him and stood in front of him. He looked her deep in her eyes. Her gaze quelled his anger. He was breathing slowly now. She began rubbing his side. He took her hand, drew her closer to himself and kissed her.

"I can't stay angry at you," he said

She smiled.

He had lit five candles and placed them on candle stands, four of the stands placed at the corners of the room. The four stands were waist high. The fifth he had placed on his study table. There was a mess of books and papers on the table. Among the books were his father's diary, Antonius's diary, the Book of Prophecy and some documents given to him by Darius earlier that day. He had spent time from noon until evening in his study going over the documents, reading Antonius's diary, still trying to make sense of what happened the night Antonius heard the scream. He remembered the night but he remembered no scream. On the table was a gold chalice of a more pristine design than the one he was already holding. He went and picked it up and showed it to Elana. The gold sparkled against the yellow light of the candles.

"This is a gift from the king of Napel," he said.

He gave her the chalice and poured wine into it.

She drank.

"It's beautiful," she said. Then she wondered and asked him. "Why did he give you this?"

"A letter came with the gift. He congratulated me on my ascension to the throne."

"Was this the only gift you received?" she asked more curiously.

"No, there were more," he said.

He thought for a moment and mentioned the gifts to her.

"A white stallion, never ridden, from the queen of Menyana, A golden amulet from the king of Venduria, some spices from Sarbu and a thousand kilograms of silver from the queen of Tynda, nothing yet from Konstuliana."

"Why is that?" she asked softly.

"As much as Antonius tried he could not mend old wounds between our nations. It has been the same since my father's death."

It was as he said. The cause of Calix death, Mitis had long blamed on Antonius. Unfortunate enough that Titus was only a year old when his father died. He had read in his father's diary of the wicked king that ruled Konstuliana before Mitis. After the war that caused Hermes the second to be overthrown, Calix appointed Mitis as king over Konstuliana. Titus was well aware of this. So it began to resonate in his mind that Mitis owed his position as king to Calix. Since this was the case, he thought, Mitis also owed respect and attention to the kin of Calix.

Titus retired to bed after sending off a messenger.

Elana lay beside him and sang sweet, beautiful songs to him. He became entranced by her. His desire for her was burning. He took a hold of her and became one with her.

The night went swiftly, the new morn brought about new possibilities for him to test the new found lengths of his power. An execution was scheduled for that evening and he was going to be there.

Events of the day proceeded as normal. Then came the evening, it was time for the execution of Tiberius. Titus smiled as he mounted his horse and rode to the Pit. The ride took him twenty minutes. When he got there he saw the bishop standing beside Tiberius. Tiberius was still alive. He got off his horse.

"You should have died when you had the chance. But you're too stubborn for your own good," Titus said.

He looked at the Pit. The soldiers had kept it going through the night till that present hour.

"Splendid," he thought.

There was a woman beside Tiberius; she was soaked in tears and deep sorrow. She was a beautiful lady in her early thirties. Once she saw Titus she ran and threw herself on the ground at his feet.

"Please spare my husband," she pleaded.

Titus felt pity for her. He bent down helped her up and looked at her with great concern. "Woman, your tears cannot save your husband. He will die and the people will know that I do not tolerate fools. All who come against the crown will suffer his fate. In a way he is doing a great service. He is an example that all should avoid."

"Please, I beg you," she said. "I beg you, I beg you, please spare hi…"

"Enough!" Titus said. He turned away from the woman and ordered the guards to take her away. The guards took her away. She was now the more drenched in tears but no sign of compassion was seen on Titus's face. It seemed as the days passed he grew colder.

He walked to Tiberius who he saw shivering. He saw the expression on Tiberius's face. No words were said for his appearance spoke loudly enough. He saw a man engulfed in fear, one who knew death would meet him but not swiftly enough.

"You look thirty. Do you need some water?" Titus asked. The cold had bitten his throat and he had been denied water since the time he was tied to the pole. Tiberius was parched, it was almost impossible for him to muster the strength to say his last words. His eyes were wondering and he looked dazed.

"Yes...please," he pleaded.

"Pitiful," Titus said "You know for one supposedly stronger than Marcus I would have hoped you put up a better fight against my guards."

Titus frowned.

"It annoys me that you're still alive. I look at your face and I see your father."

Titus turned away and got back on his horse. Then he ordered the soldiers to carry out the execution. They untied Tiberius, who upon being untied fell to the ground. He was unable to carry his own weight. They lifted his almost lifeless body and threw him into the Pit. Titus heard the loud cry Tiberius gave once he hit the ground and the flames engulfed him. Titus expression did not change as he looked dead on at the Pit and he saw the flames rise. "Ashes to Ashes, Dust to Dust." he whispered. The crowd of people around turned their heads, covered their eyes and shut their ears for they could not bear to see the misery or hear the agony of the dying man.

A thought sprang in his head that he knew would haunt him forever. "No man is spared death." He left the Pit with that thought resonating in his mind. He arrived back in the palace with his heart set on escaping the one thing he feared most, death.

He had in no way expected the execution to have this effect on his mind. Then he knew an old saying that was uttered by some wise Philonians in the past. *A close encounter with death can shake the foundations of one's soul.*

[Titus imprisoned the remaining five sons of the Elders.]

Chapter 11
A Hollow Heart: Shielded from Evil

There was a peace Antonius felt once his feet hit the base of the last step. He was making his way to the banqueting hall. The queen had wanted his presence there. He felt that since he was a guest he could not reject her request. He smelt a hint of roses and some other precious oils as he walked down the hallway. When he reached the banqueting hall he was amazed at how the room had been renovated since the last time he saw it. The curtains were a majestic white; the black and white checkered floors were polished to perfection. There was a crystal candle chandelier that hung high above the ten seat dining table.

He entered the banqueting hall to find that Mitis, Eulalie, Felix and Jeffery had already taken their place at the dining table. Mitis sat at the head of the table, Eulalie sat at his right hand, and Jeffery sat at the other end of the table, with Felix on his right. Antonius saw that they were laughing together. He took this to mean that they now had settled whatever differences they had against each other. Mitis spotted Antonius and called him. He gave him a place to sit. He told him to sit on the second seat to his left. The seat on Mitis's immediate left was reserved for his son, Galen. A young lady who sat on Jeffery's left had spotted Antonius once he walked into the banqueting hall. She was Jeffery's sister, Simona. She rose from her chair, ran to him and embraced him. Then she kissed him on the cheek.

"I was glad when Jeffery told me you were here." She said "This was really unexpected."

"Yes it was. But I am here and I am glad to see you," Antonius said.

They took their seats.

Jeffery and Felix were still conversing. Then Jeffery asked Felix a question that arose in his mind after he heard Felix's story. He remembered a story Mitis had told him. A story that Felix did not mention or allude to, Jeffery thought at least it needed some mentioning, so he asked,

"The stories you have told me of yourself seem very familiar to what I have heard from my uncle but he never mentioned your name when he told me the stories. I must ask you something."

"What is it?" Felix asked, his face showing no emotion.

Jeffery leaned closer to him and asked. The focus of the room was now centered on Jeffery and the question he was about to speak out.

"Is it true that you are among the few who have gone beyond the Blue Sea?"

"Such were the times I had the power of a king and twice the pride but those days are gone, so I wish not to speak of them ever again."

Felix leaned back and looked at an upward angle towards the corner of the ceiling and said,

"Only a few men have survived what is beyond the Blue Sea. I am still haunted by what I have seen. Even after twenty seven years, the memories refuse to fade away."

Jeffery raised his brow when Felix mentioned "Twenty seven years."

The table set before them was flourishing with all kinds of foods, from a basket of fruits, and chopped vegetables to plates of well-cooked poultry and smoked veal. The last of the prepared dishes was brought in by a servant. It was a special dish the queen made. A cake baked with ezula nuts found only in the dense jungles of Sarbu. She had prepared it earlier that day. Mitis had wanted her to give the recipe to the servants so they would prepare it but she did not want that, so he let her have her way. She had made that cake only when Antonius was present. This was the fourth time the cake was prepared.

The cake was placed in front of Mitis. He looked at it and smiled. Eulalie saw his smile, and he caught her gaze.

Felix looked at the food that was set on the table.

"May we begin this banquet?," he asked Mitis.

"Not until everyone is here."

Marcus and Xaria came into the banqueting hall. Xaria was feeling a bit better. She had been given a new dress. The dress was an emerald green. It was almost as beautiful as the purple dress Eulalie was wearing. Eulalie caught a glimpse of the mark on Xaria's neck. Her flowing hair covered most of it but the marking Eulalie saw, she was familiar with. She thought and remembered that she had seen it once in a book. She wanted to speak to Xaria but being that everyone was almost at the dinner table, she wished not to delay dinner. So she held her peace.

Marcus was given a room. In the few minutes he had before dinner, he tried to tidy himself but did not have time to trim his beard. So he combed his hair and wore the dark blue robe that was given to him by Mitis. Xaria took her place beside Simona and Marcus sat beside Antonius.

A few moments later Astra walked in with her younger brother Galen behind her. Antonius felt his heart leap for a second once he saw her. She was more beautiful than he remembered.

Galen took his place beside his father and Astra took her place beside her mother. Astra was surprised to see Antonius, her eyes lit up when she saw him the moment she walked in. She wished to speak to him, but said nothing after she had taken her seat. She knew she had kept her father waiting so she did not want to delay dinner any further.

Mitis said the blessings over the food and they began. They waited and Mitis served himself first. Then they began. Felix looked around and found that something was missing.

"Where's the wine?" he said rather surprised at its absence.

"Must you speak when your mouth is full?" Marcus said as he placed some lettuce on his plate.

"I thought you detested vegetables," Antonius said to Marcus.

"I became accustomed to new tastes on the island. I didn't have much of a choice."

At that moment a servant brought in a silver jug filled with new wine. He approached Mitis first to fill his chalice but Mitis's whispered to him to fill the chalice of Felix first. He did as instructed.

"How much more wine is there?" he asked the servant.

"Plenty." The servant responded.

"How much, I need a specific answer."

"Over ten barrels of new wine sir."

"Wonderful." Felix said then he drank from his cup. "Fill their cups, when you are done come back to me."

"Yes sir." The servant then filled everyone's cup, starting with Mitis. When done he came back to Felix but the jug was almost empty.

"Sir," the servant said. "The jug is finished but I'll return with more." The servant walked promptly out of the room. He was back in a little over a minute. He came and stood by Felix.

"Give me the jug," Felix said.

The servant gave it to him. He shifted aside some plates and made space to place the jug. After he had filled his cup, he placed it in front of himself.

"You may go. Thank you for your service," he said to the servant.

The servant left.

Everyone ate to the delights of their heart. Marcus was the first to finish his plate. He watched Xaria, who now had stopped eating and had begun to look rather ill. She stood up and walked out the room. Marcus followed after her. He met her just outside the Banqueting hall.

"What is the matter?" he asked.

"I can't eat."

"You know how cold it is, please, you must eat something. Since I received you back into my arms you have not eaten anything. Please tell me, what is wrong?"

Marcus looked into the banqueting room and saw Eulalie walking towards them.

"What's wrong?" Eulalie asked.

"She has lost her appetite."

"Are you sure you can't eat anything." Eulalie said.

"No I can't," Xaria responded softly

"Come with me. Do not worry Marcus; I'll take care of her." Eulalie said as she took Xaria's hand and led her to a room upstairs. She instructed one of her servants to bring a hot towel up to the room. The servant did as told.

Marcus was worried but went back into the Banqueting hall.

"What's wrong?" Antonius asked him.

"Xaria's condition is not getting any better. I... I don't know what to do?"

"Is it a fever? A cold?"

"I don't know."

Felix then addressed Marcus.

"There is no need to worry," he said.

"Everything will be alright."

"I hope so." Marcus said and sighed.

Marcus looked at Felix who was now gulping down what Marcus counted as his fifth cup of wine.

"Don't you think that's a bit too much?" Marcus said.

"Yes, but my friend promised me all the wine I can drink." Felix set his eyes on Mitis who was smiling back at him. Felix raised his cup towards Mitis and Mitis raised his cup towards Felix. Their motions resembled the motion one makes when making a toast.

Marcus smiled and shook his head.

"Father," Galen said as he observed Felix. "Is he always like this?"

"For as long as I have known him, yes."

Astra finished her plate and left. She kissed and thanked her father before she departed.

"Go see if your mother needs any assistance," Mitis whispered to her.

"Yes father."

As she prepared to leave, Antonius caught her gaze before she left. At that moment, the love he long felt for her rekindled.

Felix, Galen, and Antonius finished their plates at about the same time.

Felix stood and thanked Mitis for the meal. He pretended to stagger a little then smiled. Mitis and Galen laughed.

Marcus was drenched in thought about the wellbeing of Xaria. He got up and left to go find her. He found where she was taken by Eulalie. In a room, three doors from the room that was prepared for him. Eulalie sat on a small stool by the bed. Astra was standing beside her. She was holding Xaria's hand and whispering something. Marcus approached Xaria. She was sleeping. He saw the small towel that had been placed on her forehead. He placed it aside on a small tray that was on the stand next to the bed. He put his hand on her forehead.

"She feels fine," he whispered

"I know," Eulalie said. "I fear the source of her sickness might be more than we think."

"What do you mean?"

"Come."

Marcus walked over to where Eulalie was. Eulalie reached out and moved a bit of Xaria's hair and revealed the mark on her neck. Marcus was already aware of the mark.

"Do you know how she got the mark?" Eulalie asked.

"I don't know. I don't even know what it means." Marcus said a bit frightened but he tried to hide the fear in his voice. "Please tell me she's going to be okay."

"I'll do what I can." She said with a sincere look in her eyes. "Her sickness manifests in the body but the source may lie in her mind. She may be battling with her memories, things she's seen. The mark on her neck may have something to do with it."

Eulalie got up, went to the other side of the bed, picked up the towel and placed it back on Xaria's forehead. Marcus took Xaria's hand and kissed it. A tear escaped from his right eye. "Please," he whispered "I can't lose you again."

Eulalie and Astra left the room.

Down stairs, in the banqueting hall, the musicians had arrived. Once dinner was over they began to play for the king. There were female dancers. They were there because Jeffery had requested them. Simona adored the sounds of the stringed instruments, the flutes, and the tambourines. She got up and began dancing. Antonius watched her. A hint of a smile showed across his face as he watched her body move. She moved with the music as a flower does with the wind. He admired the way she turned, the flow of her dress cutting through the air, and the grace of her long hair as she bent low and quickly flung it back.

Simona caught his glance. She came to where he sat and took his hand. He reluctantly got up. Jeffery for a moment took his eyes off the female dancers and looked as his sister took Antonius's hand. It did not sit well with him, for he was very protective of his sister but he said nothing. He just watched them.

The music moved Simona and she twirled around Antonius sensually. His feet were for most of the dance in place. He did not know what to do. Simona took his hand and led.

"Place your hand here," she said as she guided his hand to the back of her hip.

She moved closer to him.

Astra made her way downstairs with her mother. Eulalie went to tell Mitis of Xaria's condition. Astra upon seeing Antonius dancing with Simona was hurt inside but she did not let her emotion be seen by anyone. She walked into the banqueting hall and watched Antonius. She watched as though she was interested in his display of mix-footed meandering. He may not have been a good dancer but with Simona in his arms, he felt calm. He let her lead.

Mitis watched on, Felix was a bit impressed but something was on his mind. He wished to speak with Antonius but did not disrupt the dance. He waited till they were done. He was standing by the door.

Upon the last twirl and final move of the dance, Simona kissed Antonius. This took him by surprise. Astra immediately left the room. He looked around the room. The music slowly died down. He had caught a glance of the hem of Astra's dress as she departed the room. Soon there was applauding by all except Eulalie. Jeffery clapped slowly.

Antonius wanted to leave and go after Astra. But he first went to Mitis and thanked him. He got on one knee and kissed Mitis's hand. Mitis saw this as a sign of sincere humility. He got up and as he was making his way out the banqueting hall, Felix took a hold of his arm.

"Please I need to talk to Astra." He said

"There are more important matters to discuss."

"I promise I'll be back."

"The more time wasted, the higher the chance of more lives being lost."

Antonius considered Felix's words and found them to be true.

"Okay" he said. "What do you wish me to do?"

"No Antonius, I need to know what you want me to do. Do you want me to stay or do you want me to return to Philonia?"

"If you return," he began but paused fearing the truth of the words he was about to speak, "Titus might have you executed. I know he is not quick to show mercy."

"And if I stay?"

"The sailors will become angry. They have families to return to. They have wives, children, brothers and sisters and many good things that wait for them."

"So what would you have me do?"

Antonius thought over what may happen if they were to return to Philonia. Knowing first the temperament of his brother, Titus, he considered for them the path they shall follow back. After a few seconds of thought he said to Felix.

"You may return with whoever wishes to go. But you must not go back the same way we came."

"So we shall not travel by sea?"

"No you can't. You shall travel going north-east from here and take the valley of Ni-keili, north of the city of Higiah, which is in Venduria. Do you know where that is?"

"I've heard of that city before. I will make sure I possess a map before departure. But going by land will make the journey back three days or more."

"Yes. When you return, make sure no sailor goes near Noble city. What concerns me as of the moment is weather. In two weeks winter will be over. Convince the men to wait till then before you set off to journey back."

"I will do that."

"In the meantime, I will speak to Mitis about readying horses for the journey back."

"Horses," Felix sighed.

Antonius smiled.

"Well you can't walk the entire journey back. Not even the skilled runners could run that far without collapsing."

"I know this already."

"I would have imagined with your years of experience, riding a horse would not faze you."

"I am a seaman. I have not taken the time to learn the ways to use such creatures."

"You're a quick man. You have nothing to worry about. If any other matters arise please come and discuss them with me."

"Alright, I will do so."

At that moment, Mitis made his way from the banqueting hall into the hallway where Antonius and Felix were conversing. Eulalie was walking with him. Galen was behind them. Antonius looked back and saw Eulalie whispered something to Galen. Galen left and headed upstairs. Although Galen was twelve, his mother relied on him for very important duties. She was proud of her son.

Mitis met Felix and Antonius once they closed their conversation. He was holding Eulalie's hand. He looked at her and nodded slightly. She understood what he wanted her to do. At the moment when Antonius was speaking with Felix outside the banqueting hall, Mitis and Eulalie were conversing at the dinner table.

She, knowing what she agreed upon with her husband at the dinner table, felt that time was of the essence. Not a second should be wasted.

Mitis spoke first to Felix.

"So, what plans have you made and does it involve me?"

"It wouldn't be a plan worth undertaking without you." Felix replied.

Mitis smiled.

"I am afraid I must be on my way," Felix said and turned to leave.

"Stay here for the night?" Mitis suggested.

"I have to inform the sailors of the plan of action, so I shall spend the night in the communal houses."

"Well I'll ride with you there," Mitis said then followed Felix. "I shall return soon" he said to Eulalie. They left the castle.

Antonius watched them depart. Eulalie took Antonius's hand.

"Come with me," she said. "I have something I must discuss with you."

She led him upstairs. They walked through the hallways of the upper floor until they got to the queen's chamber. Eulalie entered first but Antonius did not go in.

"Come in" Eulalie said.

Antonius walked in slowly. This was the first time he had entered her room. She closed the curtains and closed the door. The room was big and looked almost like a study. A bed was at the edge of the wall and a table next to it. The item that caught Antonius's attention was the giant cloth that hung on the wall on the other end of the room. Eulalie went to the cloth and removed it to reveal a grand mirror behind it.

Antonius walked to it and upon seeing his reflection he said to her.

"What did you want to discuss with me?"

He turned and saw her rigorously searching for a book from the bookshelf that was be-

side her table. She found the book she was
looking for and walked to Antonius.

"I'll show you soon. Please be patient with
me."

She turned the pages of the old book and
turned to the page she desired. She stood in
front of the mirror, Antonius next to her; she
uttered these words in an old dialect. A dialect
Antonius had heard the bishops in Philonia
using when they prayed prayers invoking the
presence of Guardians.

"The eyes mirror the desires of one's soul.
Open then mirror, for my soul desires to enter."
Eulalie said and kept her eyes on the mirror.

Antonius also kept his eyes on the mirror.
He saw his reflection began to ripple as if he
were looking into still waters that had just been
gently touched.

"Antonius, repeat the words I just said,"
she said.

Antonius did as she said and watched as
his image in the mirror was restored. Then immediately the mirror became as white as wool.

"It is true," she whispered. "Follow me,"
she said

Antonius made his way into the mirror
with her and emerged into another room. This
new room was bigger than the queen's chamber and was brightly lit. It looked as if the room
stretched forever. Antonius looked and saw
that far ahead, there appeared to be what
looked like dark clouds in the distance. He felt

anguish as he looked at the clouds. They seemed to come a bit closer, and then the light would push them back. In the room there was a wider range of books. Antonius heard singing, not of the nature he had heard when he was still in Noble city, no, these songs were different. They were calmer, without a motive to manipulate anyone. They reminded him of a more pleasant time in his life.

He felt a welcoming presence in this place.

"Where are we?" Antonius asked.

"We are in your soul," Eulalie replied softly.

"That is not true. How can this be?"

"Listen, do you hear the voice that sings the song."

"Yes, I do…"

"Listen carefully, whose voice is it?"

"My mother, it is my mother's voice!" Antonius said. He listened and a tear almost escaped from his eye. "As a child, on nights when I could not sleep, this is the song she sang to me."

Eulalie smiled.

Antonius examined the books on the bookshelf. They numbered twenty seven. He picked one and read from it. As he read he laughed for he read of his own life, memories he knew. He closed the book and turned to Eulalie. He saw that she was holding something in her hand and staring at it intently. She had found it where calix had kept it, where he had instructed her to look. It was in a small box atop a table in that big room, hidden between a stack of books.

"Can I see it?" Antonius asked.

"Your father got this for you before he died. He kept it here, within you." She opened her hands and showed him what she was holding.

Antonius saw the amulet. It was a wooden cross with what looked like the shape of a heart in the middle of the cross. The heart shape on the cross looked as if it was missing something, something that would fit perfectly in its hollowed dip. It was latched to a rope that was twice the thickness of a thread. He took it from Eulalie.

"My father got this for me?"

"Yes, he entrusted me to give it to you at the right time."

"It has been within me all my life and I did not know about it. Why now?"

"I've been praying and my visions have been stronger in the last few days. I knew you were coming. Also I know that you are ready."

"I have read of this sometime ago. It is one of the thirteen sacred crosses. Those who have possessed them were either the fallen Guardians or the ones who took their place. But I do not remember who possessed this one."

"It belonged to Sirius."

"Sirius?" he said in disbelief. "The only way to have gotten this is to have defeated Sirius."

"Which I believe your father did."

"Was he to take Sirius's place?"

"I don't know. But your father was given the gift to read and understand the prophecies, just like me. He saw that one of his sons would be a Rising Guardian. When you were young, he anointed your head with the rare clear oil that is blessed by the Great King himself. When he poured the oil on your head, your forehead began to glow as bright as the sun. That was how he knew you were the one. Soon after he became aware of how he would meet his death. So when you were two years old, he set off with Felix, and Mitis. They sailed beyond the Blue Sea to the lands of the fallen ones. They fought many ghouls to get to Sirius. After they defeated Sirius, your father retrieved this cross for you."

Antonius observed the small cross once more. He saw again the heart shaped dip in the middle of the amulet. The amulet began to glow slightly in his hand.

"Something is missing," he said.

"What do you mean?" Eulalie asked.

"It seems strange for this cross to be designed as such. The Great King made them, for his sons, but I remember a bishop telling me one late night almost ten years ago that the crosses of the Guardians all had hearts in the center, each heart representing a virtue of the Great King that he bestowed upon the Guardians."

"That is true. Your father didn't know where to find the heart. Remember that when the fallen Guardians descended to earth, they removed their hearts from the crosses given to them before they assumed the form of men."

"I remember the story."

"It also followed that when they had relations with women in those days, they bore children whose form is like the sea, forever changing."

Antonius took a hold of the string and put the cross on.

"If my father went through much trouble to get this for me, it would be best to use it. You haven't told me what it is for."

"It protects you. Since you've been born, sons and daughters of the fallen Guardians have been able to sense you. Those also who have been cursed and deceived by the Adversary have come after you."

"Like the wolf-men four years ago."

"Yes," she said as she took the cross and put it inside his shirt. "It is important that you do not let anyone know you are wearing this. I think it's time we head back."

Antonius looked in the direction from where they entered and saw a mirror, the same size as the one he saw in Eulalie's chamber.

"Come with me," Eulalie said.

"Do I have to say anything for it to work as it did before?"

"No we just walk out."

Eulalie walked through and Antonius followed after her.

They appeared back in Eulalie's chamber. The candles in her room were still lit. Galen was there. He was holding a bottle of holy oil and seated on a chair close to a closed window. He was almost falling asleep. He was leaned back on the chair, his eyes closing for a few seconds and opening quickly. He had been doing this for the past ten minutes. When he saw Eulalie and Antonius emerge from the mirror, he stood up and walked to his mother.

"I've done what you asked mother." He said then handed the bottle of holy oil to her. He had returned from the duty his mother entrusted to him, which was to bless the four corners of the castle with holy oil, and to say a little prayer after the oil had been rubbed on the wall.

"What of your father has he...?" Eulalie was about to ask when the door opened.

It was Mitis. He walked in. He had a candle in his left hand. He placed it on the desk close by the door. Then he walked to Antonius and placed his hand on his chest. He felt the cross there.

He looked at his wife and said.

"Well done." Then his attention was to Antonius again, and then he spoke. "I will do what

I can to make sure you are safe. To make sure
no one who could betray you knows you are
here but what I request of you is that under no
circumstance are you to take off that cross."

"Eulalie has explained it to me. I won't. I
care for your safety as well. My presence here
will not be a danger to you anymore."

"As long as that cross is worn, it won't."
Mitis gave a slight smile. "You should retire to
bed soon."

Antonius smiled.

"I will," he said and left.

He made his way out of the queen's chamber and into the hallway. As he walked down
the hall on his way to his room he passed by
the room where Xaria was. The door was
slightly open so he peaked in and saw that
Marcus was holding her hand. She was still not
responding. He was not adept in situations
such as these. He did not know what he would
have to say to Marcus to try to lift his spirit. So
in silence he left. Marcus looked at the door
from where he sat and saw no one.

Antonius returned to the room that was
prepared for him. He found it as it was. He removed his clothes, folded them and kept them
on the chair beside the bed. Now bare, he
looked at the cross and admired its slight glow.

He sighed.

He noticed a note on his pillow. He picked
it up and read it. 'Meet me in the knight's quarter in the Morning'. The note was signed by

Jeffery. He folded the note and kept it on top of his clothes.

There was a knock on the door.

"A moment please" He said as he took his shirt and put it on. He put on his trouser. He went and opened the door.

He was surprised to see who it was that knocked.

"Simona" he said with a slight crack in his voice. "…is something wrong?"

"No," she responded with a calm voice. "I just wanted to speak to you. Alone."

"Alright, Come in." He said as he invited her in. He was unsure of what she was going to discuss with him. As she passed him, the smell of her perfume aroused him a little.

He closed the door, then went and removed his outer garment from the chair and offered her a place to sit but she stood instead looking intently at him. The faint light from the candle was enough to illuminate her face. She was glowing. He looked at her, deep in her eyes and wondered what she was thinking.

"What is it?"

"How long has it been?" she said with a longing in her voice.

"Ten years," he replied calmly.

"It's ten years since I've seen you. I've missed you. Did you ever think of me?"

Antonius was silent for a while then he responded.

"Yes, you know I did."

"It still baffles me that you chose to rule without a queen. Amidst the sea of beautiful women in Philonia you still chose to be without queen."

"Though I loved them, I had already given my heart to someone and it is her who I wish to be my queen."

Simona smiled and walked closer to him. She embraced him. She felt the amulet he wore and wondered what it was.

"What is that?"

"Simona," Antonius said quickly, hoping to shift her interest. "You look lovely."

"Thank you," she said with a smile.

The moment felt inescapable. His eyes were on her and hers on him. For a moment he felt weak as he gazed at her and her beauty was undeniable. But his heart was not with her and he felt this should not be. He felt it wasn't right.

She leaned closer to him and slowly kissed him, but he pulled back.

"I can't do this."

"What's wrong?" Simona asked. Her voice was low and soft.

"It's late and I am tired."

"I understand. I'll leave you be. I'll see you in the morning." She said then she kissed him on the cheek and left.

He gave a sigh of relief. After she left he blew out the candle and retired to bed.

That night when he slept, he had a dream. In the dream he found himself in the middle of a garden, the garden looked very familiar to him, and the weather was unusually bright. It was quiet for the most part in the garden. He walked slowly through the garden admiring every detail. He then took rest at the base of a tree and looked at the garden closely. He kept wondering why it looked very familiar. For a moment his memory was stirred and he remembered that he had been in this garden with his father when he was a child. He quickly stood to his feet and remembered the day when he was brought there by his father. At that moment he began to hear voices coming from the shrubs in front of him. A child came running through and passed by him as if he weren't even there. He recognized the child, he was the child. Soon a tall man, with broad shoulders, dressed in a dark purple robe and wearing a crown emerged from where the child had come running from.

"Father," Antonius said with excitement. But the man did not respond to him but followed the child until the child reached a tree and noticed something about to fall from one of the branches. Antonius followed after them and watched them from a few feet behind. The young boy ran and stood by a tree on which something hung. It caught his interest. He looked up with his hand ready to catch what he saw the wind harass. It was a pupa; there were two of them next to each other. The wind blew them more and one of them fell from the tree and missed his hand. The young child went to where it fell and picked it up then he ran to show it to his father.

"Look father, what is it?" the young child said with curiosity.

"That son is the place where one of the most marvelous transformations of nature occurs."

"Really, what's inside?"

"Why not wait and see."

The pupa began to shake slightly in the little child's hand. He grew excited and wanted to help the creature he witnessed struggling to get out.

"Son, you must not do that."

"Father, look it is struggling to be free. I'm not going to hurt it."

The child insisted then he peeled back the outer scaling of the pupa and let the little insect out. It took a few meager steps on his palm and did not move anymore. The little child saw that the creature had very colorful wings. With tearful eyes he looked up at his father and asked.

"Is it dead because of me?"

The man got on one knee and placed his hand on his son's shoulder.

"Son, sometimes a creature must struggle before it is strong and ready to take on what nature has prepared for it."

The man took the dead butterfly from his son's hand. He then dug a small hole and placed the dead insect. Then he covered the hole. He sat on the grass and his son sat next to him, still a bit sad. He put his arm around his son,

"Now watch son and see the struggle that this creature must face."

The child watched the second pupa for what felt like hours to him, but only a few minutes had passed. His anticipating heart was racing to see whether the little butterfly would make it out of its casing. Then it happened, a beautiful creature with blue wings and very admirable patterns made its way out of the pupa. A smile appeared on young Antonius. Calix smiled as well.

"See son, it has won the struggle."

The child ran to the base of the tree and watched the little butterfly make its way into the arms of the wind. It flew higher and higher and then disappeared into the clear afternoon sky.

Antonius watched this from the bushes and realized that this was a day in his past. A day he had lived through, a lesson his father taught him. Struggles were a part of life. That day recollected as a dream to him.

Chapter 12
Another Knows of him. A knight is humbled

Far north in the snow covered mountains of Kismiar, west of the city of Vinimeir, there was someone who had sensed the power of Antonius when Antonius was far off at sea battling Gammon. The man had known of Antonius's nature, the power he possessed and the manner in which it displayed itself. He had read and understood the prophecies for many years. He had known a twelfth shall rise, and just like his father transcend. He waited his lifetime for the moment. Twice before he thought they had come but both were disappointments.

The man who lived in the mountains was known by one name, Peter. Only a few knew who he really was. Many times he had appeared time and again in history. He would make his mark and disappear for almost a century, only to return when the affairs of men incurred the curses of the sons and daughters of the fallen Guardians. He would fight fiercely, for he was blessed with strength, just as his father was.

He had known the father of the man whom he had long read about. He had helped him defeat Sirius and retrieve the cross of Sirius. He had seen to it also at one time that a brutal pirate who conquered the Blue Sea was captured. He had helped Calix with this quest but disappeared after he had caused the waters to rise.

Now he stood outside his cave. The mountain wind was blowing wildly on him. His clothes were as that of a shepherd but he had no sheep. He wore this as a symbol of his humility. He had with him wherever he went, a staff taller than he was. It was not the source of his power but it helped him channel the power he was blessed with. With it he had made waters rise, split mountains and defeated many ghouls.

In all the things that men awed at him for doing, he did not once take glory for them. Often after he performed a deed that attracted much awe, he would disappear and not return for a while. He did this because he did not desire the worship or adoration of men. He knew to do such would lay a curse on him, a curse he had witnessed on two men at different times of his life. He had encountered one fifty years after the transcending of his father. His father had told him that it would be his duty to guide the one who shall come after him. The first man who he thought was the twelfth also bore the same power he sensed in Antonius but the man's pride made him turn to darkness. Peter had to wage war against him and he defeated him. The second he encountered two centuries later, this time he was sure that this man would stay true till the end. But he was wrong and the man also turned to darkness and forced Peter to do to him what he had done to the first.

Regardless of the failure of his mentorship to the two men, he was sure of himself this time. When he looked back at both times he encountered those men who he thought were the twelfth Rising Guardian, he realized that they had made their choice on the path they took. "I hope this one is different." He said as he stood there looking in the direction of where he sensed Antonius's power.

He stood close to an edge on the mountain side, he thought of how he would make his way to Petra. He looked up at the clear night sky and closed his eyes. At that moment he made his decision. He took a deep breath and listened to the wind. Immediately like grains of sands, his essence was carried by the wind and he retook his form at the bottom of the mountain. He began his journey to Petra on foot. It would take him a day and a half. He chose to walk because he felt Antonius was still far off at sea. He sensed Antonius getting closer but slowly, so he was in no hurry to get to Petra.

It was a new morning. Antonius awoke to witness as far as he could see, the city of Petra baked in snow. He washed his face, clothed himself and made his way downstairs to the Knight's quarter. It was about six o'clock that morning when he arrived where Jeffery had wanted them to meet. The Knight's quarter was the west wing of the castle. It was vast and had indoor training grounds for knights. He walked in and saw Jeffery in action against another knight. Jeffery was clothed in a dark blue doublet vest with a white shirt underneath. The knight was putting up a fierce fight against Jeffery but was no match. This was a spectacle to

Antonius for he had not witnessed Jeffery duel before.

The knight swung his sword through the air in an attempt to hack at Jeffery's shoulder, but he was not quick enough. Jeffery dodged it. The swing made the knight loose his balance. Jeffery used his knee and hit the knight's stomach. The knight tried to regain his footing. He stumbled backwards and fell, then quickly got back to his feet. Jeffery was walking to him with confidence. Sweat raced down both their brows. Antonius thought it was too early to be witnessing this. He yawned silently and continued to watch.

The knight got back to his feet and swung again, this time Jeffery swung too. Their swords clashed time and again, swing after swing. The knight tried once more but was overpowered by Jeffery. When their swords clashed for the last time, the knight could not hold on to his sword for he had grown tired. It fell from his hand and slid across the floor.

Jeffery held his sword to the knight's neck, and then he smiled. He sheathed his sword

"Well done, you've improved but we need to work on your footing and your grip. If you lose your sword on the battle field it could be the end of you."

"Next time, I won't lose." said the knight with a smile. He looked a little younger than Jeffery.

"We'll see, now go get cleaned up and report back to Neemus on your progress."

The young knight gave a bow and left.

As the knight left he passed Antonius. He greeted Antonius before he departed.

Jeffery removed his vest and cleaned his brow with a small towel. As he cleaned himself he turned towards the door and saw that Antonius was there. Antonius went to him and said.

"I never knew you were that good."

"As head of the Knight's Order, I am expected to be the strongest of all the knights. I have never failed to live up to such expectations."

"Not once?"

"No, not once. I have heard people ridicule me and say that I am where I am because I am the king's nephew. I have proved them wrong."

"I don't doubt your skill. What I have seen proves that you know what you are doing when engaged in combat."

"Most of the time, I do."

"It sounds like you doubt yourself a bit."

"Is there a man in the world who is fully certain of his abilities? Though I am skilled I cannot but stop to wonder if I would be where I am had I not been part of this royal family."

"It seems that you doubt yourself more than you think the people do. You have trapped yourself in a circle of doubt."

"Why would I entrap myself in a circle of doubt?"

"That is something you have to figure out on your own."

Jeffery knew Antonius was right. He had doubted himself for a long time because of his relation to the king. But he knew he was skilled. There was no doubt about this. But he also knew who he was.

He was Jeffery Miles, the First Knight, the one who as the title implied was the best of the knights. As the First Knight, he was head of the knight's order, a council made up of a thousand of the most respected knights in the kingdom. They were only deployed at special times of war and in almost every conflict he was in he had seen the face of death and had survived.

His last encounter with death was three years back when he led five hundred knights to reclaim the lands on the eastern side of Konstuliana that had been seized by a minor lord of Venduria. The lord of a small village in the western part of Venduria had sought to expand his land without consulting the king of Venduria, Arvin Earnest. When Mitis learnt of this he thought it might lead to war if not resolved appropriately. So he put Jeffery in charge of the operation to investigate the area. While Jeffery was carrying out his order, Mitis made his way to Oreni, the capital city of Venduria. He met with Arvin, who was surprised to learn of what had happened. He sent troops immediately to the battle field but the carnage had already begun. The soldiers of the minor lord fought hard against those led by Jeffery. At a *point in the battle as Jeffery was fighting fiercely at the frontline when he got struck in the arm by a club and someone knocked him across the head with a shield. He fell to the ground almost unconscious. His eyes barely open, but open enough for him to see a towering figure approaching him with a sword. At that moment, Neemus, his second in command struck down the tall man and pulled Jeffery to safety. It was at that moment Jeffery began to doubt himself; it was the first time his life had been saved, at least, the first time as he remembered it.*

He sat there remembering that moment. Then he said to Antonius.

"If I have made this trap for myself then I will undo it or at least find a way out."

"I have faith that you will. Now the real reason I am here, I saw your note last night, is there something you wished to speak to me about."

"I have no doubt that you are a good man Antonius. I have heard many wonderful things about you and just recently one horrible thing."

Antonius knew what Jeffery was talking about.

"Regardless," Jeffery continued, "I still trust you, even after ten years your virtues are still the same. The reason I wanted to speak to you this morning was about Simona. Over the past ten years she has longed for you. She has spoken of you many times. Four years ago after she had heard of your visit and your departure, she wept because she missed you."

"I did not know this."

"There is a way she is when she is around you. She is happier."

Antonius was silent for a moment. Then he asked. "So what do you want of me?"

Jeffery stood up.

"If you don't love her as you used to, make it known to her as soon as possible. She's been hurt enough already."

"How did you know?"

"I saw the way Astra looked at you last night at the dinner table and the way you gazed back at her. You love her. It is quite clear to see. My sister loves you, so it would be best that everything gets resolved quickly so no one gets hurt."

Jeffery dropped the towel on a bench and departed the room. Antonius made his way back to the room provided for him.

❖

It was now four hours before noon. Mitis and Eulalie sat facing each other with a small table in between them and a chess board upon it. He laid his left hand upon her right hand as he waited for her to make her next move. She looked down at the chessboard, analyzing the way in which the pieces were set, she gave a slight smile. She took her husband's hand and kissed it, and then she moved her queen piece and said softly.

"Check."

Mitis placed his attention back on the chessboard.

"Impressive" he said as he planned his next move.

At that moment a servant knocked on the door. Mitis granted him permission to enter. He came in carrying a tray with two chalices that contained hot beverage. The contents of the beverage included a rare form of ezula powder, a cocoa derivative that was found only in the dense southern jungles of Sarbu. The beverage also contained milk and a little sugar. The servant took the tray to the table. Mitis took a chalice and placed it on his left side. He was wearing gloves so the heat from the chalice did not reach his skin. He took the other cup and placed it to Eulalie's right on the table. The servant bowed and left the room.

"Where were we?"

Less than thirty seconds, just after Mitis had secured his king piece, another servant came in and announced to them that the entertainment for that morning had arrived. Those who would entertain the king were setting up in the Grand Hall below. A play was to be performed that morning. One of Mitis's favorites.

Mitis decided to postpone their game. Eulalie agreed with a smile. (He placed a clear glass cuboid over the game board). He took her hand as she stood up, then they made their way downstairs. A servant came in and retrieved their drinks for them upon a tray. He followed them on their way down.

❖

Antonius had been in his room for two hours. From the time after he had spoken with Jeffery till then. He was reading through one of the books he found in the room prepared for him. He could not concentrate on what he read, for his mind wondered often. From the affairs of his kingdom, to the beauty of Astra, to the suffering he felt Marcus was going through as he witnessed Xaria in pain.

He closed the book and rose from the bed. He put on his outer robe. He left the room and made his way to the room where Marcus was staying. It was slightly open, so he slowly made his way in. Marcus acknowledged his presence. He saw that Xaria had woken up and she was sitting upright on the bed. Marcus had stayed at her side through the night. Antonius went and sat on a chair on the other side of the bed.

"How are you feeling?" He asked Xaria.

A servant came in and handed Xaria a bowl of hot soup.

"Thank you" she said to the servant. "I am feeling a bit better." She said to Antonius

"You still look pale. Do you want me to get some bread?" Marcus said.

"No, this will do. Thank you." She said then kissed him. "Thank you" she said once more.

"A servant informed me that the entertainers are downstairs, do you think you'll be able to come." Antonius asked.

"Can't you see she is still ill? What is wrong with you?" Marcus said.

Antonius kept quiet and did not answer. He felt a bit uneasy.

"I appreciate you being here Antonius but please, think before you speak." Marcus said

"I apologize."

Xaria drank her soup and when she was done, a concerned look came upon her face. She turned to the window for a moment. A tear fell from her eye, and she began to experience pain in her chest. She took a deep breath. Marcus moved closer to her.

Antonius took note of her facial expression and felt that something was on her mind but she was afraid to state it so he said to her,

"Xaria in the years I have known you, I have not known you to hide anything from your husband."

"Antonius, what are you talking about?" Marcus asked.

"Ask your wife."

"My love, if there is anything that bothers you, you can confide in me"

As Marcus wiped a tear from her cheek, she began to speak,

"Last night…I saw Gammon in a dream."

Antonius gripped the arms of his chair. Marcus was shocked. Xaria continued with more tears flowing down her cheeks,

"I saw him coming after me, as I ran I fell and he came and hovered over me. I was scared." Her hands were quivering. Marcus took her hand and kept her steady. He took the bowl of soup from her and put it aside.

"Please my love, you know I cannot bear to see you like this. Please don't cry."

Marcus wiped her tears. She composed herself and continued.

"Gammon tried to kill me but then I saw a man dressed in the cloths of a Shepherd rush from the afar and battle against Gammon. He saved me. Gammon fled because he was no match for the man. I wanted to thank the stranger but after he had saved me, he left. I did not see his face."

At that moment a servant came in and told Antonius that Mitis requested his presence downstairs at the Grand Hall. Antonius stood up, and prepared to leave, but before he left he addressed Xaria.

"I must be going but this is not over. Xaria please do not worry so much over this."

Antonius made his way downstairs and to the Grand Hall. As he approached it, he could hear a multitude of voices. He made his way in and saw the magnificent set up in the Grand Hall.

A play was to be performed for the royal family that morning. The play had been in other seasons performed in an amphitheater not far from the castle, but because of the cold, it was done inside the Grand Hall, the biggest room in the castle. The place where the king, queen and special guests were to sit was at the end of the Hall. It was a great collection of fine chairs set up on an elevated carved stone platform. The platform was thinner at the bottom and wider at the top. It appeared to be set up against the wall and painted to match the floor of the Grand hall. A rug ran in between the setup of chairs. Most of the chairs were magnificent in their design. More chairs were placed at the higher levels. The highest point which was about four meters high was the position only for the royal family. The chairs of the royal family were designed intricately to reflect their status. The colors on the chair of the queen were the colors soldier wear. The colors on the chair of the king were the primary colors knight adorn. Seats below were granted to invited guests. Ten of the twenty three nobles were present.

Felix also had been informed of the play that was going to be performed, and he decided to go. He came with about five of his sailors, those who were closest to him.

They all made their way into the Hall. After Mitis had taken his place at the top of the platform, the actors and actresses prepared to begin. Last preparations were going on behind a stage that had been built a few feet from the base of the platform. The play about to be performed was about a man who sought to find his way home, though his mind was on his home, his heart was on the one he loved.

Antonius sat in the row of seats just below the seats reserved for the royal family. Just a few minutes before the play commenced, Astra made her way in. Mitis, Eulalie and Galen had already taken their place. The last seat was on Mitis's right, reserved for Astra.

Antonius was moved by Astra's beauty once he saw her make her way into the Grand Hall. Amidst the crowd of people, and other beautiful women, she stood out in his eyes. So much so that he did not notice that Simona was closer to him. She made her way to him and took the seat beside him. He turned and beheld her, he smiled at her. She smiled back.

"Uncle adores this play. He's seen it over five times."

"What is it about?" Antonius asked as he tried to keep his eyes on Simona, as Astra approached the platform.

"It's about a man who wants to find his way home but he can't because the one he loves is not there. So he is very reluctant to return. I think it is a touching story."

"Interesting…is Jeffery going to be here to enjoy the play?"

"He will be here. He just likes to show up just before it begins, he has little patience."

At that moment Astra walked up the stairs of the platform and took her place beside her father, Antonius glanced at her as she passed by but she purposively kept her eyes off him as she passed.

A short moment later Jeffery arrived with Neemus, a taller, much older man, whose build showed through the clothes he wore. He was second only to Jeffery in strength. They took their place, in the same row Antonius sat. Jeffery shot a serious glance at Antonius.

The stage was set, and the actors began.

Antonius watched the play. He saw himself in the main character and was intrigued by every word and scene that the main actor portrayed. A man who was lost, incapable of truly finding himself without first being with the one he loved. Yet at the same time, he wanted to return to the place he knew.

At the same time at the edge of the city, the guards and some knights were in pursuit of a man who had taken two hundred pieces of gold from the chest that Jeffery had seized from Felix's ship. He ran on with great speed, some of the knights though on horses could not catch up to him. He toppled barrels, jumped from roof to roof, and ran through people's houses. The knights divided themselves. As a few chased him from behind, more knights and guards anticipated his movements and cut him off ahead.

They surrounded him at a cleared street. He was trapped and surrounded by fifty men. They stopped the hooded thief.

"Drop the gold you worm." Said the Knight in charge of the group

"Fifty, there are fifty of you…and only one of me." The man smiled. "This will be a thrill."

The knights and guards laughed

"Do you think you can take on us? Do you have a death wish?" The knight then got down from his horse and unsheathed his sword. "I will not repeat myself a third time, now worm, drop the gold."

"One, two, three, four…"The man began counting.

"What are you doing?"

"Just counting how long it'll take for you to realize that you do not stand a chance against me."

The knight in anger swung at the man, the man dodged and trapped the knight's hand, and then he twisted it. There was an audible crack, the man quickly took the knight's sword and kicked him in the side of his neck. The knight fell to the floor hard. The man removed his hood to reveal himself. It was Julian, the son of Thanos. Every guard and knight surrounding him unsheathed their swords.

"You took too long knight, now you've paid the price. I haven't had this much of a challenge in a while."

The knight that Julian kicked to the ground crawled away to safety, still holding his broken arm. His head was fidgeting.

One by one, the remaining guards and knights charged at him, with every swing at him, Julian dodged. He put up a good fight against them but after he had struck down about thirty of them, more guards arrived at the scene. A guard was able to disarm him but he quickly knocked that guard aside, another guard tackled him and soon enough more guards placed their weight on him. The knight that led his capture came forward still holding his broken arm and his heavy neck. He laughed as guards pushed Julian's face into the snow. The knight stepped on Julian's left hand. Julian yelled in pain, the pain shot through his arm and intensified when it reached the wound he had sustained a day and half ago.

"Not so quick with your tongue when you're pinned to the ground helpless and useless!"

"I say that I showed considerably how inadequate you are as a leader. If you led your men better, it wouldn't have been so easy for me."

"Oh it shall be a delight when Jeffery sees you and puts you in your place. I remember your face. You were one of the men of Philonia we captured yesterday."

"Just take me to this man who shall decide my fate, I have no interest in talking to you."

The guards and the men pilled upon Julian made sure his feet were chained before they got up from him. When they had got up from him, they held his hand behind his back and one of them punched him in the gut.

"I would have the greatest pleasure killing you right here but all cases involving the guards or Knights must be brought before Jeffery. Make sure he is bound well men."

They did as the head knight ordered. Then they began making their way to the Castle. Julian did not struggle. He kept alert of all that was happening around him. From the place of his capture till they got to the castle, he was assessing how he might escape, if the chance ever presented itself.

Peter made his way into the city inconspicuously. His face was only familiar to three people in Petra. One of those three was an old friend, the second person was that old friend's wife and the third person was a man whose capture he was responsible for but refused to take credit. When Peter arrived at the castle gate, he witnessed the knights dragging Julian in to see Jeffery. He noticed Julian's face and whispered to himself, 'The son of Thanos?' "I guess it has been a while." He thought.

The guards let in the knights but stopped him.

"What is your business here old man." A guard at the castle gate asked him.

"I am here to see a guest of the king."

"They must request your presence. You are not allowed otherwise to proceed any future beyond this point. I am afraid we cannot let you enter."

"Very well," Peter said calmly. He took hold of his staff with both hands and closed his eyes.

The guards watched in awe as a strong wind blew from behind him. The wind blew the guards off their feet but Peter stood firm. The wind was strong enough to blow the gates wide open for Peter. He opened his eyes and calmly walked into the castle yard. The guards still on the floor could do nothing but stare as he made his way into the castle.

"Let it been known if anyone asks you, you did not let me in, I let myself in," Peter said to the guards as he passed by them.

Peter walked through the halls of the castle. Things seemed unchanged. When he came to the statue of Calix in the foyer, he stopped.

"I cannot believe it has been eighteen years. I hope your son's virtues are like yours."

He sighed. Then he followed the sound of the voices of the actors, which led him to the

Grand Hall. He watched as the knights dragged Julian into where the play was going on, they did not interrupt the play. The knight who had led the operation to capture Julian walked to Jeffery and whispered something in his ear. "My lord," he said to Jeffery, "There is a troublemaker that needs to be dealt with." The knight did well to conceal the fact that his arm was broken.

"Can't it wait?" Jeffery insisted.

"He was responsible for the loss of four knights of the Order."

Jeffery turned and looked the knight intensely in his eyes.

"How is it, that one man can be responsible for the death of four of my knights?!" Jeffery said. His voice echoed across the room. The actors went silent and all attention was now on Jeffery. Jeffery stood up and walked up the Platform to a step before the row of the royal family. He bowed and said to the King.

"Forgive me for my interruption but there is important business that I wish to handle and I need your permission and presence, your majesty."

Mitis raised his hand and said.

"This shall commence another day. The play is postponed." Then he said to Jeffery. "Whatever it is that you wish to handle let it be settled here."

"Thank you," Jeffery said then he turned to the knight that came with the message and said. "Where is the low-life bastard?"

The nobles, the royal family, Felix and Antonius all stayed in their place to see the reason why the play had been suspended for the moment. The knights and guards brought in Julian with his hood over his face and his hands and feet chained.

"This is the man," the knight said as he forcefully removed Julian's hood.

"He is one of my men," Antonius said quietly.

"He is?" Simona asked.

"Yes, why would he do this?"

Felix also took note of the man, "I know his face."

Jeffery walked down the platform and towards Julian, with rightful anger he punched Julian in the stomach.

"I should pull out my sword and execute you right here and now."

"That would be wise." Julian said with a smile.

"Do not test me."

Jeffery reached into Julian's cloth and took the sack of gold. He had heard a slight clink of the coins as Julian walked in.

"Is this why you did it? For a meager amount of gold, where did you even get this?"

"I retrieved it from the chest you stole from a ship that belonged to Philonia."

Jeffery punched Julian across the face.

"You speak to me like that again, and I will cut your tongue."

"Enough." Mitis said, "This man's face is too familiar. State your name."

Julian spat out some blood smiled and stood back up. He raised his head high and answered the king.

"I am Julian, son of Thanos."

"The Thanos, Thanos of Belvain?"

"There is no other Thanos whose name is known across the four corners of the earth." Julian responded.

"That's why he was able to defeat those knights so easily" Mitis thought. Then he said,

"What you have done is deplorable. Are you aware of your crimes?"

"What I did, I did to defend myself."

"Your sharp tongue can be directed at anyone else but if you point it my way I will cut it off."

Julian nodded slightly.

"Forgive me your majesty," Julian said in a sincere tone.

"I knew your father. He was one of the greatest fighters among the seven kingdoms. He slayed many ghouls and is sometimes regarded as a hero, the only problem he had is the same you do. He could not control his tongue and his arrogance was unmatched. But though his arrogance was like a net cast over those below him, he still kept his faith and did what was right. His words may have been sharp but his heart, and mind was sharper."

"Glad to hear good words about my father."

"It is unfortunate he spent such little time with you, but still you have fended for yourself all these years. How old are you?"

"Twenty five years."

"It has been eighteen years since the passing of your father."

Antonius with his hands locked looked down and remembered that it had also been eighteen years since the passing of his father.

Jeffery feeling that Mitis had become sympathetic towards Julian interjected,

"My king, need I remind you that he was responsible for the death of four of my knights!"

"Do not raise your voice at me. I have not forgotten his crime, but you must understand that a man of his talents would be very useful."

"So then how shall he be judged?" Jeffery asked

"We judge him according to his abilities. He shall fight for his life."

"Against who?"

"That is your choice Jeffery. Since he is responsible for the death of your knights, why not have one of them restore honor to the Knights Order."

"Yes that is good, that is perfect." Jeffery looked at Julian with a smug smile then said,

"Neemus, prepare yourself, you shall be taking on this rat."

Neemus stood up. Julian was surprised at his statue. Neemus took off his outer robe. Some knights ran to the knight's quarter and brought Neemus's armor. He took it and wore it. Julian observed him and then was approached by a knight who offered to cloth him in armor. Julian said to the knight,

"All I need is for my chains to be unlocked and a sword wouldn't be much to ask for, would it?"

"You shall be dealt with well." The knight responded. "I'll bring your sword." An old rusted sword was granted to Julian. He looked at the blade with a smile. It did not surprise him a bit. They unlocked his chains. A knight offered him a shield, one that looked in better condition than the sword. He took it but it was a bit heavy for him. So he decided if it would slow him down in the duel, he would discard of it, or use it wisely.

"If it so happens," Julian began, "That I win this duel, how shall I know that you shall keep to your word and forget my crimes."

"I swear by my honor, if you win this duel, you are a free man," Mitis said.

Julian then fixed his eyes on Jeffery and said, "What of you, do I have your word of my state as a free man, if I am to come out victorious."

Jeffery responded with confidence. "On my honor, I swear, if you Julian son of Thanos somehow are victorious over Neemus, you shall be forgiven of your crimes. There you have it, a king's honor and a noble knight's honor have been put on the line before witnesses, so shall we commence with the duel."

"Yes but before we begin, I'd like to say one thing."

"No, you are done speaking." Neemus said as he raised his sword and his feet moved quickly towards Julian, he went in for the first strike. Julian moved back dodging the attack.

"All I wanted to do was apologize for my crime before we began." Julian moved a few more steps back. Then he gripped his sword tightly, he then raised his shield adequately in front of his torso.

"The dead make no apologies," Neemus bellowed as he swung once more at Julian.

Neemus was on the offensive, with every swing Julian dodged and used the shield to defend himself, but every time Neemus's sword clashed with Julian's shield, Julian felt a sharp pain in his upper shoulder. It began to interfere with his ability to effectively carry his shield. Neemus swung and struck Julian's shield again, for a moment Julian was caught off guard, and lost his balance, Neemus threw a front kick that knocked Julian off his feet. Julian rolled backwards on the floor and stood to his feet quickly. Neemus charged at him, and

swung his sword once more. Julian still a little
off balance after returning to his feet, leaned
back as the tip of Neemus's sword grazed his
left cheek.

Tiny drips of blood came ran down from
his open flesh. Neemus stopped for a moment
and smiled.

"A few inches closer and that would have
been your head."

Julian felt the blood flowing down his
cheek. He wiped it with his left hand and saw
the red cover his palm.

"Neemus stop playing around. Make him
pay for his crimes!" Jeffery yelled out.

Mitis watched with no change of expression. Some of the nobles were a bit moved by
the fight. Antonius also showed no expression.
He felt no sympathy for Julian but did not want
to see him die. He remembered that Julian had
helped him rescue those men that would have
drowned after their boat got destroyed. So it
struck him as a mystery why Julian did what
he did, though it was not his place to do so.

Julian stood firm and prepared himself.
Neemus with a fading smile recomposed himself as well. They were about to resume their
duel. Julian sprinted at Neemus, his speed in-
creasing as he got closer to Neemus. Neemus
raised his sword to strike Julian but Julian
swung his shield towards the incoming sword.
They clashed with a great force which sent
Neemus's arm flying back up. Immediately

Julian with his sword swung upwards. The double edged steel cut through the right shoulder of Neemus's doublet armor. The chainmail was no match for the blade. The steel grazed the upper part of Neemus's right bicep.

Neemus stepped back but Julian gave him no space. Julian attacked again, with every swing, the clash of his sword with Neemus's shield and the close scrapes the tip of his blade made with Neemus's flesh made Jeffery furious. Julian fought as one with much experience.

Julian could not keep this momentum going because the sharp pain in his upper left shoulder was now unbearable. So he thought quickly. He ran straight into Neemus with his shield in front of him. Neemus placed his shield in front of himself to counter Julian's force. Their shields locked in place, their faces mere inches from each other. They were staring into each other's eyes. Neither was intimidated by the other. Julian started pushing his shield more causing Neemus's leg to slide back across the marble floor. Neemus feeling insulted pushed back and stopped his motion. He tried to push Julian backwards to show his strength, but Julian's feet were in place. Neemus tried as hard as he could but Julian was as firm as a rock.

Jeffery gripped the arm of his chair. He could not believe what he was seeing. What Julian was doing, he knew was hurting himself, because the pain in his upper shoulder was now more unbearable.

Julian thought fast, he stopped pushing against Neemus's shield and leaned back quickly, Neemus was caught by surprise. His frame was launched forward towards Julian. Neemus lost his footing and was falling forward. Julian drove his knee into Neemus's jaw. Then he quickly grabbed Neemus's right arm, twisted it, there was a slightly audible crack. Neemus's sword fell to the floor. Neemus fell to one knee and looked up at Julian. The tip of Julian sword was less than an inch from Neemus's nose.

"You fought well. I honestly have no desire in killing you. As I was about to say before you interrupted me, I apologize for my crimes… Now declare me victor of this duel and you'll keep your life."

Jeffery stood up in anger and said. "You dare not say it Neemus."

Neemus looked back at Jeffery then back to Julian. He was breathing hard. He felt that if he did not declare it, his life would be taken by the man who had just humbled him. He bowed his head and said.

"Julian son of Thanos, this duel is yours."

Chapter 13
The Face of Evil. Moral Evaluations.
A Quest for Truth

Titus remembered the man's face but not his name. He remembered his voice but not what he said. He remembered the cries of pain the man yelled out as his flesh was consumed by the flames he had instructed to be lit. The sound was scorched in his memory forever and it kept him from concentrating on his duties.

"Why am I haunted by a man who defied me?" he whispered under his breath.

In frustration he scattered the mass of papers on the table in front of him. "Useless," he said, "all useless."

He rose from his desk. He was feeling a little dazed. The moonlight shone in through the open curtains. There were four candles mounted around the room. It was really late and he felt it was time to retire to bed. The last two days his mind had been wrestling with the reality of his mortality, something he did not know how to come to grasp with. "What shall become of me when I am dead, shall I even be remembered?" He heard the man's scream again. He felt it was a ploy of his conscience.

He blew out the candles and left his study. He made his way into the hallway. The hallway echoed with bone chilling silence. The torches on the walls had all been blown out by the wind and the only light on those stone floors were from the full moon.

"Where are the guards?" he thought. "Elana" he whispered and then went to look out from one of the windows in the hall. He saw into the street and it was quiet.

"Titus." A voice echoed from down the hallway. He looked to where he heard the voice speak his name. He saw no one. "Titus" the voice called out again.

"Who are you? Show yourself! I command you."

He saw the edge of a dark cloak at the end of the hallway. The shadows covered the rest of the creature. What he saw next he was not prepared for. Two snakes crawled from under the garment of the creature that called his name. They emerged from the shadows and slithered his way. He saw the snakes and his feet took off. He ran away but he was not fast enough. The snakes wrapped themselves around his legs. His knees buckled and he fell. They dragged him through the corridors, down the steps and out of the palace. The snakes dragged him through the streets, his garment scraped on the gravel streets. His eyes wandered around but he saw no one, not even the night guards.

He felt his ankle growing weaker and his back heating up. He reached to his side and was surprised to touch his sword. He pulled it out and cut one the snake's tail. The other snake noticed what Titus had done quickly and released its grip of Titus other ankle. Titus struggled to his feet. He started running in a limping motion back to the palace. The snakes looked at each other, and the snake that had been hacked at regrew its tail immediately. They slithered faster towards Titus. One snake leaped and wrapped itself around Titus's neck as the other coiled around his feet. It caught both his feet in place. Titus fell forward. The snake twisted around him tighter and tighter. He yelled out in agony. Then the snake around his neck looked into his fainting eyes. Then it spoke,

"You are only making it worse for yourself by resisting us."

Titus was in shock to hear the snake speak. He used his hand to loosen the grip of the snake around his neck so he could breathe. Then he responded,

"What are you?"

"Let's just say the Darkness gave birth to us. And you by your deeds are embracing Darkness."

"No, I...will...not...let the Darkness to take hold of my heart. I am not deceived... I know that your words are venomous and your intent forever evil. I..."

Titus was about to continue speaking but could not because the snake tightened its grip around his neck.

"Our master commands us to deliver you to him."

Fear filled Titus's heart. The snakes dragged him away from the city to the dense woods west of the city. They stopped by a section of the forest that was very damp. They released their grip of Titus. Titus was still in shock and did not stand up. He opened his eyes and saw where he was. Then he heard his name. He sat up and saw the creature that was at the end of the hall a few feet from him. The creature was clothed in a dark-hooded robe. It was turned away from Titus. It was looking off far towards the west.

"The truth is bitter." It said.

Titus took off his outer garment and saw how the gravel had ruined it. His back felt sore and he felt a sharp pain shoot up his spine to the left side of his neck. He held his neck and tried to massage the pain away. He looked and saw the snakes that dragged him slither back into the robe of the creature standing a few feet in front of him.

The clouds blocked out the moonlight as the creature turned to Titus.

"I should know. I have tasted the truth." The creature continued "What do you think of truth?" The creature asked Titus.

Titus was not at all interested in his question as he was to know where he was and who it was that was speaking to him. Fear and anger set into his heart at the same time, he rose to his feet and addressed the creature in a strict tone.

"I don't give a damn about your philosophical crisis. Who are you? Tell me!"

"The truth, it is indeed interesting, one wonders if it is lasting, if it shall hold up against all situations. What do you think of truth?" The creature asked again.

"What part of I don't care don't you understand. I need to know why I am here and who you are."

"What a fallacy it is to believe that the truth can free a man. Truth? Is it not a mystery to the wayward heart? The heart that seeks to be free does not seek after truth. It never does. I should know because my heart was once this way. Truth could not free me from what I was, nor could it keep me from becoming what I am." The creature signed "What do you think of truth?"

Titus was silent for a moment then he took a breath. Then spoke,

"I will not answer until I know who it is I am speaking too."

The creature still had its back facing Titus, for its gaze was set on the west. It slowly turned to face Titus and a strong wind began to blow. Titus shielded his eyes from debris of twigs that were flying towards his face. The creature was now facing Titus. The wind died down and Titus beheld the creature. The hood still covered the creatures face. Titus saw the hands of the creature. They were scaled like the skin of a lizard.

Silence filled the scene for that moment. Titus felt a drop of sweat run down his neck. Fear was the last thing he wanted to manifest. He stood still and tall, then he said.

"I still don't know who you are."

The creature still did not respond. A dark mist, as the one Antonius had seen fill his room began to surround the creature. The forest appeared grey before his eyes. Now, he knew that he was standing in the presence of evil.

"I am known by many names. One of which is, the Adversary."

"No it cannot be," Titus said with a whimper in his voice.

"Why are you afraid? Did you not want to know who I am?" The creature said. Its voice bellowed across the forest. The mist ascended around the scaly figure. Titus looked at his feet and saw the mist surrounding him. He looked forward and greater fear captured his heart when he saw the hooded creature standing mere inches from him. It moved fast and silently. He felt his hand shaking. He knew the cold night was not the cause of this. He was sweating and no amount of effort he exhausted could help him gather his composure so as to address the question the creature asked.

His eyes were still fixed on the creature. He was looking into the hood of the creature, expecting to see the face of evil but he saw nothing but darkness. He felt a void, yet from this void he heard the creature's voice.

"What is truth?" the creature asked again.

"Truth is that which must be for order to be." Titus replied. He felt a dryness overcome his throat. "Though it may be hard to accept at times, it is necessary because it soothes more than it hurts, heals more than it inflicts pain. In the end, it serves a greater purpose."

"Is that what you believe or is that what you have been taught to believe?" the creature said.

"It is my belief." Titus responded

"You have lied in my presence." The creature said then a strong wind blew by. Titus felt more evil flow from the creature. It shook his spine. "It is a fatal mistake to tell a lie in my presence. Had I not a soft side for you I could kill you now. But I will tell you what many do not know. Truth is a fallacy. It is a deception of a weak mind. When the truth goes against a weak person's desires the truth becomes irrelevant. So it seems that truth bare no hold on our deeds."

"That's not true. You are lying." Titus said.

"If I am lying, then tell me, how do you know that Antonius is guilty of the crime he has been accused of?"

"I don't know if he is guilty. I only sought the crown."

"So he confesses." The creature said "If you are not sure he is guilty, why then do you ride on this lie. Why not go and find him and give him back what is truly his? Give him back the kingdom."

Titus knew that if Antonius was indeed innocent, then all he had done was wrong and he would have to relinquish his kingship and grant it back to his brother.

"I cannot do that."

"And why is that?"

"I have longed to rule but I loved my brother too much to raise my sword against him. Even if I had killed him and become king, the Elders would have been a hindrance to my rule. When I learnt that they were dead and their murder was blamed on him, I could not but see it as the finest opportunity to ascend to the throne and take his place. So you see, even if it is that he is innocent, I cannot give him back the crown."

"So you would deny the truth for your own selfish desire. Just as I thought, you are weak."

"But…" Titus began about to defend his actions but was cut short by the creature.

"There is nothing you can say that will clear your case. You are as guilty as the one who killed the Elders. But know this, Antonius is not going to run forever, he will return."

"I will bargain with him. I could convince him to let me rule a portion of the kingdom."

Titus felt his words were hopeful but highly unlikely. The creature heard the doubt in Titus's voice.

"You prove how foolish you are because you continue to speak things you know are not true. What man will divide his kingdom with the man who betrayed him?"

"I did not betray him."

"Yes you did! You were not even sure if he was truly guilty. You did not care to speak to him after he was arrested. He left and when he returns, he will come against you." The creature paused for a moment. Titus's mind was on the reality of the possibility of Antonius returning. He knew that the leaders of five of the seven nations were very fond of Antonius and if he were to ask them for a favor, such as the reclaiming of his crown from Titus, they would help him. "But," The creature began, "There is something you can do."

"What is it?" Titus asked.

"Find Antonius, and kill him."

"No, I will never do that."

The mist surrounded Titus, he felt his breath leaving him, and in a matter of seconds he was suffocating and gasping desperately for air.

"I don't think you understand. You do not have a say in the matter. If you let Antonius live, he will return with an army and he will overwhelm you, then he will take your life."

Titus gasped once more and for a short moment he caught his breath.

"Antonius is not that way." he struggled to get his words out. The creature heard him clearly.

He fell to his knees. The two snakes that had dragged him there crawled forth from underneath the robe of the creature.

One of them coiled around his neck. The other went around his waist. He tried to loosen the grip of the snake around his neck. His eyes were fainting and his face turned a pale blue. He looked at the creature that towered over him. The creature lifted its right hand up, and at once Titus saw a sword appear in the creature's hand.

"You know nothing of the wickedness in the hearts of men."

Then the creature plunged the sword through Titus's heart.

He jerked and shook. Then he woke up and found himself in the palace. His pillow was soaked in sweat, his heart was racing and his fingers shook for a brief moment. He placed his feet on the floor and rested his head on one hand. He looked out the window and saw the twilight of the morning. He looked back and saw Elana sleeping soundly. He took a breath, went and washed his face. He put on his garments and went to the study room. His heart was still heavy.

Upon the table was the mass of books with his father's diary placed in the middle of two stacks of books. He saw that the window was open. He went, closed it, and then he returned to the books. He observed that the page that was open and realized it was not the page he had left it at. The wind had blown the window open and turned it to this new page he saw. He ran his fingers down the page to see if he had already read it. And he had. But something quickly caught his attention. Something he had read before but now was made clearer after the nightmare he just experienced.

It read, "One's false intentions are like snakes. Snakes that shall lead him to a well of lies, lies that are shall test him. And if he is found impure, his words shall betray him and the intent of his heart will become known."

After he re-read the passage his breathing seized for a moment. Then he closed the book. He whispered something to himself, of a sought it sounded like a little confession. He then remembered the black mist and he also recalled reading a bit about the black mist in Antonius's diary. He searched through the mass of books on the table looking for Antonius's diary. He found it and opened it quickly to the last entry. As he read of the night Antonius heard the loud scream he kept keen attention to the details Antonius used to describe his experience. He got to the part when a force broke the door of Antonius's chamber but before he could read what transpired afterwards, he heard Elana call his name from outside the door.

He looked towards the door and saw her come in. The rising sun made her eyes sparkle. Her night gown was black and had a fine silver lining the hem of the gown. On this fine morning her beauty once more captured him.

"Titus, what are you doing?" she said softly as she walked to him and wrapped her arms around him. "Are you okay my love?"

"My heart is uneasy. I couldn't sleep."

"Come back to bed. Let me sing to you and sooth your heart."

"I am afraid I can't," he said as he drew back a bit.

"Why?" she asked.

"This is a matter I must address alone."

He picked up his outer garment that he had left on the chair the previous night. He put it on, kissed her and left his study.

Elana became suspicious. She felt he may have discovered something about her. She walked to the window and waited, watching outside. There was a light fog outside. Her sight was set on the palace gate. There she saw Titus mount a horse and ride out. He put on a hooded garment over his outer garment. He covered his face before he rode off.

She opened the window. Immediately she transformed to the bird form she had assumed when she went in search of Antonius. She followed him till he reached the cathedral.

Titus got off his horse. He was unaware that he had been followed. He opened the tall cathedral door and walked in. She flew down and transformed back to her human form. She stood at the door and was hesitant to enter. She slowly took hold of the handle but when she touched it, it shocked her. She felt a sharp pain shoot from her hand to the rest of her body. She stepped back and looked at her palm, it was slightly burnt.

She clenched her hand for a moment and the burnt mark healed. She wondered why this happened. She remembered that she entered the cathedral during Titus's coronation. It slightly began to dawn on her as she felt a still presence around the cathedral, a holy presence. It prevented her from going in. She transformed back into the bird like creature and flew to one of the upper windows of the cathedral. She looked inside and saw Titus on his knees on the edge of the first pew.

He was silent.

Titus had his hands folded, his head rested upon them and his hood covered his face. Silence filled the cathedral. He wanted an answer but did not know what to say, he took a deep breath then he began,

"I have humbled myself, and I have come seeking an answer, for the true intent of my heart has been revealed. Though I am not a man worthy of your calling, I still desire to know the truth. Please, Oh mighty and Great King, father of the Guardians, answer my prayer, please I need to know if I must relinquish this crown and give it back to my brother." The last words he said with a slight dishonesty in his voice.

He was quiet.

"I need a sign. Please."

A door to his left opened. He kept still. He saw the light from a candle coming his way. He turned to it and saw the bishop.

"Who is that? Who are you?" the bishop said.

"Calm yourself. It is I," Titus said.

The bishop recognized his voice.

"Your majesty, please forgive me, I did not know it was you. But what are you doing here so early?"

"My heart is troubled."

"I must confess to your majesty, I overheard your prayer, and I am afraid that I have a truth to tell you that you might not welcome."

"What is it? Tell me." Titus insisted.

"Antonius is not responsible for the death of the Elders."

Titus was relieved to hear this.

"So I guess I won't be king for much longer. All I have to do is to grant him back this crown and the kingdom shall be his again. I find no pleasure in being king if my conscience is forever going to haunt me."

"That is not all your majesty."

"There is more you want to tell me?"

"I fear to tell this to your majesty but I believe evil has made its presence known in this city and has taken the form of a woman, the woman whom you hold dear to your heart."

"What?!" Titus said. "Are you saying Elana is the cause of their deaths?"

"Yes I believe so."

"I should have known that you also thirst for the power of this crown. So have you been conspiring with Darius on how to frame Elana? Then after her, you'll come after me? I have heard enough of this. You better grant thanks to the Great King that I have spared you from knowing my wrath though I have just heard these useless lies of yours."

Titus got up and turned to leave.

"No please, listen to me. You as well as I know that no woman among the daughters of men can do what Elana does. Her voice charms men and capture's their heart. It makes them do things that are shameful. When she walked into the cathedral during your coronation, I too was victim to her spell. I tried to anoint my ears with holy oil but I was too late. I felt my heart encircle with lust, I feel so ashamed that a man of my virtues was swayed by her voice. After she had stopped singing, and she knelt before me, I was released from my trance. I saw her and I knew nothing good can come from her presence. Since then I have re-anointed this cathedral and prayed over it, invoking the presence of the Guardians, so their spirits shall protect this cathedral. This is holy ground Titus and she cannot enter here."

Titus stopped where he was and looked back at the bishop.

"She has also affected your heart. She has made you cruel."

"That is not true, her songs do not put me in a trance, I welcome them, and they do not overcome me," Titus said.

"By welcoming them, you are welcoming your own demise. You are letting evil take over your heart," the bishop said with great concern.

Titus was well aware of the truth the bishop's words held. But his mind was on Elana, he was not quick to accept the bishop's words. Her songs were very pleasing and calming to him. She was the first person that had moved him in such a way. He thought of his mother. What would she think? Then he justified his dishonesty, 'would she not want me to be happy. Elana grants me that which I desire, happiness.' He had never felt his heart so divided on an issue before. He clenched his fist. He was silent for a few seconds.

"If that is so, then it shall be."

"No, what would your father think? He prayed over you, that you stay pure and that your heart may never yield to evil."

"Every day for the past week I have been reading through my father's diary. Everything he wrote. That is the only way I have come to know him. The more I read, the more I find that I am not like my father."

He realized the truth of his words after he spoke them. He was not like his father, he wished he was, but he knew that could not be. He was unaware that by falling in love with Elana he had opened his heart to evil desires. Her songs did not have an effect on him without his consenting to be moved by the longings they stirred in his heart. Elana's soft touch, her lime green eyes, and the curve of her face, all had made him fall even more in love with her. So, he was not very welcoming to the bishop's words.

He turned and left. When Elana saw him leaving she transformed herself back to the bird-like creature and flew in a hurry back to the palace. She was unaware that someone had seen her on that foggy morning. Darius spotted her high up on the cathedral. He was making his way to the cathedral early that morning to perform his morning devotions when he spotted her up high standing by the window ledge. Then he saw her transform and fly towards the palace. He then saw Titus exit the cathedral, he ran to him and wanted to tell Titus what he saw but Titus was in no mood to speak to him. Titus mounted his horse and rode off back to the palace.

Darius ran into the cathedral and told the bishop what he had seen. The bishop took his words as true.

Titus arrived back at the palace. One of the guards told him that they had seen an unusually large bird fly over the palace. He walked on ignoring the guard's word. His mind was set on Elana, he searched for her and when he found her in her chamber, he went to her and kissed her. She was taken by surprise.

"I have returned." He said to her.

Elana was still baffled by his action. She drew back a bit and asked,

"Is your heart content? Have you done all that you wanted to do?"

"I have," he took her hand, he saw that her eyes were welling with tears "what's wrong?"

"I feel as though you do not love me."

"Why would you say that?"

"You are hiding something from me. I needed you and I could not find you, I waited an hour for you."

Titus went closer to her and embraced her.

"My love, I was in the cathedral. I had a nightmare last night. It revealed some things, especially of the condition of my heart that I needed to address. You see, I did not leave you for an arbitrary reason."

"So what have you come to know of yourself?"

"This I have come to know, I have not been as honest as I would have hoped, especially with my brother, Antonius. I desire more than ever to know where he is. I must find him."

"Then what shall you do with him?" Elana asked expecting Titus to damn his brother.

"I will give him back the kingdom."

"But why, you are the king, is he not guilty of killing the elders?"

"No one knows that for sure. This crown is not for me. Not yet. As much as I hate to admit it, Darius may have been right. I was not ready to take on the many pressures this crown has placed on me."

"You are the king, the power is yours. To do as you please, my lord, if you love me you will do that which is honorable, you will find Antonius and punish him."

Titus turned from her and went to the window.

With his gaze set outside he said to her,

"I love you. I would have done anything else to prove it. But I am afraid that this one thing you have asked of me I cannot do. I cannot raise my sword against my brother."

This made Elana angry but she kept her composure and approached him.

"Forgive me my king, if I put you in such a situation. I can see your heart is uneasy."

She took off her garment and pulled him closer to herself. He laid his hands on her waist as he kissed her. She was bare, beautiful and entrancing. She led him to the bed. As he kissed her, he could hear her songs filling him, they took a hold of his body, and then they filled his mind. He was under her spell. He kissed her deeply and made love to her.

A week went by and Titus addressed the senate before he gathered his things to prepare to depart to Konstuliana. Spring was three days away. Things he would need on the journey were assembled according to his demands. So the day of departure arrived, the first day of spring. The flowers in the palace garden glistened in the morning sun, the air was light, and the animals that filled the forest just outside Noble city during the summer and fall months were seen by the guards at the city gate. It was a beautiful sight.

Titus walked out of the palace with Elana. Darius was there to wish him a safe journey and take any last instructions from him. Elana got into the carriage first. Darius set his sights on her as she sat down. She looked at him for a moment and then looked away. It was as if time slowed and that moment lasted longer than he wanted. Darius turned to Titus. Titus before entering addressed Darius,

"I will be gone for a week. I am placing you in charge of the affairs of the kingdom. If there are any laws that you want me to see, prepare them and set them on the table in the ballroom. I shall see them when I return." Titus was about to enter then he turned and said, "One more thing, if Antonius returns while I am gone, do not wage war against him, do not arrest him, just give him a proper welcome. That is all." Titus smiled and entered the carriage. Darius was surprised that Titus was welcoming to the idea of Antonius returning, not only that but that he should be received as one who had done no wrong. Darius wanted to say something to Titus but he was at a loss for words for his mind was set on Elana. He was more concerned as to what she really was. So he held his peace, bowed and bid them a safe journey.

There were five soldiers on horses who escorted him. They were well armed. The robes they wore were a fine black, with the symbol of Philonia on the back of their outer garment and the seal of the house of Maximus on the chest of the inner garment. They rode off with the king, a soldier stationed himself in front of the carriage, two rode beside it and the other two were stationed behind.

The route of Travel was going to require that they head west. They would rest for the night in the city of Bismotal in Venduria. Then from there they would spend a day traveling and arrive at Petra very early in the morning.

Chapter 14
Son of the Eleventh.
A Lover's Burden

Rage filled Jeffery's heart. He could not believe what he had just witnessed. His second in command was on his knees after having just surrendered to a man whose face he had

never seen and whose name he had never
heard before. He could not stand it for Neemus
had brought shame to the knight's order. He
felt it was his duty to restore the honor of the
Order by facing the man who just defeated
Neemus.

Jeffery watched Neemus concede, his nose
flared. Then he walked down from the platform and to Neemus. Neemus rose to his feet
and gave a slight bow to Jeffery as he approached.

"Please forgive me." Neemus said.

Jeffery did not respond. His eyes were intently fixed on Julian. Julian dropped his shield
because the weight had put great strain on his
injured shoulder. He could not conceal the pain
anymore. He used his right hand to massage
the pain in his upper shoulder.

"Jeffery, I did my best, I did not expect…"

"Be quiet Neemus" Jeffery commanded. "If
I had not seen it for myself, I would not have
believed it." Jeffery said, he paused for a moment and smiled. Then his expression was serious again. "I promise you, this victory will be
short lived."

He went for his sword.

"Enough!" Mitis shouted. He stood from
his place on the platform and walked down to
them. "If you fight him you will be going
against your own honor. He has won his freedom. So he can go. Put your sword away."

Jeffery looked at Mitis with a slight look of disdain, and then he looked at Julian then back at Mitis.

"Yes your majesty." He said then sheathed his sword.

Mitis ordered that the knights take Julian to someone who will treat his wounds. Then he turned to Jeffery. "He has won his freedom. Leave him be."

"He defeated Neemus. He has disgraced the knight's Order. I am taken by my obligation to uphold the greatness of our Order. I must restore honor to the…" Jeffery was saying but was interrupted by Mitis.

"Are you testing my patience?! You are not to fight him! Now get out of my sight. This charade has gone on long enough."

Jeffery turned and walked calmly out of the room. Simona saw him depart. She said to Antonius.

"I must go. I have never seen him this angry before."

She got up and followed after him.

The actors, the nobles, Felix and his crew were still in their seats. They had enjoyed the little match that had gone on between Julian and Neemus. Now Mitis had grown discontented that the play had been interrupted and thought the nobles and Felix and his crew might have been very dissatisfied about what had gone on. He went to the base of the platform and addressed them. "Please return to your homes but make no mention of what has gone on here today. You may leave."

The nobles got up and prepared to leave. They were discussing things among themselves. One made mention that Julian was bound to win because he was the son of Thanos. Another suggested that he should be considered as a candidate for the knight's tournament. Another reminded the noble that made mention of this that only knights can perform in the tournament. They discussed these things as they exited the Grand Hall.

Felix went to Mitis,

"There is no mistaking it. That is the son of Thanos."

"Indeed, he is a gifted fighter. I do not know who trained him but if he had trained with his father he might even surpass us. Even if both our strengths were combined and multiplied three folds."

Felix smiled,

"Yes, that may be so but if I were granted my youth for a day, I would not mind testing my skill against him."

"I know. He would make for a worthy challenge."

"Well, I must leave you now. The sailors and I are going to gather the essentials things we need for the journey back."

"If you need help let me know."

Galen ran to his father. Eulalie walked towards them. Astra followed her. Eulalie stood

beside Mitis, Astra made her way out of the
Grand Hall. Antonius got up. He decided to go
after her. As he approached Mitis he said,

"I apologize, on behalf of Julian. I know I
came here with him, so I am partly responsible
for what occurred here."

"Don't worry about it. He put up a good
fight."

Antonius smiled.

"If you'll excuse me, I have somewhere I
need to be."

"That's fine with me."

Peter was standing by a window, around the
corner of the main entrance into the Grand
Hall. He had heard the conversations that went
on inside. He did not watch the duel between
Neemus and Julian. But he overheard the out-
come and it did not surprise him.

He admired the snow covered city. It reminded him of the mountains, where he had
made his home for over two hundred years. He
took in a deep breath. He did not sense the spirit of Antonius as he exited the Grand Hall. But
he turned to his right for a moment and he saw
Antonius walking down the hallway. He noticed that Antonius's hair was longer than he
remembered it to be. The last time he had seen
Antonius was when Antonius was nine, the
same year Calix died. Then he had sensed a
small hint of the power he sensed when Antonius was fighting Gammon. He remembered it

all as he watched Antonius walk down that hallway. He fixed his gaze back on the city.

He sensed the spirits of Mitis and Eulalie emerging from the Grand Hall. He had also sensed Felix and he immediately remembered that he was the Pirate he had helped Calix capture. Felix had already left the castle.

Mitis, Eulalie and Galen walked out of the Grand Hall. Eulalie instructed Galen to get back to his studies. He tried to persuade her to let him go and watch the knights' train. But Mitis put his foot down.

"There will be enough time to watch them train. Now go upstairs and finish your studies for the day."

Galen as part of his studies was given the task to read three books by two prominent philosophic-historians. They wrote of stories concerning Guardians, the children of fallen guardians and how the choices of a man work hand in hand with elements of fate to produce the outcomes that are observed in a man's life. Mitis taught it was necessary to expose his son to the moral sphere at his age, so he may have a firm foundation to discern truths from lies. More importantly to know the tricks the children of fallen guardians have used to cause men to go astray.

"Yes father," Galen said, then he left.

Peter was well aware that Mitis and Eulalie had made their way out of the Grand Hall. He could sense their spirits. He did not need to look their way to confirm it. His eyes were still set on the city. Mitis was conversing with Eulalie when she spotted Peter. Mitis saw him. He observed the man whose back was turned to him. The man's skin was as the color of the bark of a white oak tree. Mitis recognized the man's structure, the man's grey hair, the dark-brown cloth he wore that resembled the attire of a shepherd. He knew for certain who the man was when he saw the staff the man held in his right hand.

Eulalie also knew Peter, for he brought with him treasured memories and unpleasant memories to her mind. She liked that he was a man of virtue. Mitis had looked up to him for years, and through the guidance of Peter, Mitis became a very understanding man. What she did not like about Peter was that he convinced Mitis to go with him, Calix and Felix, so they could quest for the cross of Sirius. The quest took three years. She missed Mitis dearly.

Peter had not stepped foot in Petra in over twenty one years.

Mitis saw him and at once a smile appeared on his face. They approached him.

"I am surprised your hair is almost as grey as mine." Peter said with his eyes still set outside.

"Your hair has been the same for centuries. Mine began to turn grey less than a decade ago," Mitis responded.

Peter turned to him. He was smiling. Mitis embraced him. Peter smelt like the mountain air. Peter looked at Eulalie, bowed and said,

"Your grace."

"Peter," she said with a smile, and then she embraced him.

"The years have been kind to you. You are as beautiful as you were the last time I was here."

"Thank you."

"I've never known you to visit casually. There is a reason why you are here isn't there," Mitis said.

"I could sense the boy's spirit when he was battling a ghoul at sea. A little over a day ago I felt it from the mountain."

"And who is this boy?" Mitis asked.

"I believe he is the second son of Calix."

"The boy is now a man. His name is Antonius."

"Antonius," Peter repeated. "Calix never told me his name. He has the same name of an old hero, in one of the stories my father told me when I was a child. Not too long ago I saw him travel down that hallway. For some reason I cannot sense his spirit. Something is blocking me from doing so but I'll try again."

Peter concentrated. He sensed the spirits of people in the castle trying to find where Antonius's spirit may be. For a moment he sensed a troubled spirit in one of the rooms upstairs, then for a slight moment he felt the presence of Gammon within that spirit.

Mitis and Eulalie saw the concern that came across Peter's face.

"What is it?" Mitis asked.

"It is not possible. No. I sense an evil that should have been destroyed."

"What do you mean?"

Peter followed what his spirit sensed. Mitis and Eulalie followed him asking him what he sensed. He explained to them that he felt the presence of Gammon but faintly. Eulalie remembered the mark on Xaria's neck and wondered if it had something to do with Gammon. Peter continued upstairs, passed the splendid corridors that had marvelous marble carvings of past heroes during the days of the War of the Fathers. As he got to the hallway where he sensed Gammon, he turned right, and found himself standing in front of the room prepared for Xaria and Marcus. Eulalie was astonished. Mitis was a bit doubtful.

"You said Antonius defeated a ghoul at sea, was it Gammon you were speaking of?"

"Yes it was."

"Then how is it that you still sense him."

"I don't know yet but I going to get to the end of this."

Marcus had been with Xaria all morning. They had talked for a while after Antonius left them. Soon after he left, Xaria was stricken with a se-

vere headache, the source of which came from
within her spirit. For Gammon who was inside
her mind, had locked himself in the depths of
her spirit. The pain prevented her from speaking, so Marcus instructed her to lie back down.
He kissed her forehead. He was holding her
hand as he watched her fall asleep. He silently
prayed that she would not sleep forever. He
hadn't eaten anything since supper the previous evening. He was losing hope that her condition would get any better. Xaria remained
that way for an hour. He watched her become
even paler than before, her body was getting
colder. He felt it and it worried him.

There was a knock on the door. He instructed the servant that was with him to answer it. The servant opened the door and saw
Peter standing there. When he saw that Mitis
and Eulalie were with him he bowed and welcomed them in.

Mitis gave word to the servant to depart.
Marcus upon seeing Peter was reminded of the
man Xaria spoke of. A man dressed in the
clothes of a shepherd. His interest was sparked.
Peter made his way in and stopped at the foot
of the bed. He looked at Marcus for a moment
and saw the resemblance he had to Calix. He
knew this was Calix's son. Then he shifted his
eyes to Xaria. He looked intently at her. He
could feel Gammon within her and he knew
Gammon was aware his presence. He noticed

Marcus approach him. Then Marcus said to him,

"Is it you? She spoke of a man who rescued her from Gammon that man was dressed in the clothes of a shepherd. These threads you wear, only shepherds wear and this is no place for a shepherd. Shepherds do not roam in this weather. Tell me who you are?"

"Watch the way you speak Marcus. This is…" Mitis was saying but stopped after Peter motioned for him to be still.

"I mean no disrespect old friend, but I will answer for myself. I am Peter. It is quite clear to see that you are a man whose pain cannot be measured, for your pain comes from the pain you see your lover endure and you know no way to cease her pain."

"Are you the one she spoke of, are you the one who fought Gammon?"

Peter was silent for a short moment and remembered the battle he waged against Gammon. It was one he could not forget, for it pushed him to the limit of the power he had then. But he remembered those days, when he was about a century old, yet he managed to survive the battle.

"I have fought Gammon before but he escaped me and left the lands to make the sea his home…"

"Tell me then can something be done to take the pain away from her. No illness of nature causes a person much distress in their spirit. She is dying before my eyes and I can tell when I hear her voice that her spirit is breaking. She is being tormented by Gammon."

"I cannot make any promises but I will search her spirit and see if Gammon is indeed the source of her distress."

Peter went to the side of the bed. He placed his hand in the air above her head. He kept still as he searched her spirit. He felt the slight presence of Gammon. He drew his hand back, opened his eyes, and left his gaze on her. Something caught his attention. He saw a bit of the mark on her neck. Most of it was covered by her flowing black hair. He moved her hair aside and saw the mark more clearly.

"That monster." he thought "So this is how he was able to tie himself to her spirit."

He focused intently at the mark and it broke his heart, for he knew the type of pain Xaria was experiencing. He looked at Marcus and asked,

"Tell me how you encountered Gammon."

"Five years ago he attacked my ship and took Xaria. He killed all my men and left me there to drown in my sorrows. The ship crashed on an Island and I was there since. I chose to stay because I felt he would have broken the promise he made to me?"

"What promise?"

"He said if I ever were to return to the Fog Xaria would be the first one I would see. I stayed because I did not believe him. Not until four day ago when Antonius came seeking my help because of some complications in our kingdom. I decided to assist him but I had my reasons for leaving the island." He gazed at Xaria for a moment. "I came up with a plan and I did not want anyone else getting involved so I compromised the wine of the sailors Antonius came with. Thereafter I took control of the ship. I redirected it and led it through the Fog. When I entered the Fog, she was the first to greet me. But she acted as if she was under a spell. I was happy to see her but I could not celebrate for I knew Gammon was close, so I watched for him and saw him above us. Not long after, Antonius made his way up to the main deck where we were and he battled Gammon. He won with ease. I was glad to have her back but she has not been herself. Every moment she is feeling ill. Her spirit is hurting."

"After you received her, did you notice anything strange on her?"

"A mark…on her neck."

Peter looked back at the mark on Xaria's neck.

"The mark on her neck is the mark of Gammon. It is the reason for her sickness. Her spirit is in distress. Gammon is alive within her mind."

Eulalie was shocked. Mitis listened carefully.

"What do you mean?" Marcus asked.

"Through this mark Gammon has kept himself alive. It is rare for a Ghoul to do this. They have too much pride in their form though they hate it. Ghouls would not resort to such an extreme measure unless they knew their end was near."

"So, Gammon knew he would lose to one stronger than him." Mitis said.

"But how could he have known of Antonius?" Eulalie asked.

"She makes a good point. When Gammon saw Antonius he acted as if he were surprised," Marcus said.

"Do not be deceived. The ghouls know many things. He only acted as such so Antonius would not know that the ghouls are always aware of his presence. They can sense him from far away. This may be why Gammon marked her. He knew he could not defeat Antonius."

"How can they sense him?" Mitis asked

"Antonius is one of those prophesied about to take the place of a fallen Guardian. He is the twelfth Rising Guardian. Ghouls know this and they make every attempt to make his life miserable especially by hurting the ones he loves."

"Is there no way to conceal Antonius's presence, so they may not sense him?" Marcus asked.

"I believe it has already been done. As I drew close to the city last night, I could not sense him. I saw him just a few moments after he departed from the Grand Hall. Even then I could not sense his spirit. If I cannot sense his spirit, I doubt that any ghoul can."

Marcus set his eyes on Xaria, then back at Peter.

"Is there anything that can be done to save her?"

Peter thought for a moment then replied.

"No, not at the moment"

Marcus put both of his hands on his head and bit his lower lip.

"What are you saying? That there is nothing we can do?" Marcus said. His voice rising with every word he said.

"I am saying the best way we can save her would be inadequate. She would already be dead by the time we take her to those who can help her."

"Where would she need to be taken, tell me, we must at least try."

"The only ones who can help her now are the Saints."

Marcus, Mitis and Eulalie were astonished that Peter had mentioned the Saints. The Saints were a small group of people whose power were thought to equal that of a Rising Guardian who has reached the peak of the power he has been blessed with. But they were not destined for Guardianship. They used their powers to serve the people by offering prayers of protection unto the Great King. No one knew their real ages, and only a few had seen their faces. It was believed that they lived on an Island, Far

East of the Main Lands. The island was said to be a mile away from the edge of the Blue Sea.

Marcus was grieved knowing his only option was to find the Saints. He had heard and read many stories about them but at this point his belief in their reality was crumbling. All the stories meant nothing. All that mattered was relieving Xaria's spirit.

A bit frustrated, he said, "the Saints cannot be the only way.

If indeed they were real, it would take forever to find them. There...must...be...another way." He went to Xaria's side. He fell to his knees and then said in despair, after he took her hand and kissed it.

"It should have been me. I wish I told you more about how much you meant to me. I am crushed and I have no more tears. My heart is bruised and my hope is gone. If only I could take your place. If only I can carry your burden."

A tear fell from his eyes and he cried there on his knees by her side, in the presence of Peter, Eulalie and Mitis.

Peter upon hearing what Marcus said knew it was possible for Marcus to take on Xaria's pain. The curse mark could be transferred. But he knew that if Gammon were ever in the body of a man he would do worse to that man than he had done to Xaria, to the point where he might try to trap the man's spirit, claim his soul and take possession of the man's body. Peter had never witnessed this occur but he heard a story from his father about a higher son of one of the fallen Guardians who took possession of the body of a man who was called to be the eighth Rising Guardian. Peter thought if the body of a Rising Guardian could be possessed, then it would be no trouble for a ghoul such as Gammon to possess the body of a mere man.

Peter felt guilty watching Marcus dive deep in sorrow. He took a breath then said,

"Marcus, don't give up hope. There is still a way to save her. But it is very risky."

"Whatever the risk, let it be done."

"I don't think you…"

"I know, I do not know as much as you. But this I know, I love her and I will do what I must to save her. Four years I was without her. I do not want to experience a second of that again. I do not care the cost, let it be done."

Peter was pleased to hear Marcus's words, for he saw a heart of sincerity in him, a heart that would be able to withstand what he was planning.

Peter placed his hand on Xaria's head. He could see that Gammon was gaining control of her mind so he felt it was time to act.

"Where is the chapel in this castle?" Peter asked Mitis

"It is far upstairs close to the tower. What reason will you need to go there now?" Mitis responded.

"The reason Gammon has control over Xaria's mind is because of the curse mark. I will transfer the curse mark onto Marcus and seal away Gammon in his spirit. But this must be done in a holy place so that Gammon's power can be properly subdued."

"If you think this is best then we shall go there. Let us lift her there."

"There is no need, I will take her there," Peter said. He looked up, then back at Mitis.

"Take my staff." He said as he handed it over to Mitis, Then he picked Xaria up. "Meet me up there, show Marcus the way. I'll be waiting."

Marcus, Mitis and Eulalie watched as Peter's essence along with Xaria's body became as grains of sand, that which they saw of Peter and Xaria was lifted up, it passed through the ceilings and went up far to the chapel. Peter retook his form and Xaria's body was restored to her former state.

"Come we must hurry." Mitis said as he led the way to the chapel.

They made their way to the chapel. They got there and found that Peter had laid Xaria's body on the altar. The chapel was circular in structure and had only a few pews.

Marcus saw her and she appeared as dead before his eyes. He approached her slowly with tears welling up in his eyes.

"Wipe your tears, for soon it will be done and you shall have her back in your arms, healthy once again." Peter said to Marcus

Mitis handed Peter back his staff. Peter took the staff with his left hand, thanked Mitis, and told him and Marcus to step back. Eulalie was standing behind Mitis. Peter stretched out his right hand and before them they saw forming from thin air, new masses of a stone substance. Together these new masses collected and formed a bed platform beside the altar. Marcus was amazed. Peter instructed him to lie upon this new platform. He did. Xaria was on his left. He looked at her motionless body, he took hold of her right hand, a motion that Peter was about to instruct him to do. Peter then said to him

"Do not let go of her hand, not until I tell you too."

"I am trusting in your wisdom Peter, please do not disappoint me."

"You need not worry, it will be over soon. When it is done, she will be well. And though Gammon will be in your spirit, his presence shall not affect you in the same manner it affected her." Peter replied. His words were reassuring. So it began, the transference of the curse from Xaria unto Marcus was about to take place.

"Marcus let your spirit be at ease and your mind still."

Marcus took a deep breath. Peter took his staff with both hands and held it in front of himself. He closed his eyes and said a silent prayer under his breath. He begged the Great king for power and it was granted to him. He felt the strength of his spirit rising, his eyes were opened and he could see the spirits of Marcus and Xaria. He placed his hand upon the hand Marcus was using to hold Xaria. He connected their spirits.

Marcus found himself in the spirit of Xaria. He saw her far in the valley of her sorrows with Gammon towering over her and torturing her. There was a mighty lightning strike on the ground a few feet from him. The dust cleared quickly and Peter's spirit was standing there in front of him. Peter turned back and saw him. Peter sensed Gammon and saw him with Xaria in the valley of her sorrows. Marcus and Peter without hesitation rushed to her. Gammon looked to the hills and saw Peters speeding his way. Marcus ran as fast as he could but he could not keep up with Peter. Peter reached before him and stood face to face with Gammon. He saw the spirit of Gammon standing tall in his human form. Xaria was on the floor behind Gammon. She was covered in bruises and dirt. She was a wounded spirit.

"Peter!" Gammon said "I knew I sensed something foul."

"You ghouls never get tired of hurting the innocent."

"No one is innocent," Gammon said with a smile.

Marcus reached them and stopped beside Peter. He saw Gammon and then his eyes were moved to where his lover laid. He was filled with fury. Though he had no weapon on him he rushed at Gammon. Gammon was about to strike him down but Peter stretched out his left hand and bound Gammon. Marcus punched Gammon as hard as he could across the face, causing Gammon to fall to the ground.

"How dare you do this to me?" Gammon said. Then his eyes turned red and he was preparing himself to take his monstrous form. But Peter would not let this happen. He took his staff, raised it high and called for lightning to subdue Gammon. From the overcast sky, mighty blades of lightning struck the Ghoul where he laid. They wrapped around him and shocked him greatly.

Once Gammon was subdued, Marcus rushed to Xaria and helped her to her feet. He cleaned the dirt off her face. He embraced her then gazed into her eyes. She was wounded but he knew in time the scars Gammon had left upon her would heal. He kissed her and said.

"My love, no longer will your spirit be burdened because of Gammon."

Xaria embraced him and wept in his arms. She turned and saw Peter. He was as he had appeared in her dream. She saw his clothes and knew it was the man who battled Gammon in her dream. She saw Gammon bound by lightning at the feet of Peter. She looked at Marcus and asked,

"What shall become of Gammon?"

"Peter has suppressed his power."

"Peter?"

"That man, his name is Peter. He is the one you saw in your dream. He has fought Gammon before and almost defeated him. But Gammon was sly and escaped him. He knew of your troubles, so he made it possible for our spirits to be connected so we could rescue you from Gammon."

"So are you going to finally defeat him?" Xaria asked.

"I am afraid that his spirit cannot be defeated here because of the curse mark that he placed on you. But we have bound him. Peter will take him and imprison him in my spirit."

"Why are you doing this? If I died, his spirit would have been defeated. My soul would have been preserved and his destroyed. It would not matter the pain I endured. It would have been for a little while."

"Yes it would have mattered. It would have mattered to me. I could not bear to see you so ill. I do not want to lose you again. I still blame myself for the first time he took you away from me and now he was about to do it again. If death took you from me, I would be lost. So I will take this burden from you. Never again shall you suffer at the hands of Gammon."

After saying this she kissed him and he held her tightly.

Peter watched on for a brief moment then he turned to the bound spirit of Gammon. Gammon was struggling to break free from the lightning that bound him.

"Marcus let us finish this."

Marcus looked at him and then back at Xaria.

"I must go my love but I will see you soon."

Marcus went to Peter. Peter placed his left hand on Marcus's shoulder and the end of his staff on Gammon. At once they were gone and the plains of Xaria's spirit were green again. The clouds cleared and the sky was pure white. A great burden had been taken from her.

Marcus and Peter appeared on the plains of Marcus's spirit. Gammon was struggling furiously. Peter was about to suggest that they look for cave so that they would place Gammon in and cover the entrance with large stones. But once he noticed Gammon struggling to break free he said.

"He shall be bound here."

"But where shall he be kept a prisoner, there is nothing above us."

Peter raised his staff high and struck the ground. The ground beneath their feet began to shake. Marcus felt the blow that Peter gave the ground. It felt as a mighty blow to his heart. He fell to his knees.

"I am sorry but it must be done." Peter said then he struck the ground again. The ground opened and swallowed Gammon. He fell till he landed in a lower place far below the surface. Peter instructed Marcus to calm himself. Marcus took a breath and remained calm. He watched as the ground that had opened in his spirit closed up. It was done. Gammon was subdued and sealed within the lower grounds in the spirit of Marcus.

"You know a little warning would have been appreciated," Marcus said.

"I apologize for that but it had to be done. If Gammon were let loose in this place he could easily take over your body, after he has claimed your spirit." Peter turned to Marcus and helped him to his feet.

Marcus watched as Peter's essences turned to grains of sand and was blown up into the air. Immediately he was gone. Marcus spirit was left there standing in those wide plains.

Peter opened his eyes. He saw that he was back in his body. He saw that Marcus and Xaria were still holding hands. Xaria was slowly waking up and so was Marcus. He looked at Mitis and Eulalie who were sitting in the first pew from the altar with their heads bowed.

"Mitis" Peter called out.

Mitis raised his head.

"Were we gone for too long?"

"Three hours to be precise. The evening sun is here as you can see."

Marcus arose. Peter saw the mark of Gammon on Marcus's neck. The mark was moving down his neck. Before the mark disappeared under Marcus's shirt, Peter noticed that it was not as dark of a shade as it appeared on Xaria. It was faded. This meant that though Gammon was inside Marcus, his power was greatly suppressed. Peter saw that Marcus was still holding Xaria's hand.

"You can let go of her." Peter said

"No. Not yet." Marcus said calmly.

They waited a minute. Xaria's skin returned to its color. She opened her eyes and saw her lover beside her. His smile was bright and welcoming. Her hand was in his. She turned and saw Peter standing close beside the altar. Mitis and Eulalie were on the other side of the altar. Marcus was seated on the platform beside the altar. Xaria was very happy to see him again. She loved him even though his body was more rugged than the appearance of his spirit. She threw herself on him and kissed him.

Eulalie smiled. Mitis was glad to see that she was well again. When she was done she thanked Peter. He gave a slight smile then turned his attention to Marcus. He went close to him and observed his body. Then he lifted Marcus's sleeve and saw the mark of Gammon on Marcus's left shoulder. It had stopped moving.

"So shall I lose my arm in order to get rid of this curse?" Marcus asked

"Gammon is sealed inside your spirit. Even if you lost your arm, he'll still be within you. He'll just have less of a body if he were to take control of yours. Just make sure that you stay clear of any ghouls because they have ways of empowering their own kind. Though Gammon's power is greatly subdued they may be able to sense him."

"There is no need to worry then. We are nowhere close to the edge of the Blue Sea. There aren't many ghouls here in the Main Lands."

"Still, you should be on your guard."

Peter said then left, Mitis followed after him and met him in the hallway.

"Are you going in search of Antonius?"

"Is he the one that was given the cross of Sirius?"

"Yes."

"Then I am going in search of him."

"But you cannot reveal yourself to him now, not with all that is going on. He is a wanted man, accused of a crime he did not commit."

"What crime was he accused of?"

"He was accused of killing the elders."

"Who are they?"

"They were a small group of men who maintained the power of the king. They were given power by Calix and their powers went into effect when Marcus took the throne."

"How do you know he did not kill them?"

"I know Antonius, I have seen his demeanor. He is not capable of doing such. Not even if he were filled with rage."

Peter took a breath. His mind was taken to the second man who he encountered and thought to be the Rising Guardian. He remembered the humble nature he saw in the man and how much hope he entrusted in him, hoping the man would stay true to the end of his trials as a Rising Guardian. He remembered the change in the man when he could not sustain himself, when his testing weighed him down and he gave his heart to darkness. The memory only made him cynical of Mitis's defense of Antonius. He said to Mitis calmly,

"No matter what you know of a man, his nature is not truly revealed until he is put under great testing. I shall not show myself to Antonius yet, but I will watch him. For now he is in your kingdom, he is a refugee and this is his test. When I make myself known to him, I will provoke him to test his patience and if he passes, I will take him under my wing and reveal to him things not even you are aware of. If he truly is the Twelfth Rising Guardian then he is destined for greatness and many troubles shall await him on the way."

Peter turned and left.

Chapter 15
A Love Restored.
Hero's Manor

Jeffery was standing outside the knight's quarter. His mind was so fixated on the recent events. His second in command had yielded to a man whose name he had not learnt till that day. His gaze was set outside on the city. The beauty of the city did not move him at all because of the anger his heart. For a brief moment he looked left and saw his darling sister approaching him. He knew she was coming to console him. Many times before when his anger got the better of him, she was there. She was the one that quelled his fury. As she approached him, he felt in his heart that this wrong that was done to him was too much for her love to vanquish.

"How are you feeling brother?" Simona said.

"How do you think I feel? I have been insulted. I am trying my best not to go against Mitis's order. I want to find that man that insulted the Knight's Order and send him to an early grave."

"Please you must not speak like that."

"Why? I must not speak my mind? Mitis may command me not to do a certain deed, and I shall yield to his command but he shall not command my speech."

"Take heart and see it this way. You are still the First Knight. Though the honor of the Knight's Order was shaken, yours still stands. Many young men want to become knights. They look up to you. Every day you train with at least seven knights. You pick out even the little weakness they exhibit and you encourage them to train harder until they are the best they can be. Have you forgotten the days when you were once in their place?"

"I struggled to get to where I am, yet some people think I am where I am because I am the king's nephew."

"But they have seen your struggles and you are where you are because of your own merits. Do not forget the agony that you went through to get here. I was with you all those years. I tended to your wounds. I have not forgotten and neither should you. So don't let this blunder that happened today make you forget your worth. You are my brother, Jeffery Miles, the First Knight of Konstuliana."

Jeffery smiled.

"You're right. I may have forgotten my worth because my thoughts were clouded. But I now see that I have nothing to fear." Jeffery paused and adored the beauty of his sister and her smile reminded him of someone most dear to his heart. Someone he missed; someone whose counsel and soft words had always soothed his heart, so he said. "You really do take after mother."

Jeffery embraced her

"I still have three more knights to mentor before the day is done. So I shall be returning to my duties. Stay well sister."

He kissed her forehead and went into the knight's training room. Simona left and went in search of Antonius.

❖

The Jewel of Konstuliana made her way far from him. Her heart was heavy and her stomach sunk when she remembered the kiss he shared with Simona. She was in the far-east wing of the castle at the end of the hall of Heroes. In this particular hallway, there were many statues that honored past heroes, many of whom had fought in the War of the Fathers.

A tear fell from her left eye. She heard footsteps coming from the end of the hall. She turned and saw him, immediately she wanted to leave but he called out.

"Astra, please wait." Antonius said from the end of the hallway.

She stopped and cleaned the tear from her cheek before he approached her. She would not turn to acknowledge him for he had hurt her and he knew it. He came closer to her and felt a little uneasy. He composed himself and said to her.

"I'm sorry that I hurt you. I know you don't want to speak to me but at least let me see your face."

She slowly turned and faced him. He admired what she was wearing. Her flowing dress was a brilliant white, striped once with a purple mix lining the hem. But most of all, her eyes caught his attention. For in them he saw the pain he had caused her. He saw how much she cared for him. He took her hand.

"It has been far too long since I have been this close to you. I cannot recall how many nights I have stayed up because of how much I longed for this moment. I counted the stars as I thought of you. Those were the times when I wrote those letters to you. When I beheld you last night, my heart was moved, for I have not felt for any woman what I feel for you."

Her eyes diverted from him. She did not fully accept his apology. Her hand was still in his. He lifted her hand and kissed it. Her eyes glistened as she stared back into his. She then said to him,

"I've kept all the letters you sent me. I've read them all at least twice. Though they were from you, they were not enough for me. I longed for you every day. When I saw you last night my heart was more than overjoyed. Four years ago you left without even saying goodbye. Since then I have waited, all the noble's sons that my mother brought for me to wed, I rejected because I still loved you. How do you think I felt when I saw Simona in your arms? You show up unexpected and you break my heart in the same night."

The truth of her words struck his heart and in her voice he sensed her brokenness. He placed his hands around her hips and pulled her closer. Then his lips met hers'. She was lost in the moment with him and forgave him. Far at the end of the hall Simona saw them. Immediately she turned around and walked away.

"I'm sorry that I hurt you. Forgive me." Antonius said. "I long to hear you play the harp as you did when I was last here."

She smiled, and then she took him and led him to a room in the castle that had been named the Center of Harmony. Within this room there were a number of instruments assembled as if prepared for an orchestra. There he saw her harp above a platform higher than the other instruments. The majestic instrument glistened gold. There she played for him and he enjoyed her melodies and her presence more.

After she played for him, she took him to a small study on the eastside of the castle.

There they talked about all that happened in the years they were apart. She told him of the knight's tournament, and the quest Jeffery went on to become the First knight. He told her of the expansion of noble city and that it is far bigger than in the days of his father. She remarked that she'd never been to noble city. He leaned in closer to her and told her that after his innocence is confirmed, he'll take her there and show her the beauty of the city.

That night at dinner Simona was not with them. Felix returned to have dinner with them, Marcus and Xaria were happy as they entered the dining hall. Antonius was surprised but happy to see that Xaria was well. Jeffery was also at the dinner table but his mind was on his sister and her whereabouts.

Peter had been invited by Mitis to join them for dinner but he refused saying that Antonius must not know of his presence until the time was right. Peter made a place for himself on top of the castle tower.

Word of his deed spread around the city. He gave no thought of what was said of him, whether praise, or insult. All he cared about now was the way the nurse was about to treat his wound. He was in a small shed close to the west gate of the city. He took off his shirt and exposed his well-defined figure. His left arm was covered in blood and the pain had stopped. He could not feel the lower part of his arm. The nurse soaked a small towel in warm water and cleaned the dry blood that ran down his arm and covered the left part of his chest.

"Is it true what they are saying about you?" the nurse asked as she wiped away the dry blood that covered his chest.

"Who are these 'they' you speak of?"

"The people of course, even some of the nobles."

"And what do they say about me?"

"Of your skill and how you humbled a knight."

"Those who saw me saw a man who entertained them. I was only fighting for my freedom and my life. I don't even want to be here."

She finished cleaning his chest then she wiped away the blood from his left shoulder and beheld the wound he had sustained from Xaria's arrow.

"How did this happen?"

"It was an arrow."

"Was this from your fight against the knight?"

"No, it isn't. Is it infected?"

"A little, hold on for a moment." The nurse said. She took a small handkerchief drenched in a strong substance on her medicine table. The content of which contained a high amount of alcohol. She slowly cleaned the wound with it. It stung Julian for a slight moment.

"Sorry" the nurse said. "I should have warned you it stings a bit."

"No worries."

She finished up suturing his wounds and wrapped a bandage around his left shoulder.

"Try not to use the arm if you can. Give it a few days to heal."

"Thank you," he said.

There was a knock on the door. The nurse got up and opened it and stepped back when she saw who was standing behind it. Neemus walked in. He was clothed in his noble wear. It was a dark red robe with a silver belt around his waist. His stature was bigger than Julian remembered, his grey hair was now the more apparent, and oddly enough Julian noticed them more in the low lit room where they were. The nurse left immediately.

Neemus approached Julian. Julian stood to his feet. Neemus looked down at him not saying a word for the moment being. Then to Julian's surprise Neemus extended his hand out, for a hand shake. Julian looked at his hand, then back at him. Julian noticed that the arm had been mildly bandaged. The long sleeve of Neemus's robe covered it, all except the bandage around his palm. The technique he used to disarm Neemus was not done to grant Neemus an injury to the degree it did. Reluctantly he stretched out his hand and took Neemus's hand with a firm grip. Both men once enemies stood there shaking hands not knowing what the other was thinking. Then Neemus said,

"Thank you for sparing my life. Under the law of the duel, you had the right to take my life and your freedom would still have been granted to you."

"I am not your enemy. I was made to be one because I took back what some other knights confiscated from us."

"I understand, this is a strange land to you and you only acted the way you felt was right. But you must understand that the king is very kind. You should have brought it up with him and he would have listened to your plea."

"Had I known, our little match could have been avoided. I did not mean to hurt your reputation."

Neemus sighed.

"I have been a knight for a very long time and my reputation has changed like the seasons. Sometimes I am loved like summer, other times I have been despised like winter. As long as war is nowhere in sight, a knight's reputation will not be firm unless he is highly ranked and his youth is with him. Like Jeffery. For four years consecutively he has won the knight's tournament."

"Is that how he became head of the knight's order?"

"No, but it helped solidify his place."

"How did you fare in the tournaments?"

"I do not participate anymore. I rarely fight for sport nowadays. I have been champion of that tournament seven times but that was a long time ago."

"Must one be a knight to participate in the tournament?"

"Yes, and also he must achieve the rank of Leo-Knight. That means he is among the top one hundred knights in the kingdom. Why do you ask? Are you thinking of becoming a citizen so you may train to be a knight?"

"No, I was just curious."

At that moment one of Neemus's servants came in. He told Neemus that his horse was ready. Neemus thanked him and told him to return to wait outside for him. The servant departed. Neemus said his last words to Julian before he made his way out.

"I am humble enough now to know this, my skill may be in need of improvement. If you ever wish to duel with me again, when neither of our lives is in jeopardy, I will be happy to go against you, son of Thanos."

Neemus left.

Julian went from that place and returned to the communal house. He spent the remainder of the day there. When the dawn broke forth and touched the landscape, calling upon the sun to follow its path, Julian arose with an intent he conceived in his heart the night before but wrestled with through his sleep.

He made his way from the communal house to the inner parts of the city. He went in search of a horse. As he walked by the people he heard whisper among them. Mostly about him but he gave no thought to what they said of him, whether praise or insult. He stopped where he thought he might be able to acquire what he was looking for. He stood outside a stable that was at the edge of the city very close to the North gate.

The stable keeper saw him waiting outside. The clothes Julian wore were what he had been wearing from his escape with Antonius. The arrow launched by Xaria that pierced his shoulder tore his shirt at the upper arm and the blood stains covered the left side of it.

Upon seeing Julian the stable keeper did not give a thought to him but continued with his duties. Julian called to him, "Excuse me, I was hoping you could help me with something."

The stable keeper was a man in his late-forties who resented the work he did until he was praised by Jeffery a day after Jeffery returned from a campaign to restore order in a northern city. Jeffery thanked the stable keeper for caring for his horses, for they were stronger than he remembered and they sustained him to and fro during the days of the campaign. From then on more people of high honor began to give their horses to the stable keeper. They paid him well to take care of them. His services became vital. The horses he tended belonged to many high ranking knights, and some, to the renowned soldiers in the army of Konstuliana. Though they did not make Petra their home, as the knights did, they kept their war horses with the stable keeper.

The soldiers stayed in a larger but older city ten miles west from Petra. A city called Vayler. Julian called the stable keeper once more. The man rather irritated responded in a harsh tone.

"What do you want?!"

"I am looking for a horse. I see you tend to many of them, so rent me one."

The man was shocked at the authoritative tone of Julian's demand. The demand he made did not line up with the appearance portrayed upon him.

The man laughed.

"You must not be from around here. If you knew who the owners' of these horses were you would not be asking for them."

"I am asking to rent, not take ownership of the animal. Now shall you grant me a horse or not?"

The man shook his head in disbelief and turned, and then as his attention was diverted away from Julian, his ears were still aware and he heard the knocking of coins upon each other. He turned back and saw seven silvers coins in Julian's hand.

"Will these cover a day?" Julian asked.

The man walked to him about to take it but Julian pulled his hand back and demanded the horse be brought out first. The stable keeper glared at him with disdain. He went to the back of the stable and brought out a black horse with a white blaze on its nose. Julian liked the horse.

The man brought it to Julian and Julian mounted the horse.

"Well" the stable keeper said.

Julian commanded and controlled the horse. He strode around with it for a short moment, then he said, "It rides well and is proper."

He took out the silver coins and gave the stable keeper.

"Have it back by sunset," the stable keeper said.

"If my conscience doesn't fail me, expect it then." Julian said as he rode off.

His set destination was a manor seven miles north-east from Petra. A manor owned by the father of one of the nobles that was present when Julian fought to preserve his life. Julian had been informed by one of the men who came with Antonius from Philonia that Felix was with the sailors at the manor. He told Julian that they had been gathering all they needed for the journey back to Philonia. The man that told him this had said of the sailors, "It is foolish for them to return without Antonius. They are accomplices, besides why would they want to leave when they are being treated as guest of respectable worth." To which Julian responded, "They have families back in Philonia, if they return it would be because their hearts led them back."

Julian rode on and reached greener pastures greater in riches compared to the grasses and the lands that surrounded Petra. But not by a degree that demeaned the great city in any way. Julian saw the manor from a mile away.

He saw how the hills glorified the sight of the grand structure that was half the size of the castle of king Mitis. When he was still a little way off, a sailor noticed him. The sailor was carrying a large box when he saw Julian riding their way. Another sailor heard the gallops of Julian's horse and looked that way too. The second sailor said to the first, "Is he not the man who we saw fight yesterday?"

"I believe so." The first sailor said.

The first sailor placed the box he was carrying in a horse pulled wagon and he spoke to Julian once Julian had come closer to where they were standing.

"Excuse me. Is there something you are looking for here?"

The second sailor then burst out saying, "You should return back to the communal houses you don't belong here."

Julian kept his composure and with a slight smirk he said.

"Are you a servant of this house? Maybe you could tell the master of this manor that I am here for someone."

"You are one to talk. You're still clothed in rags. You're a fool. I know you see full well that I am wearing the uniform of the noble sailors of Philonia."

"Yes, this is true." Julian responded, "But Philonia sailors as is known are not uncontrolled in their speech. I heard from a respectable man of my city that sailors hold themselves in high honor and their manner is proper. When he said such to me I laughed because I knew one day I shall encounter a buffoon that would prove him wrong ten times over. And here you stand."

The sailor unsheathed his sword.

"Careful now, you don't want to hurt yourself with that." Julian said with a smile.

"Get off your horse and fight me." The second sailor said.

"Aelius, don't do this. You saw the skill of this man." The first sailor said.

"Paulus this does not concern you. I know what I am doing."

Julian dismounted his horse and led it to a tree close by. He secured the horse by the tree. Then walked back and stood against Aelius.

"Where is your sword?" Aelius asked

"Seeing that you are my opponent, I don't think I'll need one."

"You'll regret this I promise." Aelius said then charged at Julian.

Julian stood in place as his attacker's feet raced towards him. The sword of Aelius came smiting through the air, fast towards Julian's left arm. Julian side-stepped the attack, five more swings were made at him. Four of them missed but the fifth swing parted his shirt. Julian took off his shirt and revealed a slight cut stretching the length of his stomach. A very thin layer of blood oozed from the cut. Aelius smiled. Some of the servants of the house saw what was taking place. A servant ran into the main compound of the manor and into the house to call the master of the house.

"Still think you don't need a sword." Aelius said. The streak of blood that escaped from Julian's open flesh stopped seeping from his wound. He wiped it and saw the red on his palm.

"I have never had blood drawn from me twice in the same week. I have been in many fights and I have walked away unscathed. You sailor are a man of the sea and battles are not much at sea as were in the days of ruthless pirates. In those days your general struck fear into the hearts of men. You were lucky to draw blood from me and it shall be the last time your sword touches my flesh."

Julian immediately rushed Aelius. The distance between them was not much but Aelius was shocked as to how quickly Julian got to him. Aelius raised his sword high to strike him down. Julian swayed away from the attack. At once he caught Aelius sword hand and twisted it quickly. Aelius let go of his sword. Julian then twisted the arm in a manner that contorted Aelius's body up to a point that Julian was able to secure Aelius head beneath his left arm. He held him tight. Aelius face was towards the sky and his neck at the mercy of Julian's arm.

The other sailors gathered once they saw the confrontation. A young sailor, the very same that had yelled when he saw the shores of

Demoir from atop the ship's main sail pleaded
with Julian not to kill Aelius. Aelius was his
elder brother. The young boy was only seventeen and a sailor. His plea did not move Julian
because Julian had no intent of killing Aelius.
Julian looked at the young boy, whose name
was Gaius and said to him. "My conscience,
though it is slow, keeps me from killing your
brother." Then Julian with his right hand gave a
mighty blow to Aelius chest. Aelius fell on the
wet grass hard. He coughed in pain.

The master of the house came out and saw
what was happening. He came out riding on a
brown stallion. He was dressed in light armor.
He was a man well in his years and whose
strength had waned only a little over the years.
He was a soldier and had a son who was a noble and another who was a knight. He had two
daughters, twins who were closest friends of
Astra. They were bold and beautiful with hair
as brilliantly bright as the noonday sun.

The lord of the manor rode to where the
confrontation had taken place. He stopped in
front of Julian and demanded to know what
had gone on. Julian took note of the man and
his attire. He assumed him to be the master of
the manor. So he answered him,

"I came in search of someone. I was told by
a friend that he takes residence here in your
manor."

"You say you come in search of a man but
it seems that you really came seeking trouble.

What is the meaning of all this commotion? My servant disturbed my meal because of you. She came saying that much bloodshed might be spilled on my land. Though I am a soldier I detest conflict, especially among like-minded people. I rushed here immediately and here I find a man such as you, dressed in rags. Why have you come disturb the peace in my household?"

While the soldier was still addressing Julian, a man, much younger than the soldier came out riding on a black stallion. He rode to where his father was and stopped beside his father's horse.

"I did not mean any disrespect to your household." Julian said.

The young man that rode out and stayed beside his father was among the nobles who witnessed the fight between Julian and Neemus. The young man immediately noticed who his father was addressing. He spoke to his father,

"Father, I've seen this man before" He said, then continued, "He is the man I told you of yesterday, the one who defeated Neemus."

"The second knight?!" His father said astonished "State your name stranger." The old soldier said to Julian.

"My name is Julian and I am the son of Thanos."

Great joy and amazement filled the old soldier. He got down from his horse, walked to Julian and embraced him. Julian was confused.

"After all these years you are still alive and well. When my son spoke of you yesterday, he mentioned your name but he did not tell me that you are the son of Thanos. Come in, come in, you are welcome in my home."

Everyone around watched in bewilderment as the soldier welcomed Julian into the manor.

"Gabriel" the soldier said, calling his son, the noble, "Go tell the servants to prepare a room for Julian."

Gabriel did not know what to make of the situation. He obeyed his father and went into the house and did what was instructed of him. Julian also did not know what to make of the situation, but he did not decline the offer, for as he looked around the manor while he was walking into the compound, the structure pleased him. The manor was much better than the communal houses.

The old soldier spoke to Julian as they were making their way into the main compound.

"You probably do not remember me." The soldier said

"Were you a friend of my father?"

"No, I was not exactly a friend. I was his rival."

"His rival? My father had a saying about rivals. A rival, he'd say, is a friend who keeps you on your toes."

The man chuckled.

"He was right in saying that." The man said "My name is John Hero."

The name sounded very familiar to Julian. A name mentioned among the men of high honor in Belvain. In the days when Julian served as a squire for a knight in Philonia, The knight had mentioned a soldier who was almost on par with Thanos, one who had been a knight in Philonia but had chosen to make Konstuliana his home after Calix had removed the wicked king. Julian had heard of the manner in which John fought, the strength he displayed and a technique of his that he used to paralyze his opponents before he finished them. But the secret of the technique was in a glove he wore before he engaged in serious combat. He had never worn this glove whenever he sparred with Thanos. But his rivalry with Thanos was unlike any other among men of great strength. Both he and Thanos were soldiers of Philonia at a period in their life. Both of them grew up from humble beginnings and knew Calix well before he became king. Both men also grew up in Belvain, but John was born in a small village on the far-east side of Venduria.

Julian now knew that he was in the company of a man who might understand his situation and would be a great help to him.

A bath was prepared for Julian and after he had cleaned himself a room was prepared for him. He found fresh robes on the bed when he entered. The robes were not equal in quality as what the nobles wore but he did not mind this. When he left his room to go meet John who had requested his presence that morning at the breakfast table, he was approached by the man in charge of security in the manor. The man was as tall as he was. He had very short hair and a scar on his neck that was partly covered by the chainmail vest he wore underneath his armor. The man extended his hand offering Julian what he held in it. Julian looked at the sword the man was about to give him, he looked at the man and questioned,

"Why are you giving this to me?"

"You'll need it."

"Does an opponent await me?"

"No, not at all, if you noticed when you entered, every man on the premise is armed, whether they are apt in using a sword or not."

"I feel like you are keeping something from me. What reason is there to arm all men in the manor?"

"There are things that roam the woods a few miles north from here. If we were in Petra, there won't be much need for this, for the walls of the city would protect us. But you see this house is far from the city, farther even from the city of soldiers. So we must take heed and be on our guard for the lives of those within these manor walls are in the hands of those who wield a sword. We protect those who cannot protect themselves."

Julian took the sword from the man. As he collected it from him, he took note of the partially covered scar on the man's neck.

"These things you speak of, what are they?" Julian asked.

"It is said by some that they were once men, but men cannot do the things they do. I have seen them and they do not look like men. Their ugliness is beyond compare. Some of them can resist the pull of the land; they take to the skies like birds and move faster than the eyes can follow. This scar came from them. I remember that day well, when they attacked." The man formed a fist as he remembered that moment, a day he wished he could forget. Then he calmed himself and said. "I'm sorry I've taken your time. My master instructed me to give you a sword and summon you. He requests your presence downstairs at the dining hall." The man turned to walk away then Julian said

"I never got your name."

"I am Jacob, son of Jorad."

"I am Jul.."

"I know who you are." Jacob said "If you need anything you can find me in the west wing of the manor."

Julian went from there to where John requested his presence. He met John in the dining room. John was seated at the head of the table, on his right sat his son, the noble, Gabriel, and on John's left sat his wife, Liana. On her left sat one of the twin daughters, Sofia, and on Gabriel's right sat the other twin, Sandra. The young ladies were not familiar with the man who had just entered their midst but they had been discussing about him with their father before he arrived, and they liked what they heard. Julian was offered to sit at the other end of the table. He took his place. They had breakfast with him. Thereafter John's daughters departed to Petra to meet with Astra.

Julian waited in the front garden of the manor for Felix. An hour had passed and in that hour following breakfast, Julian had talked in length with John about how he had managed the years following his father's death. John was shocked to hear all that happened, how the head of the city council of Belvain had become corrupt and how the knights were no longer willing to fulfill their duties because the king of Philonia had been subjugated beneath the Elders. John asked Julian what he shall do when he returns. He asked Julian if he shall take the place of his father and guide the people of Belvain to better days. To which Julian responded,

"There is no longer a city for me to return to, all that I have known, my home, the fields of my youth, they are no more."

John inquired of what had caused this. Julian lied and said a great storm had swept over the landscape and that it had happened when he was in Noble City attending a festival. Though there had been a festival at the moment Belvain met its end, Julian was not at the festival and it was not a storm that had ravaged the lands. The truth of the fall of Belvain was too terrifying for Julian to admit to John, though he was there and he had seen it happen. He had seen the madness that overcame the people. They claimed to hear songs that he himself could not hear. The people were overcome with madness and that night, the city broke out in fire. People fought among themselves because the songs had driven them insane. Julian overpowered anyone that tried to attack him but he left the city and from the hills northeast of Belvain, he watched the city burn to the ground. He knelt there and wept till the morning hours. The next day soldiers found him out on the fields and they took him to noble city. They questioned him before the courts but he refused to speak. They threw him in jail because of his silence and told him they shall release him when he is ready to talk. Antonius was not consulted on this decision made by the Elders, in the presence of ten high-ranking senators. This happened in the third year of Antonius's rule as king.

Felix arrived an hour later, by his side rode the other son of John, a man by the name of Michael who ranked eighth in the Knight's Order. Michael saw Julian sitting in the garden. He and Felix had given their horses to a servant who led the horses away and secured them in a small stable. Felix had not noticed Julian yet. Paulus was the first sailor to welcome him back. He informed Felix on the progression of things as they prepared for their departure. He told Felix that some of the snow had not melted in some of the landscape a mile north of them, where they hunted for game. So sailors who were assigned this task had not returned yet. As Paulus was still speaking to Felix, Michael looked back at the man who sat in the garden, and Julian's face became known to him, he realized he was looking at the man who had humbled Neemus. Michael had been present during the confrontation. Michael folded his arms and waited till Felix had finished conversing with Paulus. Michael did not listen to what was being said between Paulus and Felix, so he did not hear when Paulus explained to Felix what Julian had done when he arrived at the manor. Felix thanked Paulus when all was said and done.

Michael called Felix and then he pointed out to him the man who was sitting in the garden. Felix looked that way and immediately recognized Julian, though the distance from where they saw him was a bit far from where he sat. It was a mystery to him why Julian was there, though he knew Julian was on the premise because Paulus had informed him. At that moment John came out from the manor and welcomed back his son and Felix. Felix asked him why Julian was sitting in the garden. John told him that Julian had been sitting there waiting for him.

"Do you know why he is waiting for me?" Felix asked.

"He told me he heard from someone that the sailors were going to return to Philonia and that you had made my manor your place of stay before you are set to depart. It seems he is interested in returning to Philonia as well."

"You won't know the real reason for his presence if you do not go and ask him yourselves." Michael said.

"I was going to do so. I just don't want him to cause trouble as he did in the city. He has a wild nature. I don't like him."

"Well regardless of the way he is, he has a cause for being here. You must learn what it is." John said then went back inside. Michael followed after him.

Felix went to where Julian was sitting in the garden. Julian was looking up into the overcast afternoon sky. He knew Felix was coming his way but refused to acknowledge him. When Felix had come but a few steps from where Julian sat, Julian said,

"Looks like rain, maybe late this evening."

Felix looked to the skies and saw the clouds gathering. Then he said,

"Is that why you're here, to tell me things that are easy to discern?"

Julian smiled, stood up, and then he turned to Felix and said.

"Forgive me, I mean no disrespect."

"Then what do you want?"

"I want to leave this place; I want to go back to lands that I am familiar with, places I know. I am a refuge here."

"Antonius gave me orders to only take back the sailors that wished to return home. You are not a sailor and I know this, you have no home. I heard of what became of Belvain. If you go with us, you shall just be a man who is doomed to wander. And wandering men always cause trouble."

"You are one to speak of the affairs of wandering men. When you were my age did you even have a home? No, you moved from place to place, one could even say you were a wanderer. If Calix and my father did not subdue you, you would have continued to wander across the seas, pillage the land and as you say, cause trouble. You were a man of the sea. You made the Blue Sea your home, but the Sea is no place for men, at least not for sane men."

Felix was angered by what Julian had said but he controlled himself and showed no change in expression but his breathing slowed. The two men locked eyes, neither saying a word as the moment passed, and then Felix replied.

"I don't like you. I had great respect for your father, though his tongue was as sharp as yours, he knew when to be quiet. In time you will learn this, no one will teach it to you but your circumstance will force you to comply. If you want to go back to Philonia you will have to also put a hand in the work that is being done to ensure all we need is ready before we depart. Come with me."

Felix took Julian to where the sailors were gathering all that was needed for departure. There Paulus, Gaius and Aelius were conversing with a handful of sailors. Some other sailors were returning from the hunt, far from the north. The place they had been gathering things was located a few feet from the wall that surrounded the manor. It was placed in shed, the size of a small stable.

The sailors saw Felix approaching with Julian. They stepped back as Julian walked by them. Felix led Julian to the shed. He opened the door and showed him all that was inside. The shed was filled with wood, dried meat, grains, barley, and three barrels of fermented grapes, yet to be made into wine. Julian saw that the shed was half full. He and Felix walked back out, and then Julian said,

"Tell me what you need me to do and it shall be done."

Aelius had been at the door of the shed when Felix and Julian walked in. He could not believe what had been said; he approached Felix,

"Tell me this man is not part of us." Aelius said

"No he is not part of us, but he shall accompany us back to Philonia. I don't know why he wishes to return but he will help us if he is going to return with us."

"Fine" Aelius said in a simple tone

Aelius turned and walked away. The sailors did not know how to respond to Julian. They stood there looking at him, some with judging eyes, other were apathetic to his presence. Felix then instructed Paulus to tell Julian all that was needed for him to do. From then on Julian helped the sailors as they continued to gather all that was needed for departure. He spent the remainder of his time in Konstuliana there, up until an event made him question whether he wanted to leave that place.

The following day, he woke up early the next morning, rode back to Petra and met the stable keeper. Julian threw a sack of coins, containing thirteen silver coins and said to the man,

"I am taking ownership of this horse. I hope that will cover the full expenses for the creature." He smiled and rode back to Hero's manor. The stable keeper yelled at Julian trying to tell him the horse was not for sale but Julian rode on and did not turn to consider his words.

Chapter 16
A Plot for Hate.
The Daughter of Sirius and the Accursed Ones

The midnight wind fell upon her bare skin. The moonlight touched her bosoms as she stood outside the balcony of the inn she and Titus had taken for the night. Titus was asleep but she could not lay down in peace. Her mind was not steady and her heart was boiling, seeking a way she could avenge her fallen brother.

The city of Bismotal was asleep and those who kept watch at night did not look her way as she transformed into the bird like creature, the form she took upon most often at times as these. She took to the air and flew high beyond the dark clouds. Her eyes were set far on the west, set on the shores of Demoir. She wanted to go investigate the area.

As she flew high into the night sky, the winds picked up. Suddenly clouds above her began to gather and denied her the moonlight.

She decided to ascend higher. She began rising in altitude but before she ascended above the clouds, she felt something hit her from her side. Her eyes turned a bright red color. She hovered there in the air and scanned the area. There was a chilling silence. The clouds above her cleared. She turned and saw the moon. It appeared grand and mighty in form. But she saw something else, a shape, a figure of some sort, hovered there above where the clouds had been a few distances ahead from her. She spread her wings to show the figure the size of her form. The creature remained still. What she saw next she was not prepared for. A very dark mist rose from within and around the creature. A mist such as the one she saw coming from the creature, she was able to create herself but not as thick as the one she observed. The mist surrounded the creature and then she heard the creature call her name. She knew its voice. At once she prepared herself for the worst. She looked up above the creature and she saw something rise up from the mist. It was a giant snake. The snake had no wings but maneuvered around the air with ease. It kept ascending till its whole body had departed from the mist; it looked down and saw Elana. Elana knew the snake and was not intimidated by its size.

"Rudraco," she called out to the creature.

"It has been a while, daughter of Sirius," the creature said.

The mist surrounding the creature cleared. The snake twirled itself around the creature and rested its head upon the creature's shoulder.

"Oh daughter of Sirius," Rudraco began. "You have eluded me for so many years by hiding in this pretense of being a daughter of men. You take your place on thrones as you please, and become unknown to a generation with ease. How long shall you keep up this charade?"

"Do not insult me," Elana said. "I am in no mood for your games."

Rudraco laughed. Elana hated his laugh.

"What shall you do to me?" Rudraco said. "Do you not remember what happened the last time you confronted me?"

"A lot can change in two millennia. Even for beings such as ourselves. So do not think that things shall end as they did last time."

Rudraco became serious. He stretched out his left hand, with an open palm directed towards Elana. His scaly skin turned red and flames came out from his hand. They sped fast towards Elana. Elana stretched her wings back and beat forward hard against the air. A wing current was created by her motion. The fireball reversed course and started heading towards Rudraco. As the ball of fire came closer to him, he smiled. The snake on his shoulder stretched itself and swallowed the fire ball.

The snake's eyes shone red after the fire ball was completely consumed, and then it went black again. Rudraco folded his arms.

"Elana, daughter of Sirius, I will make myself clear to you. You will do as I say if you wish to live."

"Do you think you can just impose your *will* on me? Do you think that only your plans matter? I have my reason for the things I do. You are a mindless buffoon, seeking only the destruction of men. You have no goal but to see those destined for greatness fall. I on the other hand have a reason why I make the armies of men fall on their face and meet an early grave. There is a cause to the chaos I have ensued on this world in the past and it was because of this curse upon me. Have you forgotten how many of our kind were killed during the War of the Fathers. The number's pale in comparison to what we did to the armies of men.

"Trust me, I remember those years well. I remember when it was that we began to lose our grip on the hearts of men. Then when the prophecies were pronounced we thought that they had become delusional with hope." Rudraco growled "But that hope of theirs was born, blessed with incredible power, the one who they call Gordon, the First Rising Guardian. Trust me I have not forgotten. I too have a reason and to say vengeance is my goal does not do me justice. No, I unlike your father and the other fallen Guardians did not make myself known to the women of those days. Yet I fought on your side and it cost me a great deal of what was left of my being. So you see Elana that is why it has been my *will* through the years to keep a careful eye on a certain people, those who are called the children of prophecies."

"You mean the Rising Guardians."

"Precisely, I make sure that they stray from their destiny, deviate from the path made for them, for you see in time, when the darkness in their heart is revealed, they become very powerful, but they then become under my control. In the past, children of fallen Guardians have heeded my call and joined my cause, now it is your turn."

"I appreciate the offer, but I'd rather seek vengeance on my own."

"I don't think you comprehend how strong these Rising Guardians are becoming. It is like the Great King is deliberately giving them more power to spite us. It is like he taunts us because we were once cloth in glory."

"I was never cloth in glory. You and my father may have been at some point but you lost your former glory. I am not even supposed to be, yet I am. It doesn't matter how strong this Rising Guardian is. I will find his weakness and I will use it against him. I will bend him till be breaks and he surrenders his *will* to me."

"I won't let you do that Elana. There is a plan that must be executed and it involves you, and you will join me," Rudraco said calmly.

The snake on his shoulder lifted its head. Its eyes became as black as the blackest night. It lunged itself at Elana. Its speed took Elana by surprise. Elana was knocked back, she began falling, her body speeding to smack into the earth but she caught herself when she was just a little higher than the trees. She looked up. Both Rudraco and the snake were nowhere in sight. The clouds sailed by the moon and shielded its light from the earth.

Elana's senses heightened and she assumed a stronger form of the bird creature she had transformed into. Now her wing span was wider and her fingers sharper. Her size was three-fourths of the size of Gammon when he assumed his monstrous form.

It was quiet around her. She listened intently then she heard the sudden rustling of bushes from beneath her. She did not turn to see what caused the sound for she could sense that something launched itself towards her. She quickly flew away, dodged the attack, and then she stopped. The snake launched itself at her again. She began to sing as the enormous creature was approaching her. The snake stopped before her face. As she sang the snake turned red and looked as if it were being burned in a furnace.

She was unaware as she sang that Rudraco had appeared behind her. She felt a slight touch on her neck. At that moment her singing seized. She could not move any part of her body. She began to fall and she fell and she hit the earth hard. Her impact had caused a tree to be broken in half. She felt consciousness leaving her as she kept her eyes on the moon.

While she laid there Rudraco stretched his hand out and gave strength to the snake. He restored it to its normal ugly form. The snake went down and crawled beside Elana's body. Rudraco appeared beside her body and placed his scaly hands on her head. He was searching the depths of her spirit. He hated the little bits of compassion he saw within her. He decided to overshadow whatever good was in her heart. He searched her memories and saw all she had seen, all she had felt and he knew of her purpose for being in Philonia. Why she had killed the elders and submitted herself to Titus. He learnt that she thought at some point that Titus was the Twelfth Rising Guardian but after she felt the pain of her dying brother, she realized that he may not be who she was looking for. He also saw the years she spent on an Island far North-west at the edge of the Blue Sea. He saw the years when she held Peter prisoner with her and how he escaped her. Much of what he saw, he had known because he had been closely watching all the higher children of the fallen Guardians. His aim was not primarily to search her memories but to pinpoint her weakness. He reached into the depths of her being and within her planted the essence of the snake that she had fought. Through it he would be able to speak to her without being physically present.

Elana felt this as it happened. Her spirit was aware but her body could not do anything because she was still unconscious. After Rudraco had done what he wished he stood up and looked to the heavens. With the eyes of his spirit set on Pacifica, he said,

"I will reclaim that which was mine. Neither you nor your children are going to stop me."

Then he disappeared from that place in a flash of black-lightning.

A minute passed and Elana arose furiously. She sprung to her feet and took the stance of one about to engage in fierce combat but there was no one around. She felt a slight presence of Rudraco, but it was within her. At first she did not know this, but then she recalled from her spirit what had been done to her while she was unconscious. She looked at her hands. She was still in the form she assumed before she fought the snake. But now she felt different, stronger than she had ever felt. She noticed that the feathers upon her body and wings had become as the texture of scales. They were rough. The tip of her wings became incredibly sharp. She stretched out her wings, and spun thrice. The six trees that surrounded her fell. She looked at her hands again for a moment. She set her eyes west and took a deep breath. Now her mind was more focused. She could feel something prompting her to fly towards Petra. She took to the air and soared above the clouds.

She reached Petra and hovered above the great city. She was cloaked by the night. She descended unto the city walls close to the south gate. From the wall she could see the castle. She felt Peter's presence on top of the castle. Peter slightly felt her presence but because of the power Rudraco had given her, her presence was well shielded.

Peter faintly felt her from where he stood on the tower. He looked in her direction but saw nothing. At once she felt something pull her away from where she was. At that same moment, Peter raised his staff high and called upon the lightning to take him to where he felt Elana's presence. Red lightning struck him and then struck the ground a few feet from where Elana had been standing. When he appeared there, no one was upon the wall except the guards that patrolled that side of the wall. He spoke to them asking them if they had seen anything strange. They said the only strange thing they had seen was the way he appeared before them.

Elana reappeared above the clouds. She heard the voice of Rudraco instructing her not to confront Peter. He warned her that in her present state, although she might overwhelm him, she might also draw Antonius's attention.

"Know this," Rudraco spoke through the snake from the depths of her being, "The Twelfth's full strength is not yet known, so make sure you do not contend against him yet. You must weaken his *will* first, if his *will* is diminished he shall be easy to defeat."

The night, the wind and the cold did not deter Elana. Rudraco spoke to her once more instructing her to fly two hundred and five miles northwest. As she flew high above the grand landscape, her focus was set on her destination but almost half-way from her destination she felt a sharp pull to something or someone far below her. She stopped and looked down. She saw a faint light between the trees. She wondered what she felt. Immediately she became aware that her brother, Gammon had spoken to her. She felt his spirit, greatly subdued within the spirit of another.

Her vision sharpened and she saw through the leaves down at where she had felt the pull on her spirit. There she saw Antonius looking up at her. She was struck with fear for a short moment. Then she was reassured by Rudraco that he could not see her he could only sense her. To Antonius right, she saw sitting upon a log, Marcus and Xaria. She did not know who they were but she felt the slight presence of her brother from within the spirit of Marcus. She saw Marcus say something to Antonius, whose eyes were still set on where she lingered.

"You must continue on your way" She felt Rudraco say to her. "In time, you will free your brother but now focus!"

She turned and continued on her way. When she reached where Rudraco had instructed her to go, she could hear from half a mile ahead of her, growls and loud howls. She could also see a field surrounded by thick forests around where she heard the sound originate from. She flew towards the sound. There she saw a mass gathering of detestable creatures. She heard Rudraco speak to her saying,

"Land among them, and command them to submit their *wills* to you. Let them know who you are and if they do not join you peacefully, employ force and correct their rebellion.

Some of the creatures beneath her were the same creatures that attacked Antonius and Mitis on their hunting session four years back. Among the wolf-men was another class of cursed creatures that were far more gruesome. They stood eight-feet tall, and had wings like bats, a face like a hyena and fangs that always showed. These creatures were known as Guiles. These were the same creatures Jacob had warned Julian about. They were known by all who lived in the villages north of that place. Where these creatures dwelt was five miles west from the mountain where Peter had made his home. They knew of the strength of Peter and in the past had contended against him when he found them terrorizing villages around the area.

Elana watched them from above. They were speaking to one another, plotting, knowing that Peter had left his place. It was best they act. One of them had been watching Peter's mountain for months and had reported to the others when Peter had departed. Since the time they knew of his departure till then, they had been plotting among themselves to kill all the inhabitants of the surrounding villages. But some among them did not budge for they thought Peter was playing a trick. Deliberations had kept them from carrying out their plans for two weeks.

Elana saw a vast number of them, numbering almost in the early firsts of a thousand. There was a great fire in the middle of them. The smoke went up into the night. Elana felt her spirit being pushed to descend and make her presence known. But she resisted the urge on her spirit; she waited and continued to watch the creatures.

Many of them she knew. She knew that they were once like normal men but their lust for power, greed and control over their fates caused them to strike deals with some of the fallen Guardians upon the earth. They sailed beyond the Blue Sea and met with Sirius who granted them the power they sought, in exchange he took their humanity away from them and they became like the fallen Guardians and the higher children of the fallen Guardians, despising all the attributes of common peoples. Whatever outward beauty they possessed was taken and they were given these hybrid bodies between beasts of different kinds.

When they realized what had been done to them they tried wage war against Sirius and his brother, but Sirius swiftly defeated them but he did not destroy them for Sirius had planned to use them to do his will in the lands of men. Sirius feared to leave the Darkness that was beyond the Blue Sea, for fear of what a Rising Guardian or child of a Rising Guardian might do to him. But never did he envision a mere man would defeat him. After he was no more, the ones under his curse knew and felt themselves relieved but their form was not restored to them. So they hid in the world of men, from men, and only made their presence known when vengeance stirred their hearts. Then they would go forth and take out on the innocent the fury they felt in their hearts against Sirius.

Elana felt the urge once more to make herself known to these creatures but some already knew of her, they knew of the higher children of Sirius, Gammon, Elana and others whose peak of power were almost measurable to that of a Rising Guardian at their prime. But Elana did not want to make her presence known in a grand fashion. Instead she would rather the creatures slowly grow to know the depths of her power.

She flew down and landed among the trees that surrounded the open field where the accursed ones had gathered. She transformed back to her normal form, appearing as the likeness of a woman. She was not bare but she had been cloth with a dark red robe. The robe had formed from the essence of the snake and was a temporal part of her being. It covered her for that moment.

She emerged from the forest and sat by one of the trees, watching the creatures, wondering why Rudraco would want her to associate herself with such beings. When, she thought, if she separated Antonius from Peter, she could first depose of Peter, and Antonius soon after would be dealt with, though he would be a great challenge to her in the end.

As she sat there, it took but ten seconds for one of the guiles to notice her, and then a wolf-man turned back, saw her and growled loudly. Quickly she became the center of attention among the gathering.

The wolf-man who noticed her ran to her and growled again. Seeing she was not afraid it stood on its two feet, showing her its full stature. She was not impressed. Then it spoke to her, with a voice that sounded like growls encompassed every word said.

"Do you know what happens to those who wonder these woods? Do you think that mercy shall be shown to you because you are a daughter of men?"

Elana smiled. The wolf-man was not pleased with this, he raised his paw high to strike her, but he and everyone around began to hear singing when his claws were less than an inch from her face. The songs had stopped his motion. The songs resonated from within Elana and they began to manifest as streams of lights. The wolf-man saw her songs. The melodies began to wrap around its body and they began to strangle it. They crushed its bones to dust. Its death was quick. The lifeless beast lay at the feet of Elana. There was an uncomfortable silence. The guiles and the wolf-men could not believe what they just witnessed.

One of them looked at Elana more closely and then became aware of who she was. He gave a loud cry and said,

"It is Elana, the first daughter of Sirius." Immediately it flew up into the air.

The wolf-men trembled. They turned and started to run as far from her as they could. One thing they knew, she was powerful, but how powerful, they weren't willing to stay to find out.

They all tried to escape her but she did not let them. She sang a song, a harmony she rarely uttered, one that released a great amount of power from her being. As she sang, her power stretched out and encompassed the area. The snake within her also aided her. Her force

spread out like a great wave and all the creatures that heard her voice froze and were
trapped in a trance like state.

When she felt the calm around her, she
knew that she had subdued all the guiles and
wolf-men. She walked and stood close to the
fire. She looked into the raging flames. The
height of the fire grew. She gazed up and saw
the fire reaching high above the height of the
trees. Close to the fire was a frozen wolf-man.
She turned to the beast and smiled. Then she
released the beast partially, giving it back the
privilege to speak. Immediately it said to her,

"What do you want from us? We do not
deserve this…"

"Be still" Elana said calmly. "I will not
harm you. I may need your help."

"This is not the way you approach one
who you desire to help you." The wolf-man
said with contempt.

"Watch your tongue," Elana warned.

"Forgive me." The wolf-man said between
closed fangs. Its words were mixed with
growls. "So what would the daughter of Sirius
have us do?"

"Be quiet," Elana said as she could feel
something moving in her spirit. Rudraco spoke
to her reminding her of what she felt the night
her father was slain. He said to her,

"You may be aware that a mere man killed
your father but I will show you who that man
was."

As Elana focused on the fire she began to see figures of beings engaged in a great battle. She saw the figure of her father in his most terrifying form. A tall monster with wide black wings, a long snake like tail and horns sticking out the side of his arms. Elana also saw two smaller figures, one of the figures held a staff in its hand and the other a sword. She also saw the outline of a winged creature with the other two smaller figures. Rudraco used the flames to form the face of the figure who wielded the sword. Elana saw the face and saw the resemblance the face had to Antonius. Rudraco then said to her,

"The man who killed your father is the father of the one who you are trying to destroy."

Elana was about to break down in tears. Not because of what was done to her father, but because she vividly remembered how she felt the moment Calix landed the final blow on Sirius. She knew that her father had fallen at the moment the pain hit her. It took weeks before she could forget the pain. Now it was alive again, though she did not physically feel it, the emotional prospect was real.

"So why bring me here, among these creatures?" She asked Rudraco.

"You will need their help, not only to take vengeance upon the sons of Calix but on all who stand by them. If Antonius were a mere man, you could have done this on your own. But he has Peter who now watches him and instructs him the path he is to follow if he is to ever transcend and attain Guardianship."

There was then silence after Rudraco had spoken to her. The wolf-man who had been slightly unfrozen noticed that Elana had been standing still staring into the fire for about a minute. So it said to her,

"Daughter of Sirius, what shall you have us do?"

Elana returned to her senses and said,

"My name is Elana. Do not refer to me as the daughter of Sirius any longer."

She stretched out her hand and released all the guiles and wolf-men from their trance like state. They all looked her way and saw her standing close to the fire. None ran from her presence but they began to gather around her. Her form darkened and she began to transform into the bird-like creature. Her wings were as scaled feathers. Her hair was covered by black flames and her skin had become as hard as steel. She flew into the air and addressed the mass crowd of beasts as the flames raged on behind her.

"I want you all to look around, see your numbers and know this: though power was granted to you by my father, the power you possess means nothing now. For the one who granted you such power was defeated by a mere man."

They began to bicker among themselves about why then their curse was not lifted. Elana knew this and it angered her that they were not attentive to what she was saying,

"Quiet!" She shouted. "I don't need to explain to you why it is I have despised Rising Guardians for as long as time has persisted. I am under a curse myself, against my choosing not because of who I am but because of what I am. The Great King and his children have always looked down upon the children of those who he cast away but I promise you this, a day will come when the darkness will rise as high as these flames and take claim of everything from the Blue Sea to the lands of men! Then our era shall last for many millennia. Now I am not asking you to join my cause, I am telling you that you will assist me in attaining my goal. In time I will find what the Rising Guardian holds most dear to his heart and I will take it away from him and crush it before his eyes. Then after I will devour his will and he shall serve me. Until then I want half of you to slowly make your way south towards the city of Petra and watch the city. The rest of you should make your way towards Philonia and wait for me at Snake valley. The valley is a mile west of Noble city. Let the guiles lead the way since they've seen more of the landscape. Do what I have asked of you."

She flew from them into the night sky and back toward Bismotal. She flew in through the Inn window. The dawn was about to break as Titus turned towards the window and saw her in her beauty. She was bare again. He smiled and called her to bed. There was great anger in her heart. She wanted to end Titus then and there but she restrained herself, for she thought it would be more fulfilling to her goal if she finished Titus in front of Antonius. So she smiled at him, went under the covers with him and kissed him.

Chapter 17
Beneath the Clouds

The sun was yet to rise, yet to take its place in the morning sky. Despite this, Antonius was already awake, praying within the chapel in the upper room of the castle. Sweat poured down his brow, seeped from his back and soaked his nightwear. The reason for his distress was a nightmare he had a few hours prior. In it he saw many horrific things, and they appeared as visions within the dream, making him think they may come to pass. He had been there praying for over an hour, praying against them seeking an answer from The Great King as to why he would let him see such things. As he prayed, he grew tired and lay upon his arms. There was a calming silence.

In the silence of the room, he felt an approaching presence. He did not want to turn and see who it was. The person came next to him, knelt by him and held his hand. He knew the touch; he lifted his head up and beheld Astra. The altar candles made her eyes glisten. Her eyes were filled with tears because she had been watching Antonius for a while from outside and she heard some of his prayers and it broke her heart. He took note of her eyes and saw that she had been crying.

"What's wrong?" He said to her in a calm voice that cracked at the utterance of the second word.

"I heard you praying and I felt distressed because you sounded troubled."

"I'll be fine."

"Is all this prayer all because of a dream?" she asked.

"Yes, I have had dreams that turned out to be visions. I prayed asking the Great King to spare me, so that I may never live through the things I saw in my dream."

She held his hand tighter and moved closer to him. He put his arm around her and kissed her head. They prayed together until the morning sun peaked in through the small window.

Peter had been watching them from a small room facing the chapel. He heard footsteps coming from his right-side, down the hall. The door to the room he watched from was halfway open. He saw from where he sat, Mitis, Eulalie and Galen stop at the entrance of the chapel. At that hour was when Mitis, Eulalie and Galen usually performed their daily devotions. He noticed that they saw what was going on within the chapel. He stood up and went out to them.

Mitis was the first to notice Peter. Eulalie turned to him. Galen was rubbing his eyes because he still felt sleepy. Eulalie greeted Peter. He smiled. Peter looked at Galen.

"You have a son?" Peter asked in a low voice.

"Yes, his name is Galen." Eulalie replied

Galen looked up to Peter and greeted him. Peter smiled and patted Galen's back. Mitis looked back into that chapel then back at Peter and asked him,

"Do you know why Antonius is in there?"

"He had a nightmare. He is praying, hoping that the nightmare was not a vision."

"Why is Astra with him?"

"She joined him an hour ago. They've been praying together ever since. I felt his spirit become very calm at the moment she knelt by his side. He has been calm ever since. Before she stayed by him, his spirit was troubled more than a man who has lost his only love."

Mitis and Eulalie were pleased to hear this. Mitis was about to lead them into the chapel, but he turned to Peter and asked,

"Will you be joining us?"

"No, the time has not yet come for me to reveal myself to him. So I will not be joining you," Peter said.

Mitis, Eulalie and Galen walked into the chapel. Galen knelt beside his sister, Eulalie was by Antonius's side and Mitis knelt close to the altar. Antonius was happy to see them. Together they prayed until sunrise.

It was about ten o'clock that morning when two men of Philonia were stopped outside the East gate of Petra. The guards that watched from the walls saw them from a distance and noticed that they had a symbol of the Philonian kingdom on their front vests. They stopped them outside the city feeling they may be spies sent by Titus to retrieve information on the whereabouts of Antonius.

A guard went out and asked one of them what their business was. One of the messengers replied saying,

"I have a message from the King of Philonia, Titus Maximus, for the King of Konstuliana, Mitis Miles. Please permit us to enter."

"I cannot do that. I'll have someone inform the king of your presence. In the meantime, you both will wait here."

"We had heard that Petra was a hospitable city. Why can't we come in? We are just messengers."

"Exactly, you are just messengers," the guard said then went back into the city.

The messengers waited there. A guard was sent to inform Mitis. The guard who went out to see the messenger had been given the letter sent by Titus.

At that same moment, Mitis was in his study discussing serious matters with Jeffery. Jeffery had informed him that a group of squires and noble's sons were trying to take over some land. Jeffery also informed Mitis that this was going on 3 miles North-east of Vayler, and that the soldiers were not doing anything about it because the land belonged to the father of a high ranking knight.

After Jeffery had finished informing Mitis about all he knew about the situation Mitis said,

"Though this is an important issue, I cannot address it today. I have other duties I have to fulfill."

"If we let this go on, the nobles and squires could pay the soldiers to protect them. If this happens you know there will be a greater rift between the knights and the soldiers."

"The soldiers have detested the knights for a long time. That's not going to change anytime soon. It is part of this kingdom's history, even before I became king it was this way. Why do you think they rarely come to the Knight's Tournament? Only David actually shows up. Then again he is a good friend and a better fighter than many knights. He is the strongest among the soldiers and there are many more soldiers than there are knights."

"He is the General. He has to be the strongest in order for him to lead his men."

"Not necessarily but I get your point. Strength is not the greatest attribute of a good leader. You see Jeffery as king I am the mediator between the knights and soldiers. In times of war or rebellions that put the wellbeing of our kingdom at stake, petty differences between the soldiers and knights are forgotten. Then you all are united for a single cause. After all is said and done, things will go back to normal. The soldiers will despise the knights because they feel you are entitled brats who are where you are because of your affluence. I know in your case this is not true. For the stronger knights their rank was earned. But for those sons of nobles who feel it is their right to put on the cloak of honor and glory when they do not deserve it will always rank lower than those whose determination makes them strive to be better even when they have become the best they can be."

"Now I see why it was that you refused to acknowledge me as your nephew when I first came here. Those days when you told me in time I will thank you because of how strict you were on me. How you said that I should make a name for myself, independent of your influence in anyway. Well that time has come. Thank you for everything."

Mitis was pleased to hear the honesty in Jeffery's voice as he showed his gratitude.

There was a knock on the door. Jeffery went to answer the door. A guard with an important message asked to see Mitis. Jeffery let him in. The guard walked in, bowed before the king, and placed his hand on his chest before he spoke.

"Your majesty," he said, "a message from the King of Philonia."

Mitis stood up from his chair, walked to the guard and took the letter from him. He saw the authentic wax seal upon the letter. The seal had impressed upon it the crest of the house of Maximus. He broke the seal and read the letter. The content of the letter was an announcement for Mitis on the soon presence of Titus in Petra. Mitis at once thought of Antonius after he had finished reading the letter. Then his thought shifted to where the messenger who delivered this letter might be. He asked the guard,

"Where is the messenger who brought this?"

"There were two messengers. They are outside the east gate. We did not let them enter for we saw they were from Philonia and we thought they were spies coming to know the whereabouts of Antonius."

"Did anyone tell them anything?"

"No, your majesty. That is why we did not let him in, lest he sees Antonius and reports to the officials in Philonia that we are harboring a fugitive."

"You've done well. You may go." Mitis said to the guard. The guard departed. Mitis then turned to Jeffery and said.

"I have to personally see these messengers."

"You may not have the time. You have other duties. Today is the day you promised Nolan and Jasher you would judge their case."

"Those farmers have always been bickering about which land is theirs', who has extended or moved his boarders. I can see their case another day."

"If you won't see their case, at least have the queen represent you as she has done before."

"Eulalie is busy. She is with Xaria at the orphanage. A child grew very ill, so she is with them."

"If you want me to send a knight, maybe Neemus…"

"No, I know who I'll send." Mitis said. "But first I want to see Antonius."

Jeffery went out to the hallway, called a guard that was stationed by the outer door to go and find Antonius and tell him that the king requests his presence. The guard went forth and found Antonius in the third Atrium of the castle by the east wing of the castle. He was with Astra. They had spent much of the morning together. After breakfast they had spoken in length. She told him of events that had happened in the spring festivals in the years past and how she was excited for the upcoming festival. That year's festival was to begin on the fourth day of spring. When the guard came to call Antonius, he found them sitting together by a wall, observing a statue of a hero who was known as the first of the twelve children of a famed politician who ruled when the nations were one. The son's name was Konrad and he was considered to be the greatest of the three founders of Konstuliana. In the other Atriums in the castle stood similar statues but they were of the other founders of Konstuliana, brother and sister of Konrad, Sturn and Liana. All statutes depicted the founders on horses and garments that had a symbol that was attributed to the days in which their father ruled, an era of peace.

Antonius stood to go with the guard. He helped Astra to her feet and they went together. When they got to the king's study the guard asked Astra to wait outside. The guard led Antonius in, bowed and went back outside to stand at his post.

When Antonius entered the king's study he saw Jeffery. They shook hands and he stood before Mitis.

"Antonius, how are you doing?" Mitis asked

"I am doing quite well."

"Good, you see I called you here because I need your help. I speak to you not as one whom you owe a favor but as one you trust."

"Okay. What do you need me to do?" Antonius asked.

"I know when you were king, you had issues like the one I am about to present to you come your way often. So it would not be hard for you to address it."

"I cannot settle disputes here. I do not have the authority to do so," Antonius replied.

"I know, I am sending you as an escort to the person I am going to send on my behalf."

"Who would that be?" Antonius asked.

"I am sending Astra on my behalf, and I want you to escort her and oversee the case with her. Since you have more experience with settling property disputes, you'll help her come to a decision that is fair to both parties involved."

"So what is the case about?" Antonius asked.

"It is all in here." Mitis said as he handed Antonius a small scroll. "Read it. Astra is somewhat familiar with the case. She knows today is the day I am supposed to handle it but I have other matters to attend to."

Mitis turned to Jeffery and said,

"I want you to get a horse prepared for Antonius, and cloth him in light armor. Give him a helmet as well." He then said to Antonius. "It is important that you keep the helmet on whenever you are outside these city walls."

"Understood."

"Come with me," Jeffery said to Antonius.

"One more thing." Mitis said "Jeffery, tell Astra I want to see her."

"Yes your majesty."

At once when Jeffery and Antonius exited the king's study, Jeffery saw Astra. He told her that her father wanted to see her. She went into her father's study. Mitis told her that she would represent him in the case of Jasher vs. Nolan. She would settle the dispute between the farmers. She was told that she'd be escorted but was not told it would Antonius who would escort her. Mitis only said of her escort,

"He will help you settle the case. He has experience in disputes such as these. But you will make the final decision concerning the parties."

He told her to leave as soon as possible and to return before sunset. She departed and went to do what her father had instructed of her.

After he had told her everything and she left, Mitis went back and sat in his chair and relaxed for a few minutes. He looked at the letter sent from Titus again. Then he heard a voice say from close to the window.

"Are you going to let Antonius know that his brother is coming?"

The voice was Peter's. Mitis sighed.

"I don't know. This son of Calix is one I know the least about. All I know is that he is impatient. War is the last thing I want to happen. With the current situation of Antonius there is bound to be a great misunderstanding if Titus meets him here."

"The letter says he shall be here by spring, does it not?"

"Yes it does."

"So you have five days to prepare." Peter said.

"How shall I prepare? I cannot hide Antonius forever. Eventually he'll have to return to prove his innocence."

"When that day comes you'll go with him. Testify on his behalf. But you know as well as I that he is destined for greater things; greater than being a king of Philonia."

"You seem to believe in him. More than you did two days ago."

"When he prayed, I sensed his sincerity. There is no way the darkness can take his heart. I know that he could be the twelfth Rising Guardian. Soon the prophecies shall come to pass and after he transcends, my work will be done and I will be able to join my father." Peter paused. He was happy. Then he said, "Soon I will reveal myself to him, I will take him to the mountains and reveal everything to him. I am sure he knows some things about his destiny. I shall take him before Titus arrives."

"That makes my task easier then."

"We will return for the spring festivals, after the festival, we head back to Philonia to prove his innocence."

After Peter had said this, Mitis was reassured and worried less. Then he asked Peter for a favor.

"I know you are still watching Antonius. I sent Astra with him to go on my behalf to a city south of here. Please make sure they are safe."

"I will." Peter said.

Jeffery gave Antonius one of his lightweight armor. The armor comprised of fine black arm guards, a chainmail vest, a belt, and a thin breastplate that was placed over the chainmail vest. Jeffery gave Antonius one of the standard knight helmets. Antonius put on the armor. It fit him well. Jeffery sent a knight to get one of his horses for Antonius. The horse was brought. Jeffery also gave Antonius a standard sword of a special class. The sword given to him was only used by those who were Leo-knight or ranked higher. The swords of the First, Second and Third knights were of a finer quality. They were made specifically for the knights, and the quality reflected their ranks.

Antonius made his way from the Knight's Quarter to the front compound of the castle. Outside the castle gate he saw two horses, a black stallion and a white stallion. A guard held the horses in place. The guard greeted Antonius as though he were Jeffery. Antonius for the moment removed his helmet and showed the guard who he was. Then he asked the guard which horse was brought for him. The guard told him the black horse. He put on his helmet and mounted the horse. Then he waited for Astra. As he waited, he read the small scroll Mitis had given him that described the case. [He read that two affluent farmers who lived in an agrarian city south of Petra had gotten into a dispute over property lines. Jasher claimed that Nolan had encroached on his plot that was set apart for farming. Jasher had been sending word to Mitis on his case, so it might be addressed before the new planting season began]. The scroll given to him did not have much else. He rolled it up and looked towards the front door of the castle. It was at that moment that Astra stepped out. She was clothed in a fine black cotton dress. The hem of the dress was lined with patterns that resembled the crashing waves of the sea. The hem was gold. The dress reached down and stopped just above her ankles. Her hair was arranged in two braids and collected together by an ornament that held it together in place.

He was stunned by her beauty once again. She made her way to her horse. A guard helped her unto her horse. The guard asked if she needed more guards to escort her on her journey, to which she responded,

"No, we'll be fine."

They set off leaving the city through the south gate. Astra rode in front. Their set destination was Argos, an agrarian city that was a major produce supplier for Petra and Vayler.

Argos was twenty one miles south of Petra. The path they took would take them first on a road on the west side of the mountain of Pysus, then across the plains of Bello and finally through the cave of Hermes.

After they had ridden a mile from Petra, they were now close to the west valley close to mount Pysus. At this point Astra inquired from Antonius if he knew more about the case. She thought by the appearance of his armor that he was either Jeffery or the third knight, a man by the name of Chris Benday. She told him what her father had told her about the case.

Antonius let her speak. Then after she had finished telling him everything, she asked,

"So have you handled cases similar to this?"

Antonius replied to her,

"I have."

She immediately recognized his voice. She stopped her horse. She turned to him and said,

"Knight, take off your helmet."

"Your father instructed me not to remove my helmet whenever I am outside the city."

"Antonius?"

"It is I"

She smiled

"Astra, your father has instructed you to take his place in deciding this case. As I am glad to be here with you, we have to continue on our way."

"You're right."

They continued on their way. Through the rest of the journey Antonius described to Astra two similar cases he had settled in Noble city. He told her that the final decision would be up to her but he'll help guide her decision.

When they arrived at Argos, overcast skies sailed over the city. The city of Argos was not structured as a normal city. Argos had no city wall. The city was surrounded by farming lands. Much of the lands around the city were owned by eight affluent farmers. Together the city of Argos provided twelve other cities and five villages around the south and western regions of Konstuliana with produce. This was how the city made its income. City leaders had employed some soldiers from Vayler to protect the city in exchange for a small portion of the first fruit of the harvest and monetary compensation.

Antonius and Astra arrived at the courthouse of the city which was in the middle of the city. There was a crowd around the courthouse. Antonius got down from his horse, and then he went to Astra and helped her off her horse. She waited for him while he secured the horses together. After he had secured the horses, he accompanied Astra into the courthouse. At the entrance, Antonius saw a hooded man who sat by the door with a bowl in front of him. The man had a staff in his right hand. The man's clothing was dark brown. They were close in resemblance to the clothing of a shepherd. But his face was covered in dirt and he had a hood over his head. There were three young children teasing and kicking rocks at the man. Antonius commanded them to leave. Once they saw the armor he was wearing, they took him to be a high ranking knight and left at once. Astra put three gold coins in the man's bowl. Antonius and Astra then walked into the courthouse.

The people inside the courtroom were surprised to see the princess enter. They were all expecting Mitis. Despite this, they all got up in reverence for her. They welcomed her presence. A guard met her and she told him that she was there in place of her father. The guard then showed her the high seat, the place meant for her father. After she sat, the guard bowed and left. Antonius stood by her side.

Among those who were surprised at Astra's presence was the accused. A man called Nolan. Nolan had been accused by Jasher, a man who was yet to arrive at the courthouse, of encroaching on land that was not his.

Nolan greeted Astra after she took her place, he said,

"A pleasant afternoon to you, Princess."

"Thank you" Astra replied

"Though I was expecting your father, it is good to see you."

"What is your name?"

"I am Nolan. I am the accused."

"Where is your accuser?" Astra asked

At that moment a pompous man walked into the courthouse. He was dressed in an elegant robe, the same that was worn by men of high noble standings. Beside him on each side were two soldiers who walked in with him.

"Forgive me if I am late your majesty, I had something I…" the man was saying as he walked in then noticed that the person who sat on the high seat was Astra not Mitis. "What is this?" he said.

"There is my accuser," Nolan said.

"Where is the king?" Jasher asked in anger

"My father sent me in his place. I will be judging this case on his behalf. He has decreed that my judgment on the matters between you two is final."

"No I don't…" Jasher was about to contest but was interrupted.

"That's enough," Antonius said. "Take your place Jasher. We don't have all day."

"You dare not speak to me like that knight. These soldiers are under my command and if I will them to go against you they will."

"Go ahead," Antonius said calmly. "Command them to come against a knight." Antonius gripped his sword but did not unsheathe it. Astra turned to Antonius and said,

"Please, don't let him get to you."

Antonius listened to her. He released his grip of his sword and stood at ease.

"Please Jasher take your place," Astra said.

Jasher scoffed and walked to stand at the podium where the accuser was supposed to stand.

Both sides presented their case before Astra. Jasher began saying that Nolan had broken a contract formed between their families two generations ago. The contract involved the piece of land that Nolan had recently ceased from Jasher. Jasher went on to call for the greatest punishment for Nolan breaching the contract. He wanted Nolan to be sentenced to death. Astra would not have this happen. Firstly she did not think that would be justifiable in anyway because she knew of men who had gotten lighter sentences for worse crimes. Secondly, Jasher's demeanor was deplorable and she could not stand him. Giving him what he desired would only make him more contemptible.

After Jasher had said whatever accusations he had, Astra let Nolan state his case. Nolan began by revealing to Astra that he was quite knowledgeable of the laws governing the higher cities, cities such as Vayler, Petra and Argos. He explained to her that for Jasher to request the death penalty against him, Jasher was liable to be tried for ill intent because Nolan's crime was not deserving of such a punishment.

Nolan then did something no one in the room expected an accused to do. He admitted to taking the land. He gave Astra two reasons why. Though it was not in the contract, he explained that it had been documented between the grandfather of Jasher and his father, that if any of his descendants wished, they could take back a quarter of the land given to Jasher's family. This could only be allowed if the descendant had a reasonable cause.

Astra then asked Nolan what his reasonable cause was for taking back part of the land.

A smile appeared on Nolan's face. A small tear almost escaped from his eye. He took a breath then he said,

"My wife gave birth yesterday. I held my first daughter in my arms last night."

"I am happy for you," Astra said.

"Thank you."

"How many children do you have?" Astra asked.

"I have twelve children your grace. All my sons are here. What I did, I did for the sake of my family. It is not hard to see by my grey hairs that I am well into my years. Time is no longer on my side. I may not live long enough to see my daughter's wedding. I just want to leave my children with enough. I am the only child of my father. Half of what I have, I inherited from my father. Sometimes I struggled to make ends meet, sometimes it was not enough. Fifteen years ago, things started to go well for me. The crops yielded much during harvest time. I became prosperous. Now I am one of the eight higher farmers in this city. It took years but it has been done. In recent years the crops have not yielded much during the harvest. The pests are harder to control and the harvest cycle has been disrupted more than once…"

"This has nothing to do with my land." Jasher interjected.

"Let him speak." Astra commanded

"No, he is right." Nolan admitted. "We came before you today so you may settle this case involving the land that divides us. I may have extended my borders but I have given you the reason. So your grace, the final say is in your power."

Astra called for a short break. The court began to flood with conversation. Nolan turned back to his sons. Jasher talked to the soldiers that accompanied him, while Astra spoke to Antonius. She asked him what should be done. He replied saying,

"All that is needed for you to make a fair judgment has been presented. Though Nolan has no true ownership over the land anymore, his reason for taking it seems a bit just. You should judge in a way that satisfies both of them."

Astra took Antonius's words into consideration. She called over the scribe that was taking note of all that went on in the case. The man was well into his years. She asked him what he knew about the contract between Nolan's father and Jasher's grandfather over the land. The scribe told her he had been there when the deal was made. He had known personally Nolan's

father. He told Astra that Nolan's father was
not properly literate to know what he signed.
He told her during the agreement Nolan's father was coerced to sell his land. He told Astra
that what he witnessed during the agreement
was not fair. Astra took a breath; she turned to
Antonius who had also heard the story told by
the scribe. Astra called the court back into session and declared her judgment. She declared
that Nolan would keep the land. Jasher got up
in a fit of anger. The soldiers armed themselves.
Antonius unsheathed his sword.

"I am not done speaking. Soldiers put your
swords away!" Astra ordered. "Knight, you do
the same."

Astra also declared that three-fourths of
whatever the land produces shall be given to
Jasher. She said that the work to gather the
produce would be entirely on Nolan and his
servants. None of Jasher's servants were re-
quired to work that land anymore. After her
declaration, Jasher calmed down a bit. Astra
asked the scribe to draft a contract and make a
copy of all he had written about the trial. The
scribe asked politely why the copy of the court
script needed to be made. Astra replied that she
needs the copy for her father. The scribe did as
she requested. He also drafted the agreement
between the two parties in the case. The scribe
drafted up the contract and wrote a copy of the
trial script.

After the contract was drafted, Nolan browsed over it and signed it. Jasher picked the feather pen, looked over the contract a little longer than Nolan had. He signed the contract, slammed the pen and walked out with the two soldiers who accompanied him.

The scribe gave the copy of the script to Astra. Astra took the copy and gave it to Antonius. Then they prepared to leave. Antonius went on ahead of Astra and got their horses ready for departure. As he was getting the horses ready he saw her coming his way. She was holding a small basket with a couple of fruits in it.

"Nolan gave us these." She said "In case we get hungry on the way back."

Astra began to notice the color of the sky. The sky turned dark gray and the clouds were collecting in the distance above the trails that led back to Petra. Astra told Antonius of this at the moment he had readied the horses.

"This weather may not be suitable for travel," She said.

"Astra, if we leave now, we could beat the clouds. We would be in Petra before night fall."

It was about four o'clock that afternoon.

"I don't think that is possible."

"We must at least try." Antonius insisted in a calm tone.

Astra reluctantly agreed. He helped her unto her horse. He took the basket of fruits from her and put it into a bigger bag that was secured to the saddle of his horse. Antonius mounted his horse and they set off.

The heavens opened up and the rains began to cover the land. At this time, they were close to the south end of the western valley by the side of mount Pysus. Antonius began to feel a slight drizzle. Astra then said,

"We might not make it back before the rain picks up."

"We can make it. We just have to move faster."

Antonius spurred his horse on. Astra did the same. They rode fast for a mile but the showers picked up and the sky got darker.

Astra stopped her horse. Antonius noticed that she had and stopped his as well.

"What's wrong?" He asked as the rain beat down on them.

"We can't make it back in time. The rain is ruining my garment. We have to find some place to wait out the rain."

"Alright, I'll find somewhere for us to stay."

Surrounding them were dense trees. Antonius looked towards the mountain. He thought maybe that there could be some caves around the mountain for them to stay in till the clouds passed over. They began going through the forest. The terrain appeared a bit familiar to Antonius but he did not know why. They crossed over a shallow river and got to the base of the mountain. Antonius found a small cave.

He helped Astra off her horse and into the cave. He then tied the rope of their horses together and secured them close to the entrance of the cave.

Astra entered the cave cautiously. She did not know if anyone or anything was there with them. Antonius saw her going further into the cave. He called her, whispering her name. She turned to him.

"Don't go too far. We don't know if we are alone in here."

Astra listened to Antonius. She found a smooth rock to sit on as she waited for Antonius to finish securing the horses. After Antonius had secured the horses he went and sat by her. She was rubbing her arms for the cold was biting her skin. Antonius noticed this. He got up and started looking for whatever dry logs or sticks that may be in the cave. He found a small collection of twigs and shrubs not too far into the cave. He touched the twigs, they were cold and wet. He went back and sat with Astra. He removed his helmet.

"Where did you go?"

"I went to see if there was anything around that I could use to make a fire."

"I don't think it'll be easy to make a fire under such conditions. Let's wait till the rain stops."

Outside, not too far from the entrance of the cave, Peter watched them. He felt their plight. He was used to the cold winds. He was aware that the weather was making Antonius and Astra very uncomfortable. He knew of a way to improve their condition but it would require him to use a great amount of his power. Half the amount he used in his first battle against Gammon.

Peter made his way to a higher place in a cave higher up in the mountain. He stretched out his right hand, and held his staff on his left. He said a silent prayer. As he prayed, the pressure of the winds began to change, the rain clouds blew away. The moon, the light of the night, was the only thing left dominating the night sky. The winds changed in such a way that the cold air rose and warmer winds rushed in from the east, blowing north.

Antonius noticed all the changes that occurred within that twenty minute span. He noticed that the air inside the cave had become warm. Astra then said,

"Do you hear that? It has stopped raining."

"Yes." Antonius replied but was focusing on the slight presence of a person he felt not too far from them.

"I noticed something about this place." Astra said.

Antonius turned his attention to her.

"What did you notice?"

"I'm not sure but I feel like this place holds memories."

"I also noticed something familiar about this place but I don't know why that is."

Astra's memory was rekindled. It then dawned on her why the terrain looked so familiar. She said in excitement to Antonius,

"Antonius, ten years ago during the knight's tournament, this was the place we hid when the noble's guards were chasing us."

Antonius also became excited remembering that moment. With a smile he responded,

"Ah, yes that evening we spent by the river. The same one we crossed on the way here. That day on the way back to Petra you sprained your ankle."

"And you carried me back from here all the way back."

"You looked silly hopping on one foot. And I was hungry so I wanted to get back quickly. And you said it did not hurt."

"It did not...well maybe a little." She said.

"A little? It was swollen when we got back to the castle."

"It was." She chuckled.

She leaned in closer to him. He wrapped his arm around her waist and gently pulled her closer. Beneath the faint glow of the moonlight he kissed her. Together they sat in silence, enjoying the calming sound of the night breeze, soon after they fell asleep in the other's embrace.

When morning came, Astra awoke to the sound of birds chirping nearby. She gently called Antonius. He woke up and cleaned his eyes. She kissed him on the cheek and helped him up. Antonius went to the get some fruits from the basket Nolan had given them. He gave Astra an apple. After they replenished themselves they readied their horses and started back to Petra.

Chapter 18
A Knight's Pride
Lake Amore.

The knight's quarter echoed with the sound of bone bending steel. The sun was far from gracing the day. But this did not deter Jeffery from his personal training. Since the day he witnessed Neemus concede to Julian, this had become a routine of his. He would retire to bed at midnight, arise four hours later and begin training alone in the knight's quarter. On this new morning, he had set up a part of light armor, an inch thick breastplate, against the wall, which was held up by two chains. Each chain held the breastplate by the shoulder hook.

Neemus had heard from some knights that Jeffery had been doing this. Neemus decided to witness it himself. That morning he met Jeffery in the knight's quarter. As he approached Jeffery he noticed the speed of Jeffery's fist hitting against the steel increase. But Neemus was there that morning to discuss more important matters with Jeffery. Things he thought Jeffery had lost sight of.

"Is it not too early to be training?" Neemus remarked.

"That, Neemus, is a matter of opinion."

"Regardless, for the past few days you have been more concerned with training than other matters in your life."

"I don't think it is any of your business to care what goes on in my personal life."

"Yes it is. We are both knights. Our personal lives affect the way we fight. If our minds are not free of worry the quality of our swordsmanship wanes."

Jeffery stopped disfiguring the breastplate. He took a towel and cleaned the blood off his knuckles. He turned to Neemus and said.

"What happened to the quality of your swordsmanship when you fought that noname bastard? When you lost and let him insult the honor of the Knight's order."

"Is that what this is all about? This new harsher training sequence of yours is this how you shall regain the honor of the Knight's order, by succumbing to pride."

Jeffery stared Neemus dead straight in his eyes. He turned, picked up a bandage and wrapped it around his knuckles.

"I was the one defeated," Neemus said. "Yet it was your pride that was wounded. Now you can't even see the things that truly matter in your life any longer. Do you even know

what has caused Simona to feel so down lately?
Who is taking care of her if you are here training?"

"I have given Chris the duty of taking care
of anything she needs."

"You have left your sister under the care of
a madman. You are aware of how he feels
about her, are you not?" Neemus asked.

"He chooses to speak a few words every
now and then and because of this you have
labelled him a madman. His tongue may not
say much but his sword speaks a lot. That's
why he is the Third knight. Besides, I am not
worried about him taking advantage of Simona
because I know he can't."

"And how do you know that?"

"I've trained Simona to defend herself."

"You've trained a woman according to the
techniques in the Knight's Guild."

"Yes I have."

"You know that is against the Knight's
way."

"I do. But since Mitis instructed me to train
Astra a day after I became First Knight, I
thought it fair that I trained the woman that
was closest to me. Do you not remember that
Simona always followed us on the campaigns
we embarked on? Though she did not fight
with us because it is against the Knight's way,
she observed us. During those nights, and the
days in between battles, I trained with her."
Jeffery paused for moment. He thought about

his sister then said in a concerned tone. "Something ails her heart. I know this already but she refuses to tell me. Chris is capable, so I have left her under his care."

"Why can't you be there for her? Is training more important than the wellbeing of your sister?"

Jeffery was silent. He looked at Neemus with a slight frown.

"Since you won't answer that question, answer me this, recently the knights have complained that your training methods are becoming too harsh. Two days ago a knight met with me after training with you. He had sustained a dislocated shoulder."

In anger Jeffery burst out saying,

"If another knight complains to you again, tell me his name, tell him to come see me! Then I will show him what harsh is. Are we not knights? Since when were we deterred by the intensity of training? No man has time to complain about the harshness of war when he is in the middle of battle. Why then should he complain when he is doing that which will sustain him in battle?"

"I see you have already decided where you stand on things."

"I decided a long time ago. I have known what matters to me from the day I watched my mother beg on her knees before my father to spare my life. My father hated me, always saying that I was not his son. That day I watched my mother humble herself before a man I knew she could bring to his knees. I am aware of my mother's part in the conquest that Calix led to conquer this nation and dethrone Hermes the second. I know that my mother saved the queen's life. She told me many stores that at first I thought were too incredible to be true but as I grew and learnt more about this nation's history and the history of Philonia, the birth-place of my mother, I came to see that she never stretched the truth." Jeffery paused for a brief moment. "Every day I remember her words, how she always encouraged me to be better. She began training me the day I told her I wanted to become a knight. At times like these, when my heart is furious, her words would calm my spirit."

Neemus gained a bit of insight about how Jeffery was feeling. So he said to him,

"Kineta did have a way with words. She convinced me not to get the knight's involved in the war Hermes had caused. During that time, I was the First knight, and by not getting involved in the war, I had chosen to betray Hermes. When the war was over, Mitis did as Kineta promised. He let me keep my place as First Knight. I may not fully understand why it is you have let my failure bother you so much, but I will say this before I leave you to your business. You are the First Knight now. You don't have to prove anything to anyone. Don't let your pride stem from anger but let it grow from the glory of your accomplishments and the responsibility you have as the First Knight of Konstuliana."

Neemus left after he had said those words. Jeffery sat back down contemplating the true reason for his anger. Five minutes passed and the light of the morning sun began to peek in through the tall windows. Jeffery looked out and saw the beauty of the glorious city. With her high walls, gravel roads and splendid buildings. He heard footsteps coming his way. He turned and beheld Marcus in light armor.

"I am here as you requested. Shall we begin this friendly duel or should I leave you to your thoughts?"

Jeffery smiled, he got up, handed Marcus a sword and got one for himself as well. They spent the morning training. Marcus and Jeffery were similar in strength and ability but Jeffery's endurance was much more than Marcus's. After they had trained together for about an hour, Marcus began to grow tired, thirty more minutes passed before he conceded to Jeffery. They cleaned their wounds. Marcus spent the day there, helping Jeffery train some of the knights.

❖

Her room was the most quiet in the entire house. Simona had been feeling down for the past two days and she had not come out of Jeffery's house in three days. So Jeffery had told some of his servants to look after her, as well as

Chris Benday, who was a close friend of Simona, to take care of her needs. She sat on her bed, still in her nightgown. It was about an hour before noon.

Chris walked in with a cup containing a beverage that comprised of cocoa and extracts from peppermint leaves. He had squeezed two lemons into the mixture. He set the hot beverage on a small stool that was beside Simona's bed. A servant brought in fresh baked loaves of bread and set it besides the beverage. The servant left. Chris went and opened the curtains and daylight flooded the room. The sky was bountiful with light grey clouds. Simona did not welcome the light.

"Please close the curtains." She said.

"I'm sorry but I won't." Chris replied. "The light will help you heal."

"The light cannot heal what ails my heart."

Chris took a seat on the fine chair that was close to Simona's bed. He leaned in closer to her and said.

"In the many years I have known you, I have never seen you like this. You have brought joy to everyone you meet, and not a day goes by that I do not adore your smile. But you are not smiling today. Tell me, what is the reason for this?"

A moment of silence passed. Simona leaned back and wiped the tear that just escaped from her eye. She felt Chris did not understand the cause of her distress. She loved

Antonius and she had felt that though at some point he loved her, he always had a special place in his heart for Astra.

Simona was about to respond to Chris but then there was a knock on the door. The person behind the door called out to Simona. Simona and Chris recognized the voice. The door opened and Jeffery walked in. Chris stood up as a sign of respect to Jeffery.

"Give us a minute." Jeffery said. Chris gave one last look to Simona before departing. Jeffery went and sat by Simona's side.

"How are you feeling?" Jeffery asked.

"I've had better days," Simona said.

"Do you think, you could train the squires today?"

Simona sighed, looked away from him and shook her head.

"No I can't," she said. "I don't care for the squires or anything that has to do with the knight's order."

"Simona," Jeffery said calmly. "I know you don't mean that. You know the squires need you. They are willing to take lessons from you than from other knights I have assigned to train them. Please do this for me."

Simona did not respond. Jeffery kissed her forehead and left. He told Chris, who was waiting outside the door, to make sure Simona's needs were provided for and that if she decides to continue training the squires he should make sure her horse was prepared and anything else she requests. After Jeffery departed, Chris returned to Simona. He met her in tears. She was clinging onto a necklace. It was given to by her for Antonius a few days after they met. The pendant on the necklace was a royal blue and had the crest of the house of Maximus encrusted in it. The necklace brought many memories to her mind. She wept for she longed for things to be as they were in those days. Simona looked up with tear filled eyes. It was then that she noticed Chris's presence. He did not know what to say or what to do. Chris noticed what she was holding. He had seen her wear it on several occasions, most often during the summer months. Chris felt incapable. He did not know what to do to soothe Simona. He turned around and left. He waited outside her room.

In that moment of tears, Simona's memory was spurred because she gazed at the necklace intently. So much so that her mind took her back to the day she met Antonius.

In the later days of that summer, the summer of Queen Annabelle's last visit to Konstuliana, Antonius was seventeen years old. Queen Annabelle had brought Antonius along with her because she knew of his fondness for Astra. It had been eight years since Antonius had been in Petra before that summer. The Knight's Tournament for that year was about to begin.

The queen and her son were graciously welcomed into Petra. Astra greeted Antonius at the footstep of the castle. On that same day Simona had

set off for Petra from the Manor of her father which
was close to the border between Venduria and
Konstuliana. She arrived in Petra three days after
Annabelle and Antonius. But Petra was not her first
stop after she left her father's house. She knew of
Jeffery's ambition to become a knight. She knew that
Mitis had given him a place to stay, a cabin in the
woods close to the North Garden. During this time
Mitis refused to acknowledge Jeffery as his nephew,
after he learnt of his reason for coming to Petra. Jeffery did not understand at the time why Mitis did
this, but Mitis assured Jeffery that he would in due
time understand. When Simona met Jeffery in his
cabin, she spoke to him and found that his heart was
dismayed. She began to see that he was about to give
up on his ambitions. She stayed with him for five
days before she went to Petra.

Simona was well learnt and knew of many nat-
ural things that enhanced the strength of the body.
She had studied immensely during her time at her
father's Manor and learnt of a very dangerous yet
powerful fruit that had enhanced the strengths of
men who took them. The effect of the fruit was even
passed on to their children. She read of a man who
took the fruit in due season of the fruits ripening. The
fruit granted him great strength that lasted his lifetime. His name was also known around the world for
the feats of strengths he performed and the skill he
displayed when he fought. She had never met the
man but she knew three things about him, given in
the account she read. The man was a friend of Calix
Maximus, he was a soldier in Philonia and he died
on the same night as Calix. The account of the man

*she read was written by his sister. In the account,
Simona saw a sketch of what the fruit looked like. She
was also given a warning by the author of the account. The warning stated that if the fruit was not
eaten in due season, the one who consumes it would
fall ill and would die. There was no specification in
the account of what the fruit looked like in due season
but it was written it was the same size of a pome-
granate and only the seeds of the fruit should be eat-
en. In the account the locations of where the fruit
would be in abundance were given, one of these places was close to the Manor of Simona's father. She
found the fruit. It was as described in the account.
She kept it and took it with her when she departed to
see Jeffery.*

*Jeffery was overjoyed to see her. He told her of
his struggles and how because the king had refused
to publically acknowledge him as his nephew it had
been hard to gain the favor of people, especially the
well-established knights. He told her he was planning to take part in the Knight's Tournament but
because of all the recent events, his hope was waning.*

*She embraced him and encouraged him. On the
third day of her stay with him, she prepared a meal
for him with the seeds of the fruit in it. Jeffery ate it,
giving no thought to the seeds in the food. That afternoon while he was training he lost all feeling in
his legs. He crawled to the door of the cabin, calling
out to Simona as he crawled. She ran to him and
tried to help him to his feet but he told her he could
not walk. She helped him to his bed, and he laid there
wondering what caused this. The night was worse.
He was sweating badly and had lost all feelings in*

his arm, and he could no longer move his neck. He could speak but he spoke slowly and in a slurred manner. Simona was scared and in tears. She thought he would die that night. She sat by him and held his hand. She prayed. She could not stop crying, but she continued to pray until she fell asleep on his chest. The next morning she was awoken by his voice. She could feel his hand grasping hers.' Simona woke up and was happy to see Jeffery alive. Jeffery showed her that movement had been restored to only his right arm. She was happy and embraced him. She promised that she'd take care of him until he was back to full health. He improved greatly as the day went on.

On the fifth day, Simona told Jeffery that she would be going to Petra to see Astra. Jeffery wished her well and told her first to see Mitis and make her presence known to Eulalie also. Simona did as Jeffery instructed her. When she had presented herself to Mitis who welcomed her graciously, she went to Eulalie, who was also glad to see her. She asked about Astra, for she had not seen her cousin in years. Eulalie informed Simona that Astra had sprained her ankle while in the woods with a friend. Eulalie told Simona that Astra was in her bed and she was being taken care of by her friend.

Simona went from the queen's presence to Astra's chamber. There she met her cousin in bed, with her ankle bandaged. Simona embraced Astra. Astra was glad to see her. Simona told Astra of her journey, of how nice people were to her in the Inn's she stayed on her stops. As they spoke, a young man dressed in noble apparel walked in. At once Simona *noticed him and he noticed her. There was silence for that passing moment. He approached her and said.*

"Good evening fair lady. Please don't mind me asking, but who are you?"

Simona tried to speak but she could not muster any words, for her eyes were caught in amazement of the beauty of the young prince. She admired his fine chin, his short curly hair and his stubble face.

"Simona," Astra said, she then tapped Simona lightly.

"Yes…I'm…Simona…my name is Simona," Simona said.

The young prince smiled.

"I am Antonius, the second son of Calix Maximus and a Prince of Philonia. It is a pleasure to meet you, Simona." He gave a slight bow. "Please sit."

Simona sat on a fine chair beside Astra's bed. Antonius went to Astra's feet, removed the bandage and began massaging her ankle with an ointment given to him by his mother. While doing this he asked Simona more questions to learn more about her. She told him all she had told Astra. They kept Astra company for the remainder of the day.

The following day marked the beginning of the knight's tournament. Early that morning Antonius had spotted Simona making her way north, through the North gate and towards an area known as the North Garden. He followed her and saw that she went beyond the North Garden into the forest. He followed after her keeping his distance. He found where she had ventured too. She was outside Jeffery's cabin when Antonius revealed himself to her. She was surprised at his presence. He got down from his horse and approached her.

"Simona" He said "Forgive me. I know you were not expecting me. I was curious, so I followed you here. But please tell me, where exactly are we?"

"No it is alright." She said "I am not too familiar with the names of places here. But this is the cabin that my brother stays in."

"The nephew of Mitis stays in a cabin outside the city. I find that hard to believe."

"Are you calling me a liar?" Simona asked

"No, I am not. I just don't believe you."

At that moment Jeffery walked out to them. He had a waist-high branch in one hand that he used to support himself as he walked around. He hadn't regain movement in his left leg yet.

"Why is it hard to believe the king would make his nephew live in a lonely cabin in the middle of the woods. I mean the weather is nice now that summer has come. I awake to the birds chirping, I hunt my own food and I live as they did in the days after the War of the Fathers."

"It's hard for me to believe that Mitis would do this to his own blood without good reason."

"Good reason" Jeffery smiled. "Yes I guess my desire to be a knight is good reason enough for him to refuse to acknowledge me as his nephew." Jeffery sighed. "Come in, come in." He said as he invited Antonius in. "By the way what is your name? I see that by what you are wearing you are someone of high standing."

"I am Antonius Maximus, the second son of Calix Maximus and a prince of Philonia."

Upon hearing who Antonius was, Jeffery smiled. They were now inside his cabin. He led them to the kitchen and began preparing a meal but Simona took over and told him to sit. She pleaded with him not to stand for so long until he regained feeling in his other leg.

As Simona prepared the meal, Antonius and Jeffery conversed. Jeffery told Antonius many stories that his mom, Kineta had told him. Antonius found them interesting; he was also surprised to learn from Jeffery that his late father and Jeffery's mother were very close friends. Many of the stories Jeffery told to Antonius were similar to stories he had heard from his father. Years later when Antonius became king and was allowed to read his father's diary, he found that Kineta was mentioned several times. And that the stories Jeffery had told him were almost identical to the ones he read in his father's diary.

That evening Antonius took Simona to a lake half a mile west from Jeffery's cabin. The lake was surrounded by four hills and looked as if the water had collected into a valley forming what they saw. Simona was astounded by the beauty of the lake and how the evening sun set upon the waters from a distance.

"Never in my life have I seen such a beautiful place." Simona said

"I know what you mean. It is amazing. They call this place Lake Amore. It is believed that this was the place where the poet Yanis composed many of his poems."

"Let the winds speak of the ways of love." Simona began "Let the songs of Guardians rain from *above. Speak to the sea and it shall speak to you. It shall speak of a love that is bold and true."*

"You've read some of his works."

"He speaks a language only the heart can understand."

Antonius smiled. Together they admired the setting sun. Antonius returned later that evening to see Astra. She was very glad to see him. She asked about his day and he told her everything, leaving out the detail about taking Simona to the lake. Antonius spent the remainder of his time in Petra like this. Spending the day with Simona at the Lake and returning to Astra in the evening.

Astra learnt from her close friends, the daughters of John, Sandra and Sofia, about Antonius's interest in Simona. They were careful in the way they told her as to not slander or insult Antonius in anyway because Astra did not take kindly to anyone insulting Antonius in her presence. Upon learning this Astra became sad but she did not let Sandra or Sofia know of her distress, nor did she ever bring it up when Antonius met with her in the evenings.

Annabella, the queen of Philonia, and mother of Antonius also learnt of her son's new interest and she did not like it. For she knew of Antonius's love for Astra and though she spent much of her time with Eulalie and Mitis watching the Tournament matches, she had people who informed her of the activities of Antonius. She called her son into her chamber a day before the last match of the tournament. She reprimanded him for what he was doing and she told him not to play with Astra's heart. Antonius did not argue or try to defend his actions. He *sat in silence as his mother spoke to him. When she was done, he apologized and returned to his chamber. He took his mother's words to heart.*

The day after the tournament ended was the day that Annabella set to return to Philonia. The night before, Antonius had met with Simona outside Jeffery's cabin. He bid her farewell but before he left he removed the necklace he was wearing,

"I don't know when I'll return but until we meet again, remember me." He said then he put the necklace on Simona. Simona was moved and she threw herself on him and kissed him. At that moment, he thought of Astra.

All this Simona recollected as she gazed upon the necklace. She cleaned her eyes and got up from her bed. She opened her door and saw Chris standing outside. He was standing by the window at the end of the corridor. She went to him and requested that he send for her horse to be brought. He went immediately and got things ready for her. In the meantime, Simona went, cleaned herself and adorned herself in a beautiful gown. When her horse was brought, Chris asked where she was going but she did not tell him. She rode off without saying a word to anyone. She was making her way to Lake Amore. It was around two thirty that afternoon.

The plains half a mile west of Hero's manor were starting to turn green. The shadow of spring had fallen open them. The sky was still overcast. On that same day, Julian, Paulus, Aelius and Gaius had been instructed by Felix to gather more firewood. Paulus had gone with Aelius northwards, while Julian and Gaius headed west. Julian and Gaius had crossed the plains west of Hero's manor. They were about to enter a mildly dense forest. From the time they left the manor till then, Gaius had tried to converse with Julian but Julian rarely responded. So Gaius started whistling. The melodies he whistled Julian knew of, so he began whistling along. They got to the end of the plains about to enter into the forest. Julian stopped. He looked behind and saw that Gaius was looking through his telescope at something, south of where they were.

"What are you doing? This is not a good time to admire the landscape. There's still work to be done," Julian said.

"It is not the landscape that has captured my eyes," Gaius responded.

"What are you taking about?"

"Here take a look," Gaius said as he handed Julian the telescope.

Julian took the telescope from him and saw for himself. He directed his vision south but did not see anything.

"Look a little more west," Gaius said

Julian did and saw something moving. At first he could not make out what it was because it was moving fast. He got a better look at it and saw that it was a person upon a horse.

"Is that a woman?" He said

"I believe so. It looks like she is heading into the forest," Gaius said.

"Yes, I believe you are right."

"But for what reason?" Gaius asked.

Gaius felt a drop of rain land on his hand.
He looked up and saw the clouds thickening.

"We should be heading back. We could try
again tomorrow morning before we leave,"
Gaius said.

As Gaius was still speaking, Julian watched
as the person he saw rode into the dense forest
and disappeared from sight. He lowered the
telescope from his eye before he responded to
Gaius.

"I want you to head back now. I will return
later." Julian said in a stern voice. He handed
Gaius back the telescope.

"But what…" Gaius started but Julian rode
off before Gaius could finish speaking. Then he
shouted to Julian who was riding away. "What
shall I tell Felix, if you don't return before we
depart?"

Julian stopped, turned back and responded.

"I will return on time."

Gaius knew that Julian was going to investigate what they saw. But Gaius was not interested in going because he was not familiar with
the landscape and worried about getting lost.
He turned and headed back to Hero's manor.

Julian rode after the person and entered into the part of the forest he saw the person disappear. He stopped his horse and saw tracks.
He followed steadily but not too fast. As he got
farther into the forest the tracks became hard to
see. To his surprise he stumbled upon an abandoned cabin in the woods. He was about to go
in and explore it but he saw the tracks he was
following lead from the front of the cabin further into the woods. He continued on the terrain until he got to a very steep descent. The
descent was not that far down. He stopped his
horse. At that moment a light rain began to fall.
He looked ahead and saw a lake. From where
he was it looked like it was slightly hidden by
the surrounding landscape. He secured his
horse by a tree close by and slid down the descent. He was amazed at the beauty of the
place. He saw that the tracks were leading towards the lake. He snuck his way forward, using the trees to hide himself from the person he
was following. He had not seen the person yet
but felt that they were at the lake. He stopped at
a place that overlooked the lake. It was at that
moment he beheld her. He squatted and kept
still. He saw a very beautiful lady standing
close to the lake. She was clothed in a fine blue
dress. Her feet were bare. He adored her figure
and her long hair.

Julian saw that she was holding something
in her hand. He could not make out what it was
but when he saw her put it on, he assumed it to

be a necklace. He saw her standing beside the majestic lake as the rain began to pour down harder. He was not sure what to expect from her. It seemed like time slowed and he felt every raindrop that touched his skin. He watched her take slow steps towards the lake. Immediately he knew what she was trying to do.

As she walked into the waters, the rain began to intensify. Julian stood from where he was and ran quickly towards where he saw her enter the water. He dove in without hesitation. The cold waters did not deter him from swimming into the majestic deep. It was hard for Julian to see where she was. He caught a quick shimmer that reflected off the necklace she had put on. He wanted to swim up for air but felt that if he did so he wouldn't reach her in time. So he swam towards the faint glow. As he swam, he felt the water weigh down on his back, he was finding it hard to hold his breath, but he could see her and he was getting closer. In the moment when he almost reached her he felt his last breath leave him. Never in his years had he felt himself divided between saving another or saving himself. He did not care for the moral implications of either action. In that moment he decided in his heart if he could not save her then he'll drown with her.

He swam deeper and caught her hand. With the last of his strength he swam up to the surface. He reached up out of the water and caught his breath. He held her head above the water as he swam with her to shore. He laid her down on the wet grass. He coughed up water. The heaviness he felt in his chest was unbearable. After he had regain his composure, he went to attend to the lady he pulled from the water. He wanted to attend to her but the rain was a bother. As he moved closer to her he saw that she began to slowly cough up some water.

He remembered the cabin he encountered on his way to the lake. He carefully carried her and started for the cabin. When he got to the cabin, he kicked the door open and met the place in a dusty mess. It became clear that no one had been there for a while. He saw a bed setup close to the wall at the end of the cabin. He took her to it but saw it was crawling with insects. He cleared space on the floor and laid her down on her side. A few short moments passed. It felt like an eternity to him before she coughed again and woke up. He gave a sigh of relief.

There was a moment of surprise. A light hit her eyes as she felt water rush out her mouth. Simona arose to find herself in the old cabin that belonged to Jeffery, with a stranger looking down at her. She recognized the face of the man looking at her.

"You." She said.

"You're alive." He said with a smile.

"It is you. Julian?"

"Yes, I am Julian."

Simona sat up.

"Why did you save me?" She asked softly. "You don't even know who I am?"

"I didn't need too." Julian responded.

Simona started crying and holding onto her necklace. Julian noticed this and asked her.

"Why do you cradle the necklace as though it were your child? What memories does it hold that make you weep when you touch it?"

Simona cleaned her eyes but did not respond.

"Who gave it to you?" Julian asked.

"Antonius." Simona said underneath her breath, low but enough for Julian to make out the name.

He reached for the necklace and slowly removed it. He studied it carefully and noticed the design was distinct and something in the range made for the royals in Philonia. He looked behind it and saw the inscription written to honor Antonius, a Prince of Philonia.

"You are not Antonius, are you?"

"No" Simona responded.

"Then you knew him, and you once loved him?"

He saw Simona's eyes tear up a bit.

"He once loved you," Julian said.

"Yes."

Julian gripped the necklace tightly and began to crush it in his palm. Simona heard it and tried to stop him but he said,

"To him you are the past. Do not dwell on your memories so much, if not you will forget to live."

Only the outer layer of the necklace had been shattered. The jewel within it was still perfect in form. After he crushed the necklace, he threw it outside. It fell in the mud and the earth covered it.

"Now, tell me, what is your name?"

"I am Simona."

He helped her to her feet. He told her that he would not let her out of his sight unless she was returning to Petra. But Simona did not wish to return to Petra instead she requested that Julian take her to Vayler. He told her that he does not know the city but she should guide him to it. The rain began to slow in its intensity and the grey clouds began to scatter to reveal the early night sky.

Julian instructed Simona to wait for him. He went from the cabin in search of his horse. He found it where he had left it. When he returned to the cabin he saw Simona hide something inside her sleeve as he entered in. Simona's hands were covered in mud. Julian knew what it was but he did not confront her about it.

"The horse is ready, let's go."

"Is it not too late?" Simona asked.

"We expose ourselves to greater danger if we spend the night here. We are leaving now."

Simona stood up from the bed and went outside with Julian. Julian mounted the horse first before he helped her up. He asked her which way they should go from there. Simona told him to first head south until they were out of the forest, then they'll have to head west a few miles to Vayler.

Julian reached underneath his belt and pulled out a compass given to him by Felix. He used it to know his way. From there till Vayler took about an hour of travel. When they arrived and were approaching the Northern City gate, an arrow was shot that landed a few feet in front of them. Julian brought the horse to a halt. Then a voice said.

"Do not come any further."

Julian and Simona watched on as they saw the city gates open and a young man dressed in light armor rode out to meet them. Two guards carrying torches rode behind the young man. Simona told Julian to be calm, she knew the man coming their way.

The man got to them and said,

"I am Hector, son of David and the lord Brigade Commander of the royal army of Konstuliana."

Hector noticed the lady behind Julian and said,

"Simona is that you?"

"Yes" she responded with a smile.

"The years escape me too quickly. You do not visit as often as you did a few years back. Who is this man with you, and why have you come at this late hour?"

"My name is Jul.." Julian began but was cut off by Hector.

"I was not speaking to you."

"He is a friend," Simona said. "He journeyed far from Philonia and I am showing him the glory of our nation."

Hector smiled.

"Vayler is a great part of the glory of this nation. You're both welcome, come in."

As they were making their way into the city Simona whispered to Julian warning him he should not let them know who he is because word of what he did to Neemus had spread to Vayler. He agreed.

They spent the night in Vayler. After David was informed of Simona's presence, he sent for her and gave her a room to stay in his castle. Simona made a request to David when she met with him. She requested that a place should also be prepared for Julian in his castle. David refused to grant her request. In response, she politely declined to stay in his castle and spent the night in the moderately managed inn with Julian. There was only one bed in the small room given to Julian in the Inn. He let Simona sleep on it while he sat by the door and rested his head on the wall.

All this happened on the day Antonius and Astra left for Argos and the day before Felix and the sailors departed for Philonia.

Chapter 19
Peter and the Twelfth

The morning was a grand splendor of sunlight, calm winds, and beautiful pastures. Antonius and Astra beheld all this as they made their way back from the mountains back to Petra. When they arrived at the great city, they were welcomed by the guards at the gate. A guard went ahead of them to inform Mitis and Eulalie of their return. It was about half-past seven that morning.

Antonius and Astra arrived at the castle and made their way in. Astra was whispering to Antonius, asking him how they were going to explain their being late to Mitis so he would not get angry. Antonius reassured her that all was going to be well. They passed the foyer and came into the first atrium where they met Eulalie and Mitis. They looked disappointed. Antonius went to Mitis, reached into his armor and handed Mitis the summary of the court proceedings.

"Where were you?" Mitis asked in a stern tone. He did not collect the scroll from Antonius.

"We were held back by the rain. We had to take shelter in the mountains."

Mitis took a breath. He glanced at his daughter and said,

"Antonius, I want to speak to you alone."

Mitis and Antonius went from that place to an upper room in the castle. Eulalie took Astra to get herself cleaned up. Some of Astra's maidservants prepared a hot bath for her. She cleaned herself and put on a new dress.

When Mitis and Antonius got to the upper room, Mitis took the scroll from him and put it away in an arrangement with scrolls containing similar cases.

"I want you to tell me what truly happened Antonius. I will not be angry with you," Mitis said.

"What I have told you is the truth. I will never forgive myself if I betrayed your trust. I am a guest in your household, a refugee in your kingdom. Even when I was king, though I loved Astra so much I restrained myself. I have longed to be with her for so long but I know how you felt about me then and I respected your opinions of me and only sent letters to her. This was the way we kept in touch in years past."

"I was aware you were sending her letters, though I did not like you then, I let her receive them because they made her happy. But I do not understand you Antonius, if you love her so much, why then have you not asked my permission to be betrothed to her?"

"Please forgive my response…I had many matters in my kingdom I had to attend to be-fore I was ready to take a queen. I saw what

Marcus went through with the Elders and I did not want anything to strain my relationship with Astra. I know what I had to do to restore power to the crown and surely I could not have given Astra the time she deserved if I had taken her as queen then. I was waiting for the appropriate time, when the power of the crown was more than that of the Elders. I love Astra with my whole being. Please understand I was constrained by my circumstance. As a king yourself you know the demands of a crown sometimes makes us overlook the ones we love for the sake of those who need us, our subjects."

Mitis sighed. He was not angry at Antonius. He understood the burdens of the crown. He knew it was harder for Antonius because he had five other men who had the same power as he. Mitis had heard of the things Antonius had done in Philonia to restore the power to the crown. He knew only a truly humble person would do what Antonius did. It was unheard of for a king to work alongside common men, or for a king to wear the attire of craftsmen, blacksmiths or even simple fishermen in order to get closer to his subjects. This was how it was in Philonia when Antonius was king. Even the nobles appreciated his rule because he reduced the portion of the people's income that went to the crown. Antonius did this to spite the Elders because they were in charge of the king's treasury.

Mitis stood up, went closer to Antonius and said,

"I trust you. Not as much as I trusted your father…but I trust you enough to leave you with my daughter through the night and believe that she is still pure in the morning. Do not break that trust."

"I promise you, I would never do anything to make you doubt me."

"Good…In a little while I will be going over to Hero's manor, care to accompany me?"

"Of course" Antonius said. "Hero's manor, is that not where Felix has taken to stay?"

"Yes it is. Go get cleaned, wear a new robe and meet me by the castle gate in an hour."

Antonius went to his chamber. After he cleaned himself and put on the new robes that were sent by Eulalie, he began making his way to the castle gate. When he was walking through the Hall of Mercy, which was in the center of the upper northern wing of the castle, he began to see birds flying past him. Immediately the purple rug he was walking on began to change and took the form of a purple stream. Antonius stopped. He looked down and saw his feet sinking into the rug, but he did not feel what he saw. He looked up and saw the sky, it was blanket white. Bright as a summer day but there was no sun to be found.

"An illusion" he thought. "But who or what?"

Around him, he could see much of his memories begin to pass him as streams of light. He could hear voices. He heard his father's voice, his mother's voice and the voices of many people he had met in his life. In his mind he had decided that none of what he saw was real. He closed his eyes and opened them. He found himself in the middle of the Hall of Mercy. From within his spirit he could sense the spirit of another coming towards him, but it did not cause a rise in his power. He turned back, there was no one there but when he faced forward Peter was standing in front of him.

"You're much different than I remember." Peter said

"It was you, wasn't it? You cast the illusion on me."

"Do you know who I am Antonius?"

Antonius took a good look at Peter. His memory was not stirred, so he answered Peter simply,

"I don't believe I've met you before."

"You can't remember…because you were far too young."

Peter stretched out his hand and placed it on Antonius's head.

"What are you doing?" Antonius asked.

"Be still," Peter said.

Peter revealed to Antonius the conversation he had with Calix after Calix found that Antonius was to become the Twelfth Rising Guardian. Antonius saw and heard it all. He heard his father instruct Peter not to reveal himself until when the fire in Antonius's heart begins to burn. In that moment as Antonius witnessed the conversation, he realized that his father knew that his time was soon running out.

When Peter drew his hand back and Antonius came back to his senses, he was speechless.

"Though you may not know me," Peter began, "I have known you for a long time. I have seen the struggles you went through after your father died. I have waited till this moment to reveal myself to you because I believe the fire in your heart has started burning. I believe you are ready."

"Ready for what?"

"I believe you are ready for me to reveal things to you that few will ever know. I believe you are ready to begin your journey as a Rising Guardian."

"I was ready a long time ago, when my circumstances were better. But now, I am a man who is yet to clear his name. I have known of my destiny since when I was a child. When I became king and read my father's diary, it was then I knew the truth. He was destined to be what I am." Antonius paused. Peter was silent.

Peter did not understand why Antonius was resistant.

"I am not naïve Peter." Antonius continued. "I know that being a Rising Guardian is nothing of ease. If it is true that I am the Twelfth

Rising Guardian, then you are the son of the Eleventh. I know how the Great King has ordained things. The first children of previous Rising Guardians are not let into Pacifica until they have instructed the next Rising Guardian according to the Noble Way and helped them understand the depths of their destiny."

"If you know all these things then you know why I am here."

"Yes I do, but why now?"

"You'll have to trust me," Peter said. "Five days is all I'll need to help you understand your destiny, show you the depths of your strength and help you understand why it is you who is suited to be the Rising Guardian and not your father."

"Fine, I'll grant you five days."

"Good," Peter said. Antonius passed by Peter and was about to leave his presence, then Peter said.

"You'll need to do one more thing for me…I cannot instruct you here."

"Then where shall be convenient for you."

"There is a mountain far North-East from here, close to the village of Kindlar. It should take you two days to get there. Travel by way of the river close to the forest of Ashburn. When you get to Kindlar, the people will welcome you and will show you the mountain. It would be best to leave tomorrow, for time is not on your side. But be warned, do not travel at night and do not travel alone."

"No I cannot leave tomorrow…" Antonius started as he turned to Peter, but no one was there. He was alone again in the middle of the Hall of Mercy.

Antonius went from there to the castle gate. There Mitis was waiting for him. Mitis could see that Antonius was not very attentive as he approached him.

"Is everything alright?" Mitis asked.

Antonius just realizing what had been said to him turned his attention to Mitis and responded.

"I'm fine."

A guard brought over the horse that Antonius had used on his journey to Argos. Antonius mounted the horse.

"Let's go," Mitis said as they began towards the manor. He led the way.

When they were about half a mile from the home of the old soldier, they saw the grand assembly of sailors outside the compound. Antonius spotted Felix and rode his way. Felix was directing the sailors to move what they had stocked up for the journey to particular wagons.

"Felix" Antonius called out. Felix saw them approaching and went to greet them.

"I am glad you could make it." Felix said

"When are you set to depart?" Antonius asked.

"Before the sun goes down our wagons shall leave this place."

"Remember the path I told you to follow," Antonius said.

"Yes I remember."

At that moment John Hero rode out and saw Mitis, Antonius and Felix conversing. He went to them, got down from his horse and got on one knee before Mitis.

"My king," he said with great joy in his voice. "I am here to serve you, what may I do for you?"

"Please stand John. I am here to see an old-friend off."

"Yes your majesty," John said. He greeted Antonius with a calm bow. They conversed for a little while. Then John invited them into his home for lunch. The daughters of John were delighted to see Antonius. John's sons were not present for they were attending to their daily matters at that time. Liana also took pleasure in Antonius's presence. She welcomed Mitis graciously. She instructed her servants to prepare a small banquet. It was done. After lunch, they all went out to see Felix depart with the sailors.

Thereafter Mitis and Antonius rode back to Petra. It was about half-past three in the afternoon.

The guards at the gate of the old soldier's manor saw a horse approaching them. They recognized the man on the horse. Jacob, the son of Jorad spotted the man from his station on the manor's wall.

"So he has returned," Jacob thought.

The guards stopped Julian at the gate of the manor and informed him that Felix and the sailors had already left. As they were telling him this, Gabriel the second son of John came out to welcome Julian.

"I am glad you have returned but if you have come for Felix, I am afraid to inform you he has departed with the sailors."

"The guards just informed me of this. But I am not here for that. I am here to see your father."

"Okay...alright. Come with me."

Gabriel led Julian to where his father was. They met John in an upper room in the house. The room had a simple design, the simplest room in the house. It was the study place of the old soldier. Upon seeing Julian, John was excited; he got up and went to him. Julian got on one knee before John and said,

"I am eternally grateful to you, for the hospitality you have shown me. But I cannot stay with you any longer."

"Of course you can. Just because Felix has departed does not mean you are no longer my guest."

"Please sir, respect my decision. Once again I thank you." Julian stood up. The old soldier embraced him. Julian turned to Gabriel, shook his hand and left.

As Julian was making his way out, Gabriel caught up with him at the gate and asked,

"If you are not staying here, where are you going to stay? Do you know the lands, how to get from place to place? It is not safe to be alone in a lot of these parts."

"Gabriel," Julian said calmly as he mounted his horse. "Don't worry about it. I'll be fine."

Julian rode off, leaving Hero's manor and heading towards the cabin he found in the woods. He stayed there for the time being. He wished to be alone. He liked the solitude, a place to resolve his thoughts. He felt it was a place close enough to Simona but far enough from Jeffery.

It was about six o'clock in the evening when he left Hero's manor.

Antonius arose that evening from a nap. It was about nine o'clock that evening. He cleaned himself, changed his clothes and sat upon his bed contemplating what to do. He knew what he was and he knew that his destiny had finally caught up with him. He had expected it earlier but he knew it would not happen on his terms. Antonius stood up and went to the window. The wind blowing into his room was warm, calm and soothing. Two people were on his mind at that moment, Marcus and Astra. He had already informed Mitis of his plan to leave the following morning while they were on their way back from Hero's manor. Mitis was not surprised. He told Antonius he expected Peter to take him earlier. He encouraged Antonius not to worry; Peter was someone he could trust.

Antonius did not know how he was going to explain his situation to his brother and to Astra. Remembering the words of Peter he thought if there was anyone that would be best to travel with to the mountain it would have to be Marcus. Antonius closed the window, left the room and went in search of Marcus. As he wandered through the castle halls he could hear music. He heard laughter, singing and a myriad of conversations. He followed the sounds and found himself standing outside the upper ball room of the castle. The room was three-fourths the size of the Grand Hall. As he walked in he recognized some of the faces. There was a great number of sons and daughters of nobles, Lords and Soldiers in the ballroom. Some knights were also at the gathering. Antonius made his way through the crowd. He felt a touch on his shoulder as he walked through the people. He turned and saw the daughters of John.

"Sandra, Sofia, ladies." He said with a smile.

"Antonius." Sandra said then she and Sofia curtseyed before Antonius.

He smiled and gave a bow.

"You seem to be enjoying yourselves."

"We are. It is a marvelous gathering that Astra has put together. Everyone is elated for spring is close and the festival this year is going to be outstanding," Sofia said.

"Indeed," added Sandra. "This year there are going to be performers coming all the way from Tynda. They shall be performing with us."

"That sounds delightful. What sort of performance will you be doing?" Antonius asked.

"We will be dancing. Astra will play the harp while we dance and she will sing during the second celebrations."

"That reminds me…do you know where I may find Astra?"

"She is here. I believe I saw her…there she is." Sofia said then pointed to where she had spotted Astra.

Antonius turned and saw the Jewel of Konstuliana sparkle as she danced and moved in harmony with the music that filled the room. The tambourines, drums flutes and harp all in perfect harmony moved the Jewel to dance, twirl and become as graceful as a dove gliding through the calm spring air. She was like a blooming flower, as beautiful as the blossom of the morning.

Antonius went to Astra and met her in the middle of a twirl. She stopped and saw him.

"Antonius" she said with great joy in her voice. He smiled. She embraced him.

"Come with me. There is something I must tell you but I cannot tell you here."

He took her and led her into the hallway.

"What is it?" Astra asked. "Is something wrong?" She noticed that he looked slightly distressed.

"I'm leaving tomorrow." He said.

"Leaving…why…where are you going?" She asked.

"I cannot say but I will return before the start of the spring festival."

"So you won't be gone for long?"

"No, only for a week. Your father told me after the festival, he shall return with me to Philonia to prove my innocence." Antonius noticed that Astra was still a bit sad so he said to her,

"I promise you, I'll be back before the festival. I'll be back before you perform the new piece you've written. The people will come to know what I have known for a while now, that you are as graceful with the harp as an eagle is with the summer wind."

Astra smiled.

"I'll hold you to that promise."

Antonius smiled. He pulled her closer to himself and kissed her. He could feel her smile as his lips met hers. He could also taste wine on her lips.

"Come we must return to the celebration." Astra said as she led him back into the upper ballroom.

A little while later Antonius found Marcus standing close to a window.

"Marcus," he called out to his brother.

"Antonius, this is a surprise. I have not seen you as often as should be."

"I have been busy with other matters Mitis assigned to me. But brother there is something serious I must discuss with you."

"Yes what is it?"

"I met a man today."

"Alright. What about this man makes you come to me in concern?"

"I felt in him a power similar in magnitude to Gammon but his spirit was pure."

"What is his name?"

"At first he did not reveal his name to me but he showed me his memories about encounters he had with our father. I believe the man is Peter, the very same our father wrote about in his diary."

"Yes, I know. I met him earlier. He was the one that made Xaria well again."

"How did he do this?"

"He found the source of Xaria's distress. It was the curse mark of Gammon. He and I entered Xaria's spirit, we found Gammon and he subdued him. He took Gammon from her spirit and sealed him in mine." Marcus revealed the mark on his shoulder to Antonius. "In time, after your innocence has been proven, I will go with Peter to find the Saints, so that this curse shall be removed permanently. So what has Peter told you that you need come see me?"

"He has requested five days with me, but he shall not instruct me here. He says I must travel north but I should not travel alone. That is why I am here. I need you to accompany me on my journey."

"Why are you making this journey?"

"I cannot say because this is not a fitting place to speak the reason."

"Alright, when do we leave?"

"Tomorrow morning."

"That seems sudden but I'll be ready by sunrise."

As they were still speaking, from across the room they heard the crashing of plates and the gasps of guests. Someone had fallen. Marcus and Antonius along with everyone in the room focused on the place where this had happened. A few people were in Antonius view of the incident but as they cleared and moved aside, he caught a glimpse of the dress of the person who had fallen. It was Astra's dress. Immediately he rushed to her. When he got to her, the son of a noble had helped her to her feet.

"Astra are you alright?" Antonius asked.

"No, not really." Astra replied. She looked dazed.

After she rose to her feet, he tried to help her make her way out of the ballroom but she was stumbling so he swept her off her feet and carried her to her chamber. Her maid servants followed them. When they got to her chamber Antonius entered carrying her, he gently let her on the bed. Astra opened her eyes and saw where she was. The candles in her room had been lit by her maid servants. She spotted Antonius about to leave, so she called to him, he turned.

"Stay, please." She pleaded in a soft voice.

Antonius went to her bedside and sat on the fine chair by her bed. On the lampstand by her bed sat a lyre. Antonius took particular notice of the lyre, the instrument brought memories that he loved. Astra noticed Antonius's interest in the instrument. She remembered that he had played it once during the days of the Knights Tournament ten years prior. When she found him playing it, he stopped and was hesitant to play for her then. Now she said to him,

"Do you remember how to play it?"

"Yes…"Antonius responded. "My mother was the one who taught me."

"Play something…please." Astra pleaded.

Antonius picked up the lyre and massaged the strings. He played a tune that was indicative of Philonia's origin. It was soft and mellow, sweet and somber. After he had finished playing, he laid the lyre back on the lampstand.

"That was beautiful." Astra said. Then she smiled and giggled. "I was speaking with a fair lady today; I believe her name was Xaria."

"She is my brother's wife. Yes, what did you discuss with her?"

"She is a very intelligent lady and she told me of many things, fascinating stories and truths, mostly about the affairs of the heart."

"And what of the affairs of the heart did she reveal to you?"

"She said that there is no love that exists that was destined. But can this be true? I mean, what about us?"

Antonius in the depths of his heart agreed with Xaria's words, to an extent. He had been taught by his mother how to discern true love from false desire. He noted Astra's question and concluded that she believed that their love was destined, so he chose his words carefully and responded saying,

"Our love is such that even the stars sing of us. We have known each other since you were five and I was nine. At that time we knew not what love was but that did not stop our hearts from aligning at the moment we met. Astra, if it is true our love is destined then I am glad that you are the one chosen for me."

Astra smiled. He leaned closer and kissed her.

"I love you," Astra said.

"I love you," Antonius said softly then he kissed her again. "Goodnight."

Antonius went to the outer part of her chamber and wrote a letter to her informing her of what he had told her earlier, in case she did not remember when morning graces the land. He gave one of her maid servants the letter and instructed her to give it to Astra in the morning.

Chapter 20
Journey to the Mountain

The morning was calm and cold. The dew was still set upon the leaves in the royal garden. Around this hour was when Antonius prepared himself for the journey. Eulalie had instructed him on the path to follow to the mountain. After he had informed her of his encounter with Peter, she was not surprised that Peter requested he leave immediately for the mountain. She told him to travel north-west until he makes it to the Novarian River, the river that cut through Konstuliana, starting from the high north and ending in the lower west side of Venduria. She told him to follow the river on the east side, and to continue north. She instructed him not to travel at night.

Antonius thanked the queen and made his way to the castle gate. There he saw Marcus and Xaria awaiting him. He was surprised to see Xaria. Xaria was clothed in an armor that was worn by female soldiers in Konstuliana. The armor comprised of a brass breast plate that curved with her body, arm guards extending from her wrist to her lower elbow. She also wore knee high boots made of fine leather. The horse given to her was one of Eulalie's horses. When Antonius got to Xaria and Marcus, a horse was brought for him by one of the guards. He mounted his horse and smiled at Xaria.

"Good to see you are doing well." Antonius said "Your complexion has returned. I was not expecting you to come with us."

"I insisted she come with us." Marcus said. "Do you think it's too dangerous for her?"

They started heading towards the north gate.

"No, she is well and she has her weapons with her. So I think she'll be of use in our company. Xaria are you fit to fight?"

"Yes" Xaria responded calmly. "If I may ask where are we going?"

"We are heading to a mountain north of here. We will first head northwest till we reach the Novarian River which is close to the forest of Ashburn. Then we shall continue north following the river's path. This is the way Eulalie says is best."

"How long do you think the journey should take?" Xaria asked.

"Two days, three at the most," Antonius responded.

Mitis and Eulalie stood at the high steps of the castle door as they watched them depart. The king and his queen felt a gentle breeze blow before they felt the presence of another beside them. Eulalie wondered why the air smelled like the mountain. Mitis smiled.

"You are not as discrete in the way you reveal your presence anymore," Mitis said.

Eulalie turned to see why her husband spoke. She saw Peter standing beside Mitis. She neither heard any footsteps nor seen anyone approaching them from behind.

"Perhaps I should try harder." Peter said

"Perhaps." Mitis said with a smile. "If you came looking for him, he just departed not too long ago."

"I am aware."

"Don't you think you should be going ahead of them? They will be expecting to see you at the mountain."

"I know." Peter turned his gaze to the east. He had been feeling something approaching the city for a while. But the presence of what he felt had stopped. It worried him a little. He would have gone on his own to know what it was if the circumstances were different but he stayed in the city for the time being, waiting for the approaching presence to reveal itself. The presence he felt approach was familiar to him, it was a presence he had felt many centuries back but his memory did not aid in identifying who it was that he sensed. All he knew of the presence he sensed was that the being was a child of a fallen guardian and had the spirit of a woman. Peter turned back to Mitis.

"I have no use for this." He said as he stretched out his hand and gave Mitis three gold coins. "Your daughter is very kind. I have to return to the tower. I can get a better view of the city from there."

"Is a good view of the city the only reason you are heading to the tower."

"No." Peter said then left. He chose to walk back down the hallway and take the long way to the Tower. He did this because he needed to think. And he thought of many things, most of all at the center of his thoughts was the fate of Antonius. There were things he knew he would have to reveal to Antonius and if Antonius was anything like Calix, he thought, Antonius was not going to take his message well. He arrived at the tower and set his eyes northwest, in the direction Antonius, Marcus and Xaria had gone. The winds picked up and the clouds rolled in. It was going to be an overcast spring morning.

The grass was greener closer to the Novarian River. Antonius noticed this. They arrived on the eastern side of the forest Ashburn close to where Antonius and Mitis had encountered the wolf-men four years back. Antonius did not like the feeling he was getting remembering the event. They continued until they saw the river. The river flowed south with great speed. The trees around the rivers were so tall it seemed as though they touched the clouds. Their leaves were a heavenly green, lush in splendor and majestic to behold. Xaria admired the scenery as Antonius and Marcus took their horses closer to the river for a drink. After the horses had drunk, Antonius, Marcus and Xaria refreshed themselves.

Four hours had passed since they departed Petra. Antonius could tell because the noon day sun was high above the earth. They continued heading north on the east side of the river until they met the evening sun. The sun set far out in the west above the trees. It was at this hour Antonius suggested they stop and set up camp for the night.

They set up camp close to the river bank. The scenery was bountiful with tall trees, rich green grass and a few collection of murky wet soil closer to the river. After they had secured their horses they sat together, built a fire, sang-songs and told stories of the old days. Xaria sang a song with Marcus, a song known to be sang by two people who had a united heart. Antonius enjoyed their song and smiled as he saw the love they had for each other blossomed with every word sang. Antonius sat across from them as they sang. When they finished their little duet they embraced.

"That was beautiful," Antonius said.

"Forgive me brother we did not mean to leave you out. Let us sing a song from our childhood, Perhaps a hymn. Xaria you are familiar with "The Rose" by Hayadus."

"All who know the freedom of love know the words of that song," Xaria said.

"Then sing with us," Marcus said.

Together once again they sang and they sang with great joy in their hearts, their voices soft synchronous and harmonious. As they still sang Antonius could feel something approaching them fast not from the ground but from above. He stopped singing, stood up and watched the night sky. His gaze did not move from a particular area for from this area he sensed something. Though he could not see it, he felt it was the cause of the rise in power he felt in his spirit. Marcus and Xaria stopped singing and shifted their eyes to where Antonius had focused his attention.

"What's the matter Antonius?" Marcus asked.

Antonius did not respond but kept still with his hand ready to unsheathe his sword. Marcus and Xaria stood up as well and took up arms. A few seconds passed before Antonius began to feel the rise in power in his spirit subside. He knew the danger he sensed had moved on.

"I thought I saw something," Antonius said. "It was far above the clouds."

"Maybe it was a bird," Xaria said.

"No, I don't think so," Antonius said.

"We should rest. The day's journey has weighed hard on us," Marcus said.

The next morning they continued on their way following the river northwards. When they had journeyed over a hundred and fifteen miles from dawn till the sunset, stopping twice only to replenish themselves, they stopped to set up camp as the sun bid farewell to the day and the night arrived. Antonius got the fire started, Xaria secured the horses and Marcus went in search of food. Xaria followed after Marcus after she had secured the horses. After about an hour they returned with an Antelope, which Marcus had hurled across his shoulders. Antonius brought out a small knife and skinned the animal. He washed the blood off the hide and saved it. Marcus observed Antonius as he was doing this and asked.

"What are you doing?"

"I am saving the hide," Antonius answered.

"We don't need it."

"Yes, we may not need it but perhaps there are people we may encounter that we could sell this too. We have to repay Mitis for his kindness."

"We have to focus on the journey. We can't wander off hoping to sell it."

Antonius continued setting up the hide to dry.

"Antonius," Marcus said. "This is not the time to worry about such things? If you want to sell it, fine. But do not worry so much about repaying Mitis now. When your innocence is proven and you are king again then you may pay him back," Marcus said to reassure Antonius and get him focused on the journey.

"Come now brother, put the hide away and let us eat."

After they had eaten and replenished themselves, Xaria felt tired and slept with her head upon Marcus's lap. Antonius was seated facing Marcus. The fire he built flared between them. Antonius stared into the flames. He was not aware he had been doing this for the half hour that passed. Marcus had been watching him and he wondered about the blank stare on his brother's face.

"Antonius," Marcus called out.

Antonius looked up from the fire, his face had no expression.

"Is something wrong?" Marcus asked.

"No," Antonius responded and continued staring into the fire.

"You are good at many things brother but lying is not one of them," Marcus said. "Whatever worries you, you can confide in me."

"I am not worried, I am just concerned. I am concerned about the state of things…Why now? Why would Peter choose now?"

"I do not know the answer to that question but what I can tell you is this: be quick to listen but slow to speak. Remember the destiny you now bear was once father's." Antonius turned his attention from the flame to Marcus. "Yes Antonius I was able to decipher father's messages in his diary. I don't think I have ever heard or read of the destiny of becoming a Rising Guardian passed on to the next generation but it seems this is our situation. So Antonius the trials you are about to undertake father has gone through and persevered. So have courage, do not stumble, stand strong and all will go well for you."

Marcus's words reassured Antonius's spirit. He smiled.

"Thanks brother. My spirit is a bit more at ease now." Antonius said. Then he began to think not of his destiny but of his kingdom.

"What about Philonia?" He asked Marcus. "We still have a responsibility to the fate of our nation."

"You have a responsibility to the fate of our nation. I gave you the crown. You are king." Marcus smiled. "The king's diary is written by every king in Philonia meant only for the eyes of the king. Father had one, and I had one. Did you ever read my diary Antonius?"

"Yes, you wrote a lot about how the elder's frustrated you. How they hindered the progress of our kingdom for their own personal interests."

"Yes I wrote of those things but I also wrote of someone who is very important to me and plans that concern them."

"You also wrote of Xaria. It was from your diary that I learnt that she longed to see her sisters." Antonius was saying then paused. He looked sad. "After I heard of your accident at sea, I wrote a letter telling her sisters of you and Xaria's passing. They came to Philonia the summer of your death and a memorial service was held in honor of you and Xaria. The nation wept at your passing, even some of the elders."

"Well Xaria and I are alive and soon days of celebration will follow after all that needs to be done is done. You will begin your journey as the Twelfth Rising Guardian. We will return to Philonia after the spring festival and clear your name. Once you are king again, I will take Xaria to see her sisters. Thereafter as Peter has promised, we will find the island of the Saints so that this curse mark shall be removed. I will not be able to fulfill all these things as king. Philonia is a kingdom that needs great leadership, we are after all the youngest of the seven kingdoms…Don't worry brother, The Great King will grant favor to our endeavors. So let us rest for we have a long Journey ahead of us tomorrow."

The night went by fast. Antonius arose to a touch on his shoulder. He opened his eyes and beheld Xaria. She was very close to his face.

"Wake up Antonius," Xaria said.

Antonius could smell apples and honey on her breath. Xaria drew back once Antonius fully opened his eyes. She gave him an apple.

"Eat, we'll be leaving very soon," She said.

She took his hand and helped him up.

"Where's Marcus?" Antonius asked.

"He went to feed the horses. He'll be back soon."

A minute passed and Marcus returned with the horses.

"Antonius you are finally awake," Marcus said as he brought Antonius's horse to him. "Here you go brother."

Xaria mounted her horse and started going on a little bit ahead of them. The brothers were conversing as Marcus took his time to mount his horse. Xaria turned around and saw them taking their time.

"What are both of you waiting for? The river keeps widening as we head north, so the mountain must be close." Xaria said with slight excitement in her voice.

"She is a lot livelier this morning," Antonius said.

"It must be the honey," Marcus said.

From there they continued north, following the path of the river, keeping close to it and admiring the beauty of the lands they passed. Around noon Antonius began to feel hungry. His stomach growled so loud that Marcus and Xaria heard it. Xaria giggled. She reached into a leather bag strapped to the side of her horse, brought out an apple and tossed it to Antonius. He caught it, thanked her and ate.

The gentle wind made the length of the journey bearable. When the early evening hours came, minutes before sunset, they stopped and went to the river for a drink.

"How far do you think the mountain is from here?" Marcus asked.

"I do not know but we are doing as Peter said," Antonius replied.

"Then perhaps we must keep heading north until we see the mountain," Xaria said. "Don't worry I believe we'll get there soon."

They rested by the river for about half an hour. The beauty of the area was breath-taking. The lands were untouched and flourishing with wildlife. They saw deer emerge from the forest on the other side of the river bank. The sound of bird songs filled the area. All they saw was a marvel to behold, especially the sunset through the trees when they set their eyes west.

Though the scene was moderately calm Antonius could not shake the feeling that they weren't safe. He felt that they were being watched.

"I think it's time we continue on our way." Antonius said.

"I think it's best we stay here and set up camp for the night," Marcus said.

After he spoke they heard the leaves among the shrubs behind them rustle. Then it went silent again.

"Did you see that?" Xaria said in low voice.

"See what?" Marcus asked.

"I saw something move between the bushes," she said.

"It's probably just a deer," Marcus said.

"It was no deer," Antonius said.

He and Xaria had their eyes fixed on the same spot in between the shrubs. Marcus was not certain where the sound had come from but once he saw that Xaria readied an arrow in her bow, he readied himself as well. Antonius stood up as Xaria drew back her arrow against her bow.

For that short moment silence reigned over the area. It was uncomfortable for them. Then Antonius said, "There is no need to keep hidden. We mean you no harm. Come out now."

After he spoke there was movement among the shrubs. Then someone stepped out. It was a man who was a little taller than Antonius. He had a spear in his right hand and a wooden shield in his left. He was cloth in an indigenous attire that was worn by a tribe that were known to be a nomadic tribe in the ages before but rumors from traveling merchants had suggested that the tribe had settled somewhere around the northern mountains of Konstuliana. The attire comprised of trousers made of moose hide and a sleeveless vest that seemed to be made out of white fur from an animal that inhabited the mountains around the tribe.

The man came out curiously but with high caution as he approached them. He sought to know who these people were. The man did understand what Antonius said to an extent but Antonius did not know what to expect from this strangely dressed stranger. The man approached Antonius. He looked over at Xaria who was still armed with her arrow pointed at him. Antonius turned to Xaria.

"Lower your bow," he said.

She did as he said.

Antonius noticed the man was looking at him with particular curiosity to the point that Antonius began to feel uncomfortable. Then the man spoke, saying but one word, a name and a question.

"Calix?"

Antonius, Marcus and Xaria were astonished. Antonius was speechless for he did not know how to process the fact that a young man about his age from a secluded tribe would know his father's name.

"How do you know that name?" Marcus asked as he made his way closer to the man. He approached him rather aggressively, angry almost.

"Calix." The man said again. "He is the one who saved the tribe. He and a man, name who was Peter saved the tribe from the beasts that came from the west. They saved my father. Are you he?" The man asked Antonius again then he turned to Marcus. "Or is it you, both of you look like him. He never spoke of a brother."

"No, we are his sons." Marcus replied.

After Marcus had declared this to the man about their relation to Calix, the man became relieved and a smile appeared on his face. He bowed before Antonius and Marcus.

"Great Princes" the man said. "My name is Ivo and I am honored to meet you. If I may be of service to you, please speak and I shall do."

Antonius helped the man back to his feet and said,

"Thank you for your reverence but we are in need of help getting somewhere. We were hoping you could tell us how to get to the village of Kindlar."

"That is my home. Of course I can take you there. Come with me, I show you the way."

The man led them east through swamp lands, valleys and small hills until they came to a cave. The entrance of the cave was fifteen feet tall. Antonius was not particularly thrilled to go into the cave. He asked Ivo if there was another way to get to the village but Ivo said that the cave was the shortest path to the village. He explained to Antonius that the cave was like a tunnel, though at first Antonius did not see it immediately he trusted Ivo and they continued on their way. The exit of the cave led them into a valley with a small stream that flowed beneath their feet. Marcus was taken by the size of the mountains around them. In the distance they could hear singing and chatter. They also saw smoke rising from brightly lit points surrounded by stone-mud houses. Ivo continued on towards the stone-mud houses. Antonius, Marcus and Xaria followed him. Marcus still was not fully supportive of the idea of following a stranger, even if that stranger knew their father but Antonius was eager to find the mountain before the dawn of the next day. He had decided that following Ivo was a progressive step in their journey.

As they approached the village the sound of songs got louder. Ivo started moving quickly. Antonius, Marcus and Xaria kept pace on their horses. Soon enough they entered the village with Ivo still dashing towards the celebratory songs.

"Why is he in a hurry?" Marcus asked.

"I guess we are soon about to find out." Xaria said as they saw Ivo push through the crowd and stop in front of an elderly man. Ivo bent low to the floor and apologized to the man saying.

"Father please, forgive my lateness. I stumbled across some strangers."

During this moment the celebration had died down a bit and the people made way as Antonius, Marcus and Xaria made their way to the old man. The old man was seated outside the center hut of the village. He had a cane in his right hand. When he saw Antonius and Marcus coming his way, he took hold of his cane with both hands and tried to stand up. Ivo saw this and helped him up immediately.

"No I can stand by myself," the man said to his son. Then he started walking to Antonius who had stopped just a few feet in front of him. Antonius saw the wonder in the man's eyes. The man looked as if he had just seen a ghost.

Antonius saw the old man was about to cry. Antonius out of respect got down from his horse and approached the old man. Antonius could hear whispers among the people of the village. He heard his father's name five times among the mumbles.

The man almost fell when he approached Antonius. Antonius caught him and helped him stand up straight.

"Calix" the man said with a tear almost escaping his eye.

"No I am his son, Antonius and this is my brother, Marcus and his wife, Xaria."

"His son...sons?" the old man smiled. He wiped his eye then he welcomed them into his home. The celebration continued outside.

"I am Dizu, chief of this village and fourth son of the late great Damyn. What brings the sons of Calix to my village?"

"We have come in search of a mountain," Antonius said.

"Mountain?" Dizu said "Go outside look around you. We are surrounded by mountains."

"We are looking for the mountain where Peter lives." Marcus said. "Do you know how to get there?"

Dizu was silent for a moment. He told one of his helper to go get his son. Ivo entered and went to his father. Dizu instructed Ivo to take Antonius, Marcus and Xaria's horses to the east side of the village. He instructed him to wait there.

"I can take you to the mountain."

"Can you take us there now?" Marcus asked.

"Marcus, please be a little more considerate." Xaria said "If it's too much of a burden for you to show us the way. Just tell us the path to follow and we will find our way there."

"No it's alright." Dizu said as he took hold of his cane and struggled to get up. "I'll show you the way. Follow me."

Dizu led them from his home to the east side of the village where Ivo was waiting with their horses. Ivo followed his father as they led Antonius, Marcus and Xaria towards the mountain of Peter. They continued four miles east till they came to a hill. Ivo and Dizu stood at the base of the hill. Dizu pointed up towards the top of the hill.

"Go up there" He told Antonius. "You should be able to see the mountain from up there."

"There are other mountains around the area. How would I know which one is the mountain of Peter?"

"You will know the mountain when you see it," Dizu said.

Antonius, Marcus and Xaria ascended the hill and when they got to the top they beheld the glory of the mountain. In the distance they saw it. The presence of the moonlight glorified the mountain even more. The surrounding mountains were like hills compared to the mountain of Peter. It was a wonder to them why they had not seen the mountain from the distance. It then dawned on them that they had been seeing the tip of the mountain behind surrounding mountains but now atop that hill they saw the rest of it. And with three words Antonius said what he, Marcus and Xaria were thinking,

"There it is."

Chapter 21
The Arrival of Titus

Titus could feel it. Something about this morning was not right. He smiled for a short moment and wanted to be happy but he could not because he saw the distress on Elana's face. He went over to her as she brushed her hair. They were preparing to leave Bismotal on that early morning. He sat by her, held her hands and looked into her eyes.

"Your smile is the light of my morning. Tell me what I must do to see that light."

Elana did not respond, she got up and walked calmly out of the room and to the enclosed carriage that was going to take them to Petra. Because Titus loved her, he was patient with her. When he got to the carriage and met her, he tried again.

"Please Elana, let me help. I am here for you. I love you."

As he was saying this to her she was looking out her side of the carriage. When he revealed that he loved her, she sighed, a sigh she felt in the center of her being because she knew what was coming. She knew what she had orchestrated and the danger that had set itself ahead of them. She turned to Titus and smiled but she did not say anything.

They set off on their way, following the Gylin Road which was a straight cut path from Bismotal to Petra. After they had journeyed for about thirty three minutes Titus heard the man who controlled their carriage scream out. The scream was so terrifying that Titus's hands began to shake. Titus's yelled out asking what all the commotion was about. As he continued to listen he heard more screams come from outside. He started sinking into his seat. He dared not stick his head out to see what was causing the men to scream. But from the growls he heard, he knew it was some kind of beast. He turned to Elana but she had disappeared. He began to panic. His breathing increased and his palms were very sweaty. In a short moment after, there was silence after he heard a last cry of pain from one of the guards behind him. He heard loud and slow steps. They were getting louder. The shadow of the creature that was approaching was cast upon the carriage. He saw its size was terrified. The creature took hold of the carriage door and pulled it out of its hinges. Titus saw it; he had read of it but never thought that he would encounter a wolf-man. He kept still as the creature came closer, then it said in a growling voice,

"Son of Calix!"

Titus gasped. He turned and tried to escape from the other side of the carriage but the creature took hold of his leg and pulled him out from its side. Titus rolled on the dirt road. The stones on the road ruined his outer garment. He took off and started running. But he could not run far because he saw another one of them standing in his path. The wolf-man that had pulled him out commanded him to remove his garment. He stripped down till he was naked before them. Another wolf-man came and took his clothes. The one that had commanded him to strip approached him slowly. When it was close to Titus, it stood on two feet to show Titus its great statue. Titus was shaking. He could feel that this creature that stood before him hated him but he did not know why. The wolf-man growled and struck Titus with its back hand. Titus was thrown a few feet back. He fell and ate dirt. He tried to get up but another wolf-man rushed and kicked him while he was still down. They struck him three more times, slashes from their claws marked his back. Then they heard a voice yell for them to stop. They knew who commanded them. They turned and saw Elana in her bird-transformation, standing on top of the carriage they pulled Titus from. Her feathers were not scaly as when she was flying from Petra to the domain of the wolf-men in the high north lands in Konstuliana.

"I commanded you to take only his clothes from him and nothing else. You have defied me."

The wolf-men stepped away from his body. Elana flew to Titus and landed close to him. As she approached him, he opened his eyes. His vision was blurred and he could not tell that the person approaching was Elana.

"Be still Titus." Elana said "It's alright."

She laid her hand on his head and he slept off. She then laid her hand on some of his wounds and healed them.

"Why are you helping him?" One of the Wolf-man said in a high and angered tone.

Elana after she had healed parts of Titus got up, turned to the wolf-man and said,

"My vengeance will be more complete with him alive." Then she looked up. "You've come just in time."

Two guiles landed before her and bowed. She commanded them to take Titus back to Noble City. Then she instructed the guiles and the wolf-men,

"I want you to take the city. Do not destroy it but bring it under your command. Do not kill excessively but enough to instate your dominion. Tell those who are waiting in Snake Valley that this is what I have commanded." She plucked out one of her feathers. "Take this feather and show it to them if they do not believe you. I have matters to attend to in Petra. In two days I will join you."

"One more thing," Elana said "Under no circumstance are you to harm him."

They left that place to do as she commanded. The guiles lifted Titus and flew towards Noble City with him. When they had left the place Elana transformed back to her human form and sang to herself. She sang softly until she took on the image of Titus. She put on his clothes, mounted one of the horses that was attached to the carriage and started towards Petra.

Mitis was clothed and ready to begin his daily duties. He left his chamber and went to the queen's chamber. He made his way in and found Eulalie still in bed. He went to her side but she was not sleeping, she was laying there with her eyes open. They were set on the window as the morning sun peaked in. She turned to him when she saw him approach her.

"Forgive me my love. I did not hear you come in."

"That's fine. Is everything alright?" Mitis asked as he sat by her as she sat up.

"You always seem to know when something bothers me."

"That is because I care and because I care, I listen. Have I ever not known when you were worried?" Mitis said with a smile. "So tell me, what bothers you?"

"I believe I had a vision. One of those visions," Eulalie said. Mitis understood what she meant by "those." Most of the time when visions were given to her, she could clearly discern what they meant but the vision she just had was hard to decipher. She had such visions rarely but when they occurred she knew something bad was going to happen.

"What did you see in the vision this time?"

"I saw a white lion and a blue bird. In the vision the lion and the blue bird were friends."

"Friends?"

"Yes, I was confused as well but then I saw darkness surround the blue bird and it pulled it away from the lion. The lion chased after the blue bird to save it but the darkness was too strong for it and it surrounded the lion and crushed it."

"I...have no idea what that could mean?" Mitis said then he stood up and thought for a while. He walked towards the window then he turned back with an answer. "Perhaps the white lion in the vision refers to Venduria. The white lion is the beast on their banner. The blue bird may be Napel. One of the animals on the crest of the royal house is the Pascuset bird, and it is blue. To make matters even better both nations are allies. One of the daughters of a prominent noble in Venduria married the prince of Napel two years ago, so I know they are in good terms."

Eulalie stood up from bed.

"What of the darkness?" she said with concern in her voice.

"Perhaps it could mean war, maybe not between the two nations but from an outsider. Should we send word to them to warn them?"

"I don't think this vision has to do with the well-being of nations," Eulalie said.

"Then what do we do since we know nothing about what it means?" Mitis asked.

"We wait. Maybe things will begin to fall into place and we will eventually learn more about what the vision means."

"Alright, that seems reasonable." Mitis said

After he spoke they heard commotion outside the queen's chamber, then there was a knock. Mitis went to the outer room of the chamber and answered the door.

The guards upon seeing Mitis bowed and one of them said,

"My king, forgive us for coming to meet you here but he has come earlier than we expected."

"He?"

"Titus, your majesty, the king of Philonia, the guards on the east gate spotted him not to long ago."

"What?!...Alright go and inform Jeffery and tell him to welcome Titus and those he came with."

"Your majesty the king came alone."

"What? Why would anyone travel alone? The roads are very dangerous and the journey from Noble city to here is quite long. Alright I will be down soon." After the guard left Mitis returned to Eulalie and informed her of Titus's arrival. Eulalie was surprised that he had arrived that early. Mitis told her to get ready, while he goes to welcome the king of Philonia.

Jeffery was informed by the guards and immediately left his training with the younger knights. Neemus also caught word of why Jeffery left the training session suddenly. He went with him and left Chris in command of the Knight's quarter. Jeffery put on his finest light armor, and so did Neemus before they went out to meet *Titus*. They waited just outside the castle doors. Soon Mitis made his way out to join them. The castle gate slowly open as the man they came to see slowly strode in on his brown stallion. The second Mitis saw *Titus* he thought that his resemblance to Calix was even more prominent than Antonius's resemblance. Jeffery noted what Mitis had commented on before.

"He came alone?" Jeffery said.

"It seems so," Neemus said.

"Do not bring this up when he meets us." Mitis said, "I don't want him to feel unwelcomed by us in anyway. From what I have heard, this son of Calix is the most impatient."

"If he is more impatient than Marcus, then I should not be held responsible if I act out of hand if he speaks ill to me." Jeffery said, "King or not, the boy should know his place. Look at how arrogantly he walks to us, as if he has won many battles, I bet you he has not even been in one."

"Jeffery, enough." Mitis commanded "He has the power to start a war against us. I will not go to war against Philonia."

Jeffery took a breath and held his peace. *Titus* walked up to them and met them in front of those high castle doors. With a smile and an extended hand reaching out to him, Mitis welcomed *Titus*. *Titus* shook his hand. At the touch of *Titus's* hand, Mitis felt a dreadful chill run up his hand, down his spine and to his feet. It was horrifying. The smile on his face faded away. Neemus and Jeffery gave a slight bow.

"Thanks for the warm welcome Mitis, it is Mitis right?" *Titus* asked with a smile.

"Yes, yes it is. Come with me, I'll show you around," Mitis said. His voice was rough for a moment when he began speaking. Mitis took *Titus* into the castle and they began walking through the corridors. As they walked they conversed. Mitis began by saying,

"We did not expect you to arrive this early. Things were planned for your arrival today but at high noon. A big feast was planned for that hour."

"We can still have the feast. And I can join you for breakfast beforehand," *Titus* said with a smile.

"As it soothes you, so shall it be done. You are my guest." Mitis said. "I must say among you and your brothers, you bare the most striking resemblance to your father. It is a shame you did not know him that well. Your father was kind and noble. A man I hope you are or will become."

"Only time can decide that," *Titus* said.

"That is not true. Time bares no hold on what we should strive to be."

"Mitis, but it does. Who can say what events will occur in the future, and how they will shape our will. No man, no matter how good can hold on to his character when the flames of trial become unbearable. Noble men are not exempt from the reach of temptation. And like the rest of us normal people they can fall. For if the Guardians fell, what makes noble men special that they cannot be taken to the temptations that visit them."

Mitis was shocked to hear *Titus* speak in such a way. *Titus* spoke as though he had lived a thousand years and only seen the cruelty of the world, the wickedness of men and nothing more. As if he had seen nothing good, neither of the privilege of freedom or the blessing of love, the touch of kindness or the wonder of new life. Though *Titus* did not speak in a spiteful tone, his message still sounded as though he hated the world.

They were still walking and after *Titus* had finished speaking they stopped. They were standing in a hallway with tall windows behind Mitis. The morning sun was blaring down from behind him. The hallway was well lit. A purple rug ran underneath their feet. The tapestry on the wall facing the window stretched across the hallway. On it was a story and Mitis knew that story. Mitis laid his eyes on the tapestry and asked Titus to turn and see it.

"This castle is over two thousand years old, yet it still stands. This tapestry is older than the castle. Do you know the story that is told on this tapestry?"

Elana was very aware of the events that were displayed on the tapestry and she knew more than what had been recorded in the history books. But she also knew of the legends and stories that had been passed down over generations. So in the form and voice of Titus she limited the wealth of her answer to what she knew most people knew.

"The story displayed here is of the man they called the Father of Freedom, Hayadus."

"You are correct. This tapestry was made by his eldest daughter, Liana. It is said that it took her and two of her maid servants twelve years to complete. Look closely here." Mitis said as he pointed to a portion in the tapestry that displayed soldiers rushing into battle against an army of what looked like guiles and men who had hybrid bodies with beasts of different kinds. "These soldiers, these here that are rushing into battle are noble men. They are noble not because of their status but because the virtue they are fighting to achieve is priceless. These soldiers all believed in the reality of Hayadus's dream, the dream of a world where men could be free from the rule of the accursed ones. Where kings and queens would be kind to their subjects, not treat them like cattle, slaughtering them by the millions as the wicked emperor Nextyn did. After the war it became known that Nextyn was accursed himself. He made a deal with Vain, the elder brother of Sirius. That was how he became powerful and conquered the earth. But he was foolish to underestimate the passion in Hayadus's heart." Mitis walked over to another scene on the tapestry that depicted a group of people holding up a floating crown towards a man who held his hand out as if he did not want to accept the crown. Mitis continued, "After the great victory, the people sought to make him king but he refused and said he'll be as a friend to them. He became like an advisor to the people, a senator of sort. With his brothers, he made laws that he did not force upon the people but instructed them, if they wanted lasting peace across the land they should follow these laws. The people took to obey the laws he set up quickly, they were more lenient than those Nextyn had set in place. Hayadus, though hopeful as he was, was a realistic thinker and having studied conflicts of the past, he knew to leave an empire encompassing the entire world to the first of his twelve children might arouse some jealously among his younger children. So two years before he died, he divided his empire into twelve nations, knowing where a majority of the resources such as gold, silver, brass and spices were, he made it so that certain nations lacked what others had in surplus. This way, the nations would have to reason among themselves if they wished to get what they wanted from each other. After his death, some of his children united their kingdoms. Konrad, Hayadus's eldest convinced Sturn and Liana to join him and they did. That is how Konstuliana came to be. The eldest siblings always looked out for their younger siblings. There was a time when Veniam and Duria tried to join their armies to take land from Hayadus's youngest, Philonia. Konrad made sure they did not dare enter the land. As punishment they took lands from Veniam and Duria and gave to Philonia. A few years later Veniam and Duria united their kingdoms. That is how the kingdom of Venduria came to be."

"Is there a point to this story?" *Titus* asked

Mitis sighed and with a smile responded. "Titus, now you are king, your people will look to you not only for guidance but also for protection. When I became king of this nation I did not know if the people would trust me but they did because Hermes had turned on them, he lost their trust. So they'd rather have a foreign king who looks out for them than a king with their own blood who abandons them. And they began trusting your father and me, well before I was made king by your father. We would not have been able to win the war if Kineta had not convinced the knights not to get involved."

"Who is Kineta?" Titus asked.

"She was my sister. She passed away twelve years ago. If not for her I don't think your father would have been able to unseat Hermes as king. She has done a lot for this kingdom and also for me." Mitis clenched his fist. "Oh Guardians' day, I miss her." He paused for a second. He almost wept but he kept his composure. Titus folded his arms and kept quiet.

Mitis took a breath and said,

"I'm sorry you had to see that. Come, join us for breakfast."

They left and went to the upper dining room. The room was a lot smaller than the banqueting hall. It was a comfortable size for the royal family. When Mitis and *Titus* arrived at the room, the servants were setting down the freshly baked bread that they had just finished preparing for the royal family. The servants set down all the food and left the room. Mitis invited *Titus* to seat on his right. *Titus* complied and sat next to Mitis. At the moment Mitis took his seat, Eulalie walked in. There was laughter coming from down the hall behind her and footsteps approaching fast. Galen ran passed her, because he was being chased by Astra. He went and ran behind his father. He was laughing. Astra stopped chasing him when she noticed the man on her father's right. Mitis laughed as he told Galen to welcome *Titus*. Mitis then stood up and said,

"Eulalie, Astra come and welcome our guest, Titus, the new king of Philonia."

Titus did not stand but he calmly nodded and said,

"Please Mitis there is no need. Ladies please take your seats," he said.

Eulalie and Astra approached cautiously. Eulalie sensed something wrong, the longer she stared at *Titus*, the more the vision of the white lion and the blue bird flashed in her mind. She diverted her eyes from him and went and to take her place at the other end of the table. Galen greeted *Titus* kindly and sat at his father's left hand. Astra was concerned because this was her first time seeing *Titus*. Her father had informed them that *Titus* would be arriving on that day but Astra did not expect to see him joining them for breakfast. She took her place beside her brother and they had breakfast together. Eulalie felt very uncomfortable throughout but she held her peace and tried to keep calm. She was quiet for the most part and spoke only when Mitis or *Titus* asked her a question. She ate light and left immediately she was done. She thanked Mitis and curtsied towards *Titus* before she left.

"Do you think she's alright?" *Titus* asked.

"I don't know. She only acts this way when she is worried about something." Mitis said.

"Do you know what may be worrying her?" *Titus* asked.

Mitis had a feeling Eulalie's strange behavior might have been related to the vision she had earlier. He was not certain of this but the thought occupied his mind. Only he, Calix, Peter, Antonius and a few close friends of the royal family knew that Eulalie on occasion had visions. Mitis did not want to tell *Titus* just yet of Eulalie's gift, so he replied Titus saying,

"I'm not sure."

Throughout breakfast Galen was most vocal. He spoke about many things telling *Titus* of his studies. *Titus* let him speak. Specifically Galen remembered what his father had informed him and everyone in Petra prior to *Titus's* visit. No one was to speak of Antonius. The guards, nobles and all had been informed that as long as *Titus* was in the kingdom, Antonius's name or whereabouts were not to be mentioned. Mitis also made certain that the prisoners from Philonia who had chosen to stay in make Petra did not leave the communal houses while *Titus* was in the city. But in a moment of excitement while Galen was talking about being taught to string a bow, he mentioned that his mom first showed him and Antonius helped him perfect the craft. At the mention of Antonius name, Mitis turned his eyes to *Titus*. Titus asked,

"How long ago was that?" *Titus* asked

"About four years." Galen replied. Then he caught a look from his father he did not like but he understood what it meant. He did not speak much after that.

Later that Afternoon, Mitis took *Titus* to the Knight's quarter to watch the knight's training session. When they walked passed the tall doors into the quarter the knights bowed as the kings walked by. They made their way into the inner courts and into the training ground. The training ground was located around an open area in the castle. Sometimes the area had been called the Knights wing.

There were seven training squares. Each of different sizes, the biggest was where Jeffery usually trained fast rising knights. When Mitis and Titus made their way closer to the main training square, the talking around them began to die down. Jeffery stopped his session with the knight in training and turned to see what caused the sudden silence. Even the other knights in the other squares had stopped fighting. When Jeffery saw *Titus* standing right outside his square he turned towards him and said,

"You are impressed by what you see, aren't you?" Jeffery said. Some knights chuckled.

"Hardly," *Titus* said.

Mitis interjected before anymore more words were exchanged between the two.

"I was showing Titus around and I wanted to show him a great part of the pride of this nation, The Knights of Konstuliana. I…"

"I'd like to test my strength against you." *Titus* said. There was an uncomfortable silence. Mitis put his hand on *Titus* shoulder, trying to advise him against fighting Jeffery but at the moment his hand touched Titus's shoulder a quick flash of the scene of the War of the Fathers appeared into this mind. But Elana knowing that this happened shrugged off Mitis's hand.

"With your permission my king, I will grant his request." Jeffery said to Mitis.

"Very well," Mitis said.

Titus stepped into the square. But Elana knew what she was doing. She knew that even though she was weakened because she had taken the form of Titus, she could still make short work of Jeffery. Her purpose for fighting was not to show her skill but to get information from Jeffery.

Titus requested beforehand that they fight without swords. Jeffery after the request was made thought it would be more fitting so he could get a chance to humble the new king. But

Elana knew that in order for her to get the information from Jeffery, they were going to have to get in close contact, and using swords would delay the chances of that happening. So she stood in the form of Titus, at one end of the fighting square. Elana took on an old fighting stance, one that Mitis recognized but could not remember where he had seen it before. Eulalie was watching from a place at the end of the Knight's quarter. The place was set higher, along a hallway that cut through the side of the Knight's quarter and into the main castle. Eulalie saw the fighting stance that *Titus* took and immediately she recognized it. It was a fighting stance that she had seen Peter assume before.

Jeffery also assumed his fighting stance. He placed his right leg half a pace behind his left, he lifted his hands, formed a loose left fist and a firm right fist, and he placed both hands in front of his face. The knights had come to know this stance ever so well. But they knew that Jeffery was a dynamic fighter, and though his stance was always the same, the way in which he moved varied based on who he was up against.

There was silence for a brief moment, and then Jeffery began taking small paces closer towards Elana. Elana stood still. She greatly suppressed the power of the snake within her. If she fought Jeffery with even a little of its power, she would kill him instantly. So she fought, in the form of Titus. Though in her

weakest state, she did not fight very aggressively but she knew she had to put on a spectacle.

Jeffery got close enough to her and began
throwing quick left jab to test Titus's reflexes.
Elana knew this was a test. She evaded the five
quick jabs Jeffery threw, but then Jeffery threw
a swift right towards the side of *Titus's* face.
Elana saw it and stopped the punch. She held
Jeffery's right hand in place. Immediately she
began searching his memories. She looked deep
into his eyes. Elana saw the moments from
when Jeffery captured Antonius and his crew,
the fight Jeffery witnessed between Neemus
and Julian and also the night when Mitis had
informed Jeffery about Antonius's journey and
his soon return for the spring festival. But the
memory from Jeffery that caught her interest
the most was the night Antonius had dinner
with the royal family. She saw the way Jeffery
saw Antonius notice Astra when she walked
into the dining hall. It became clear to Elana
that Astra was very dear to Antonius.

Jeffery felt frozen, he saw that Titus's eyes
for a quick moment looked like those of a snake
then it transformed back to normal. He pulled
his hand back and jumped a pace back and
assumed his fighting stance again. Elana came
rushing in with a swift right punch. Jeffery was
ready for her attack. He quickly dodged the
attack by moving his head back, and then he
took a hold of Titus's arm and pulled him forward. In the short moment he gripped Titus's

hand, he felt an uneasy presence. He felt an evil presence invading his mind. This made him very angry and in that same movement, he drove his knee into Titus's chest. But his knee did not hit Titus's chest, for Elana had stopped it with her left hand, and she had done it with ease. Elana pushed Jeffery backward. Jeffery almost lost his footing but caught himself quickly.

"You're stronger than you let on." Jeffery said. His words were not meant to flatter but to slight *Titus*. Despite his quick words, his mind kept on why he had felt the strange evil presence coming from *Titus*.

Elana decided that she was going to throw the match and let Jeffery maintain his reputation so no one would be suspicious and ask how a young king was able to defeat the highest ranking knight in Konstuliana with ease. Elana took her stance once more as Jeffery came rushing in with left swing. Elana dodged the punch. Jeffery continued on the offensive, throwing more punches, and moving closer with every swing in an attempt to disorient *Titus*. Then out of nowhere he threw a kick, which Elana saw coming but she let it hit her. Jeffery's shin brought *Titus* down.

The knight's quarter fell silent. Mitis unfolded his arms and walked closer to the square as *Titus* slowly got up. Jeffery took his fighting stance. But to his surprise *Titus* conceded and with a smile said,

"You're not as weak as you let on. Good fight," *Titus* said then left the fighting square and began making his way out of the Knight's quarter. Mitis walked with him to make sure he was okay but there was no bruise on his face.

Eulalie witnessed all this. And she felt it all as well. She knew that evil followed *Titus*. At least the man they thought was Titus. The feeling of evil made her uncomfortable because it was a familiar presence she felt. Through the day, she thought on why the presence felt familiar. Then she realized around the early evening hours, just as the sun was setting that the presence she felt was almost identical to that of Sirius.

To say it was a beautiful evening would not do justice to the marvel she saw. The sun was setting in the distance as Astra set her eyes west. The winds were slowing picking up but the evening for the most part was delightful. She admired the city and the distant setting sun from the west balcony in the upper ballroom of the castle. After a long day, this was the place she came to be alone, a place for her to collect her thoughts. As the final light of the day faded away a voice said from behind her,

"Princess."

She turned and beheld *Titus*. It was almost as if all around her froze and time was still. She was not expecting anyone and he was the last person she would have expected to come and see her. But she was calm as he approached.

"It's beautiful isn't it?" *Titus* said as he looked out into the city. The torches that hung from houses on the streets had been lit and the city had a beautiful glow. Even at night the beauty of Petra was still seen.

"It is indeed," Astra affirmed.

The cool spring air began to blow just as *Titus* started speaking again. Astra felt slightly uncomfortable by his presence but held herself and made sure he did not sense her reluctance.

"Princess," *Titus* began. "All day I have been thinking about you. The moment you set your eyes on me this morning you, my soul was set on fire. Since that hour, you have overcome my thoughts." *Titus* took hold of Astra's hand. This made Astra even more uncomfortable. But this was part of Elana's plan. To make Astra so uneasy that she would give word about the whereabouts of Antonius. But following the instructions of her father, Astra knew not to speak of Antonius in the presence of *Titus*. But her heart was bothered because of *Titus's* touch and she could not but think of Antonius. So as Titus was still speaking she drew her hand away and said.

"I'm sorry but my heart is given to another."

"Another?" Titus said. "And where is he? Where is this person who has kept me from taking place in your heart?"

"He is not here," Astra replied.

"Is he dead? If he is not then he has no reason not to be with you. Tell me princess who is it that has won your heart? I am sure he is no king. I am sure his stature is not as well framed as mine."

As Titus continued to speak, Astra tried to keep still. At least she tried as much as she could not to speak but *Titus* was getting too arrogant with his words.

"This man who has won your heart, does he know of me? Does he know that though I may be a young king, my worth is immeasurable? You know that the wealth of Philonia in the years of my father equaled that of this nation but now it is twice as much as it was before. Can the one who has won your heart buy you the purest silver in the land, dress you in the finest cotton, provide for you a diamond untouched by the hands of man, and shower you with the love of a true king?"

Astra outraged responded.

"He has given me much more than you ever will." But after she spoke she drew back a bit, for she did not mean to speak in a harsh tone to *Titus*. But his arrogance annoyed her.

"Be careful with your tone princess. Remember you are speaking to a king." *Titus* said. Then he tried to place his hand on the side of her face to comfort her but she slapped his hand away before he touched her face.

This angered *Titus*.

"It seems that you are committed to this man who has won your affection. Tell me princess who is he? I know he is no king. Is he a noble or the son of a noble? Is he a knight or a soldier? Or is he a common man and you are embarrassed to speak him name."

"Why does it matter to you who he is?" Astra asked.

"I want to know this man, so I may personally shake his hand and seek his advice on how to win the heart of a beautiful woman such as you."

Astra was quiet and did not answer him. She faced the city and acted for a moment as if he was not there. This made Elana angry. Though she knew who had won Astra's heart, she wanted Astra to confess it. As Titus, Elana was getting impatient. She tried as Titus to reach out and turn Astra to face her so she could receive an answer but Astra knocked her hand away again and pushed her back. She fell down.

"The man who has won my heart is a man who you shall never become. He has the heart of a true king. He is brave, selfless, determined and without a doubt a better king than you. And you know him well for he is your brother, the true king of Philonia, Antonius Maximus." Astra declared and walked away, leaving Titus at the balcony.

❖

Never before had the queen's heart been so distressed. Evil was within the walls of her castle and she knew it. Eulalie taught it an imperative that she informed Mitis at once. It was around the same time when *Titus* met Astra at the balcony that Eulalie found her husband in his study as the evening sun gave way for the moon's light.

The king was in the outer room of his study. Ten candles illuminated the room. Mitis was at his desk looking over some documents when he noticed his queen enter. He did not see her face but he noticed her garment first and from the splendid design, he knew it was her. She approached him. When she was closer he could see she looked worried.

"I don't like that look." Mitis said. "What's wrong?" he asked.

"I want to tell you something that has lain heavy on my heart all day but I don't know how to say it or if you will believe me if I tell it to you."

"You can tell me anything, my queen." Mitis stood up from his chair and went to her. He held her hand and he saw she became more distressed. "Speak before your heart bursts."

"I think we are being deceived."

"What makes you think this?"

"I do not think Titus is who we believe he is."

"What do you mean?" Mitis asked.

"I was there watching from a higher place overlooking the knight's quarter. I saw him fight and every time he had his hand on Jeffery I felt a familiar evil."

"What are you trying to say?"

"I believe a ghoul has taken the form of the Titus and come before us."

"So what shall I do? Shall I go confront him about it? Shall go accuse him?"

"No that is not…"

"I know you mean well my love but there is no way to handle a matter like this that would not incur great consequences. Even if I brought this up in a casual manner, he would think I have insulted him and could declare war against us. I know right now Konstuliana far out-matches the troops of Philonia but to go to war with him is like taking a knife and slicing my own throat. Philonia was my first home, I still have relatives there and I must do all in my power to make sure that I do not offend this son of Calix."

"I don't want war either."

"Good, and there is no reason for it. Let's keep it that way. Accusations of being the child of a fallen guardian have a dark place in the history of Philonia. There was a king about seven hundred years ago who was overtaken by madness and thought that ghouls were seeking to kill him. He began suspecting his own subjects to be ghouls and many people lost their lives because of the king's superstitions. A hundred thousand died in four months. It was a great massacre. But people close to the king knew he was not mad but he was being controlled. When one of the priests came to realize that there was indeed a ghoul in the kingdom. All the while this ghoul sat right next to the king every day, shared his bed and ate meals with him. The ghoul was his queen. When the people were informed of this they gathered themselves and came against her but she was nowhere to be found. And they found the body of their king in his bed, in a pool of his own blood."

"Why did you tell me this?"

"I don't want another ghoul-hunt to take place. If Titus becomes defensive he may accuse the guards, the maids, servants or knights of being ghouls. I would have to prove to him they are not to appease him and often it is hard to prove a person is not a ghoul without causing them great pain or taking their life."

"I am not saying we accuse him."

"Then what do you want me to do?"

"I want us to keep watch and wait. If he is a ghoul then our lovely daughter and our precious son are in danger. We are all in danger. I love you and I love our children and I would not want us to not be on our guard if we are to be suddenly attacked. So all I ask is that you be cautious for my sake, the sake of our children and for the sake of this kingdom as well."

"Alright, I will be on my guard." Mitis said to reassure her. Eulalie left his study and retired to her chamber.

❖

About an hour before sunrise, the guards at the gate of Mitis's castle saw a figure walking out from the castle. They armed themselves and prepared to fight but when they saw it was *Titus* they lowered their weapons and bowed and asked how they may be of service. *Titus* commanded them to bring his horse and they went to the castle stable and retrieved it. *Titus* mounted his horse. The guards noticed he was in his royal apparel. They opened the castle gates and *Titus* rode east, to those who saw him, he was heading back to Philonia. But about a mile east of Petra, Elana dismounted the horse and transformed back to her own skin. There was a wolf-man waiting for her behind one of the trees in the forest on the side of the road. She approached him and called him to come forward. He came before her and knelt. She began to sing a song and as she sang, the wolf-man began to change in form and began to resemble Antonius in every-likeness. His voice changed and his eyes were the same color as Antonius's. Then Elana breathe into the transformed body. A black cloudy mist came out from her mouth and into the nostril of the transformed body. Then she spoke saying,

"You will be my eyes as I leave this place. I need you for a greater part of my vengeance, so wait till you hear my voice, and I will instruct you on what to do."

Elana then transformed into the bird-like creature and flew back to noble city.

Chapter 22
Days on the Mountain

Antonius was the first to reach over the hill. He set his eyes east. He could see the mountain and in the distance he saw the first ray of sunlight. Marcus and Xaria reached the hill as well and they saw what he saw. It was beautiful. They continued. When they were about a quarter mile from the base of the mountain, they saw red lightning strike a place a little higher on the mountain. They looked up but there was no cloud in the sky. It was an odd sight. The birds were singing on that fine morning. The jungles around the base of the mountain were beautiful. They reached the mountain base and saw a rising pathway that continued along the side of the mountain.

Peter met them there. He was standing in the middle of the pathway, looking down at them as they emerged from the jungle.

"Peter!" Xaria said with excitement.

"I told you not to travel at night. Why did you disobey me?" Peter said with a commanding voice.

"When we saw the mountain, we immediately started ..." Antonius began.

"If the wolf-men saw you they would have torn you to pieces. You may be a Rising Guardian but you know nothing of the power that is within you. Evil can sense your ignorance." He took a breath and calmed himself. "But regardless, I am glad you are safe. Come with me," he said.

They followed him as he led them along the pathway which continued towards the upper east side of the mountain. They continued until Peter stopped and they were standing in front of a cave. The winds picked up for a brief moment. Peter went into the cave and invited them in. Marcus was the first to step in. The cave was dark. Xaria followed after him, and then Antonius went in. Peter went to a corner in the cave and created a small fire.

"Where are we?" Marcus asked.

"This is my home," Peter said.

The outer reach of the cave was not small but was also not very impressive to behold. There was not much to see except a small bed made of the fur of a mountainous animal, a small pile of books and a hole in the cave wall that housed many scrolls. Peter took a torch that hung on the cave wall and lit it with the fire he just made. He told Marcus and Xaria to follow him and he instructed Antonius to wait for him near the cave entrance. Antonius took the latches of their horses and secured them near the entrance of the cave. He sat on a rock next to the horses and waited.

Peter continued further into the cave as Marcus and Xaria kept pace. It seemed that the inner part of the cave kept descending slightly. They had been walking for about thirty five minutes, Xaria was patient but Marcus wasn't.

"I wish I could say I was enjoying this, but I would be lying. Where are we going?"

Peter did not respond. Marcus sighed.

"Please be patient." Xaria pleaded as she took his hand.

After about seven minutes they began to see a light at the end of the pathway. They heard the chirping of birds and could smell the scent of flowers. When they reached the light, they emerged into a garden. The garden was surrounded by mountains and there was a small lake within the conclave of trees. It was not as vast as the gardens north of Petra but it was by far more beautiful and serene. There was all manner of small animals. There were rabbits, squirrels, and many kinds of different colorful birds.

Marcus was speechless when he saw it all. Xaria smiled and said.

"This place is beyond belief."

Peter was glad that they took pleasure in what they saw. Then he said to them.

"Antonius and I will be gone for a little while. So I wanted to show you this place because I know the cave can get a bit dull. You can spend the nights in the cave if it gets too cold out here. The food you need get only from here. The trees are always in season and many fruits grow here. Do not wonder to the forests surrounding the mountains outside the cave. It is very dangerous, especially at night."

"How long will you be gone?" Xaria asked.

"We will return in five days and then we shall return to Petra for the spring festival. Thereafter as Mitis promised Antonius, he shall help him prove his innocence in Philonia. But don't worry too much of it. I want your hearts to be at peace. That is why you are here. Now I must return to him. Stay safe."

Peter turned to start going back but Xaria called to him. He turned and she said,

"Thank you."

"Wait Peter, I am coming with you" Marcus said, he turned and said to Xaria, "There is something I must tell Antonius. I will also return with the horses."

When Peter and Marcus got back to the outer part of the cave, they met Antonius, seated on a rock resting his arms on his legs. Antonius appeared as though he was sleeping but he was still awake but very tired from the night's journey. Antonius heard someone coming. He turned to his left and saw Peter and Marcus coming his way.

"Where did you go?" Antonius asked.

"Don't worry about that," Peter said.

"Where's Xaria?" Antonius asked.

"She's fine," Marcus confirmed.

Peter put out the torch and placed it back on its holding. Marcus went to Antonius to encourage him. Antonius stood as his brother approached him.

"Antonius, how are you feeling?"

"I'd be lying if I said I was doing well. I am still sore from the journey."

"I think I've come to know why Peter brought you here. I want you to keep this in mind Antonius. Our father went through the same thing. All the Guardians who have transcended and are now in Pacifica have been tested greatly. I don't know how it is that you inherited father's destiny but that does not matter now. All that matters is that you do not let your heart become discouraged by whatever trial you face. Hold fast to your courage and you shall overcome anything. Good luck brother."

Antonius felt reassured by Marcus's words. He thanked his brother, stretched out his hand to shake his, but Marcus embraced him.

"See you in five days brother."

Peter was waiting outside the cave for Antonius. Antonius went out to meet him after he had bid his brother goodbye. Peter continued further along the pathway that led up the mountain. Antonius followed. But as they continued up the path, Antonius's occasionally set his eyes towards the top of the mountain, which was surrounded by a choir of clouds. As they continued along the path, he gazed up at the daunting grand rock, missed his step and slipped. Peter sensed a sharp distress in Antonius spirit, turned around quickly and grabbed Antonius's hand. He pulled Antonius back up.

"I know you are eager but keep your eyes and your feet on the path."

"Thanks."

Peter did not respond. They continued for about an hour along the rising path until it suddenly stopped on the north side of the mountain. Antonius looked up. The mountain was now more daunting. The cold winds began to blow again. Antonius shivered.

"We'll have to climb from here."

"But it's too steep. Can't you just tell me what you need to reveal to me of my destiny in a cave. It would be great to get out of this cold."

"Be still Antonius. Take a breath, calm your spirit."

Antonius tried to do as Peter said, but the air was too heavy to breath and the cold made things worse. Antonius fell to his knees and coughed.

"I can't do this."

"You can, and you will," Peter said.

Peter took Antonius by the back of the light armor Antonius was wearing and pulled Antonius back up to his feet. Peter reached into his robe, pulled out a small knife and handed it to Antonius.

"This should help you."

Antonius took a breath, stood up straight, looked up, formed a fist and said,

"If it must be done, then so be it."

Peter was pleased with Antonius's change in attitude. He could also feel that power was rising inside Antonius, not much but enough for Antonius's body to get used to the surrounding. Peter secured his staff on his back and together he and Antonius started climbing.

The ascent took about three hours. At the third hour, the cold winds died down and Antonius felt unusual warmth surrounding him. He was exhausted. The mountain was surrounded by fog so dense that Antonius could no longer see Peter. Peter had been climbing just a few feet above him. Antonius stopped to catch his breath then he felt someone grab his wrist and pull him up.

"This is the place," Peter said as Antonius rose up and walked away from the edge. He tried to stand but his knees gave way and he collapsed backwards on the grass. The scenery was plain in its appearance. It seemed to stretch on for a while. There was a forest in the distance. Antonius's eyes were set on the forest. But he could not keep them open. He closed his eyes and still in thought, he wondered how such a place could be set upon a high mountain. It was a greater mystery to him why it was warmer up there than it had been around the caves. Though it was warm, the air was heavy and this made it impossible for Antonius to recuperate efficiently. Antonius opened his eyes for a short moment and saw the clear sky.

"Antonius, stand up. There is much I have to reveal to you."

"Five minutes, grant me five minutes," Antonius pleaded.

"You will be given time to rest after I reveal what I must to you."

"Five minutes Peter, is that too much to ask for?"

Antonius heard a voice respond. A voice that was deep and commanding. It came from his left but he did not open his eyes until the one who spoke finished.

"In five minutes" the voice began, "A battle could be won, a life saved, an empire toppled. Five minutes is too precious a time to waste."

Antonius opened his eyes and turned them to where he heard the voice speak. At the sight of the one who spoke, he leaped to his feet and unsheathed his sword.

"Put your sword away," Peter said.

"No, it is good he's quick to react. Would you like to fight me Antonius?" the creature said.

"What are you, and how do you know me?"

The creature that spoke to Antonius appeared in the form of a white lion with a blood red mane and large translucent wings. It stood six feet high with a wingspan of eighteen feet. As the creature approached Antonius, Antonius gripped his sword tighter. The creature laughed and then said.

"There is no need for alarm Antonius. Though you may not know it now, you actually know me, rather I should say, you know of me. To answer your question of what I am, I am a Faracot. I was made the same day the spirit of the Twelfth was created. The spirit which lives in you and because of whom, you are called a Rising Guardian. I was made to be the spirit's companion in light. To serve the Twelfth as the spirit is sometimes called. But I do have a name Antonius and it would have been nice of you to ask who I am... I am Josiah, the Faracot of the Twelfth, formed in flames, molded by lighting and awoken on the day that the Twelfth came to be."

"You're the one my father wrote about. But he spoke little of what you looked like. Because of the way you instructed my father and your great reasoning I assumed you to be a man, a man of great age."

Josiah smiled and said, "Men are not the only creatures that can reason."

Day 1: Union of Once Parted Rivers

Later that afternoon, Peter began revealing to Antonius many important aspects about being a Rising Guardian. They sat on the ankle high grass, facing each other as Peter began. Josiah was seated four feet to Antonius's right.

"There are many things I have to reveal to you Antonius. I will start with the basic truths. Then when your mind is ready, I will reveal to you truths that will shake the foundation of your belief. First Antonius, I want to know how much you know. Josiah has confirmed because he knows much more than I that you are the first to inherit the destiny of being a Rising Guardian. Your father was the second royal to be chosen to be a Rising Guardian but he was not a royal when he was called. Though I have studied the prophecies for many centuries I have come to understand more why it is the Great King answered your father's prayer and placed his destiny upon you. Every Rising Guardian that was and those who transcended are part of a greater plan, one that will be unwoven at the end of time. But you need not worry about that yet, in time you'll understand more of this Greater Hope."

Josiah got up and walked closer to Antonius and said reassuring him.

"When your father was first here, he was very hesitant to accept the things we revealed to him. But I can sense in your spirit unlike your father, there is no ounce of vengeance in your heart."

"There was vengeance in my father's heart and you still revealed much about his destiny to him?"

"Yes, it was our hope that one day when he was confronted with the chance to attain the vengeance he so sought that he would realize that vengeance harms the one who seeks it more than the one whom it shall be impacted on. But it turned out much better than we expected. He got his chance to attain the vengeance he so sought but his heart was overcome by love that he could not do it and he forgave the one who wronged him instead."

"I remember the story. Yes the one who wronged him was the then king of Philonia."

"Because of your father's choice he won the complete love of your mother and the king had a change of heart during his later years. It was no surprise he chose your father to succeed him even before he wedded your mother," Josiah said. Then Peter added,

"It was on that day that Josiah revealed to me what I had been hoping to see for a long time. The prophecy was being fulfilled that day and I was witness to it."

"What prophecy?" Antonius asked.

"It was something I don't even believe your father was aware of but when I revealed it to him he did not believe me until the Twelfth spoke to him personally. Have you heard of the prophecy called The Union of Once Parted Rivers?"

"Yes I have read it."

"Your existence and that of your brothers is a greater testament to the fulfilment of that prophecy. As you know it is impossible for many to read prophecies in the Book of Prophecy until the prophecy has been fulfilled. It will appear as ripples of watered words before the eyes of those who have not been blessed with the ability to understand them. Rising Guardians are not even given this gift. Only a select few have this gift, your father after you became the Rising Guardian was given this gift and Eulalie also possesses this gift. But I will tell you of the prophecy, what it means and how it pertains to you."

Peter told Antonius the meaning of the prophecy in its entirety.

"Your father believed that he became a royal the day he married your mother but that was not true. He had been a royal from birth. Your father was a descendant of Maximus."

"Maximus? He must be the one my family name honors."

"He is. Maximus was a prince of Philonia and the only son of Davus, one of Philonia's most affluent kings. All who knew Maximus said only good things about him. He was beloved by the kingdom and by his parents. One day during a grand celebration held in honor of Maximus's academic achievements, Maximus went on a hunting trip where he encountered a beautiful woman who he saw was being pursued by pirates. He confronted the men who were chasing her and stopped them. But someone struck him from behind. He fainted and found himself on a Pirate ship. The first one who he saw was the woman he was trying to save. It turned out that she was Amelia, the daughter of the most ruthless pirate at that time, Baydus. Maximus was held ransom for more than half the king's wealth. Davus wanted to wage war against Baydus but the queen advised him not to, for the sake of Maximus's life. But Maximus was a cunning prince. He waited patiently for the perfect situation to present itself. One day at sea, he could feel it through the cabin window where he was held prisoner. A storm was coming; he knew this was his chance. He deceived the jailer, stole the keys and escaped to the main deck in the middle of the storm. He was quick to find a lifeboat while everyone else was trying to keep the ship afloat. During the commotion Amelia went to check on Maximus and when she saw he had escaped she ran back to the main deck and saw him at the moment he released the lifeboat. She jumped into it with him and they fought, she with sword in hand, him without. Maximus was able to restrain her and held her down as the storm blew their boat away from the ship. When the winds had died down and the waters were still, Baydus noticed that his daughter and the prince were missing."

"Maximus must have survived the storm," Antonius said.

"If he hadn't we would not be having this conversation." Peter said then continued "After Baydus realized that his daughter and the prince had been lost during the storm, he hum-

bled himself and went before Davus and
pleaded for him to lend more men and ships to
search for both the prince and his daughter.
Davus almost lost himself and killed Baydus
there but the queen stopped him from doing so.
She kept his mind on what truly mattered, finding the prince. Davus agreed to lend more men
and ships to help in the search for Maximus."

"Where were they? Maximus and Amelia,"
Antonius asked.

"They had hit shore on an island close to
the edge of the blue sea, an area where ships
rarely travelled. It took three years before they
were found. They found Amelia in a cave. She
had in her hand a three month old baby when
they found her. They asked after Maximus but
she wept at the sound of his name. The only
one she spoke to of his fate was Davus. Davus
wept and the kingdom mourned for two
months. The queen at that time was too old to
bear any children, so Davus sought to make the
daughter born to Amelia his heir. Every time he
looked into the child's eyes he saw the eyes of
his son. But Davus's younger brother, Myenius
would not allow this. He stated that because
Amelia was not of royal blood and being that
she was the daughter of a pirate; it would be
reprehensible to allow any offspring of hers'
even if it were truly of Maximus to be in line to
the throne. The council of Senators sided with
Myenius and warned if Davus did not stop
trying to make the child an heir it would be on

his head if anything happened to the child because not many supported his pursuit. Davus disagreed. The next day Davus was found dead in his bed. When word of this got to Amelia, she escaped and fled with her child to a small village in Napel. Myenius became king and it was from his line that your mother was born. From the child that Amelia bore, your father descended. All this happened about four centuries ago. It was at this point in history that the rivers parted. Do you understand Antonius?"

"I believe so," Antonius said.

"Then explain to me the significance of the story," Peter said.

"Amelia and Maximus had a child who could not become an heir in the royal lineage in Philonia, because of this, the child though a royal, was never allowed to be one, so in effect, they had been broken from the Philonia royal lineage. This was when the prophecy began. But as you said earlier, because my father was a descendant of this child and he married my mother, who was a descendent of Myenius, their union restored the royal line to the way it was before Maximus's offspring was cut-off from it. The significance thereof is the restoration of the true lineage of Philonia back to the throne. And as the prophecy states, the spirit of the Twelfth shall be upon the one who shall unite the rivers. So that is why my father was a Rising Guardian."

"I'm glad you were listening," Peter said.

"He is correct," Josiah proclaimed.

"But what I don't understand is why my father's destiny was placed upon me."

"That should not be your concern now, in time, you will come to know the answer but neither I nor Josiah will be the ones to reveal that truth to you."

"Then who will reveal it to me?" Antonius asked.

"The one who is within you," Peter said.

Evening came and the light of the new morning broke forth. That was the first day.

Day 2- A Calm Spirit Keeps the Body Whole

The winds picked up the scent of the flowers from the forest that was a bit away from them and blew it in their direction. Antonius arose to the scent of roses, pine and lavender. He woke to find Josiah staring at Petra while Peter was praying. Peter held his staff in both hands, his head bowed and his outer shepherd's robe had been set on the floor beside him for they had been soaked by sweat. At the utterance of the last word of his prayer, Peter opened his eyes and turned to Antonius. He was surprised to see Antonius awake. He went to him and asked,

"Did you rest well?"

"Yes. I did. Is there any water?"

"Yes there is, go into the forest, there is a creek there," Josiah said as he approached them.

"Thank you," Antonius said.

He went into the forest, found the creek, washed his face, drank and returned to them.

"What shall you reveal to me on this fine day?" Antonius asked as he sat on the rich green grass that still felt the touch of the morning dew. He sat facing Peter.

"It is a fine day. But today Antonius I will not be teaching you. I will just be revealing to you things you may not be aware of but the principles of which you understand."

"What do you mean?"

"A calm spirit makes the body whole," Peter said.

"Yes I know the saying, it was one of my father's," Antonius said.

"Is that so?" Peter smirked. "Anyhow do you understand what it means?"

"My father explained to me that it pertains to the state of one's mind when they are injured, sick or healing. One's mind must stay calm, preferably positive, for the body to heal properly."

Peter was silent.

"He is correct," Josiah said.

"As a Rising Guardian Antonius," Peter began, "This saying still applies to you but it is much more crucial in your case because if you are injured and your mind is not calm, your pain will get worse and your wounds will rot upon your skin. No matter how much you wish you die, death will not come for you, for Rising Guardians are denied death even in the most challenging times of their lives."

"Then no matter what, I will try to keep a calm spirit."

"I'd like to hope so but I cannot be too sure. I am going to test the calmness of your spirit."

Josiah got up and went to Antonius.

"Take off the armor and your shirt Antonius." Josiah commanded.

Antonius did as he was told. Peter saw that Antonius was wearing the cross that Eulalie had given him. Josiah went behind Antonius and said.

"Almost a month ago, when you were on the island where your brother had chosen to exile himself, a creature that looked like me attacked you."

"Yes. It did," Antonius confirmed. The tone of his voice was shifting.

"As I look upon your back now, I see no sign of this attack, not even a scar."

Antonius reached to touch where the lion had struck him and he felt it was smooth, he felt no scar only his shallow hair.

"That is strange."

Josiah brought the claws on his right paw and said before he slashed across Antonius backside,

"Pardon me."

Antonius let out a scream. The wound stretched across the length of his back and was a centimeter deep.

"Stay calm," Peter said.

Antonius began to breathe slowly and tried to keep calm. His pain began to subside. Josiah kept firm eyes on the wound. In two minutes, blood had stopped flowing from the wound, three more minutes passed by; now the wound had closed, after seven more minutes the scar had disappeared.

"It has completely healed," Josiah said.

"Interesting, it took your father about an hour to heal the first time we tested the calmness of his spirit," Peter said.

"Please don't do that again," Antonius pleaded.

"We have to test the calmness of your spirit under more tense conditions, so we will inflict upon you a similar injury," Peter said.

Antonius sighed. "Tense conditions?"

"I must know that you are strong enough within yourself to control the state of your spirit. Those Rising Guardians before you who could not keep their spirits calm saw the darkness as a place of escape and they paid dearly for it. So it is important I know where you stand."

"I will never give myself to the darkness," Antonius said.

"You say that now but you do not know what trials you shall face that may corrupt your mind."

"No matter what trials I may face in the future, I will stand by my convictions."

"Stand by my conviction, he says, have you ever even been close to the face of death, do you know of the incomparable sorrow those who plot against you wish you to suffer, you are…"

"Peter! That's enough." Josiah said. His voice resounded across the mountain and shook the skies. "Do not let the past make you cynical. Antonius is different. Have faith in him."

Peter sighed. "Fine, I just can't afford to waste the little faith I have left."

"Was your faith in Calix wasted?" Josiah asked.

"No, it wasn't."

"Then assuredly you should know it shall not be wasted on his son. I can feel he is like his father, even so more determined."

"Alright" Peter said "Forgive me if I spoke unkindly. But the trials that befall a Rising Guardian can break the ideals of strong men easily. I don't want to waste my faith on someone who is bound to fail. The faith I have left is as small as a mustard seed."

"Then it is enough," Josiah said with a smile.

Peter stood up and approached Antonius. He stretched out his hand and helped Antonius to his feet. He knew what he would have to do to test the calmness of Antonius spirit under tense condition and he knew Antonius would not like. It might in a sense send Antonius spirit into chaos if Antonius let his emotion get the better of him. But Peter had faith in Antonius and said before he placed his hand on Antonius's head.

"I am going to place a great burden on your spirit. Thereafter we will inflict on you wounds like before to see if you can keep your spirit calm and heal yourself."

"How will you do this?"

Peter placed his hand on Antonius head and said,

"Relax your mind."

Antonius took a breath, closed his eyes and kept still.

"I hope you will forgive me for what I am about to do," Peter said.

Antonius opened his eyes to ask Peter what he was about to do but once he opened his eyes it was done. Antonius saw that all around him had completely changed; in fact it was too familiar. He was not in the mountain anymore but he was standing in the middle of a hallway, in a palace. He knew the hallway, and he knew the palace.

"How? How did he do this? I am home. But it cannot be," Antonius said in disbelief.

He slowly bent down, felt the ground and it was as real as could be, he touched his face and it was ever so more real. He smiled. But then he began to wonder if there was a reason Peter had sent him back to Philonia. He looked outside the window in the hallway and saw that it was night time. Clouds sailed by a blood moon. Antonius's breathing stopped once he saw the color of the moon. Something from his memory sparked terror in his heart, he slowly backed away from the window. He began to hear footsteps from the corner of the hall. He ran to a room close by and hid. He cracked the door open a little to see who was coming. At the sight of the person a tear escaped from his eye because he knew now not only where he was but when he was.

He saw his father dressed in full armor. All but his helmet was put on. When his father was coming closer about to pass the room where Antonius had hidden, Antonius came out and calmly called out to his father. He stood in front of his father but his father walked through him as one does through the wind. This frightened Antonius. He saw the grief on his father's face and it broke his heart. When Calix walked through Antonius, he stopped. Antonius turned to him and thought his father had acknowledged his presence though he could not see him. Then Calix said,

"I thought I felt the presence of an old friend." Calix sighed and closed his eyes. "All this time I knew this hour was sure to come and I thought I'd be ready. Now old friend, I am not so sure of myself. But my sons they keep me going. And my queen, her love keeps me strong."

Antonius heard his father's words and could feel wholeness in his father's spirit. Immediately he saw Calix start running down the hallway. He followed him. Calix arrived at a room that was at the other end of the palace. Antonius knew the room far too well. And he feared what he might see when Calix opened the door. Calix opened the door and Antonius's fear was confirmed. He saw his mother holding a baby in her hand, with young Marcus on her right and Antonius as a child pulling on her gown asking her what was going on. Antonius took a deep breath when he saw himself, for the pain fell upon his spirit again, and his spirit began to weep. Tears fell from his eyes as he watched the events of a night he wished to bury in his memory for all time.

He saw his father approach his mother and he greeted her with a kiss. Young Antonius hugged his father tight and did not let go until his father explained why he had to go. Antonius remembered that he felt weariness at that moment as a child. He knew that that would be the last night he saw his father, and that was why as a child he held on to his father. Calix gently pick up young Antonius, held him in his arms and upon the young child's forehead, he laid a kiss.

"I must go soon my son."

"No father…please." Young Antonius pleaded.

Calix gently put young Antonius down and got on one knee to plead to his sons. He looked up to his darling wife for a moment then back to young Antonius and Marcus. He consoled them with kind words, and encouraged Annabelle that all was going to be well. Annabelle knew Calix would not be returning, so after he had spoken to Marcus and Antonius, she pulled him to herself and kissed him hard. A tear escaped from her eyes when their lips met. Antonius's spirit bowed his head low and he fell back against the wall. He could not bear to see this moment again. Calix kissed the head of the baby Annabelle held in her hands.

"My precious Titus, I want you to know that I love you my son. Take care of your mother for me."

Titus began to cry and his little hands held on to the finger of his father.

"It's alright little one. It's alright."

Calix gently pulled his finger from the baby's grasp. Calix led Annabelle and the children out of the room. Just outside two guards were waiting. Calix commanded them to take the queen and the princes out of the city and not to bring them back until they got word it was safe to do so. Antonius's spirit watched the

guards lead his mother, his young self and his
brothers away. His spirit was standing beside
his father.

Calix left that place and started for the palace door. Antonius's spirit followed his father
through the hallway and on his way outside.
But when Antonius got to the door of the palace he watched his father run out but he
stopped and thought of what the consequence
of helping his father might be. His spirit did not
care and he sought to run after his father but
when his foot reached outside, lightning flew
down from the clouds and struck right in front
of him. The guards by the door saw the flash.
Calix turned and saw the crack it had made on
the marble step leading into the castle. Antonius looked into the heavens and he saw the
clouds gathering. He stepped back as he
watched his father turn away, mount a horse
and ride towards the south gate of Noble city.

Tears began to falls from his eyes; he fell to
his knees, hit the ground hard and yelled at the
top of his lungs. When he opened his eyes, he
was back on the mountain again. Blood was
flowing from open wounds in his back. He did
not notice them. He looked up to Peter with
murderous eyes and said.

"Why would you do that to me?"

Peter was silent. Antonius's sorrow turned
to rage then he felt grief overcome his spirit. He
fell on his side and wept. Josiah observed the

wound for about three minutes. Peter could sense the restlessness in Antonius spirit.

"Try to keep your spirit calm Antonius," Josiah said.

After a few minutes passed, Antonius's wound had gotten worse. Peter observed Antonius's wound. He placed his hands on them and healed Antonius.

"There was no way he could have healed himself. His spirit was too troubled. Let him rest we'll continue in the morning."

"I thought he could do it. Take heart Antonius, your father went through the same testing." Josiah said to reassure Antonius. But Antonius did not want to speak to them.

"Leave me Alone." he said with a broken voice.

Evening came and the light of the new morning broke forth. That was the second day.

Chapter 23
Days on the Mountain (pt-2)

Day 3: Not by Will Alone

Antonius felt a light rain fall on him around the early morning hours. It bothered him so he put his hands over his face. A short moment later he felt the rain stop falling on him but he could hear that it was still raining. He opened his eyes and saw Peter sitting in front of him. He looked up and saw that Josiah had spread his wings above them. Peter was holding a small bag. He opened it and brought out two apples and a peach. He gave them to Antonius.

"Take, eat, and replenish your strength."

Antonius half-heartedly took the fruits. Peter could see that the effects of the previous day's training still lingered.

"How are you feeling?"

Antonius looked at Peter but did not respond.

"I could take away the memory from you but a memory like that believe it or not makes you stronger. It keeps your heart set on things that are important."

"It was a memory, a memory Peter. That is what it should have been, yet you made me relive it. I could not do anything for my father though I knew his fate."

"You are right to feel this way. I do not blame you. If I took such a memory from you I would be taking a great part of yourself away as well.

Antonius took a breath and calmed himself.

"A part of me is still angry at you. But a greater part of me understands that what you did you did for the right reasons. I cannot be angry at you for this, so I forgive you." Antonius placed the base of his thumbs together in the upper valley of the apple and pressed his palm hard on the side of the apple. In one motion he split it in two and wanted to give half to Peter.

"No thank you, eat all of it. You'll need it for what we have to do today."

"Really, what do you have planned for today?"

"Antonius, how much do you know about the previous Rising Guardians before yourself?" Josiah asked.

With a mouth half-full Antonius answered him,

"I know as much as has been written in the history books. Why do you ask?"

"Do you know that it was a Rising Guardian who split the earth and banished the fallen guardians to the darkness that is beyond the blue sea?"

"Yes, it was Alick Gordon, within who dwelt the Spirit called The First and it happened during the last year of the War of the Fathers."

"That is correct. During those days I watched the war from Pacifica. The Great King did not permit any being in Pacifica to join the war. He believed that Alick could unite the armies of men to go against the fallen guardians and their children. And Alick did so but at the end of the war, he was still a Rising Guardian and he used the powers given to him to break the earth and banish the fallen guardians to the Darkness."

"The proof of his deed are still manifest to-day," Peter added. "One-fourth of the world is still covered in darkness that most men do not dare to tread. But Gordon was not the only Rising Guardian to perform incredible deeds. Of the eleven who have transcended, all performed acts at some point in their calling that were beyond belief. But their power came from the Spirit within them. Dana Lounge within who dwelt The Sixth saved the grandson of Sturn from an avalanche of falling rocks the size of castles, and Florence Voudon within who dwelt The Eight fought and defeated three higher sons of Belshire who had taken Menyana under their control."

"Who is Belshire?" Antonius asked.

"He was the elder brother of Sirius and the eighth to fall," Josiah said.

Antonius finished the second apple then said,

"I do remember reading of the deeds of Florence but I did not know that Dana saved the grandson of Sturn."

Peter rose and went to Antonius; he got on one knee and placed his left hand on Antonius shoulder. His staff was in his right hand. Antonius felt uncomfortable for a moment, Peter felt this in his spirit then he said to Antonius.

"I am going to make you aware of the power that is within you. If I do not test you

harshly you will never reach your full potential."

Antonius looked at Josiah. Josiah looked
very serious, more so now. Josiah stood up and
went closer to them. Antonius noticed that Josiah tucked in his wings. Immediately Peter
raised high his staff and lightning struck his
staff and in a blinding light they disappeared
from that place.

Antonius opened his eyes but he saw nothing. He knew his eyes were open but the darkness was overwhelming. Peter's hand was no
longer on his shoulder. He called out to Peter.
From the darkness not too far from him he
heard Peter telling him to keep still. Antonius
called again to Peter as he tried to stand up but
he hit his head on a rock above him. The ceiling
was low. Peter advised him to stay low. Antonius then began to see a faint light coming from
in front of him. The light shone from Josiah's
wings. The light was faint but was enough for
Antonius to notice all around him. He saw Peter seated beside Josiah. The ceiling where Peter
sat was a bit higher but not high enough for
either him or Antonius to stand straight up.

"Peter, where are we?" Antonius asked.

"We are on an Island far west of the mountain."

"This does not look like an island. It looks
like a cave with no entrance or exit."

"This is not a cave Antonius. We are in the
belly of a mountain."

"Why have you brought me here?" Antonius asked.

"I want you to lift this mountain," Peter said.

Antonius was shocked for a moment. He was about to speak then he smiled and looked baffled.

"You cannot be serious," he said.

Peter's expression did not change. Josiah still looked very serious. Antonius was not intimidated by their expression not one bit because he was astounded by what Peter wanted him to do. He thought it was ridiculous to lift a mountain despite whatever magnitude of power Peter and Josiah thought dwelt in him. Antonius laid flat on his stomach on the cold ground and looked up to Peter and Josiah and said,

"That is not going to happen. This is ridiculous."

"You have not even tried and you have given up," Josiah said.

"Have a little faith Antonius," Peter said.

"Faith? I have a lot of faith. Maybe not as much as you but to lift a mountain takes strength not faith," Antonius said.

Josiah was angered and disappointed by what Antonius said and Antonius felt his disappointment.

"How do you think the Twelfth's power manifests itself in you?" Josiah said. "Do you think that he submits himself to your will and he'll give you the power you request on your own terms? Do you think you were given the power to defeat Gammon because you had strength?! Was the strength even your own?! Faith, Antonius, that is how you were able to defeat Gammon. Whether you believe it to be so or not, at times like that the Twelfth can sense the courage in your spirit, he senses your determination and faith and he gives you his strength to go against your foes. Now without even trying you have given up. A Rising Guardian who lacks faith is just as bad as those who aligned themselves with fallen guardians and lost their humanity."

"I am nothing like them." Antonius said

"Then show us, have faith and lift this mountain."

Antonius got back to a vertical position as much as the low ceiling above him would allow. He got into position and tried to lift. He kept at it for seven minutes then he fell back down. He felt out of breath. Peter told him to take off the light armor he was wearing. Antonius did so and gave it to Peter. Now he had only his pants, his boots and the necklace Eulalie had given him. After he had rested for about two minutes he got back into position again. He tried this time for about twenty minutes but nothing happened. He fell on his face again. His body was sore and all his muscles were swollen.

"You can do this Antonius," Peter said trying to encourage Antonius. But Josiah understood the Twelfth's power more than Peter, so he instructed Antonius saying,

"It is not from sheer will that the power within you shall manifest itself. Remember, it is the spirit of the Twelfth that dwells within you that possesses the power to lift this mountain. You must first understand the circumstance under which the Twelfth will give you the power you need. Remember, the power is given when faith is exhibited but in order for faith to manifest, there must be a need."

"A need?" Antonius asked. His breathing was still hard. "Well I need to lift this mountain."

"That is not the need I am talking about," Josiah said.

"Alright I'll try again." Antonius said as he slowly picked himself up. His muscles were still burning and they felt as though they had been ripped a thousand times over. Peter felt sorry for Antonius for he knew all this time the Twelfth had not given Antonius any power at all. Antonius was lifting with all he had. The ceiling had scarred his back and some of his muscles were torn. When Antonius got back into position, he took a deep breathe but before he tried again Peter said,

"May be I can help."

"Antonius has to do this on his own," Josiah said.

"I can provide the need."

"How so?" Antonius asked.

"I'd rather show you than explain. Stay as you are." Peter said as he stretched his hand forward and placed two fingers on Antonius forehead. He searched Antonius mind and found the person who was most precious to Antonius. He had a suspicion it was the daughter of his friend Mitis, and he was right. When his suspicion was confirmed he placed a thought in Antonius's mind. One that Antonius saw as a vision passing. This was his need. Peter pulled his hand back. Slowly they began to feel the power of the Twelfth rising in Antonius. Josiah watched Antonius and looked into his eyes. Antonius looked as though he were in pain but there was a determination in his eyes that they had not seen before.

"What did you do?" Josiah asked Peter

"I placed a thought in his mind. I put the one who is most precious to him in danger, now he is seeing things as if he were there. I have made him believe that the only way to save that person is to lift this mountain. He has his need, now we wait," Peter said.

Josiah looked back to Antonius. He saw Antonius eyes began to well up with tears, and then Antonius frowned and looked angry. He began to lift the mountain with all his strength. Peter could feel the power within Antonius rising exponentially. Antonius's leg began to crack the ground beneath him and the mountain began to rumble. Josiah did not set his eyes off Antonius. He began to see red flames pour out from Antonius's heart. Peter could not see the flames. The flames were from Antonius's spirit and they engulfed his body. Josiah warned Peter,

"He is using rage to draw power from the Twelfth. If he uses rage he shall corrupt himself."

"Have faith in him. He will not be overcome by whatever rage is within him," Peter said.

The mountain continued to rumble and the cracks beneath Antonius feet stretched and reached where Peter and Josiah were sitting. Josiah continued to observe the red flames, they raged on higher. Though Peter could not see them, he felt all around them get warmer. The warmth he knew was coming from Antonius. The mountain continued to rumble more, and then it began to feel as if an earthquake caught them. Josiah saw the red flames that covered Antonius began to turn white. At that moment, it happened. Peter saw the walls all round began to break and crack in a thousand places, Antonius was slowing rising up with the mountain above him. He continued to lift it higher till he stood in a fully erect position. He felt all his muscles rip apart but as they ripped they healed quickly. His bones felt like unbreakable steel. Now the mountain had been lifted, Josiah and peter rose to their feet. Antonius face was red and his body flushed red with blood. Antonius was still seeing the vision while carrying the mountain and in a loud voice he yelled out a name, the one who was most precious to him.

"Astra!"

Peter took a hold Antonius hand and Josiah put his wing over both of them. Immediately they disappeared and reappeared on the mountain north of Petra. The vision Antonius was seeing passed and he got back to himself. He looked and saw they were in the mountain. He was still standing with his hand raised high. The power in him subsided and he began to feel all his muscles burning. He fell backwards, coughed and rolled on his side.

"What happened?" he asked.

"You did it." Josiah said with a smile.

"It feels as though my muscles were set on fire. Everything within me feels like its burning."

"You've done well. You should rest," Josiah said.

Peter went to the river and brought some water back for Antonius. Antonius drank and fell asleep.

Evening came and the light of the new morning broke forth. That was the third day.

Day 4- Spirit of the Twelfth

The next morning the air felt lighter and the wind calmer. Antonius woke up and tried to get up but his muscles were still sore. He forced himself to sit up but as he did so he groaned. He turned and saw Peter behind him, seated facing Josiah. There was a small mat in front of Peter with a couple of fruits on it. Peter saw that Antonius was awake and he called him to join them. Antonius tried to stand but he couldn't. Peter saw this, Josiah chuckled. Peter gathered the fruits together and moved closer to Antonius. He gave Antonius a peach and a guava. Antonius thanked him.

"How do you feel Antonius?" Peter asked

"Everything, everything is on fire," Antonius responded. Josiah smiled.

"Have you tried calming your spirit and healing yourself?" Peter asked.

"I have, my muscles are whole but they are still sore." Antonius responded.

"You'll feel better soon, so don't worry. Eat and replenish your strength," Josiah said.

After Antonius had finished eating he asked Peter,

"What challenge awaits me today?"

"None. Today we'll talk about those who were before you. I want to know how much you know of the history of the guardians before you."

"But before the day is done there is one more thing that you'll do," Josiah said.

"What's that?" Antonius asked.

"You'll meet the Twelfth. Last night while you slept he spoke to me."

"How will I meet him? He is within me."

"Through meditation, Antonius," Peter said.

"Meditation? Hmm, it's been awhile since I've had time to meditate."

Antonius and Peter began their discussions about the previous Rising Guardians who had transcended but before they began, Peter proclaimed a truth that all Rising Guardians before Antonius were told. He revealed to Antonius that the greatest gift a Rising Guardian could give the world is their love. He also warned Antonius that a Rising guardian who is angry at the world is more dangerous than three fallen guardians. The discussion carried on began with the first Rising Guardian, Alick Gordon, who Antonius had read about. He confirmed to Peter that he was aware that Alick was called during the War of the Fathers. He knew that Alick ended the War of the Fathers after he split the earth and banished ten of the thirteen fallen guardians to the darkness. Peter mentioned that there were hearts, taken as virtues of sort, attributed to Rising Guardians when they transcended. He asked Antonius if he knew the heart given to Alick. Antonius did not know so Peter revealed it to him.

"The heart attributed to Alick was the First Heart," Peter said.

Much of the remainder of the discussion carried on in this manner. Antonius would name the Rising Guardian, some great deed they accomplished and the heart that was attributed to them. He named Enoch Dimini, who was the Third. He was known to be a great healer and to whom was attributed the Lion Heart. Philemon Salon was also mentioned. He was the Fifth and one of the most important because he was said to be the father of the new world, or sometimes was called the father of the father of Freedom. Hayadus was his disciple, and unto him was attributed the Free Heart.

As Antonius continued to mention Rising Guardians before him he mentioned a name, Marloway, but Peter stopped him when he said the name. Peter warned that they shall not speak of those who did not transcend. Antonius told Peter that Calix had told him of Marloway, and that he was called to be the eight Rising Guardian. But Peter corrected him saying,

"Though Marloway was called to be the eight Rising Guardian, he did not transcend because a higher son of one of the fallen guardians took over his body. He became cursed. The one who took his place is Florence."

"Is she the one who saved the grandson of Sturn?" Antonius asked,

"No, she fought three higher children of fallen guardians. You should pay more attention Antonius. But just like you she was a royal," Peter said.

"She was the first royal to be called to be a Rising Guardian," Josiah added.

"Yes she was and unto her was attributed The Noble Heart," Peter said.

Antonius continued naming the remaining Rising Guardians. He mentioned Eleazar Effne, the Ninth, Cristus Love, the Tenth and, Paul, The Eleventh, who was the father of Peter. When they began speaking of Paul, Peter revealed to Antonius that his father was a Shepherd and the staff he had belonged to his father. He received it on the day of his father's transcending. Peter revealed to Antonius that Paul was from Sarbu and grew up as a wandering orphan. Paul had no home. But Peter never understood why his father had such a calm demeanor, nothing seemed to worry him. He never wept in front of anyone nor did he burst out in anger when those he loved were in danger. Paul was always collected but never distant from those he loved. Peter smiled as he remembered all these things about his father. Then he told Antonius the heart that had been attributed to his father, The Willing Heart.

Later that evening Antonius was relaxing by one of the trees close to the lake. Josiah came to him and told him that the Twelfth has instructed him that it is time for him and Antonius to meet. Antonius went from there to where he and Peter had discussed, in the open field. Antonius saw Peter looking south in the direction of Petra. Antonius asked Josiah,

"Is he alright?"

Josiah was silent and did not answer Antonius. He could sense Peter was distressed and he knew why. He and Peter had felt the presence of wolf-men and guiles heading south towards Petra a day before. About a week before that they felt the presence of many wolf-men and guiles heading east. Usually this did not bother Peter but he felt as though they advanced with a purpose and this worried him. In years past they would attack random villages around the northern mountains and he would stop them and drive them away from the villages. But now they moved further south than they had done before. And he worried the most about those moving east because wolf-men had never ventured pass the border of Venduria since he made the mountain his home. Josiah did not want to make Antonius aware of this for he felt it would distract Antonius. So he said to Antonius, choosing his words carefully,

"Peter has things on his mind that he does not want to discuss."

"What things? Do you know?"

"Private matters Antonius. Do not worry about him. It is time. Take your place."

Antonius sat on the grass and rested his hands on his knees. He closed his eyes, his breathing slowed and he kept still. Josiah sat facing him. Almost all was quiet around them. The wind was the only thing that spoke. But it was more of a whisper. Antonius began to feel as if he were floating. He took a deep breath and exhaled through his mouth. The sensation of floating he felt got stronger and the air around him got colder. Then he felt a stillness that was perfect. He knew he was now in his spirit. He opened his eyes and found himself floating above a quiet lake. His reflection was calm and still, but then he saw it began to change and took the resemblance of his father.

"Father." He said but the image did not reflect what he did but it spoke back after he spoke.

"Antonius." The image said as it moved closer to him and came out of the water. Antonius frightened flew back, but before he flew away the person that came forth from the water grabbed his arm. Antonius felt a peace that was familiar and it rekindled treasured memories. The last time this same peace filled his heart was when he sat upon his father's lap as a young boy and his father told stories to him, Marcus and a number of other children of his father's close friends and subjects.

"Be still Antonius," the person said.

Antonius did not need to ask who the person was for their touch had revealed it to him.

"You are The Twelfth," Antonius said.

"Yes I am." The Twelfth said. His voice was calm and soothing. He flew with Antonius from the middle of the quiet lake to the shore and landed gently on the lush green grass. Antonius looked up to the sky and saw a ball of light that shone upon the land in a similar fashion as the moon does. The Twelfth saw Antonius took particular interest in the light so he said.

"Do you know where we are Antonius?"

"I believe we are in my spirit," Antonius answered.

"That is correct. That light in the sky Antonius is your soul." The Twelfth said,

"I never thought I'd live through a moment like this."

"Within the Light is where Eulalie took you, that is where your father sealed the cross of Sirius, The cross that you are wearing."

Antonius looked inside his shirt but the cross was not there.

"The cross is worn on your body not on your spirit, Antonius." The Twelfth smiled. "Long ago before the lands of men were laid and the oceans took their place, the cross of Sirius and those of the other now fallen guardians were forged by the hands of The Great King. They represented the virtues that The Great King had placed upon them to protect and proclaim. But when they fell their virtues became the vices we now know. Sirius was given the virtue of Sanctity but when he fell he became the most vile of all the fallen. Well second most vile, Rudraco's impurity is unmatched. Now the cross serves a different purpose. The cross shields my presence."

"Why does your presence need to be shielded?" Antonius asked.

"Antonius, the fallen guardians, their children and the accursed ones go against you because they want to get to me. They want to use you to imprison me. On the day they fell, I was born. I came forth from the spirit of the Great King, me and my siblings. The power you get from me comes from the Great King."

Antonius fell on his knees when the Twelfth revealed this about himself. Antonius wanted to worship him saying,

"If you are part of the Great King, who am I to stand before you as your equal. I am not worthy."

But the Twelfth took Antonius by the shoulders and helped him up and said.

"You are worthy. That is why you were chosen. Antonius the destiny might have been your father's but it is yours now. There is no mistake to this."

"Why then was I chosen if my father could not do it? What happened, please tell me."

"I will tell you but first you must promise me something." The Twelfth said as a concerned look came over his face. Antonius looked into his eyes and waited to hear his request. "Promise me that no matter what trials you face, you will not let sorrow overcome you. You will not let the darkness cover your soul and you will not give up on the promise of the Great King."

"My father told me never to make a promise I cannot keep. I don't know what lies on the road ahead so I don't know if I'll be able to keep that promise."

"Promise me at least you'll hold on to the promise of the Great King so that darkness will never have a place in your heart."

"I promise you this; I will never give myself to the darkness."

The Twelfth knew Antonius's words were true. He sensed in Antonius sincerity and a desire to seek that which was good. So he had faith in Antonius's promise. The Twelfth said to Antonius as he sat on the shore,

"I trust that you'll keep your promise, if you don't Peter will be forced to stop you from misusing my power. He is already heartbroken from having to do it twice before. Spare his heart and stay on the good path."

Antonius sat with him and responded.

"I will. I promise…About my father…"

The Twelfth smiled.

"Yes, you want to know why it is that you inherited your father's destiny." The Twelfth began. "The Great King loved your father immensely. Your father lived in such a way that reflected the principles the Great King wants all people to live by. Your father even at the point of attaining the vengeance he so sought all his life, though it would have been just for him to take it, he chose to forgive the one who wronged him for the sake of the one he loved. Mere words cannot describe how much your parents loved each other. When I was within your father's spirit I came to realized that he drew more strength from his love for your mother than from me. Whenever he felt down, he would think of her and it kept him going. My power intensified his love for her. She admired him greatly for all he did. But your father had many enemies. Most of who were children of Sirius and those who served them. After your father defeated Sirius, the eldest son of Sirius, Sythe, came alone against your father. He attacked Noble city but your father was able to defeat him. But before Sythe breathe his last, he launched a spear at Annabelle. The spear barely missed her heart. Annabelle was pregnant when this happened. She was pregnant with you. Your father finished off Sythe and turned to your mother. Peter was present as well and he witnessed everything that happened. Your father rushed over to your mother as she was gasping for air and letting out what he feared were her last breathes. His spirit was broken but he tried to keep calm. I granted him much of my power so he could heal your mother but the damage done was too severe. She was going to die. You were going to die as well. But your father did not give up hope, he cried and he prayed to the Great King. He pleaded that Annabelle's life and your life be spared and in exchange his destiny be given to whomever the Great King thought worthy. At that moment I felt myself being pulled from your father's spirit and into yours. The Great King gave me greater power than I had when I was in your father and with the power I was given I restored yours and your mother's life. Your father was eternally grateful."

"So if my father had not said that prayer what would have happened to him?" Antonius asked.

"I am not at liberty to say but I am glad he did because if he hadn't, we would not be having this conversation right now." The Twelfth said in a comforting voice.

Antonius smiled.

"One day Antonius our spirits will become one." The Twelfth continued. "On that day, you will transcend and become a Transcended Guardian, having all the privilege, strength and duties assigned to the Pure Guardians. Until then do as Peter has said and never let your circumstance turn the love within you into hate."

"I will do my best," Antonius said.

"Good. You may go now. Whenever you need me just keep your heart still and you will hear my voice. I will give you the strength you need whenever the situation calls for it. I trust you'll use it wisely."

Antonius in his spirit closed his eyes and took a breath. When he opened his eyes, he was back on the mountain again. Josiah was still seated across from him, sleeping. Peter was still by the edge of the mountain but he was sitting now. Antonius called Josiah, Josiah woke a bit groggy. Antonius noticed that night had fallen upon them so he asked,

"How long did I meditate?"

"About three hours," Josiah said. "Get some sleep, tomorrow you head-back to Petra with Peter. Rest now Antonius." Josiah said then he went back to sleep. Antonius laid back on the lush grass and rested peacefully under the glory of the moonlight.

Day 5- Last Words, Plans of Returning

A calm breeze tickled Antonius's nose causing him to sneeze. He woke up and beheld the clear morning sky. The sun was peeking from the mountains east in the distance. Antonius admired it for a moment. He took a breath then turned to Josiah. Three sparrows had taken to play around the sleeping Faracot. The sight of the birds flying around, landing on Josiah's paw and picking at his hair made Antonius smile. Antonius called out to him. Josiah woke up groggy and yawned loud. He got up and stretched out.

"Where's Peter," Antonius asked.

"I am sensing his spirit by the river."

"Should we go to him?"

"No wait for him, he'll be here soon," Josiah said.

Antonius and Josiah conversed in the meantime while they waited for Peter. After about fifteen minutes, Peter joined them. He came with a couple of fruits in a small bag. He brought out an apple and tossed to Antonius. Antonius ate then he stood as they prepared to leave. Peter walked to the edge and Antonius followed after him. But Josiah stayed in place. While he and Antonius conversed he told Antonius that he did not want to leave the mountain. Antonius turned and saw him watching them, he was curious to know if Josiah had changed his mind and was considering following them back.

"Have you changed your mind?" Antonius asked. "The festival is going to be grand."

Josiah smiled made his way to them. When he was about ten yards from them he sprinted fast at them. He leaped over them, over the edge and started gliding down the mountain.

"See you at the base," Josiah said.

Peter laughed. Then Antonius said,

"He's fast. But it is not a race. Besides there's no way we are going to get to the base before he does."

Peter took a hold of Antonius's armor and pulled him as he leaped off the edge of the mountain.

"Are you insane?!" Antonius yelled at the top of his lung. "You cannot fly."

"Be still Antonius," Peter said with a smile.

They were falling fast but Peter was not fazed a bit. The same could not be said of Antonius. He was waving his arms up and down in a panic, making the same motions birds make when they fly. Peter was still holding onto Antonius's armor with his left hand and in his right hand he held his staff. He kept keen eyes, watching movements below him so he could seek out Josiah. He saw Josiah; he was about fifty feet below them. Peter concentrated and collected his power in his staff. As he had done when Antonius and Astra were cold in the cave, he began to change the wind pressures around them and created a small wind current surrounding he and Antonius. Antonius opened his eyes and saw that they were not just falling but soaring through the air. Peter saw Josiah soar closer to the mountain then he began to fly along the pathway that they had taken up the mountain before they started climbing. Peter changed the wind current so it could guide them along that path as well. Josiah looked back and saw that Peter and Antonius were catching up to him. Josiah raised his wings and beat against the winds once then he tucked his wings close to his body. This put him further ahead of them.

Peter smiled. Antonius now had gotten used to the winds. He was able to see ahead and all around him. He saw what Josiah had done and he urged Peter to make the winds push them faster. Peter was glad Antonius was used to one of his means of travel. Peter concentrated more of his power from his staff and spread it to the last fiber of his being. Because he was holding Antonius, Antonius was also affected by what he was about to do. In a matter of seconds their essence became as grains of sands. Everything of him and Antonius became as grains of sand except his staff. The wind current continued along the pathway and blew their dispersed essence down the pathway till they overtook Josiah and stopped in front of the cave where Peter had told Marcus and Xaria to stay. Josiah saw Peter's staff overtake him and he could feel Antonius's presence close to the staff. He knew they had over taken him. He smiled and continued along the pathway until he saw Peter and Antonius in their full bodies by the entrance of a cave.

"It seems once again you have bested me," Josiah said.

"Did you expect any less of me?" Peter said.

Antonius collected himself, took a breath and stood up.

"You only won because of the wind. Had I done the same you would not have even seen my tail."

"True," Peter said.

"Are we here for the man and the woman?" Josiah asked.

"Yes, Marcus and Xaria." Peter said then he revealed to Josiah that Marcus was Antonius's brother and Xaria was his wife. Josiah knew that Marcus and Xaria were married because he could sense a certain union between their spirits. He knew that Marcus was Antonius's brother because the character of Marcus's spirit was similar to that of Calix. Josiah waited outside for them. Peter and Antonius made their way into the cave to find Marcus and Xaria resting together on a gathering of leaves. Marcus saw his brother enter with Peter. He woke Xaria and they stood up. Antonius embraced him.

"You haven't changed much brother," Marcus said.

"The greater change happened within." Antonius said with a smile. He turned to Xaria. "It's nice to see you are well, both of you."

"Get the horses we must be leaving soon." Peter said then he saw Marcus and Xaria freeze in fear. He turned and saw Josiah walking in slowly. "I thought you'd wait outside for us."

Marcus unsheathe his sword and Xaria armed herself to shoot at Josiah but Marcus urged her to stay back.

"Calm down Marcus. Josiah will not harm you."

"Josiah?" Marcus said with a shaky voice.

Josiah smiled and introduced himself to them.

"Yes, I am Josiah, Faracot of the Twelfth and a friend of Calix."

"You are the one my father wrote about in his diaries. But he never…"

"You expected to see a man?" Josiah asked

"Yes, I did." Marcus said as he put his sword away. "Forgive me."

"There is no need for apologies. We must hurry back to Petra before the festivities begin."

"Agreed." Antonius said "But Josiah what if the people see you. I don't think they'll welcome you kindly."

"I can hide my presence from whoever I wish. Only the four of you will be able to see me. Now come let's go. Daylight burns away."

Marcus and Xaria unloosed the horses and gave Antonius his horse. Marcus granted Peter a horse and rode on one together with Xaria. They began back for Petra, heading south along the Lanii forest. The path they followed would make the journey only a day and a half long. It was about two hours before noon when they departed. The festival was to begin two days from then at noon.

Chapter 24
In Time for the Festival

The morning was brisk and beautiful along the plains, fields and forests that stretched from Vayler to the city of Knights, Petra. Simona that morning left Vayler after spending a few days with David. Hector and his twin sisters, Helena and Hedona, who were also high ranking soldiers, welcomed and hosted Simona. Jeffery had been worried about her so he sent a small scout of knights to know of her whereabouts and when they confirmed her presence in Vayler he sent a letter to her pleading for her to come back to Petra so she may continue training the squires. Jeffery's letter was one of the reasons she left Vayler, the other being to search for Julian. The day after they shared the room in the inn, he left early that morning, leaving nothing, not even a note saying goodbye to her. This made her worry and she wondered about his whereabouts. She left the inn after he did and spent the remaining five days in David's castle. David gladly welcomed her.

Now she was heading for Petra in search of Julian. The festival was to begin in two days, and though she was going to perform with some dancers that had journeyed from Tynda, her mind was so fixated on finding Julian that she did not care to practice. Simona arrived in Petra in the early afternoon hours and was welcomed by guards at the castle. They took her horse away as she made her way to the knight's quarter. Though she knew not where to start looking, she wondered if some knights might know more about Julian's whereabouts since his name was on their tongues for days after he defeated Neemus.

She ventured the halls of the grand castle and when she reached the knight's quarter, she sought out Chris. She found him training in one of the fighting squares. He was going against a young knight who had been showing promise, so Jeffery assigned Chris to continue to train him so he may become fit for war. The young knight showed some skill but when he thought he was beginning to overpower Chris, Chris finished him and laid him to the floor in order to teach him a lesson. In an instant, Chris told him, the tide of a battle can change. Chris helped the young knight up and when he looked to the door of the knight's quarter he saw Simona looking at him. She was smiling. He observed that she was wearing a black dress with gold stretching the sleeves and the helm. Simona also had on red earrings, a red scarf and a red belt. Around her neck was a necklace that was beautiful though the outer shell was cracked. After Chris cleaned himself he went to her.

"You've been in Vayler only five days and you adorn yourself in the color of soldiers." Chris said jokingly.

"Well I'm not sworn to Knighthood so I can wear what I wish."

Chris laughed.

"I know, the colors suit you well."

"Thank you."

"What brings you here? Did you come to learn from me or see me teach rising knights a lesson in humility?"

"I came because I am looking for someone." Simona said

"Oh alright, who may that person be?"

"His name is Julian."

"Be careful to speak that name around here. Jeffery has banned that name from being spoken in these quarters because many knights spoke a bit too much about him. I didn't care so much. Why are you looking for him?"

"Please just tell me if you know anything about his whereabouts."

"I need to know why you want to find him. Jeffery would not be pleased if he finds out you're out searching for the man who disgraced a knight."

"Please, it's important." Simona pleaded

"Alright, I don't know much." Chris said. "But I do remember a knight say that Julian was staying in the Manor of his father."

"Do you know who owns the Manor?"

"I believe it is owned by a soldier, John Hero. I also got word that some sailors that came with Antonius were there as well."

Simona thanked him wholeheartedly, embraced him and then she kissed him on the cheek. Chris smiled and wished her well on her quest for Julian as she departed. She left Petra within the hour. When she was around the east gate about to leave the city, some of the squires she trained saw her and caught her attention. She apologized for her absence and instructed them to continue training using the techniques of swordplay she taught them. She promised she'd resume training with them after the spring festival. They felt neglected but couldn't stay mad at her because they looked up to her.

Simona set course for Hero's Manor. She knew the way because she had been there on several occasions before. Jeffery once invited her to go with him when he was training to become a knight under the tutelage of high ranking soldiers one of whom was John. Then most soldiers did not know of Jeffery's interest in becoming a knight. Another time she had gone with Astra, Mitis and Eulalie for a banquet Sandra and Sofia hosted in honor of their father turning sixty five.

Usually she only went to the Manor when invited or with Astra because Astra was close friends with the daughters of John. Simona was not sure how her presence would be received being that she was going alone. She got to greener fields and knew that she was close to the Manor. A calm gentle breeze started to blow as she arrived at the Manor. She noticed something strange as she approached the manor. The archers on the wall of the manor had their arrows set on her but lowered them when she got closer to the manor. The gate of the manor swung open for her and she rode in and headed towards the house. Hero's servants welcomed Simona as she rode by. She greeted all of them with a smile. The head servant of the house welcomed her and asked her if she needed anything. But she said she wished to see John. As she spoke to Simona the head Servant noticed John making his way to them. She bowed greeting John. John with a smile greeted her and gave orders for something to be prepared for Simona to eat. When the servant left them, Simona thanked John saying,

"I am eternally grateful for your kindness but I cannot stay long."

"Not even for tea. My lovely servant, Mye has gone to prepare something nice for you."

"I came looking for someone I cannot stay long."

"Come, whatever you need to discuss we can discuss over tea. Liana will be pleased to see you."

Try as she might, John would not let her speak to him unless it was over tea. So she gave in and went with him to the dining room. John sat at his place and Simona sat next to him.

About a minute passed and Mye brought in a jug that contained barley tea. Another servant came in with a small cup that was filled with ezula nuts that had been crushed to fine powder. The servants set a cup for both Simona and John and served them the barley tea. Then they put in each cup a little of the ezula powder. They curtsied before John and left. John carefully picked up the mildly hot cup and took a sip. There was a satisfied look on his face after he took that sip.

"Perfection. Try it."

Simona took a sip and was surprised at the sweet and creamy nature of the tea.

"It's delightful."

"Two years ago at a banquet the queen served us these. They were more incredible than plain barley tea. We had to know how she made barley tea so delightful. She told Liana and I that it was the ezula nut powder. We've always made our tea this way since then."

"There is a cake she prepares on certain occasions that tastes very similar to the tea. It's delightful as well." Simona said.

"I'll have to try it sometime. Hopefully I'm present when she prepares it. So what did you want to discuss."

"Please I need to know where the man Julian is. I believe he is the son of Thanos." Simona said but pronounced Thanos wrong.

"Thanos," John said and laughed. "Why didn't you say so earlier? Well he stayed here a while back. Yes when the sailors were still here."

"Did he leave with them?" Simona asked concerned.

"No. But he came back on the day they departed and thanked me for my kindness. Then he left heading west into the forest. I thought it was strange."

Simona smiled because she finally realized where he might be. All this time it had not crossed her mind but knowing now that the last place Julian was seen heading was into the forest she was certain she knew where he was.

"Thank you I think I know where he is." She said to John as she stood up. She thanked him for the tea before she departed.

"You are leaving in haste just like he did. At least stay for some cake."

"I really appreciate your hospitality but I must find him before it gets dark. Send Liana my regards." She said then she departed.

"Alright I'll tell Liana you came by." John said. Then he whispered to himself after Simona left. "These young ones are always in a hurry." Then he smiled. "To be young and carefree...I'll give much of my wealth to live one day like that again."

Simona left the manor and set course west. She set course for Jeffery's old cabin. When she saw the cabin from the trees as she approached, her suspicions of Julian's whereabouts was confirmed. She saw him carrying some firewood

making his way to the cabin. She hid the necklace she was wearing as she rode closer.

Julian heard the gallops of her horse. He set
the firewood by the door and turned. He was
surprised to see her. She dismounted her horse
and with a smile she greeted him.

"Why are you here?" Julian asked. His tone
was strict.

"You sound like you are not happy to see
me."

"No that's not the reason…"

"I'm here because I was worried about
you. You left without even saying goodbye. I
thought something might have happened to
you and I'd never get the chance to say thank
you."

"For what?" Julian asked.

"For being there when I was not well."

"Is that the only reason you came? To say
thank you." Julian said with a slight smile as
Simona approached him. Simona smiled.

"No I also wanted to invite you to the
spring festival. I'll be performing and I'd love
for you to be there."

Julian had planned on leaving Jeffery's cabin in two days and heading to Venduria. He
thought that since his name was well known
now among the soldiers and knights it might be
hard for him to establish himself among the
knights without them feeling he was a threat.
Or among the soldiers for fear that those who
were high ranked will do anything in their

power to make sure he did not rise in rank. So he wanted to start anew. His plan was to head to Venduria and submit his service to one of the higher lords. Slowly he would reveal his skill to them and join the Vendurian royal army if need be. But he did not want to reveal this to Simona yet so he said,

"I'll be there."

"Great. It is in Petra and come early because the festivities begin at noon…" As Simona was still speaking, he noticed that she was wearing a necklace but the emblem was hidden in her dress. He noticed the design of the lace. As she still spoke he slowly reached for it and brought it out from underneath her dress. It was the necklace Antonius had given her.

"I can see you are still living in the past. I will not speak to you until you are fully present with me. There is no future for us if you keep holding onto your past." Julian turned and started making his way to the cabin

"How dare you?!" Simona said. Julian stopped. "You don't know me enough to judge me. He gave me this to remember him by."

"He is not dead is he?" Julian said in anger. "No! As I am speaking to you, you are not fully here with me because a part of you is still with him."

"It was a gift!"

"I don't care." Julian said. Then he walked into the cabin and slammed the door behind him. Simona was standing outside yet she could hear his frustration as he threw the fire-wood into the hearth.

"Fine then!" She yelled. "I don't care if you come to the festival."

Simona got back on her horse and left. After a little while, Julian feeling a bit guilty went out to apologize but Simona had already gone. He closed the door behind him and took a breath. Now Simona was heading back to Petra, distraught and broken. She could not hold back her tears but she was angry at Julian. But she also thought of Antonius and had hope he might someday love her again.

The forest was not as thick on her ride back to Petra. Above the sky became overcast. As she rode back she began to see a dark mist appear about a hundred yards away. She stopped her horse but the mist started to get closer to her. It crept closer to her and from within the mist she heard a voice.

"You cannot give up on love. You cannot give up on Antonius."

Simona was uncomfortable. She tried to turn her horse around to run back to Julian but the mist surrounded her and the voice spoke again.

"Do not give up on love Simona."

"How do you know my name? Who are you?"

The mist began to move in closer to her. It rose and was just beneath her nose. She turned but the mist went up her nose and her eyes saw the one who spoke. He was floating in mid-air in front of her. The creature had on a dark hooded robe. She was afraid to speak but the creature assured her.

"Simona, you cannot give up on love. Antonius still loves you."

"He does?"

"Yes but part of his heart is given to another. He cannot be yours if she is in the way. I think you know who I am speaking of."

"Astra." Simona whispered. "What are you saying?"

"I will not harm her. I will only take her away for a little while so Antonius can realize his love for you once again."

"No I don't believe you…" As she spoke the mist inside stirred her memories. She saw memories of Antonius and her at Lake Amore. She remembered every word from the letters he sent her the years following that summer. Her love for him intensified.

"Deliver her to me." The creature said. "Antonius will return in two days. He shall come from the north and he will be in the garden waiting for her."

Simona opened her eyes and was back in the middle of the forest. The mist had dissipated and she was alone. All that happened to her felt like an apparition but the love she felt for Antonius was still intense. She rode back to Petra. She spoke to no one about what had happened.

Petra was bright and bustling with activities a day before the festival. On the morning of that day Mitis was in his chambers waiting for Jeffery who he had summoned for an urgent matter. Jeffery rushed from the knight's quarter to the king's chamber. After he was let in by the guard Jeffery went to Mitis and bowed. Mitis was standing in front of a mirror when Jeffery greeted him.

"My king, you requested my presence for an urgent matter?"

"Yes." Mitis said then he turned around. He was wearing a new robe designed by the royal seamstress. "What do you think?"

Jeffery was confused. "What do you mean?" he asked

"What do you think of the new robe? What do you think?"

"Is this the urgent matter that you summoned me for?"

"Yes it is."

"Forgive me uncle but I fail to see how this is urgent."

"Is how the king appears before his people not important?"

"Of course it is."

"Then this is an urgent matter. So what do you think about this robe? I have four more I need your opinion about."

"Why is my opinion important to you?"

Mitis smiled and turned back to the mirror. He fixed the cuffs of the shirt he wore beneath the robe.

"On the strolls we've taken around the city I've noticed the way the women look at you. There is a desire in their eyes. That look is only given to well-dressed men. Whether you are in armor or in noble-wear they are drooling over you."

Jeffery smiled. "Well I never noticed."

Mitis laughed. "Are you actually being modest?"

They both laughed. Then Jeffery told Mitis the robe he was wearing was too bright to be a king's apparel. Mitis looked once more in the mirror and he agreed. While he tried on the second robe he conversed with Jeffery about the exhibition match that was to take place on the day of the festival.

Every year the names of the ten highest ranking soldiers and knights were placed in two bowls. One contained the soldiers' names and the other the knights' names. This year Jeffery's name had been picked from the knights' bowl and David's name from the soldiers' bowl. This was the first time in seventeen years that the first knight and the General had been paired up against each other. This had been one of the traditions held at the festivals alongside the dances and singing and play performances. The exhibition match between a high ranking soldier and a knight was always looked forward to by the great masses. Never had the match disappointed.

"Are you ready for your fight against David tomorrow?"

"Actually there has been a change in plans. Neemus will take my place."

"Really? The people are not going to like that. Why is he taking your place?" Mitis asked as he was putting on the last piece of the second garment.

"Neemus pleaded with me to take my place. He says it's a personal matter. I think he is trying to gain back the adoration of the people. Ever since he lost to that bastard he has not been adored as before. If he defeats David tomorrow, things may get back to the way were."

"Bastard? Do you mean Julian, the son of Thanos."

"I don't care what his name is."

Mitis laughed.

"Well Neemus and David both deserve to go against each other. It will make for a very interesting fight nonetheless. It's really amusing. They are almost alike in every way. They are both well in their years and both of them are very experienced and have fought side by side in many battles. Though I respect Neemus, I think David will come out victorious in this pairing."

"Why do you think so?" Jeffery asked.

"David is a fighter just like you but he is much more experienced. Many say your skills outmatch his but his experience far outmatches yours'. David fights in a manner that is hard to study. He has five different fighting styles but he adapts to his opponents fighting style. He learns the way every punch is thrown. The way every kick flies. The manner in which his opponent is going to swing based on their stance. He is an intellectual warrior." Mitis finished putting on the garment. "What do you think?"

"It does not go well with your beard. It looks like it's strangling you."

"It is a bit tight." Mitis said then he began to take off the garment. Then he continued.

"David was born to a Sarburn father and a Napelian mother. His father was a scholar and a fighter and his mother, a scholar as well. She was more learnt than his father. David is not to be taken lightly. If Neemus makes one mistake he'll pay dearly for it."

"David always boasts of being a descendent of a Rising Guardian so his skills may be inherited if his claims of linage are true. Besides Neemus will not make the same mistake with David that he made with the bastard"

"David and the last Rising Guardian were both from Sarbu but I cannot affirm anything he claims. As for Neemus, he was too proud when he fought Julian. It was plain to see. He moved carelessly and he underestimated Julian. David once fought Thanos. It was a year after the war. Though Thanos won that duel, he left with his shoulder out of place. Thanos confessed to your mother, Calix and I that David was the toughest man he has ever stood against. He said that David is even more vicious than wolf-men and more conniving than guiles. Though their fight happened twenty five years ago, I assure you the only thing that has changed about David is the color of his hair."

Mitis tried on the fifth garment and both he and Jeffery agreed upon that one.

On the evening of that same day Julian gathered more firewood for the hearth in Jeffery's old cabin. The night of the day before was pleasurably warm but Julian could feel that the approaching night was going to bring with it a cold front. He set the firewood into the hearth. As he was trying to start a flame going he heard the rustling of leaves outside not too far from the cabin. He kept still and listened. He listened for a sound to know if it was an animal or a person passing by. He kept still for a few passing moments. He turned to resume getting the fire started but before he could begin he heard the leaves rustle again and growls came from outside. But there was something strange about the growls. They sounded as if they were mixed with words. He quietly set aside the rocks he was holding. The cabin was dark and the moonlight was just about to peak through the clouds. Julian slowly snuck to the window to investigate what made the sound. What he saw shocked him.

From between the redwood trees Julian saw two wolf-men emerge. A third one jumped down from the trees and landed in front of the other two. Their eyes were set in the direction of Petra. Julian kept still and watched them. To him it appeared as if they were speaking to each other, plotting something. Julian knew of the immense strength of wolf-men and he was not about to let himself get noticed by them. The moonlight burst through the clouds, shone through the leaves of the giant trees and on the wolf-men. Julian was afraid but he kept calm. He slowly backed away from the window. As he was backing away he saw one of the three of them had set its eyes on the cabin. He snuck and hid in the shadows in the corner of the cabin away from the touch of the moonlight. Julian reached for his waist but his sword was not there. He saw it under the bed where he usually placed it before he slept. He knew it would be unwise to go and get it but he wanted to. As he pondered if he should rush for his sword, a wolf-man burst through the door of the cabin and let out a loud roar.

A cold chill ran down Julian's spine. He was frozen in fear. He did not utter a word nor did he move. He even feared to blink. But slowly his fear turned to anger and his anger to rage. He remembered his father telling him: "fear should have no place in your heart." Now he

was angry but he knew he was outmatched so
he kept still. The wolf-man sniffed three times
and slowly it started taking short paces towards
the corner Julian had hidden. From outside
Julian heard a growl, then a roar. The wolf-man
in the cabin turned around and was about to
leave but before it left, it looked towards the
corner where Julian hid and growled. It ran off
with the other two heading south. Julian took a
deep breath and held his chest. His heart was
beating rapidly. He slowly stood up and went
to collect his sword. He looked out the window
and waited for about an hour. Silence reigned
for that passing hour. In that hour he was lost
in thought for every passing minute on what to
do. He decided that he'll head back to Hero's
manor to tell John what he saw. He felt John
might believe him, if not him then Jacob, the
one who warned him of strange creatures. He
wanted to leave immediately but he thought it
would be madness to do so. But he knew to
wait any longer might mean an attack on Petra.
He thought of Simona. She had left for Petra.
He got up, snuck quietly out the cabin and
started for Hero's manor.

The morning of the spring festival had finally
come. About thirty five miles north of Petra,
Antonius, Peter, Marcus and Xaria came up
onto a hill from which they saw the landscape
for miles. Josiah came up last and after he saw
all that was ahead he confirmed that Petra was

within their sights. Peter covered his eyes from the morning sun to try and see without strain. He still could not see the great city. But Antonius said he could see the north garden. Peter turned to Antonius who was on his left and gave him an odd look. Peter could feel power slowly rising in Antonius. In the distance Peter saw something in the sky flying towards Petra. It was about two miles east of where they were standing. He saw Josiah had also turned his attention to the creature two miles from them. Marcus and Xaria were still trying to scope out the garden in the distance but they could not see what Antonius saw. Marcus asked him if he was sure of what he was seeing but Antonius did not respond. He was quiet and was looking in the direction of the North garden with particular curiosity. The power inside him was rising. Josiah felt it and he turned to Antonius.

"Something is wrong." Antonius said "I don't like this feeling."

"What do you mean?" Marcus asked.

"I can sense something close to Petra, near the North garden, a familiar feeling." Antonius said then he recognized what he sensed, the same feeling he had sensed when he and Mitis had gone hunting about four years ago. But now because there were more of them the feeling intensified. Immediately Antonius spurred his horse on for the North garden.

"Antonius!" Marcus yelled out.

Peter followed after him. Josiah warned Marcus and Xaria that they should not fall behind. He urged them to follow after Peter and to keep on Antonius's trail. Josiah leaped into the air and flew keeping sight of Antonius from above the trees. It was about nine o'clock that morning.

❖

At that same hour the Jewel of Konstuliana was in her chamber with her two closest friends, the daughters of Hero, Sandra and Sofia. She was elated that the day had come but she was also eagerly awaiting the arrival of Antonius. She knew he would keep his promise to her. Not once had he made a promise to her he did not keep and she trusted him to be on time before the festivities began. As she deliberated on the two garments that had been made for her to wear, she practiced some of the songs she was to sing at the festival with Sandra and Sofia. They harmonized together, their singing was heard from outside her chambers by the guards that stood at the end of the hallway. They were glad that the princess was happy. Sandra played the lyre while Sofia danced with Astra for a while. After they had gone and exhausted themselves, Astra urged them that they had to be ready in time. There was still the decision to make about which dress to wear.

Suddenly there was a knock on the door. Sofia ran and opened the door.

"Simona!" Sofia said excitedly. "Come in."

Astra turned to welcome her cousin in as she finished putting her hair together in a braid. She embraced Simona and was glad she had come because she felt Simona could weigh in on which dress she should wear. The daughters of Hero were split on the two dresses Astra had narrowed down. The first was an elegant purple dress that had a beautiful etched design around the curve of the neckline. It flowed down like a river and hugged Astra around the waist when she tried it on. The second was a blue dress of a more simple design but the beauty of it was its simplicity. Sofia had decided on the purple and Sandra on the blue. Astra asked Simona which dress she thought would be best for her to wear. Simona looked at the dresses for a moment, then back at her cousin. Before she decided she asked Astra.

"How do you feel?"

"I feel happy but at ease."

"You should wear what fits your mood. The blue is better for you."

Astra looked at the dress once more

"I agree. Thank you. Do you think Antonius will like it?"

"I know he'll love it."

Astra giggled. After she had put on the dress she turned around and Sandra and Sofia both agreed that the blue was good on her. Simona then revealed to Astra that she had heard from some of her squires that they had spotted Antonius a little way north of the North garden. Astra asked how long ago that was. Simona confirmed that that was the reason she came to see Astra. She suggested Astra go welcome him. Astra agreed. She collected her sword which was in a sling strap sheath. As she made her way fast down the hallway she ran into her father who stopped her. Eulalie was at the hallway talking to a knight but she started making her way to them after she finished speaking to him.

"Where are you going in such a hurry?" Mitis asked

"I am going to welcome Antonius."

"Where is he? Has he arrived yet?"

"No he is at the North garden. I'm sorry father but I must be going."

"Should I send a guard to go with you?"

"No father I have my sword. I'll be fine." Astra said then she ran off. Eulalie wanted to speak to her but she embraced her mother, greeted her and continued on her way.

Eulalie made her way to her husband.

"Do you know where she is in a rush to?"

"She said she is going to welcome Antonius? I wanted to stop her but there is no stopping her when she has her mind set."

"She is stubborn." Eulalie said. "Just like her father."

"Really?" Mitis responded with a smile. "If she's stubborn because of me what does she get from you?"

"Her beauty and her wit."

"Is that so?" Mitis responded with a smile as he took Eulalie and swept her off her feet.

They both laughed. In that moment they felt happy. The love they had for each other was quite clear to see. The queen embraced her king as he carried her. She stared into his eyes in love, she ran her hand through his hair and upon his lips she laid a kiss.

Chapter 25
A Dark Day in Petra

The guards on the wall of Hero's Manor saw someone approaching from the west. It was very early in the morning. That very same morning the spring festival was set to begin. The archers on the wall readied their arrows at the command of Jacob. He told them to stay on form while he looked through his telescope to see who it was that was approaching from the west. At the end of his telescope he saw Julian staggering in their direction. Every step he took, he made with great effort. Jacob saw him stumble and fall. He commanded that every archer lower their bow. Jacob descended the wall on the inner side and ran to his horse. The gates of the manor swung open and he rode out to go help Julian.

Jacob brought him in and took him to lay in one of the guest rooms. He ordered a servant to fetch him some water. It was brought to him, he splashed some on Julian and when Julian regain full consciousness, he drank, replenishing himself before he spoke.

"Where is John?" Julian asked "I have to see him."

"John left for Petra last night with Sandra, Sofia and Michael." Jacob said. A servant handed him a hot towel which he gave to Julian. Julian used the towel to clean his face. "What happened to you out there?"

"I need to speak to John." Julian insisted.

At that moment Liana entered in with Gabriel. Julian wanted to stand and greet her but he was still sore. She urged him to conserve his strength. She came closer to him and sat by his side.

"I overheard you say you need to speak to my husband. John is not here but whatever you need to tell him you can confide in me."

"In us," Gabriel added.

"If I told you what I saw, I am not sure you would be quick to believe me," Julian said.

"You are among people you can trust. We opened our home to you. No one will ridicule you for what you have to say. Now tell us what happened."

Julian revealed to them what happened to him the night before. As he spoke, everyone listened intently and kept silent. He told them everything in its entirety, sparing no detail from the time he saw the Wolf-men till the moment they departed heading south. After he had finished speaking, he saw a great look of concern on Liana's face. Liana stood up and commanded Jacob to ready two horses, one for Julian and one for Gabriel. She told them they must leave as soon as possible. Julian stood up, but he groaned as he did. When he got on his feet he agreed with Liana. Liana thought it very urgent for them to relay the message to John so he may tell Mitis.

"The king needs to know what's going on before something horrible happens."

Julian and Gabriel left Hero's manor within the hour and started for Petra.

❖

The heavens appeared as if they were about to weep. Astra witnessed the clouds gathering as she rode between the plains and into the forest a little ways from the north garden. All before her and behind her seemed dull because she was excited to see Antonius. In haste she continued, through the forest and she came into the opened field on the south end of the garden. There she saw what she thought was him, for in her excitement she saw with her eyes and not through them. For if she had seen through her eyes with an understanding of Antonius's nature, she would have known immediately that it was not truly Antonius who she saw but one who had mimicked his form to deceive her. She saw him standing by a tree and she went to him, dismounted her horse and ran into his arms. But she felt something strange as she embraced him. He did not embrace her back and when she pulled back she looked into his eyes and knew that this was not the man she loved. She tried to pull back but he grabbed her arms and held her in place.

She pleaded with him to let her go but the creature that took Antonius's form did not. Since he did not release her, she kicked him in the gut, jumped a pace back and unsheathe her sword. She warned him,

"Whoever you are, I don't care if you have taken the form of the one I love, I will not hold back."

The creature smiled. It took a strange stance. It stood with its leg apart, looked to the sky and let out a howl. Astra was scared but she stood her ground. From the forest behind the creature leaped out two wolf-men. Astra stepped two paces back. She continued to look on in fear as the one who took the form of Antonius transformed into the likeness of the creatures she saw emerge from the forest. She tried to run but one leaped in front of her. She was afraid but she thrust her sword upwards at its neck. It barely dodged the attack. Astra kept on trying to put up a fight against one of the wolf-men while the other two watched on. She kept swinging but the creature kept dodging every swing. It grew tired and caught her sword, pulled it away and threw it on the ground.

Then with words mixed with growls the creature said to her

"Precious Jewel. He shall not save you. He will not be here in time." The creature was about to take her but before he grabbed her they heard a voice yell her name from the north end of the garden. She looked north and saw Antonius. There was a slight glow around him. The wolf-men saw it but she did not.

"Antonius." She cried as one of the wolf-men grabbed her, threw her over its shoulder and started running into the forest.

"Astra!" Antonius yelled. A wave of fear and fury rushed over Antonius. He unsheathed his sword and started his horse after Astra. He gave no care to the two wolf-men that were standing in his way. Though they knew his strength they were not going to let him through. They charged at him; and he at them. Their razor sharp teeth did not deter him, their huge physique did not scare him and their claws did not make him back down. When they had gotten about ten yards from each other, the wolf-men leaped into the air at Antonius. But a moment before they clashed, lightning flew down from the sky, split in two and struck them down. Antonius stopped his horse. One of the wolf-men tried to get up but before it rose to its feet three arrows in succession struck it in the neck. Antonius heard Peter call his name. He turned and saw that they had caught up with him. Marcus and Xaria emerged from the forest after Peter. Josiah landed beside Antonius.

"Go after her, Antonius," Peter said.

Josiah warned them before Antonius left.

"The wolf-men are not working alone. Look above you."

They looked to the skies and saw two guiles diving fast towards them.

"Antonius hurry," Josiah said. "We'll handle them."

Antonius started after Astra immediately. He continued on into the forest following the path of the wolf-man. He could not see its tracks but the power rising inside him made it possible for him to sense Astra and the wolf-man as well. Antonius yelled Astra's name as he raced closer to her. He could feel it, he was getting closer. She yelled back. He was glad she was still alive. Then he caught sight of her through the trees ahead of him. The power within him kept rising and the gallops of his horse began to increase. The power had spilled over into the horse. It jumped over logs and fallen trees with ease.

Antonius began to become aware of his surroundings. It became clear to him which part of the forest he was racing through. He knew that the Novarian River was ahead. He also knew that this portion of the river had a steep drop. He knew he had to get to Astra before the wolf-man got to the river. More power began to rise within him. His horse galloped ·faster.

Antonius's senses were heightened because of the power that was rising in him. He knew that two guiles were coming in fast from his left and right. Antonius quickly unsheathed his sword and struck down the guile that came in from his right but before he could take down the one coming from his left in time. It tackled him. The impact knocked the wind out of him. He fell off his horse and dropped his sword. He was dazed for a moment but regained his composure in time to stop the guile from gnawing off his face. In the corner of his eyes he saw his horse running away. He felt Astra's spirit get further away. He knew without his horse he would not get to Astra in time. With his hands still restraining the jaws of the guile he looked in the direction of where he sensed Astra's spirit. The Twelfth gave him more power because he sensed the weight of Antonius's need to save Astra. Antonius kicked the guile off himself. It flew back a few feet. Antonius ran for his sword. The guile rushed Antonius. Antonius stood his ground and prepared himself. But before it could get close to tackle him, lightning fell from the sky and brought it down. Antonius heard Peter call his name. Antonius turned and beheld Peter and Josiah racing towards him. Marcus and Xaria were a little ways behind them.

"Antonius, are you alright?" Peter asked when he got to him.

"I'm fine but I may not get to Astra in time."

Josiah sensed that the power in Antonius started to fall after he said that, so he encouraged Antonius because he knew Antonius doubted himself.

"Do not give up easily Antonius, Peter, give him your horse."

Peter immediately got off his horse. Antonius took the reins and leaped on the horse.

"Continue after Astra now. Go!" Josiah said. After Antonius left, Josiah told Peter to get on him. "We'll take to the skies and watch over Antonius." Peter got on Josiah. Josiah leaped into the air and flew after Antonius, watching him from above. He made it his initiative to make sure no guiles or other wolf-men attacked Antonius. He sensed the power in Antonius had risen again. Antonius was heading fast towards the wolf-man. He was about a three hundred yards behind Astra. He looked on ahead as he continued to race closer to her. The wolf-man had reached the edge of the river drop.

His horse kept pace and continued running fast approaching the wolf-man and Astra. The wolf-man dropped Astra on the floor and turned back at Antonius. A huge guile landed by Astra and took a hold of her. The wolf-man looked at the guile and the guile knew what it was to do. It picked up Astra and was about to fly away. The power in Antonius surged. The power flowed more into his horse that it began to run so fast that its gallops made the ground beneath quiver.

The wolf-man rushed at Antonius as the guile took to the air with Astra. Antonius was less than fifty yards from the edge. From above Josiah and Peter saw this. Marcus saw his brother far ahead of him through the trees. Antonius's eyes were on Astra but he knew he would have to dispose of the wolf-man first but he had no intention of stopping. The wolf-man rushed at him and jumped to knock Antonius off his horse. But in a swift moment, Antonius unsheathed his sword, impaled the wolf-man in its chest and threw it over his head. It landed dead behind him. He continued after Astra. Antonius was just about close to the edge as the guile was about to fly further away and without a second thought he led his horse to leap off the edge. But before it went off the edge Antonius squatted on the horse and took a hold of the harness. The horse leapt fifteen feet in the air. Astra saw Antonius as he was about leap off his horse. She felt he might try to reach her so she hit the guile on the back of its head. It lost its grip of her but caught her quickly. Antonius launched himself off the horse, forward and upward. He stretched himself to reach Astra but his fingers grazed hers before the earth began to pull him down and the guile flew away with Astra. In that moment as he fell he knew he had failed. He saw fear overcome Astra. All around him seemed to become slow. Time was moving like a snail and reality was merciless. He hit the water hard and was knocked unconscious.

"Is he insane?!" Marcus yelled after he witnessed what Antonius had just done.

"Why would he do that?" Peter asked.

"Oh no," Josiah said.

Marcus and Xaria had caught up enough to see Antonius disappear over the edge. Xaria yelled out his name as they raced closer. When they reached the edge of the river drop, Marcus looked down into the river but Xaria set her eyes downstream. The current was relentless. Xaria saw him.

"There, downstream," she said.

Marcus started his horse downstream and continued until he got sight of Antonius. He continued riding till he was a little way ahead of him. The drop from where he was now was not as daunting, so he dismounted his horse and dove into the water after Antonius. He reached his brother and started pulling him towards the shore but the current was unforgiven. Marcus persisted and got to the shore with Antonius. Marcus coughed up a lot of water and when he was alright he checked on Antonius. Peter and Josiah landed by him and Xaria rode up to them. Marcus pressed his ear against Antonius's chest.

"He's still alive," Marcus said. "What was he thinking?"

"He was doing what he thought was right," Josiah said.

"It was not right. It was insane." Marcus said "That is the length he is willing to go for her." Josiah said, "You of all people should know how much she means to him." "This is neither the time nor place for an argument." Peter said "Marcus I think it is best you take Antonius back to Petra but do not tell Mitis what has occurred here today. Josiah and I will go after Astra. We will try to bring her back but until we return do not tell Mitis what has happened. He will act rash if he knows Astra is in danger."

Josiah kept his eyes on Antonius and could feel that the power the twelfth had given him had not subsided a bit. Even in an unconscious state, Antonius's need to save Astra was still strong. Peter got on Josiah and they took to the skies after the guile that took Astra.

Marcus picked up Antonius and put him over his horse and they started back to Petra.

Chapter 26
Terror in the skies

The skies above the south-eastern side of Konstuliana rang out with the shrieks of guiles. But the shrieks did not last long for Josiah's mighty roar ran across the sky as he flew with great speed at the guile that was carrying Astra. Peter was on him as they raced together towards the guile. Perhaps he thought, somehow they could save Astra before it was too late. But both Peter and Josiah knew this was not going to be an easy task considering that more guiles were behind them and were coming in with great speed. Josiah looked to his sides and saw guiles on each side of him flying at the same speed as him. He raised his wings and flapped faster to gain speed. He got ahead of them and continued soaring but they caught up to him. Peter looked behind and saw another guile fast approaching.

"Josiah another one of them is behind us."

Josiah turned and saw it. Then he thought up a plan on how to rescue Astra but he would have to make sure the guiles following him did not get in the way.

"Peter, can I rely on you," Josiah said.

"Of course."

"I have a plan but you must trust me. Do not hesitate when the time to act comes."

"I will do my best."

Josiah kept on course but started flying at an angle, ascending higher into the clouds. The guiles kept on him. He flew faster and started to glide for a bit till he caught sight of Astra again. The air was cold. Josiah tucked in his wings and dove towards the guile. He broke forth from the clouds and Peter saw why he started diving.

"Peter now, dive after Astra now. I will handle the guiles that are following us."

"Good luck my friend."

Peter got into position and leapt off Josiah. He put his arms very close to his sides and was falling fast. At the rate and angle at which he was falling he was going collide with the guile that was carrying Astra. This was Josiah's plan. He had told Peter on their ascent that after he takes care of the guiles he'll come for him and Astra. As he was falling Peter took one last look behind him and he saw that Josiah was in fierce battle against the three guiles. He turned back to the guile that was carrying Astra and from behind him he heard the shrieks of the guile followed by Josiah's mighty roar.

Peter focused. He was getting closer pretty fast. He stretched his left hand out and grabbed the wing of the guile when he collided with it. The guile spun twice but held its grip of Astra. Peter struck it with his staff on the back of its neck. It let go of Astra. As Peter let go of its wing he struck it one more this time on its side before he dove for Astra.

Peter and Astra were both falling fast and he feared he would not reach her in time. He kept his arms close to his side but he still was not approaching Astra fast enough. He thought quickly and created a wind current as he transformed his essence to grains of sand. The wind took him faster towards Astra and he retook his form a little below her. He took a hold of her and tried to calm her but her screams made it hard for him to concentrate. Peter could sense that Josiah was still above the clouds. Peter tried to calm Astra for she began to become more frantic as they were getting closer to the ground. So he said to her, speaking in a calm voice

"Everything will be alright princess I promise. Don't look to the ground. Close your eyes. Be still princess."

His words were soothing but he could still feel the restlessness of her spirit. Above he saw Josiah burst forth from the clouds with great speed. There was a loud sound that followed after. Josiah's wings appeared as streaks of white light as he rushed towards them. But what Peter saw behind Josiah he knew would be a problem to them all. A guile was still following Josiah but as Peter kept keens eyes on the guile, he saw three more behind it. The guile behind Josiah looked to Peter as if it was gaining speed. It flew faster and caught up with Josiah. It stretched out its neck and with its sharp teeth bit Josiah's tail. Josiah spun quickly and used his wing to knock it away.

Peter knew at this rate Josiah was not going to make it to them in time. It was up to him to get Astra to safety. Peter kept still and concentrated his power into his staff. Everything seemed to slow down, and then he lifted his staff towards the skies. From the clouds, lightning raced down and passed Josiah and the guiles and was coming in fast to strike his staff. But a guile struck him hard from the side before the lightning stuck his staff. The lightning incinerated the guile. The impact knocked him unconscious and he let go of Astra and started falling. Another guile flew quickly, caught Astra and laughed as it watched Peter fall to the earth. Josiah saw this happen a moment after he disposed of the third guile following him.

"Peter!" He yelled. Though he knew Peter was alive he could sense that Peter's spirit was in a dire state of stress. But Josiah could not get to Peter's aid because one more guile stood in his way. Josiah rushed at the guile as he released his claws. He drove his claws into the guile's neck and he placed his hind legs on the guile's chest. In one swift motion he separated the guile's head from its body as he pushed the body of the guile towards the earth.

Josiah set his eyes east and saw the guile that had taken Astra. There were seven more guiles flying with that guile. He could sense's Astra was trembling but to go after them would mean he would have to leave Peter.

"Peter." He said and remembered. He looked to the earth and saw that Peter had landed among some ferns in the marshlands beneath. His fall had caused him to bring a tree's roots closer to the surface and his body was lying close to the edge of a swamp. Josiah flew down to him immediately.

"Peter can you hear me."

Peter was lying face down in the mud. Josiah saw Peter's hand twitch after he called his name again.

"Peter hold still." Josiah said as he placed his paw on Peter's back and healed him to the point where he was able to move. But every fiber of his being was sore. Peter got up to one knee and Josiah tried to help him up but Peter refused.

"Thanks but I can stand on my own." Peter struggled to his feet. He leaned on his staff as he got back to his feet and when he was standing he moved a few paces back and leaned against a tree.

"I have to go after them." Josiah said.

"Alone? That's not wise. Something tells me there are much more of them than we think."

"If we wait what change will come about? I will go not to confront them but to know where they are taking her and who is behind this? I have a feeling it is a ghoul. In the meantime you should return to Petra and tell Antonius what has happened. I'll return when I find out more about what's going on."

Peter watched Josiah fly away heading east. Peter bowed his head and took a deep breath. With the last bit of strength he had left he raised his staff and called for lightning to take him. He disappeared from that place and appeared at the north gate of Petra. He fell to his knees and started breathing hard. The guards on the wall saw what happened and they sent out two horsemen to help him in.

The great city of knights was bustling with activity. The people knew not of the things that happened outside their gates. Not of what happened in the North garden or above the skies east of their city. The people cared only for the festival that was about to begin. And it was soon about to begin. It was about thirty minutes before the festival was to commence. The guards on the wall of the north gate felt that such a day of celebration might be cut short because they had kept watch in the direction of where Astra had left towards the north garden to welcome Antonius. They were worried because she had not returned. From the bushes into the forest that they saw her depart they saw three people appear. Two of them were on a horse and the third person led the horse. The head guard on the wall looked through a telescope and saw that one of the people on the horse was Antonius. He called for an escort of three horsemen to go welcome them and to inform them that Mitis was worried and was waiting for his daughter's return. But when the horsemen saw how battered Antonius was they feared to ask what happened to him.

When they asked about the princess, Antonius, Xaria and Marcus left them without an answer.

"Excuse us." Marcus said as he walked past them. Xaria held Antonius steady upon the horse. He was slowly regaining consciousness but he kept swaying with every step the horse took. Marcus went from there to the castle. As he walked through the city and saw all that was going on in the city he felt sorry for the people. A guard had gone ahead of them and informed Mitis of their return.

Mitis refused to leave to begin the opening ceremonies of the festival until Astra returned. When the guard informed Mitis of their return, Mitis was in his study room with Eulalie and Jeffery. He stood up immediately and started for the castle door and he met Marcus, Antonius and Xaria in the first hallway, left of the foyer. The grand statue of he and Calix was behind them. Marcus and Xaria supported Antonius as they walked in. Antonius's head hung low and his steps were slow. When Eulalie saw the condition Antonius was in she wanted to go to him and help him but Mitis held his hand in her path, she stopped and stepped back. Marcus did not like the stare Mitis gave them. He knew Mitis would want to know what had happened to them. But to explain it all to him, Marcus felt Mitis would not understand nor would he be willing to listen to reason. Mitis with a stern voice asked calmly.

"Antonius, where is Astra?"

Antonius did not look up to him but he heard Antonius whimper. Marcus hung his head low and then looked up to Mitis to try and explain to him what happened.

"We were on our way back when…"

"I was not speaking to you Marcus. I was speaking to Antonius" Mitis said. His voice was still calm. He asked again. This time his voice was a little higher and strict. "Antonius, where is Astra?" Antonius still did not respond or look up to acknowledge him. But a tear escaped from his eye.

"We were attacked." Marcus began. "It's not his fault."

In a fit of rage Mitis rushed Antonius, grabbed him and slammed him against the wall.

"Where is Astra?! Where is my daughter?!" his voice bellowed and ran down the hallway. Xaria tried to get Mitis to release Antonius but he shoved her back with one arm. She fell to the floor. Marcus rushed him as well but Mitis used his elbow and struck him in the jaw.

"Where is she?!"

Mitis did not stop slamming Antonius against the wall until Eulalie called out to him,

"Mitis please stop it!"

Her voice seemed to keep him in place and he slowly let go of Antonius. Mitis was still furious but he tried to keep calm. Jeffery did not dare speak to him when he was like this. Only Eulalie could attempt to reason with him when he got this angry. But Mitis felt regret, guilt and a sudden realization as he stepped back from Antonius. Antonius fell to the ground. Xaria rushed to help him.

"I was right." Mitis began. "All these years I was right to treat you as a curse. I kept you at arm's length for the sake of my family. But you made me feel guilty and out of guilt I welcomed you into my home. I blamed you for the death of your father. He died because of you. Eulalie knows it's true. You are a curse."

"Mitis please stop," Eulalie pleaded.

"No you will not defend him! Not this time…not this time. He is not a child Eulalie." Mitis turned back to Antonius. "Your father died because of you. I'll be damned if I let my daughter die because of you as well."

Mitis turned and left them. As he walked away from them he ordered Jeffery to summon David. Jeffery left immediately. Eulalie ran to Antonius and apologized for Mitis's words but Antonius did not respond. From the corner of the hallway they heard someone coming their way. They turned and saw Peter. His cloth was torn in several places, he was covered in dirt and he was walking with the help of his staff.

"I'm sure you heard all of that," Marcus said.

"It is best to leave Mitis alone for a while. Josiah has gone on to learn more about who is behind this. Guiles and wolf-men do not act this organized without a leader. We have to know who we're dealing with before we act."

Peter saw the concern on Eulalie's face. Eulalie knew of Josiah and she knew he only involved himself in the affairs of men if ghouls were concerned. Peter went to Eulalie and embraced her.

"Do not weep fair queen. We will bring your daughter back." Peter turned to Antonius and pleaded with Eulalie. "Please clean his wounds, I will go and speak with Mitis. Perhaps I can reason with him before he does something rash."

Peter went on from there to find Mitis.

Chapter 27
A Father's Heart

It was about half an hour into the second hour after noon when Peter found Mitis. The sky was overcast and looked as if it was about to rain. Peter did not want to speak to him yet. He watched Mitis from the hallway window that faced the throne room. He saw Mitis give instructions to Jeffery and a man of taller stature, who had silver hair and wore an armor that was equal in glory and splendor but had a different set of colors to the one that Jeffery wore. Peter watched him give instructions to Jeffery and this man who looked familiar to Peter. But Peter did not dwell on the man too much. He watched Mitis trying to discern what he was saying but could only gather something about the assembling of men, nothing more. He waited for about half an hour. In the time that passed he treated some of his wounds. Then he went to speak to Mitis.

Mitis was staring east out of one of the tall windows in the throne room. There was a chilling silence in the room. The only thing he heard was the wind. Then he began to hear footsteps coming his way. He turned expecting to see Jeffery and the man he sent coming to confirm they had done what he sent them to do. But once he saw Peter, he turned his eyes east again and started breathing slowly as Peter approached him. When Peter got closer, Mitis began,

"As a father, there are many things you worry might happen to your child. You prepare yourself to handle such things to the best of your abilities when they happen. Many worries begin from the day they start walking, on the day they fall and hurt themselves, sprain an ankle or bruised a knee. Many things I have prepared my heart to handle but nothing like this, nothing like this."

Peter heard the slight crack in Mitis's voice. When Mitis turned to Peter, Peter saw that Mitis's eyes were wet but his cheeks dry. A tear escaped Mitis left eye. He felt surprised.

"What? Am I crying?" he tried to smile but it faded quickly. "I can't remember the last time a tear escaped my eye."

"Twelve years ago I could feel from the mountain your spirit was greatly distressed as the day when Calix passed away."

"Twelve years ago?" Mitis said and remembered the event. "Kineta's funeral," he said then he sighed deeply.

"Mitis there is no need to feel grieved, Astra is still alive." Peter said trying to lift Mitis's spirit.

"But for how long?" Mitis said.

"Don't speak like that. Antonius and I were not the only ones who tried to save her. Josiah was with us as well and he has followed after those who took her to know where she was taken and who is behind this. Wolf-men and guiles do not act this organized without a leader."

Mitis upon hearing that Josiah was involved felt a bit reassured because he had seen Josiah's power at play and felt they may have a chance at saving Astra.

"I know what you are going through Mitis." Peter said. "It still hurts me to say but I outlived my children, my grand-children and two generations after them. The closer I kept to my descendants, the more they were made targets by wolf-men and guiles. I drew back and stayed in the mountains for their sake. As the years passed, my descendants forgot me, soon they forgot my name but they always knew that they were descendants of the eleventh Rising Guardian. As long as they did not forget this I was happy."

As they were still speaking a strong wind blew open the doors on the others side of the room that led out to the balcony of the throne room. Peter and Mitis turned and saw Josiah land on the balcony and he made his way in slowly. Mitis's hands quivered for a moment. He still hadn't gotten used to the nature of Josiah's form. Josiah always looked intimidating whenever he first met someone but after they heard him speak, his voice reassured them that he was kind at heart. Josiah made his way to Mitis and Peter. Peter noticed that Josiah had been hurt on his left side. It appeared as if he had been hit there and the bruise was apparent of this. The skin beneath his white fur was bright purple and the mix of the white of his fur made it appear a lighter shade of purple. He spoke to them revealing what he knew,

"I know where they took her and I know who is behind this. I met them, or rather I should say they met me." He looked at his left side.

"Where did they take her?" Mitis asked

"Who is behind this?" Peter asked.

"It is Elana, the daughter of Sirius, she is the one behind all this."

"No, please no, it cannot be!" Peter said

Peter was shocked but remembered that the day Antonius left for the mountain he felt a spirit of a similar nature to that of Sirius when he watched the city from the walls. But Elana, he never thought would do something like this for he had once been on an Island with her and she did not kill him. She was merciful to him and he believed she let him escape. In the time he spent with her he saw a different side of her heart and hoped that she would be among the few children of fallen guardians who did not bring pain upon the lands of men. This was years before he first encountered Gammon.

"Where did they take her?" Mitis asked again.

"They took your daughter to Philonia. She is in Noble City. Wolf-men and Guiles have taken over the city but as I flew close to it I could sense a great collection of spirits in the Cathedral. I think someone foresaw the attack and knew to gather the people into the Cathedral."

"What good does that do?" Mitis asked

"No guile, wolf-man or children of a fallen guardian can enter a cathedral without risk of burning to dust," Josiah answered.

"Who struck you on your side?" Peter asked "Did Elana do that to you?"

Josiah looked at the bruise on his side and revealed the source of his injury.

"Yes, ten guiles attacked me at the same time and after I had disposed of them, I was suddenly struck by something and I fell to the earth. She appeared before me, choked me and lifted me as if I was nothing! Though she could have made me suffer she let me go."

"How can she be this powerful?" Peter asked.

"While she held me I felt darkness in her spirit Peter, a snake of sort is manipulating her will. She demands that Antonius be brought to her. She wants to battle against him to avenge her father."

"Why does Astra have to be brought into the middle of this?" Mitis asked.

"She is testing him. Elana knows Antonius loves her. Antonius's nature is such that he would refuse to confront her given a choice. But now she has given him an incentive." Peter replied but he knew that often higher children of fallen guardians did this not for the incentive but to have an upper hand against those who they challenged. But Peter knew that Elana was not only powerful but cunning, there had to be another reason for her taking Astra other than incentive and an advantage over Antonius.

"Why Astra?" Mitis said then he yelled. "Why my daughter?!" he fell on his knees and struck the floor. Peter took his hand and brought him back to his feet.

"Mitis, I promise you, Josiah and I will do everything in our power to make sure we bring back Astra alive."

"No, you've already tried and failed, it is in my hands now. I will not fail my daughter," Mitis said.

Peter and Josiah forgave Mitis's arrogance. They felt sorry for him so they did not hold what he said of them against him.

At that moment a guard opened the throne room doors and ran to give the king a message but at the sight of Josiah he froze in place and he stumbled on his words.

"Speak now! What is it?!" Mitis commanded.

"Your Majesty, David and Jeffery have returned."

"Send them in now!"

The guard went out and permitted Jeffery and David to enter. Jeffery walked in and behind him walking at a calmer pace was David, the General of the Army of Konstuliana. He was a tall man, well into his years, he had broad shoulders and most of his hair was silver gray. His posture and demeanor made him out to be a man to be respected and rightfully so because of all he had done for the nation. Mitis was the third king he had served under and under' whose kingship he was made General. When David and Jeffery entered the throne room they saw Mitis, Peter and the great white winged lion behind them. Jeffery went for his sword but David walked up further in front of him and commanded Jeffery,

"Put away your sword knight." David observed Josiah for a moment and had a suspicion of what Josiah was. Then he acted as if he knew when he proclaimed it.

"I know what you are. You are a Faracot are you not?"

Josiah was silent. Peter smirked and went to sit on the last stair that led up to Mitis's throne.

"A Faracot, what is that?" Jeffery asked.

"Do you not study the history books? Faracots and Rising Guardians are as vines and grapes. One cannot thrive without the other. I don't know who it is he has been assigned to by the Great king but whoever the Rising Guardian is, he must be a person of great honor."

"How do you know these things?" Jeffery asked. "I've always said it but many have doubted me. I am a descendant of Paul the eleventh Rising Guardian. His Faracot was the great bear of the south. Paul was the first and only Rising Guardian to be chosen from Sarbu."

Peter slowly turned his attention to David and stared him down carefully. He could see that after so many generations his father's features were still apparent in his descendants.

Mitis had other matters at hand and wanted to confirm with David and Jeffery if they had done what was requested of them. So he asked them after he silenced David and called their attention,

"Is everything ready?"

"Yes my king." David said

"How many soldiers are there?" Mitis asked.

"Four thousand strong and ready to mobilize within the hour as you commanded," David replied.

"How many knights are there?" Mitis asked.

"Four hundred ranked knights and six hundred of the best from the reserves my king," Jeffery responded.

Josiah sighed and was about to speak but Peter stood up and said what he was thinking,

"An Army is not going to stop Elana. You cannot save Astra like that." Peter said trying to reason with Mitis.

"So what shall I do? Wait around like you are doing? Unlike you Peter I have a plan."

"War is not a plan. It is best we wait until Antonius recovers."

"I don't care if he is the Rising Guardian, I don't need him to help me kill that whore. I will bring Astra back. I will see to it that anyone who stands in my way, whether wolf-men, guiles or offspring of Sirius, will meet their end at the edge of my sword."

"I see you've made up your mind," Peter said. "Fine I'll go with you."

"It is best we wait for Antonius," Josiah said.

"Let us face the facts Josiah. I know you
can feel it as well. Antonius's body is not the
only thing that is broken. His spirit is still distressed and it takes longer for the spirit to heal.
It's going to be a while before Antonius can
heal himself after he overcomes whatever ails
his heart."

Mitis turned to David and Jeffery and
commanded them to go wait for him by the
castle gate. He told them he'll be joining them
soon. They left. Peter a bit confused thought
Mitis was about to leave immediately, after
hearing the instruction he had given David and
Jeffery he asked,

"You're not going with them yet?"

"No, I have to get my home in order before
we depart." Mitis said then he left them. Peter
and Josiah went to find Antonius.

The heavens above the great city wept and
earth drank its tears. The heart of the nation
was broken and the heart of the one most precious to the princess was shattered even more.
At about the same time Peter had finished
speaking with Mitis, Marcus had taken Antonius to the room that was prepared for him and
Xaria. Eulalie was with them for a while. She
and Xaria helped clean Antonius's wounds and
dress them with bandages. Antonius sat on a
chair next to the window. He looked out into
the city and saw the wet day. He was silent. He
had not spoken since he had been pulled from

the river. A servant brought in something for him to eat but he refused it. Marcus was speaking to Eulalie who was about to leave them when he saw Antonius turn away from the food that was brought to him. Marcus thanked Eulalie and she departed. The servant left as well. Marcus went and sat on the bed close to his brother. Xaria stood close to the window. The tray that had been brought to Antonius had on it a bowl of soup, a few carrots and an Apple. Marcus took the apple and with his palms hard on the side of the apple, he split it in two equal halves. He extended his hand to give Antonius a half but Antonius would not take it. He pleaded with him.

"Please brother, take and eat."

Antonius's gaze was still set outside. He looked to his brother, then at the apple. He took the apple from Marcus's grasp. He bit into it and chewed slowly. Marcus took a bite of the half he was holding and watched his brother for a moment. He saw brokenness in Antonius's eyes. He had seen the same brokenness in his eyes when he looked into the ocean the day he landed on the island alone. He could remember feeling that he had lost Xaria forever. He looked to her. Her gaze was on Antonius, she looked very concerned. When she caught his gaze he called her to come and sit beside him. He took her hand before he spoke to Antonius. He spoke words of encouragement to his brother.

"You feel you have failed her." Marcus began. Antonius turned to him and listened in silence. "No one can do what you did to try to save her. Antonius you must not give up hope. I know she is still alive. Take heart brother. You have not failed her. And you should not feel as if you have."

Marcus took a breath.

"Seventeen years ago, exactly a year after father passed, Can you remember what mother told us? Do you remember what she said when we found you in the garden weeping by a tree that night? She carried you and told you something. I heard what she said. Can you recall what she said Antonius?"

Antonius recalled her words well. Like a rushing wave they crashed into his memory the moment before Marcus spoke them.

"She said, know that my eyes are always on you whenever you fall my son, for I shall never leave you in the dirt. In the days I am not here, your brother shall help you up. Those same words mother spoke to me when I was hurt myself and even on the lonely nights on the island I could hear her spirit whispering those words to me. Though my body was down, she lifted my spirit up." Marcus leaned in to his brother and affirmed. "I will not leave you lying in the dirt Antonius."

At that moment the door creaked opened and Josiah and Peter entered. Antonius was now looking down towards the tray and did not acknowledge their presence until Josiah called his name. He slowly turned to them. Josiah could sense the deep distress that hung over Antonius spirit. He knew Antonius was blaming himself for all that had happened. But just like Marcus he tried to encourage Antonius. Josiah approached him and said.

"It is not your fault. You are not the one who sent the wolf-men and guiles after her. You may feel you have failed her because you were not there in time but trust me there is still a chance to save her before it is too late. But it cannot happen without your help. I know where she is. I know who is behind all this."

"Who did this?" Marcus asked.

"The daughter of Sirius, Elana," Peter said. He was standing by the window.

Josiah could sense Antonius had an idea of who it was, so the news did not surprise him as much. And though he did not move much they could see in his eyes that the news did not move him. Then Peter revealed to them where they took Astra.

"The creatures that took Astra have taken her to Noble City."

When Antonius heard where they had taken Astra his eyes widened and he sat back up against the chair. He looked very concerned. He tried to speak but his words were stuck in his throat. It appeared as if he were having a slight convulsion.

"Antonius be still," Marcus said as he took Antonius's hand and tried to calm him. "It's alright." He turned to Peter when he remembered his brother. "What of Titus, is he alive? Were you able to sense him?"

Josiah answered him, "Elana attacked me before I could learn if he was alive. There are still many people in the city I could sense them. But they are gathered in the Cathedral, maybe Titus is among them."

"We can only hope," Peter said.

"What of Mitis? What does he plan to do?" Marcus asked them.

"Mitis has assembled an army and they are soon to leave within the hour."

Marcus stood up.

"Do you know where he is?"

"Why?" Peter asked.

"I want to join him, for Astra but also for Titus and my people."

Xaria stood up.

"If you are going then so am I."

Marcus turned to her. He took her hand and said. "Alright, but under no circumstance are you to wander from me. I need you by my side at all times." Marcus asked Peter again. "Do you know where he is?"

"I can sense that his spirit is upstairs around the chapel. I don't know if he'll be there for long."

"Thank you. We'll go meet him before it's time to depart."

Marcus turned to his brother one last time before he departed with Xaria to find Mitis. He patted his brother on the shoulder and said

"I hope you resolve the ailment in your spirit so you can join us. We'll need you out there."

After he said this, he and Xaria left. Now Peter and Josiah were in the room with Antonius and they did not have many words for him. They knew the state of his heart. They would have to give him some time alone with himself so he could heal himself after he has resolved his thoughts. But before they left him Peter spoke to him saying,

"I know you may feel afraid. There is no shame in feeling fear Antonius. I can sense in your spirit you want nothing more than for Astra to be safe but you are afraid you'll fail if you try to save her again. Your fear has crippled your spirit and because of this your body stays broken. I have also been under the burden of fear but I have not let it cripple me. Sometimes it is okay to be afraid but it is never okay to let fear cripple you from doing what you know is right."

❖

A simple silence filled the hallway on the path to the chapel. The guards still stood at their places and as Marcus and Xaria passed them they could tell the guards were all aware of much that had happened. When Marcus and Xaria reached the corner of the hallway close to the chapel they heard voices. Marcus peaked and saw that Eulalie and Galen were standing outside the chapel. He motioned for Xaria to be still. She stretched her head to see what Marcus had seen. She saw Eulalie and Galen. Marcus and Xaria kept still and kept watch. About a minute passed and Mitis emerged from the chapel. He was clothed in full armor but without his helmet on.

Mitis got down on one knee before his son. He rubbed his son's shoulders and said.

"I am proud of you my son." Then he embraced him. "I promise I'll bring your sister back." Mitis kissed Galen on his head and held him tight. The young prince held onto his father and tried to hold back tears.

Marcus overheard what Mitis said and the sight of the moment made him remember the events that happened the night of his father's death. Calix spoke to Marcus in the same manner that Mitis was speaking to Galen. Mitis stood up and with love in his eyes he gazed at his queen.

"I'm sorry for what I said earlier. I hope you can find grace in your heart to forgive me."

"All is forgiven my love," she said as he took her and embraced her tight.

"I love you" Mitis whispered in her ear. He whispered something also to her about Galen's coronation if he did not return. After he had said this he gazed at her and saw that tears filled her eyes. He laid a kiss on her lips while in her embrace. As he wiped the tears off her cheeks he heard footsteps approaching them. Mitis turned and was surprised but glad to see Marcus and Xaria. A slight smile came across his face.

"It's good to see you," Mitis said.

Marcus smiled.

"What happened earlier…" Mitis started with intent to apologize.

"There is no need to apologize Mitis. All is well between us. In fact we have come to join your army."

"Thank you," Mitis said. "We'll be leaving soon, so perhaps we should get going."

"Yes but one more thing." Marcus said then he turned to Galen. He got on one knee as Mitis had and made a promise. "Look at me. Your father will return. I promise you. I will do all in my power to make sure he returns alive with your sister. So take heart and do not let your spirit linger in despair. I was your age when I lost my father. I can remember the pain of loss too well. I won't let you go through the same thing. A child should never have to suffer that much." Galen bowed his head as Marcus was still speaking. "Look at me," Marcus said gently, "I promise you."

Eulalie felt a great comfort after Marcus made his promise. But Xaria was concerned about the lengths Marcus would take to keep his promise. She knew that Marcus was a man of his word and his heart knew no bounds when it came to staying true to his words. Marcus stood up and shook Mitis's hand. From there they went to the castle gate. Eulalie and Galen watched them depart from the front door. The rain had stopped and the clouds scattered as the last light of the evening sun graced the land. Eulalie and Galen waved goodbye as Mitis, Marcus, Xaria, Jeffery and David departed. They left Petra heading to where the army and knights had assembled by the Gylin road. When Mitis reached he saw the army had formatted themselves in a fashion that was used during wartimes. The knights had stayed in a section in front amidst soldiers on the outer row and on the further left.

Among those leading the army was David, who was upfront. On his right and left were his twin daughters, Hedona and Helena. And on David's further right was his son, Hector. Leading the knights was Jeffery. Neemus moved with him on his right side and Chris on his left. Mitis lead both groups with Marcus on his right and Xaria on his left. Behind them was the setting sun. Mitis saw a shadow fall on him as they started marching. He cast his eyes to the sky and saw Josiah and Peter flying ahead of him. Peter looked back at him. Mitis felt assured of victory.

Chapter 28
An Unlikely Friend
Visions of Hope Courage Found

Grave like silence haunted the halls of Mitis's castle. The silence penetrated the room in which Antonius stayed the most. The door was open. A small candle had been lit by Peter before he left. He set it on a small stool that stood beneath the window. The evening sun made way for the night as the wax of the candle melted away. Antonius could sense that the silence had not only overcome the castle but also the city.

Outside his room Simona kept still and listened. Her heart sank when she thought of all that had happened and she blamed herself. She peeped into the room and saw the blank stare on Antonius's face. He was staring at the flame of the candle. She could feel her stomach clench up. She leaned against the wall and held her chest. She groaned in silence and started breathing hard as she kept herself from wailing. Initially she wanted to go with Jeffery but he pleaded with her to stay and console Antonius so he could come to himself again. But she felt she could not do it because her heart was still shaken from all that had happened. Because of the power in him his sorrow spilled out and she could feel it and it weighed heavy on her heart.

Tears ran down her cheeks. She took a breath and kept still then she heard footsteps coming her way.

When she turned and saw that Julian was coming her way, she wiped the tear off her cheek and stood up straight. Julian was clothed in the armor soldiers of Konstuliana wore. The armor had been lent to him by John Hero. The armor was one of John's older ones and though he could not fit into it as he did in his younger days, the armor suited Julian pretty well. He had all of the standard bearing on except the helmet, which he was holding in his right hand.

Julian noticed Simona from down the hall as he was making his way to her. He saw her and slightly smiled but the smile disappeared from his face rather quickly.

"What are you doing here?" Simona asked

Julian did not answer her. He peeked into the room and saw Antonius and responded.

"I now see why you're here."

"Please Julian not now. I had to be here for him. After I learnt of what he went through trying to save Astra I...I had to come" She said as her voiced cracked and she kept a low tone. She was about to break out in tears but she held herself. "He almost died trying to save her." Julian wiped the tear that slid down her cheek. He took her hands and drew closer to her.

"It is alright," he said trying to comfort her.

"I want to go in and console him but his sorrow weighs heavy on my heart. I can feel it. I can feel how hurt he is."

Julian could feel Antonius's sorrow as well but it did not lay heavy on his heart as it did on Simona's heart because he felt no guilt about any of the recent events that transpired.

"I'm sorry if you are angry to see me here but this has nothing to do with us." Simona said

"You're right. I did not come here for you. I came here to speak to Antonius."

Simona raised her eyes to him and asked, "Why?"

"I was in the front ranks of the Army with John Hero as we waited for Mitis east of the city. When I was with Hero he thought it strange that Antonius was not in front of the army ready to lead with Mitis to war against those who took Astra. He told me of the love Antonius had for Astra. He thought Antonius would have gone on his own to save Astra. I told him that Antonius would come but he did not believe me. He told me under such circumstances a man would have one of two reactions, he would either be ready to take down all that stand in the way of him and the one he loves, or he would hide away afraid of acting because he fears the possibility of failing the one he loves. Hero asked me to return and check on Antonius and make sure he joins the war because Antonius has encountered wolf-men before. I agreed and while heading back to the city I met Marcus along the way. Mitis, and a few others were with him. They went on while he discussed some things with me. He told me what happened to them on their way back from the mountain and their encounter with the wolf-men. He says he also tried to encourage Antonius but Antonius did not respond much to his words. But he also revealed to me something about Antonius that I had suspected before but I let my doubt overrule my suspicions."

"What about Antonius did he reveal to you?" Simona asked.

"He told me that Antonius is a Rising Guardian. When I was a child rumors around my town and Noble city suggested that Calix, his father was the Rising Guardian but somehow it is Antonius who is truly the Rising Guardian." Julian said then thought back to how easily Antonius defeated Gammon on the ship. He knew no mere man could stand against a ghoul such as Gammon not even Thanos, his father. "If this is true…" Julian continued. "We'll need his help against the wolf-men. I'll go and speak to him. I think he'll come around. But this is so unlike him. On our voyage here he never once backed down from anyone that threatened our lives. We escaped death together. I owe him my life."

Julian slowly went in. The candle vaguely illuminated the room. The light did not travel to far from Antonius. When Julian entered in he stood at the door,

"My king." He said addressing Antonius.

Antonius turned and acknowledged his presence but could not see who it was that addressed him. Julian walked closer to him and saw what he was wearing. The shirt Antonius had on was stained with fresh blood on the right side of his lower rib. Julian sat on the bed as he observed Antonius wound. Julian asked politely if he could examine the wound. Antonius slowly lifted his shirt and Julian saw that Antonius was bleeding through the bandages. Julian carefully removed the bandages. He took the towel that was on the stool close by and cleaned the blood off Antonius side. He saw the wound clearly now. He could tell it came from the fangs of a wolf-man. There were fresh bandages on the stool from which he got the towel. He took the bandages and dressed the wounds. As he was doing this he told Antonius that Marcus had spoken to him. After he finished dressing the wound he picked up the towel and cleaned his hands.

"I know I'm the last one you expected to see. There is not much that we share, not in possession or in personality. I am the son of a soldier and you the son of a king. Very little is common between us but this one attribute I know we share. We are not cowards. I've heard some of the things the people of the city have called you on my way back. They have called you a coward for not going with Mitis for the sake of Astra. But they have not seen what I have seen. A coward does not jump into the roaring sea to rescue prisoners he does not know. A coward does not stand against a ghoul like Gammon to protect those dear to him. And a coward does not risk his life to go against wolf-men and guiles to try to save the one he loves."

While Julian spoke Antonius did not turn his eyes from him. Julian leaned in and continued.

"Do you know what tomorrow signifies Antonius?"

Antonius kept silent so Julian continued.

"Tomorrow marks the start of the nineteenth year since our fathers passed away. Neither of our fathers were cowards. We are sons of brave men, men who gave their lives to protect the ones they loved. You were willing to risk your life to save men you did not know, you stood against Gammon for the sake of the ones dear to you and though you tried to save Astra you couldn't and now you feel defeated. Are you afraid you'll fail again or are you afraid you'll lose her?" Julian stood up. "If you do not gather the courage to go fight for her, then you will fail her and you will lose her. Think on these things Antonius because we need you... she needs you."

Julian left Antonius in the silence. Antonius was alone with his thoughts again. The night had fallen upon the land. He kept his eyes on the shadow the flame cast on the wall. He swore he could hear laughter but it was only his thoughts. But the laugh he knew too well, the laugh of Astra. She filled his mind in the silence of that passing moment. In his thoughts he could see her smile, he saw her dance and loved the way she moved, he remembered the smell of her perfume, the mixed scent of apples, pear and honey. He coughed and held his chest. He wondered why he felt so broken.

Antonius was tired and he began to fall into a deep sleep. As he drifted off he heard someone call his name. The voice was that of a woman. The voice was familiar to him. When he opened his eyes he was in a garden. The same garden he had come to with his father when he was a young child. He was in the middle of some shrubs. The voice called out to him again. He stood up and ran in the direction it came from. He emerged from the shrubs and saw the one calling his name. It was Annabelle. She was cloth in a bright white dress with a golden belt. To Antonius she appeared very tall. He did not care. He ran to her and when he stretched out his arms to her he saw that his hands were small. He then realized he was as a child. Annabelle picked him up, embraced him and kissed him on the head. He held her tight and wept in her arms.

"I'm so sorry mother," he said. "I'm so sorry."

"What for my son?"

"I was not strong, mother."

"My son, there is no need to apologize. You are strong."

Antonius heard another voice call out his name. He knew the voice and turned at once. He saw his father coming their way. Calix was cloth in a fine purple robe and had a golden belt around his waist. When Calix came to them, he held both Annabelle and Antonius in his arms and kissed them.

"I'm proud of you my son."

"I have done nothing for you to be proud of."

"Don't speak like that son. Remember the promise I made to you before I left you. I promised you that whenever you need me I'll be there. I saw the lengths you went through to try to save Astra. That took great courage. But you have begun to doubt yourself because you could not save her. You should not fear to go to such lengths and beyond for her sake my son."

Antonius looked down. He was tearing up but he wiped his eyes.

"Antonius, do you love her?"

Antonius looked up to his father and answered.

"With all my heart."

"Good, then let your love keep you strong. Love is a tree and courage is one of its fruits. I understand your brokenness. I have gone through the same thing." Calix said then locked

eyes with Annabelle. He smiled. "No matter
the fear that filled my heart, I thought of your
mother and how much she meant to me. How
much I loved her. My love for her kept me
strong, my strength always returned to me
when she filled my mind. I know you love Astra. Let your love for her be your strength. Your
brother was able to do this after he was desert-
ed on the island alone. I spoke to him and he
kept hope that one day he would hold Xaria in
his arms again. I can see that you love Astra
and you would do anything to make sure she is
safe. Wouldn't you?"

Antonius nodded. Just as Calix finished
speaking a butterfly landed on Antonius's arm.
He was taken a bit by surprise and was about
to move and startle the creature away but Calix
gently rubbed his shoulder. Then he said calmly.

"Be still my son."

The Butterfly flapped its wings softly as it
sat on his arm. Then it took to the sky in peace
and Antonius watched it as it flew away.

Antonius knew he was dreaming and in
that calm peaceful moment he opened his eyes.
When he woke it was morning and the wound
on his side had healed. He felt it when he
touched his side. He ripped off the bandages
and stood up. He looked outside and felt anew.
Courage burst from the core of his being. He
could feel the Twelfth giving him power because he had overcome his fear. He took to

heart the words of his father and knew what he had to do. Then he said under his breath before he walked out of the room.

"Astra I will not fail you."

When Antonius walked out into the hallway, he saw Julian and Simona sleeping opposite the wall that faced his room. Julian was resting against the wall and Simona was resting her head upon his lap. Antonius called to Julian in a calm voice. Julian did not wake so he went to him and gently nudged his shoulder. Julian woke up groggy. When he saw Antonius he knew something was different about him. Antonius stood straight. Julian called Simona to rise. She woke up and saw Antonius. She could also sense something different in him. There was a slight glow that resonated from him. Antonius helped both of them to their feet.

"What made you finally come around?" Julian asked.

"It is as you said; we are sons of brave men. To waste away in my self-pity is to dishonor my father and abandon Astra. It is also true what you said, she need us."

Julian smiled. Simona was happy to see Antonius smile.

"Alright then, there is no time to waste we must head out now," Julian said. "If we ride for a day without stopping we may be able to reach them before the battle starts."

"I agree but I need a new armor. The old one given to me is broken in many places."

"New armor?" Julian said. "This one is not even mine. I can't loan what I don't have."

"I know where you can get armor," Simona said.

"You do? Show us the way," Antonius said.

Simona led them to the armory room which was close to the knight's quarter. This room contained armor that was used mostly for training purposes. These armors were light weight and the shield not as strong as the standard war shields used by knights. Antonius did not mind this. After he put on the new armor, Simona brought him a new sword. It was the training sword used by Jeffery. It was as a real blade but the material was not the same durable material used to make standard war swords of knights. Antonius swung the sword in the air, testing its handling. He liked it. He turned his attention back to Simona and asked.

"Are you not coming with us?"

"No…I fear I might be a burden to you."

"We could use you out there. Your brother trained you did he not? Do not doubt yourself. Put on some armor and let us leave."

Simona did as he said. The armor she wore was one of Jeffery's older armors. The same he wore when he first fought in the knight's tournament. Originally it was beaten up but Jeffery had it restored and secretly made it to fit Simona after he became first knight. This was one of the armors she used when she trained squires. After she put on the armor she met up with Antonius and Julian outside the armory. When Julian saw her he was impressed. She had tied her hair back and held it in place with a band.

"Alright let's go," Antonius said.

They went on to the castle gate. The horse secured close to the gate was Julian's. That was the only war horse available to them. Julian knew where they could get horses fast enough to cover the distance they had lost. As he rode out Antonius and Simona ran on foot following him. They came to the stable that was cared for by the man Julian had bought a horse from to journey from Petra to Hero's manor. The man saw them coming his way and thought that the two running were knights and the one on the horse was a soldier. He was just arriving to tend the remaining horses when they met him. When Julian came close enough the stable keeper recognized him.

"You... I did not know you were a soldier please forgive me for the way I spoke to you before..."

"It's alright old man. I did not come here for retribution. I need two horses. The fastest you have."

"I don't have too many fast horses left."

"It doesn't matter. Bring us two of the fastest among the remaining lot," Antonius said.

"Yes, yes of course." The stable keeper said then he ran into the stable and brought out two horses he judged to be the fastest among those he had left. The first horse was a brown stallion and the second was a Tyndarian White Whisper. The White Whisper was about the same height as the stallion but it had bigger legs and a hairier mane. It was also slower than the stallion.

"Do you not have anything faster than the Whisper?" Julian asked.

"No this one is faster than most White Whispers. That is why it was brought back."

"It'll do. We'll take it," Antonius said.

"Are you sure?" Julian asked. "Surely he must have something faster."

"We shouldn't waste any more time." Antonius said then mounted the horse. Simona took the brown stallion. Antonius turned to the stable keeper and thanked him before they rode off. They left heading towards the East gate. Antonius rode a little bit ahead. Julian rode on his left and Simona on his right. They rode on heading east. The power in Antonius began to rise. Julian and Simona could feel it. He urged them to stay close. As the power flowed into his horse it also spilled over into theirs and their horses galloped faster than any horse had ever done before.

Chapter 29
The Battle at Snake Valley

A day had passed since they began marching. The evening sun was about to make way for the night as the army led by Mitis stopped to set up camp. Many had grown tired from the march so David convinced Mitis to stop so they could rest. Mitis's heart wanted to go on for the sake of his daughter but he could not deny his body's need. He was worn from the journey as well. They set up camp thirty miles from the borderlands between Venduria and Philonia. To the south their position was wet lands and further south beyond the hills were the shores. To the East of their position the land carried on with valleys and hills and dense forests. To the West of their position the land was plains and green fields on which they had marched on for quite some distance. North did not have much to offer but flat lands and grand mountains in the distance.

Many of the soldiers rested between the plains and on the side of the hills. Many of the knights rested atop the hills and a few on the sides with the soldiers. Mitis rested beneath a tree. He sat alone for a while. Meanwhile Jeffery went with Neemus and Chris to consult with David on how the knights and soldiers would align on the battlefield. David asked

Jeffery to sit. On David's right and left hand side were his twin daughters and leaning against a tree behind him was his son. Jeffery sat down and they began to discuss on how the soldiers and knights would format themselves so they would be able to break through the wolf-men as fast as possible.

"It is not going to be easy taking down one wolf-men let alone an army of them," David said.

"This is true but I've encountered them before so I know how vicious they are."

"So have I. The last time I stood against a wolf-man I was in my late fifties. Twelve years ago. Mitis sent me to personally deliver a message to a lord in Venduria. Lord Aiden, Hector you were there with me, remember?"

"Yes father, I remember," Hector said. "You scared the beast more than it scared us. It tried to escape but you put it out of its misery quickly."

"I didn't want to be cruel to it. It was once human. I was just being merciful to the poor creature."

"It was the third that attacked us that day," Hector said.

"...and the last," David said. "What of you Jeffery, when did you last encounter a wolf-man?"

"It was four summers ago. I led a campaign to reclaim land taken by a noble or a lord I can't remember. When we were returning from the battle we were attacked by about fifteen of them. Neemus some other knights and I were able to finish them off before they escaped us. They almost killed Simona but Chris got to her in time." Jeffery said then continued. "But we are not only going against wolf-men. We also have guiles to worry about."

"This is true," David said. "So we must be mindful of the skies. But what of that man on the Faracot, perhaps he could be of much help to us."

"Peter? I don't know much about him but he is fighting with us so I hope he keeps the guiles in check."

As they were still speaking Hector noticed Mitis coming towards them, Helena and Hedona also saw him and they stood up. Jeffery turned and saw Mitis and stood up to greet him but Mitis said they should stay as they were. Mitis was holding in his hand three loaves of unleavened bread. Mitis gave a loaf to Jeffery which Jeffery split between himself, Neemus and Chris. Mitis gave a loaf to Helena which she split with her siblings. Mitis broke the last loaf he was holding and gave half to David. Jeffery looked on at the army and noticed that everyone was sitting in different groups but all eating something. Some soldiers were among knights and vice versa.

Jeffery felt a bit sorry for some of them and for himself.

"For some of them, even for us, this could be our last meal."

"Don't speak like that Jeffery. To speak as one defeated is to already admit defeat," Mitis said as he sat with them.

"Forgive me your majesty," Jeffery said.

"It's alright. We should keep our spirits up," Mitis said.

"I wonder if it was like this during the days of the War of the Fathers," Jeffery said.

"The armies in those days fought against children of fallen guardians. They could take forms more terrifying than wolf-men and guiles. In a way we have it easy," David responded.

"Though this is true we will not in any way be careless," Mitis added.

When Mitis finished speaking Josiah landed a little ways behind him. Peter was with him. When Helena and Hedona saw Josiah they shook a bit and drew closer to their father but David told them that they need not worry. Josiah was not going to harm them. Hector was startled for a moment but held his place. Josiah and Peter went to Mitis and informed him of what they had seen ahead.

"As suspected there is an army of them," Peter said.

"How many are there?" Mitis asked.

"A little over a thousand wolf-men but I'm not sure how many guiles there are," Peter said.

"They cannot be over a hundred," Josiah added.

"That is true. As of now many of them are around Snake Valley."

"That's only a mile and a half from Noble City," Mitis said.

"I think it best the army confronts them there than to bypass them for the city. We should finish them off before we head for the city," Peter suggested.

"I don't think we have a choice," Josiah added. "We couldn't bypass them even if we wanted. The guiles would give away our position."

"Alright. We confront the wolf-men at Snake Valley," Mitis said.

"What of the guiles?" David asked.

"Leave the guiles to Peter and me. We will keep them from interfering. Just focus on breaking through the numbers of wolf-men that stand in your way." Josiah said then he and Peter left them.

David and Jeffery finished strategizing on how to integrate the knights and soldiers to effectively fight together. When they decided upon the formation to use David sent his daughters to inform the soldiers the agreed upon course of action while Jeffery sent Neemus and Chris to inform the knights.

A little ways east of where David, Jeffery and Mitis were, Marcus was sitting atop a hill by a tree with Xaria by his side. His eyes was set east in the direction of Noble City. He wondered how much the city had changed since he left. If the people would recognize him or forgive him for he felt he abandoned them in some way. Then he began to speak his thoughts,

"It has been too long, far too long. After all that is too happen, if the people see me, will they remember me, will they forgive me, will they welcome me?"

"Of course they will welcome you. They will be even glad to crown you as king again." Xaria said.

"I have no desire of being king, at least not now." Marcus said "Not until the Saints cleanse me of Gammon's mark and I present you as alive before your father and sisters. Antonius told me how broken they were at our funeral." His voice was calm and his spirit open. He slowly stood up with his eyes set on Philonia. "Can you hear it? It's beautiful."

"Hear what?" Xaria said as she stood up as well.

"That beautiful song," Marcus said.

"I don't hear anything. Marcus please sit down. We've journeyed a whole day we need to rest."

"But I can hear it as clear as the morning birds. You can't hear it?" Marcus said. His tone was a bit louder. He was sure of what he heard.

"No my love. Come let us sit," Xaria said as she took his hand and they sat back down and rested against the tree. The last light of the evening sun departed the land and the stars came out. They all slept beneath the stars.

Mitis was the first to arise an hour before dawn. Peter was close by and had kept watch through the night. Josiah was beside him resting but not asleep. Mitis mounted his horse and started towards where Marcus and Xaria were. He stopped beside them. Marcus heard him and woke up slowly. Xaria arose as well. They got up and mounted their horses and took their places beside him. Josiah with Peter flew over to them and landed. The ranks of knights and soldiers started waking up and when they became aware their king was set to depart they started to gather themselves quickly.

"We'll go ahead you," Josiah said.

"That's fine," Mitis said.

"We'll keep the path clear and make sure no guiles interfere," Peter added.

"Good luck," Mitis said.

"The Great King will grant us victory. See you soon my friend." Peter said then he took to the skies with Josiah. As they flew away Josiah revealed to him something that worried him. Josiah told Peter that he had been watching the moon and plotting its path and it appeared by its movement that sometime around noon the shadow of the moon will fall upon the earth.

"Wolf-men are stronger whenever darkness covers the land," Peter said.

"Then we have to end this before noon," Josiah said.

When the first light of the morning flared across the horizon, the army led by Mitis began marching. The archers stayed on the peripheral line of the group. Many of the archers were soldiers and a few knights. The biggest soldiers and knights stood among the front ranks. A few of the most skilled knights and soldiers were given the duty of leading into battle a group of soldier and knights they were assigned the day before. They had been informed by David that an average person cannot take down a wolf-man easily but if four or more attacked at once, the beast could be brought down much faster. This was the plan. To attack in groups led by highly trained knights or soldiers. David could stand against a wolf-man alone but he knew many soldiers had not encountered such a beast so he thought this the best means of attack. He also kept in mind the safety of his soldiers and knew this form of attack will garner fewer casualties.

They marched on for two hours and came upon a great hill. Ahead in the sight of many of them was Snake Valley. Mitis looked up and saw Peter and Josiah returning.

"They're coming our way and quick. They are as an army themselves." Peter said. "Some guiles spotted us when we were scouting the land." Josiah said "We must attack very soon."

Mitis looked on ahead and he could see the wolf-men in the distance. Those vile beasts were even uglier than he remembered and they were coming in great numbers. He took a breath and looked to the mass of soldiers and knights gathered behind him. In some of their eyes he saw fear, in some he saw hope, in some he saw a determination to overcome whatever odds stood against them. He could feel for those who shook in their boots. So as their king he rallied their hearts and spoke to them,

"Soldiers, Knights, I am before you, speaking to you not just as your king but as a father, a father whose daughter has been taken from him. All who are fathers and mothers among you know what it is to love one who is as your own, in flesh, in blood, in glorious likeness. So I plead with you, take this burden of mine upon your hearts and let it be your strength. I beg you, please guard your hearts. Guard your hearts against fear, for fear has no place in the hearts of the sons and daughters of Konrad, Sturn, Liana, and Philonia." Mitis locked eyes with Marcus at the mention of Philonia. "Make no mistake this is not going to be easy for no great victory is handed to anyone. We are gathered here today for one cause, to save Astra. And we will not spare anyone who stands in our way whether they are beast or man or son or daughter of fallen guardians, I do not care! This is not a battle, this is not a war; this will be a massacre. We will destroy every one of them. Those things we are about to fight were once men, but they betrayed humanity, and now look at what has become of them. There is no fight for honor, nor for glory, we fight for Astra." Mitis put on his helmet "Ready your arms! Let us finish what they started!"

His words struck their hearts and a wave of affirmation from the knights and soldiers rang back at Mitis. They beat theirs shields twice and raised their spears high. Peter smiled. Marcus and Xaria enjoyed the little spectacle then they turned their attention to the sea of wolf-men and guiles coming their way. Peter and Josiah were about to take to the sky but Mitis said.

"Not yet."

Josiah waited. Jeffery gave the call for the archers on the right wing of the army to raise their bows. David called for those on the left wing to do the same. In unison David and Jeffery gave the command to fire. The first wave of arrows flew fast and struck down a hand full of wolf-men and knocked down a guile from the sky. The archers did this three more times. When the archers readied themselves to release the fifth wave, Mitis, Marcus, Xaria and many of the knights and soldiers unsheathe their swords in preparation to charge. The spearmen readied themselves as well. After the archers released the fifth wave, Mitis let out a battle cry that ran down the valley and shook the hills. Josiah roared. Then he and Peter took to the skies. The soldier and knights united charged at the hordes of wolf-men coming at them.

Mitis nostrils flared as his horse galloped down the hill and into the valley towards the wolf-men. All his fear turned to rage. He griped his sword with such intensity that the hilt and his palm were as one. Nothing was going to stop him from getting to his daughter.

Then it happened, the sons and daughters of the mighty army of Konstuliana clashed with the vast number of wolf-men. Mitis dodged the first wolf-man that jumped at him. He used his shield to knock aside the second that came lunging itself at him. He thrust his sword into the heart of the third wolf-man that attacked him and in that same motion threw it aside. But the forth caught him by surprise and knocked him off his horse. He regained his composure quickly, rolled, collected his sword and sprung to his feet. A wolf-man came charging at him, but he side-stepped the creature. When it turned back to attack him, he put up his shield and blocked its claws. With three swings of his sword he brought the wolf-man down.

In the early goings of the battle, Marcus and Xaria fought close together and made sure they weren't too far from Mitis. Peter and Josiah kept the guiles in check. Peter and Josiah had learned to fight in a harmonious manner. Peter would on occasion jump off Josiah and onto a guile's back, then he would strike it and as he fell Josiah would fly to catch him. Sometimes he would call down lightning to take a hand- full of guiles down. The guiles kept their focus on him. The army pressed on because they did not have to worry about the guiles interrupting.

Jeffery advanced with the group Neemus and Chris commanded. They took down wolf-men in perfect succession. Because they moved together and watched each other's back, there were very few casualties among their group.

David and his children were a group and they pressed through the wolf-men as well but David fought too intensely and broke through the numbers of wolf-men in their way. Helena, Hedona, and Hector found it hard to keep up with their father. They started falling a bit behind. When Hector realized this he encouraged his sisters to keep fighting so they could catch up with David. As David broke through he met up with Marcus, Xaria and Mitis. Five wolf-men were charging their way. Hector and his sisters caught up and saw the beasts charging at them.

"We can't back down now," Hector said.

"No, we can't," David said then he and Mitis leading started charging towards the wolf-men with Marcus, Xaria, and, his children keeping pace as well.

As Jeffery fought on he noticed the soldiers were advancing faster than the knights. He did not like this so he encouraged those who were with him to fight with more vigor. He started to fight more intensely and recklessly but nonetheless his method worked and he advanced as well and was able to catch up with Mitis and the company with him. Now they had come out further from the center of the valley and over a new hill. Marcus was the first to see it. The gate of Noble city was a mile away in the distance.

"There it is!" Marcus said. All of them saw it but there was still a considerable amount of wolf-men in their way. They could see more guiles and wolf-men coming out from the city. They waited for a short moment and the number of their company increased as more of the army got to where they were. Mitis and Marcus stood together in front of them ready to lead the charge. Mitis gave the word and they charged together. But from above a guile swooped down and picked up Marcus.

"Marcus," Xaria yelled.

The guile flew on with him towards Noble city. Peter in the corner of his eye saw a guile carrying someone and when he saw it was Marcus, he told Josiah and they flew fast his way. But Marcus was not one to wait for help. With his sword still in hand, he thrust upward at the guile's heart twice. The first blow made it shriek and it sunk its claw into his armor and its nails began to pierce his shoulders. He took hold of the guiles hand with his left hand and shrugged his right hand out of the guile's grasp. With a greater force he thrust his sword into its heart one more time as he pulled it to-

wards himself. The guile shrieked even louder
and clawed at his hand. He lost his grip and
started falling. The beast died in the air and
started falling. They were twenty five feet in the
air. Marcus managed to land on his feet. He
heard a crack and felt a quick snap around his
lower left ankle. He yelled in agony. He tried to
stand but he fell back down.

Xaria was the first to see where he landed
and she immediately started towards him.
There were five wolf-men in her way. Mitis
supported her and those with him rushed on
following behind her. The first wolf-man saw
her coming its way and it stood tall to strike her
down but she slid through its legs. Two others
came running at her but she side stepped them
and continued. As she was escaping them, Mitis and those following her were finishing them
off. The fourth wolf-man caught her by surprise
but she dodged its claws at the last second. She
jumped back and the beast roared at her. She
was not intimidated. She unsheathed her
sword and charged at the wolf-man. It tried to
strike from overhead but Xaria used her shield
and knocked its claw away. With four slashed
and a fifth thrust into its throat she brought
down the beast. She put her sword away and
readied her bow and arrow and took aim at a
fifth wolf-man who had noticed Marcus and
was rushing to him. She shot four times in
quick succession at the temple of the beast. It
fell down at Marcus's feet. Marcus was still

trying to stand when he looked up and saw Xaria running his way. She came to him and took his hand.

"Are you alright?" Xaria asked.

"I'm fine," Marcus said.

"Don't lie to me. You're not fine. You can't continue fighting."

Josiah and Peter landed by them as Mitis and those with him caught up to them.

"Marcus I'm sorry I didn't make it in time," Josiah said.

"How bad is it?" Peter asked as he approached and observed Marcus's leg. Xaria had taken off his boot.

"I think it's broken. I can't stand."

"Be still," Peter said. He placed his hands on Marcus's ankle then said. "It'll take a while to completely heal it but I can do it."

"Do what you need to do we'll keep the wolf-men out of your way," Mitis said.

David's eyes were on the gate of Noble city when he saw many more wolf-men rushing out of the city and the guiles high above grew in number. He gripped his sword and frowned.

"My king, it seems this battle is far from over," David said.

Mitis turned to him and ahead noticed the wolf-men and guiles coming their way.

"There are far too many guiles. Peter how long do you need?" Mitis asked.

"I don't know. Maybe fifteen minutes. Josiah do you think you can hold off the guiles for that long?"

"There numbers are more but..." Josiah said then he stopped speaking because he could feel something coming from the west. A strong wind started to blow east. The power Josiah felt was familiar. Peter could feel it to. He and Josiah had their eyes set west.

"Do you feel that Peter?" Josiah asked.

"Yes but who is it?" Peter asked.

"Yes, yes it is him. It is..."

"Antonius!" Peter exclaimed.

Chapter 30
The Power of the Twelfth

The hoofs of the Tyndarian white whisper stomped on through the forest seven miles from the battlefield. It was about thirty minutes before noon when Antonius, Julian and Simona emerged from the forest west of Snake Valley and onto the path to the hills before the valley. Antonius could sense that the tide on the battlefield was changing. He could sense a growing number of wolf-men and guiles pouring into the further part of the valley. He could also sense the spirits of the soldiers and knights on the battlefield. Their hope was waning because of the numbers of beasts coming their way. He knew this. Then he felt someone else. He sensed the spirit of Marcus and he could feel something was wrong. Julian riding behind on his left noticed the change in express on his face.

"Antonius is everything alright?" Julian asked.

Antonius heard him but did not respond. The power in him began to rise and he sensed spirits further away in the distance in Noble City. He could feel that there were a vast number of people in the cathedral but he also sensed people in the palace. It was then he felt a faint spirit and he knew whose it was. He could tell it was Astra's spirit. Beside her spirit he felt the presence of a great evil within the spirit of another.

It began to dawn on Antonius that this was the same presence he felt when he looked to the trees at the shores of Demoir. The same presence he felt that caused him to look to the skies on the night he was with Marcus and Xaria. The same presence he felt in a dream days before the death of the elders.

"We must hurry," Antonius said. The power in Antonius continued to rise and now he could not only sense the spirits of those on the battlefield, he could now see them. They emerged from the forest and in the distance Julian and Simona saw the soldiers and knights in fierce battle against the wolf-men and guiles.

Antonius's vision was sharper now and he saw where Marcus was. He could tell that Marcus was hurt and he also saw Xaria, Peter, Mitis and those around him. But further he saw the wolf-men pouring out from the gate of the beautiful city.

Julian kept his eyes on Antonius as they rode on. He began to notice something very different about Antonius. He watched on as Antonius's armor started to slightly glow and the aura spilt over onto the white horse. The aura continued to extend itself and began to surround his and Simona's horse. He could feel his horse galloping faster. He looked to Simona and she was looking back at him and it was confirmed without speaking that they were not hallucinating. They both set their eyes on Antonius who rode on in front of them.

"Julian, can I rely on you?" Antonius asked.

"Of course," Julian answered.

"Have you encountered a wolf-man before?"

"I have never stood against one before but I am aware of their strengths."

"I want you to prepare yourself. I need you to do something for me. I need you to ride on ahead of me and go to the frontline of the battle. Many of the soldiers and knights need more skilled people among them. Simona I want you to stay by Julian. Watch his back."

"If anyone should be there with them it is you," Julian said.

"I can't join them yet. I have to go check on Marcus."

"Is something wrong?" Simona asked.

"What happened?" Julian asked.

"I don't know. What I do know is that he is hurt." Antonius answered. "There are some others attending to him now. Xaria, Peter and Mitis and a few others are standing guard..."

As he was still speaking the power in him was still rising and he became more aware of every single person on the battle field. At that moment they were at the back fields in the lower valley of the battle field. They rode on passed a few bodies of dead soldiers and knights with the bodies of wolf-men already turned to ashes. Ahead Antonius sensed a wolf-man was charging straight for someone whose spirit was familiar to him. He looked on and saw John Hero standing back up after having taken down a wolf-man. His back was turned to the creature charging at him.

Antonius reached for a spear sticking straight up from the ground and launched it towards the wolf-man. The spear flew fast and passed just above John's head. He felt its force and it made his hair flap for a second. The spear brought down the creature and it growled in pain just as it turned to ashes. John turned and saw the creature changing. Then he turned and Antonius who was riding his way. Julian and

Simona were still with him. He smiled before he fell to one knee then he fell on his side. Michael was close by and after he brought down a wolf-man he rushed to his father's aid.

John was surprised to see Antonius. He smiled when he realized that it was Antonius who threw the spear. Antonius got down from his horse and rushed to John's side.

"Perhaps this battle was not mine to fight." John said then he coughed up blood.

"Father, please don't speak. Conserve what strength you have left." Michael said in concern.

"I should have listened to Liana. She desired I stay and not get involved but Sophia and Sandra understood that I had to go. They want nothing more than to see Astra safe again. I'm here helping that cause. But I should have listened to Liana. She always complains I'm too stubborn." He tried to laugh but he started coughing again. "Even now when death has come for me, I'm too stubborn to die. But this old soldier is not ready to go yet. Today is not the last day that I witness the break of dawn." John struggled to his feet. Michael helped him up. "Antonius, go on ahead, I'll be fine."

Antonius smiled and shook his hand. At the moment their hands met, John felt power flow into him and it made him feel a little better. Antonius mounted his horse. Julian and Simona got back on theirs as well. Before they rode off John nodded in Julian's direction. Julian understood the sentiment.

Julian and Simona rode on to the front ranks where the fighting was more intense. Antonius had seen that David and Jeffery were also there and he pointed Julian and Simona in the direction of Jeffery. He wanted them to assist Jeffery and those in the front ranks. Antonius rode to where Marcus was. Mitis, Xaria, and Peter were still with him. Upon seeing Antonius, a smile appeared on Marcus's face. Then he said when Antonius was close enough to hear.

"If it isn't the one man cavalry, just in time!"

"It is good to see you to brother." Antonius responded with a smile. "How bad is the injury?"

"I've healed him enough so he can walk but he may walk with a slight limp. The ankle was damaged severely." Peter said. "It's hard to concentrate with all that is going on around."

Once Peter finished speaking, Antonius looked to the sky and saw a guile falling quick and about to land on them. He caught it and threw it aside. He turned his eyes to the skies again, scanning the heavens for Josiah, then he saw him closer to the city in a fierce struggle against many guiles. Antonius extended his hand and helped Marcus up. Marcus put his arm over Xaria as he stood up. He put a little pressure on the ankle.

"It does not hurt as much as before," he said.

"Good. Stay here and rest a while," Antonius said.

"I have not come this far to sit this one out brother. We will finish this and we will finish it together."

"Agreed." Antonius responded then he said to Peter, "I've sensed Astra's spirit and I'm going for her but I'll need you to create a path for me."

"Astra is alive?" Mitis asked.

"Yes she is," Antonius said.

"It can be done. I'll meet up with Josiah and we'll clear a path for you."

Peter said then he started running towards the front ranks closer to where Josiah was fighting. Antonius mounted his horse. Mitis and Marcus insisted on going with Antonius so they both caught stray horses. They mounted the horse and set on. Marcus and Xaria shared a horse. But Xaria commanded the horse because she did not want to take any chances on Marcus putting too much stress on his leg. He was hesitant to let her but when she told him this he agreed.

They continued on and Antonius set his eyes to the skies again. He saw that Peter had made his way to Josiah and they were engaged in a heated battle against many guiles and were being successful in their efforts. The number of guiles in the skies was reducing quickly. Antonius's presence seemed to be giving them hope. Suddenly Antonius looked on in front and saw a wolf-man coming his way. The beast jumped at him but he felt a burst of power rise up in his spirit. He did not go for his sword instead he stretched his hand at the beast with an open palm. His power manifested itself with a great force that pushed the wolf-man several feet back. Marcus, Mitis and Xaria were astonished by Antonius's display of power.

Antonius looked on after he broke through the front ranks and was running on ahead of the army. There were still a great number of wolf-men coming his way. He called to Peter and once Peter spotted him, he knew it was time for him to create the path for Antonius. The gate of Noble city was about a quarter mile away from them. Peter still on the back of Josiah took a hold of his staff in his right hand and with his left hand up towards the sky he called down lightning that struck his left hand and flowed through him. It came out of the head of his staff splitting seven ways and taking down seven wolf-men. But there were many more coming so he thought of another way to clear a path for Antonius. He called down lightning again and it landed a few feet in front of Antonius. Antonius horse stopped and raised its front legs. Antonius looked to the skies and was about to reprimand Peter but he saw Peter was still concentrating his power. He turned and saw the blade of lightning started to move and then he realized this was Peter's way of making a path for him. No wolf-man or guile dared get close to the bright blade and all in its path were burnt up. He, Mitis, Marcus and Xaria continued on following the blade of lightning until they made it to the gate of the city.

Now it seemed the army was pressing on as well and the tide on the battlefield was changing. The knights and soldiers began to have an upper hand on the wolf-men and they followed Antonius. Jeffery mounted Simona's horse, pulled her onto the horse and together they followed after Mitis. Julian mounted his horse and stayed on course as well.

As Antonius rode through the city streets he saw the dead bodies of Philonian soldiers all over the place. This made him furious. As he passed by the cathedral he caught the glimpse of someone looking at him from an upper window. He could sense the spirit of all who were in the cathedral from Darius and the senators to many people he had met in the city. But he did not sense Titus until he was half-way from the palace. He saw it in the distance. He looked up and saw Josiah and Peter flying on towards the palace.

Jeffery, Julian and Simona were following along, as well as David, his children and the remaining soldiers and knights. When Antonius reached the palace gates two wolf-men charged at them. Antonius did not stop but rode straight at the first beast coming his way.

It launched itself at him. Antonius in an instant unsheathed his sword and drove it into the heart of the beast. He then threw it aside. Antonius stopped his horse and looked dead in the eyes of the other wolf-man. It was standing a few feet from him. The power in him was still flowing. His clothes began to glow a faint white. The beast felt scared and turned to run but Antonius threw his sword at it. It struck its neck and it came down. Antonius dismounted his horse, went and collected his sword then he pushed the gates open.

When he reached the front door he could clearly sense where Titus, Elana and Astra were. He could sense that Elana was in the west side of the palace and Titus was in the east. Peter called to him as Josiah flew down to him and landed close by.

"I know what you are thinking but you cannot face Elana alone. We'll go with you," Peter said.

"Peter is right, Elana is much stronger than you think. You cannot fight her alone," Josiah added.

At that moment, Jeffery, Julian and Simona arrived.

"I don't care how powerful she is; I will put an end to this. But first I have to make sure Astra is safe."

"Where is Astra? Where is she?" Mitis asked.

"She is in the palace but we may have to search around," Antonius said.

"Wherever you go, I go," Mitis said.

"Same with us brother," Marcus said. He was standing with Xaria supporting him.

Julian approached Antonius.

"I don't know the limits of your power but do you have an idea of where she is," Julian said.

Antonius puts his hands on Julian shoulders and said.

"Can I trust you to do something for me?"

"Name your request," Julian said.

"I want you, Jeffery and Simona to head east of the palace. If you meet Elana, do not confront her at any cost. Just run or call my name."

"I am not going anywhere with this man." Jeffery said.

"After all we accomplished together on the battlefield. I thought we really had a connection," Julian said.

"I disagree."

"Enough," Simona said. "Good luck Antonius and be safe." She said then embraced Antonius before she started heading to the east side of the palace. Jeffery followed after her and so did Julian. But he kept his distance from Jeffery.

They continued on searching room after room and came upon a large study room in the upper far-east corner of the palace. After Jeffery kicked the doors open, they saw that there was someone sitting in the chair at the other end of the room. It was Titus. His eyes were as the color of blood. He stood up slowly walked out from behind the desk. He walked out before them.

"Who is he?" Jeffery asked.

"I know him. He is Titus. Antonius's brother," Julian said. "Titus," he called out to him. But Titus did not respond.

"He does not look well," Simona said.

"No I don't think so. Look at his eyes. Those are not the eyes of a man who is in control of himself," Julian said.

"Perhaps it is the siren that is controlling him," Simona said. But Jeffery did not care so he said.

"Whether he is being controlled or not, I know the look in his eyes and those are the eyes of a man who is looking for a fight."

Meanwhile Antonius, Mitis, Marcus and Xaria, along with Peter and Josiah were heading towards the upper west area of the palace where Antonius, Peter and Josiah had sensed Elana's and Astra's spirit. As they ran down the hallway a wolf-man came from around the corner launching itself at them. But Antonius was quick and he tackled the creature broke its neck. They continued on and reached a room with very tall doors. It was the second throne room in the palace. Antonius pushed the high doors open and when they entered in, they beheld Elana.

Elana was sitting on the throne. She was not wearing a crown and she appeared to be in a milder form of the bird-creature transformation she sometimes assumed. She was sitting with her eyes closed and there was a spear laid across her feet. Two wolf-men much larger than the many they'd encountered were standing at the base of the steps that led up to the throne.

Antonius looked towards her right and saw Astra lying on the floor. Her spirit was faint and he was hurt seeing her like this.

Chapter 31
A Cursed Existence. The Siren's Last Trick

The sight of Elana on his throne was not his first concern. Seeing Astra lying where she was cast a burden on his heart and he could not stand it any longer. But he knew it would not be wise to act rash because he did not know much about this daughter of Sirius. All he knew was just that, she was a daughter of Sirius and knowing this alone he knew he would have to be careful in his dealings with her.

Antonius, Xaria, Marcus, Mitis, Peter and Josiah walked in slowly. There was silence as they walked in for they did not know if Elana had acknowledged them. Josiah looked outside and as he had foreseen the shadow of the moon was about to fall over Noble city. They walked half-way between the throne and the door before Elana opened her eyes and acknowledged their presence. The wolf-men that stood at the base of the steps leading up to the throne had made it known to Antonius and those with him that they were aware of their presence. They had gotten down on all fours and assumed a stance ready to attack but waited for Elana to give the command.

When they saw Elana open her eyes they stopped. Peter's gripped his staff tightly. Josiah's claws came out. Elana appeared very calm before them. This worried Peter especially because he knew her nature and she was most vindictive when she was even-tempered. This is what set her apart from many of her siblings. She did not seek out the destruction of men unless they crossed her and wronged her one way or another. She took a breath then said,

"Not a single one among you can comprehend the pain I have suffered since the day I was conceived until this very moment. Even now I am hurting. Not a single one of you know what it is like to be unwanted, what it is like to be alone, what it is like to be cursed. I was conceived of a forbidden union and because of my nature I could understand all that was said even when I was still in my mother's womb. Like my brothers and sister I tore my way out of my mother's womb and before she died she cursed me. Three millennia's and I still clearly remember her words and the bitterness in her voice. In time when I understood what I was I came to realize this one truth. I am not supposed to be, yet I am. This was twenty five years before that cursed war between the fathers of men and our fathers. My father had many wives, many who he deceived and made bare children who would bring pain and death to their mothers at child-birth. I have many brothers and sisters. Or rather I should say I had many brothers and sisters. Some of whom died during that cursed war. Over the years those that survived and tried to escape into the shadows were hunted down by Rising Guardians, children of Rising Guardians or the armies of men. I am one of the higher children of Sirius not because I was among those who were first born as is rumored but because I was conceived when Sirius was at the peak of his power. I never fought in that cursed war. My father and many of my elder brothers did but I never favored man nor fallen guardian. Their quarrels were all nonsense to me. But because of the curse The Great King laid on all the children of fallen guardians, I felt the demise of all of my brothers and the few of my sisters that met their end on the battlefield. Tell me Rising Guardian, do you know what it is like to suffer the pain of another? Do you know what it feels like to suffer because of the transgression of others? No Rising Guardian ever gives this thought though they know the nature of those who they persecute. You will never know such pain so you can never understand those who you hunt down and kill without regret." Elana bowed her head and gripped the arm of the throne. "It is one thing to suffer the pain of your siblings, and feel their death but that pain is nothing to the pain I felt when my father met his demise at the end of your father's blade with the help of that lovely man standing on your right."

Antonius turned to Peter who was standing on his right. Peter did not look back at him but kept his eyes on Elana. Elana was staring back at Peter.

"It is good to see you Peter."

"I don't believe you," Peter responded. His tone was strict.

"I am not surprised you don't believe me. You have always doubted my sincerity. Even though I kept my word and let you leave my island. It has been quite some time. How long has it been Peter?"

"Four centuries," Peter said.

"And yet it feels as if it happened last night. I trusted you to keep your word Peter that is why I let you leave. Do you remember the promise you made to me?"

Peter kept silent and bent his head low. He clearly remembered the promise he made to her. His silence and the gesture he made confirmed to her that he did remember. He had promised her before she let him leave her that he would not in any way cause her pain. He knew that the promise meant he could not battle against any of the children of Sirius. He had no choice but to make this promise to her before she let him leave.

"Did you forget that I could feel the pain of my brothers and sisters? Not only did you wage war against my brothers but you killed my father as well." Elana said and her voice shook when she spoke about her father.

"Gammon forced my hand." Peter replied. "He had no business being in Menyana. I was already fighting him when he revealed to me that he was a son of Sirius. I was conflicted because I remembered my promise to you and I knew battling him would bring you pain but I only caused him to flee from Menyana. I did not kill him."

"What about my father?" Elana asked.

Peter had no answer for her so Josiah stepped forward and said,

"The fate of Sirius was already sealed the moment he betrayed The Great King. All the fallen guardians who were banished after the War of the Fathers met their end at the hand of Rising Guardians who were going to take their place. It was no different with your father."

After Josiah spoke there was an uncomfortable silence that fell on the room. He, Antonius and Peter could feel Elana growing stronger. They watched on as she slowly stood up. She stretched her wings out to its full length and showed them her glory. They could feel a strong wind coming from her and encircling the room. The force of the wind pushed Xaria, Marcus and Mitis a bit back but Antonius, Peter and Josiah stood in place. Even the wolf-men bent low to keep steady. The windows and the balcony door in the throne room were blown open. Some of the feathers on her body began to turn to scales. Her eyes turned from mist green to dark red. She then responded to Josiah saying,

"How dare you speak to me like that?!"

She stretched her hand towards Josiah. At once he and Peter prepared themselves for the worst. But as they kept watch, they saw the spear at her feet rise up and enter her grasp. She put the head of the spear to Astra's neck and said.

"Perhaps I should return the favor."

"Astra!" Mitis shouted. "Leave her alone."

"Mitis don't," Marcus warned.

Mitis unsheathed his sword and started for the throne but Antonius put out his hand in his way.

"Get out of my way Antonius."

Antonius turned to Mitis and did not say a word. Mitis looked into his eyes. Antonius's stare was cold. Mitis put away his sword.

Peter and Josiah still assumed a stance ready for Elana to attack. But they kept still.

Antonius started walking towards the throne. As he walked closer he unsheathed his sword and to everyone surprise he dropped it. He stopped a few feet away from the steps leading up to the throne. The wolf-men wanted to attack him. But they watched on. Even Elana was curious to see what he was going to do. Antonius unlatched his armor and removed it. He removed all until he was in his trousers and boots. He still had on the cross of Sirius around his neck. When Elana saw this she was furious and wanted to turn the spear on him. She realized this was the reason she could barely sense him. She had only sensed him twice, both times were when the power within him had risen beyond the point the cross could conceal. He looked up at her and fell to his knees.

"Whatever hatred you have towards me, Peter or Josiah, we can settle it. But please I beg you, leave Astra out of this."

"Antonius!" Josiah called out angrily. "What are you doing? Stand up! You are disgracing yourself by kneeling before her."

"I don't care what I have to do for her to spare Astra's life. If Astra dies all our efforts are in vain." He looked up to Elana. "I may never truly know your pain and I wish I could undo the wrongs that have been done to you but it is not within my power. Whatever act you seek to take to attain your vengeance, take on me. Punish me anyway you desire. If I meet my end at your hand, so be it. But I beg you, please spare Astra."

The room went silent. Everyone watched and waited for Elana's response. She bit her lower lip and with a little hesitation retracted the tip of the spear from Astra's neck.

"I will punish all who have wronged me." Elana said. "Not only you Rising Guardian. I will spare her life and give her back to you because I see how much you love her. Also because you have done me a big favor by bringing me what I want."

Antonius did not understand what she meant nor did Josiah and Peter. They kept their eyes on her as she stretched her hand towards Astra. Astra's body was lifted off the ground and began to float. Elana brought down her hand but Astra's body continued to float. Slowly Astra's body floated Antonius's way. He opened his arms and received her. She could not stand on her own so he held her gently as he knelt to the ground with her. Her skin was cold and her breathing shallow. He embraced her. She wished to embrace him but she lacked the strength to lift her arms.

"I'm so sorry," Antonius whispered. "I'm so sorry I didn't come sooner."

"Antonius?" Astra murmured. Then she opened her eyes and saw him. She tried to smile but it faded quickly.

"It's alright."

"Antonius is she alive?" Mitis asked.

"Barely," Antonius responded.

Antonius picked her up, sweeping her off her feet. With great care he held her as he walked to Mitis. Mitis was glad to see his daughter and to be close to her again. He opened his hands to receive his daughter. As he was about to receive her from Antonius, he saw a spear pierced through Antonius's upper right chest. The spear extended far through Antonius and pricked Astra's left shoulder. Antonius took a step back and Mitis froze. He felt his grip of Astra slip. His right hand collapsed and he was about drop her but Mitis caught her before she fell from Antonius's grasp. Antonius fell to his knees.

"Antonius!" Marcus cried out.

Peter and Josiah were about to rush and help him but Elana swooped down quickly. With a backhand she smacked Peter across the room. She kicked Josiah across his face. The blow knocked him back. He slid across the floor and hit the wall close to the throne. Elana turned to Mitis, whose feet were still in place. He was holding Astra and looked terrified. His sights were on Elana and he felt powerless to do anything after just witnessing what she had done to Peter and Josiah.

"You better get her out of here before I change my mind. She is of little importance to me now."

Elana was now standing behind Antonius. Mitis carefully started walking backwards with his eyes on Elana until he left the room. Antonius kept trying to control his breathing. He tried to stay calm but the pain was insurmountable. His hands were on the floor as he was bent over still on his knees. He tried not to fall on the spear or on his side. He knew this would make things worse. Perhaps, he thought if he could pull it out he could keep his spirit calm and start healing himself.

He felt a presence behind him. He looked to the door and saw Mitis as he left with Astra. He felt a bit happy. At least she was safe. Elana took hold of the spear and with her left foot she stepped on his spine and forced him to the ground. The spear came back up until the head of the spear was in his upper chest. Antonius coughed out blood and felt a sharp pain shoot through his body. He was losing a lot of blood. But despite this he kept trying to keep himself calm. He reassured himself as long as Astra was safe he did not need to worry again. But it was hard for him to do anything for himself.

"Rising Guardian, oh Rising Guardian, I can tell you are trying to keep your spirit calm. Do not stress yourself trying to stay calm before you lose more blood. But as long as this spear stays in your body you cannot start healing yourself."

"Antonius, hold on." Marcus said then he unsheathed his sword. Xaria readied her bow and arrow and took aim at Elana.

"Do you even have an ounce of courage to let that arrow loose?" Elana asked Xaria. Xaria drew the arrow back against the bow but when she looked down at Antonius lying as if dead underneath the foot of Elana, she felt it was pointless. She had seen what Elana had done to Josiah and Peter. She slowly let down her arrow and lowered her bow. Elana heard Josiah growl as he got back up. Josiah looked at her with great rage in his eyes. The white fur underneath his eye had become a dark purple.

"Stay where you are Faracot unless you want to see him in worse pain. His life is like a thread in my hands now."

Josiah got back up and after Elana had spoken to him he was blind-sided by the wolf-men. They attacked him, he roared and tried to fight them but he was overpowered by them. One of the wolf-men held his head down in its arm and the other sunk its claws into his back. He roared in pain as they pinned him down.

Peter still hurting from his collision to the wall picked himself up and tried to plead with Elana but she silenced him. She proclaimed that it was too late for his apology. Four centuries too late. Elana stepped on Antonius again and she moved her leg up towards the lower part of his neck. She turned the spear-head. Antonius yelled out in pain.

"Let it out Rising Guardian. Call to the Great King. Let him hear your cries. Do you hear it? Not even a word. He is silent towards your pain as he was to mine. Keep screaming; now you only feel a fraction of the pain I felt when I woke up screaming the moment my brother met his end at your blade. I know you killed Gammon. Though his body is dead his spirit still lives and his spirit has been calling me for weeks. Calling me to free him and you have done me a great favor by bringing the one in whose spirit he speaks from."

She turned her eyes to Marcus.

"Open your eyes Rising Guardian and watch the rebirth of Gammon."

Immediately Elana's form began to change and she glowed with a frightening light coming from the center of her being. Her songs started to flow out of her as streams of light and it filled the room. All her feathers became like scales and the light that moved from her began to circle around Marcus. Everyone could hear her songs but only Marcus was affected because she focused much of her power on him. Marcus felt his head get heavy. He fell on his knees and held his temple. He let out a horrifying scream. Xaria was terrified and ran to help him up but he warned her to stay away. He looked to the ceiling and his eyes turned blood red. Xaria was persistent. With one hand he pushed her away and she slid back across the floor. Antonius with the last of his strength turned to Marcus and saw the horror that was overcoming his brother.

"No...Marcus," he said in pain.

Marcus groaned and yelled out again. His scream sounded like Gammon's roar.

"No, please, not again," Peter said.

"Fight it Marcus," Josiah said. "The battle is your spirit. Do not let Gammon overcome you."

Antonius watched on with a broken heart as his brother held his chest, struggled to stand to fall down again.

"Don't give up Marcus."

The lights began to enter his heart and he yelled again. Xaria in tears watched on. She felt there was no help for him. All would be lost if he let Gammon overcome his spirit and take over him. But she could not bear to see him suffer any longer. There was a stirring in her heart and she found a little courage. She ran, picked up her bow and arrow, and took aim at Elana. She fired but the arrow turned to dust before it touched Elana. Elana did not even turn to acknowledge what Xaria had done. She did not even consider her a threat at all.

Elana's song got stronger and pierced deeper into Marcus's spirit. Marcus was lifted up by the streams of terrifying light that surrounded him. As he was lifted up he let out one last cry before his body was no longer his. They watched on as his physical appearance began to change though he still appeared human. His hair got longer, thicker and more curled and he appeared taller. The manifestation of Elana's songs let him down slowly and everyone in the

room kept watch in silence. Elana stopped singing and the body landed on its feet.

The body was changed and different but
still appeared human. It was done. Elana had a
grin on her face. Antonius, Xaria, Josiah and
Peter beheld Gammon in his human form.

Chapter 32
A Plot for Redemption. A Brother's Decision

The whole shadow of the moon fell upon
Noble City as Gammon stood in his human
form and observed his body. He looked at his
hands, clenched and unclenched his fist. He
touched his face and smiled. Then he started
laughing. His laugh was terrifying and filled
the room. He turned Elana's way and started
walking to her.

"It's been far too long. I never would have
ever conceived the thought of you subduing
Antonius as you have. But then again you were
one of the few who could rival father so it's not
much of a surprise."

"I heard your spirit calling me. You bothered me even when I slept. So I had to come up
with a way to free you. So you'd stop whin-
ing."

Gammon smiled. "There is something different about you Elana." He said. "I can feel it

and see it. This new form is unusual for a siren."

Antonius stretched his hand towards Gammon. The effort it took to do just that caused him severe pain because the spear was still in his back.

"Marcus," he said with a shaky voice.

When Gammon heard what Antonius said he looked down at him and smiled.

"Marcus is dead," he said. "Take a good look around. Do you see your brother anywhere?"

Elana swiftly pulled the spear from Antonius back. She took a hand full of his hair and lifted him to his knees.

"This cannot be happening again. Not again," Peter said as he held his side and watched on.

Gammon took grabbed Antonius's by the neck.

"The last time we saw each other, I was the one on my knees . . . begging for mercy. Oh how the tables have turned Rising Guardian; or would you rather I call you by your name, brother?"

Antonius frowned and in anger reached up and took a hold of Gammon's neck. But his grip was weak and Gammon smiled as he pushed Antonius's hand off.

"Though Marcus is dead, his body was the foundation for my new body. So you could say we are brothers now Antonius."

"I...don't...believe...you. Marcus ... is alive." Antonius said struggling on each word uttered.

Antonius struggled to get himself free from Gammon's grasp. He could feel consciousness slipping from him. He kept one eyes open and controlled his breathing by taking shallow breathes when he could. His tried to keep his spirit calm. Gammon could feel this and he did not like it.

"Grant me another chance at him." Gammon said to Elana.

"Fine but do not kill him. That pleasure will be mine."

Gammon sighed. "Of course." He replied. He threw Antonius to the ground.

"It has been a long time since I have felt like this. Far before the years of that cursed War. Indeed, this is a new birth." Gammon then turned and said to Peter. "I know you never thought you'd see this day come again." He smiled, closed his eyes and took a deep breath. The ground began to quiver. Parts of the ceiling broke off and fell. A great force of power burst forth from Gammon. Seven of the twelve windows in the throne room shattered to dust. Gammon let out a loud roar as he started to transform. Gammon's body began to grow as he assumed his monstrous form. His wings burst from his back and they were unbroken.

As Gammon was still undergoing his transformation, Josiah let out a loud roar. He shook off the wolf-man that held his head. He leaped into the air with the wolf-man that still had its claw in his back. He flew up and smashed into the ceiling with the wolf-man. Though this caused him pain he did not care. He turned upside down and the wolf-man fell. He flew down fast charging at the wolf-man he had shaken off himself. He brought out his claw and sunk it into the side of its head as he pushed its head to the ground. The wolf-man's skull shattered beneath his paw. Josiah then let out a roar so terrifying that it shook the foundation of the palace. The second wolf-man ran away. Elana turned to him for a moment. She was surprised at his power.

Peter saw that Elana was distracted by what Josiah had just done. He was not going to let this chance escape. He focused his power and through his staff he called down lightning. From the sky a blade of lightning rushed in through an open window heading for Elana. At the moment she saw it she covered herself with her wings but the lightning still struck her and knocked her back. Elana used her wings to create a resistance that stopped her from hitting the wall. She landed and glared at Peter. Peter saw her form changed slightly again. He also began to feel a greater evil in her growing stronger as she changed. This same evil he had felt when he was a child and his father fought one of the higher child of the fallen guardian whose place his father took. His father after he defeated the fallen guardian's child explained to Peter that the higher child of that fallen guardian was very powerful because it had given its will to Rudraco and Rudraco had given a portion of his power to it. He told Peter that Rudraco's presence is distinct. It is colder than any guile, wolf-men, or child of a fallen guardian and viler than any of the fallen guardians. He told Peter that he'll know when he feels such an evil. And that when he does, he should know that Rudraco's hand had something in it.

Elana rushed Peter. Peter was still a bit shaken when he realized the source of the evil presence he felt in Elana. He came to himself and tried to dodge her but it was too late. She tackled him and flew out the throne room. Josiah immediately followed after them. Elana flew higher then she took Peter's hand, spun and threw him towards the earth. Josiah was quick enough to stop Peter in the air. Peter got on Josiah's back.

"Elana has aligned herself with Rudraco," Peter said. "It's not going to be easy taking her down."

"I had my suspicions about this," Josiah replied. "I felt something familiar in her the moment she began to transform herself."

"Though she has aligned herself with Rudraco, she still has a strong desire to kill us for what we did to Sirius. Her will is still intact."

As they spoke between themselves they could feel the power in Antonius falling and his spirit fading. They knew he should have been dead but the Twelfth was the only one standing between him and death.

"Maybe we should go back and help Antonius," Josiah suggested.

"Look at who is before us," Peter said. "Do you think she is going to let us?"

"I see your point."

They saw Elana spread her wings then she pulled them back. She started diving fast towards them.

Meanwhile in the throne room Antonius took a breath and as he kept calm he could feel the power in him rising but at a slow rate. He struggled to his feet but once he stood up straight Gammon kicked him back down. He slid close to his sword. As Antonius struggled to his feet again Gammon heard Xaria whisper Marcus's name. He turned and saw her on her knees weeping. He said as he walked her way.

"Marcus is dead. And you'll be joining him."

He was about to take a hold of her but Antonius called him.

"Gammon, your battle is with me."

Gammon turned his way. Antonius was now standing again but with a slumped posture. His right side was heavy. He was holding his right shoulder with his left hand. He had his sword in his right hand. He could barely move the arm let alone swing it. But he tried to keep his grip of his sword tight while staying calm. The wound on his upper right chest stopped bleeding and the hole seemed to be closing.

"Look at yourself." Gammon said. "You can barely stand and you aren't even holding your sword well. It is sad. And saddest of all I know you don't even have the will to fight me." Gammon shrugged. "Very well. You are making this too easy for me." He rushed Antonius.

Antonius breathing was heavy. He saw Gammon coming his way fast. For a moment everything around him seemed to slow down as he took control of his breathing. Much of the strength he had he was using to maintain his balance but after he breathed deeply he began to feel his power rising again. He readied himself for Gammon but as Gammon drew closer about to tackle him, he heard a voice call his name. He recognized the voice of the one who called his name. It was Marcus's voice. Gammon rammed his head into Antonius chest. Antonius flew back and slid across the floor until his back met the base step leading up to the throne. He heard something crack.

Antonius felt all the air leave his lungs in that moment. He coughed and tried to catch his breath. He held onto his side as he tried again to get back up to his feet. This made Gammon angry and he went after Antonius again. He lifted Antonius and threw him out of one of the windows. Antonius landed hard among the shrubs somewhere in the palace garden. He lost his grip of his sword as he fell down. It landed somewhere close by. He rolled on his stomach, looked around and when he saw it he started crawling towards it. But Gammon from above came down on him and landed on his back. Antonius felt his ribs shatter. In that moment as he laid there broken he could feel death slowly falling on him like a creeping shadow. But Antonius felt someone push this shadow away every time he felt it coming closer to him. He knew it was the Twelfth who kept him from passing on. His hope was gone but yet the Twelfth would not let him be. Antonius closed his eyes and within his spirit he pleaded with the Twelfth.

"Leave me to die." He said in his spirit and the Twelfth heard him. "My body is broken and the pain is too great. Please leave me to die."

After Antonius made this plea he felt stillness all around. It was awfully quiet. Then he heard a voice calmly call his name. It was the voice of Marcus. Antonius felt the shadow of death move faster but the Twelfth pushed it away again. But the manner in which he felt it was different. All the pain in his body was subsiding and he heard Marcus call his name again. It sounded as if Marcus was very close to him. Antonius opened his eyes and found himself in the middle of a field. He was lying on his stomach. All the pain he felt faded away. He rolled over on his back and when he looked up he saw Marcus standing next to him. Marcus stretched his hand to help him up.

"Brother?" Antonius said surprised to see Marcus. He was confused by all that was going on. The sky above them appeared red and lightning shot across the sky. The landscapes in the distance were quaking.

"I thought you were dead." Antonius said

Marcus appeared very displeased with Antonius. Antonius could see it but did not understand why.

"Why are you restraining your powers Antonius?" Marcus asked.

"I don't understand what you mean."

"You're still not very good at lying. You know what I mean."

Antonius looked away from his brother, and then he clenched his fist and said.

"I couldn't fight Gammon knowing that there could be a chance that your spirit was still alive within him. The longer I stood against him that chance became a truth. I could still sense you. I know that your spirit is still alive within him."

"And you fear that if you fight Gammon and defeat him, you also shall bring about my end."

"Yes." Antonius responded with regret.

"Look around you Antonius," Marcus said.

Antonius set his eyes to the skies and as he kept still he could feel the slight rumble of the ground beneath them. He saw that the lands around and the skies above appeared to be unsettled. The grasses in the fields they stood were slowly losing their lush green appearance and becoming a dead grey.

"Do you know where we are Antonius?"

"No I don't. But it seems as though life is leaving this place."

Marcus closed his eyes. A small smile appeared on his face. He opened his eyes, set his sights to the skies then he turned around and looked far into the distance.

"We are in my spirit. Life is leaving this place. My spirit cannot sustain itself here because of the presence of Gammon. It is slowly withering away, seeking to be free. But once my spirit is free, my time on the earth will be done. I will soon die Antonius." He turned to Antonius and Antonius saw the tear that escaped from his left eye. "I am prepared to die Antonius."

"No, no, brother, do not say that!" Antonius said. "There must be another way. There must be another..."

The ground beneath them shook very violently as Antonius was still speaking. Antonius was shaken off his feet. Marcus was still standing. As Antonius picked himself up Marcus said to him.

"The Twelfth is the one who sent you here and he is the one who holds you from being overcome by death. But he cannot do it for much longer. If you let Gammon overcome you, he and his sister along with other children of Sirius that may still be out there will set humanity under their feet. And things shall be that way until another Rising Guardian is chosen and stands against them. But who knows when that will be? The lives lost between those times will forever weigh on your conscious brother. Even in death you will not be able to forgive yourself."

Marcus went closer to Antonius then he embraced him. Then he said while in his embrace.

"Defeat Gammon and do not worry about me. I have said my prayers and I have heard the Great King's voice. I am ready to go."

Antonius held onto Marcus and did not want to let go. Marcus said while still in his brother's arms.

"I can already hear the songs of Pacifica. The voices of the pure and transcendent Guardians are clearly falling on my ears. Be still and win brother."

Antonius could feel himself fading away from there. All around him went dark again. He heard someone yell him name. It was Peter. He could hear Peter yelling from the skies telling him to stand and fight. Peter and Josiah still had their hands full with Elana. She was proving to be of great difficulty to them.

Antonius could feel the pain again. He knew he was back in his body. He opened his eyes to find himself in the palace garden. He was next to a tall statue. He noticed his sword was nowhere close by when he looked around. He saw Gammon coming his way and as he got back up to his feet, using the statue to pull himself up, he saw his sword behind Gammon. When he was up to his feet, he could feel the power rising in him. The pain in his upper shoulder was dissipating and the wound was closing up.

Antonius controlled his breathing and kept calm. He could hear Gammon's wicked laugh. He looked Gammon's way and saw him standing about fifteen meters away.

"I'm surprised you can still stand after all this," Gammon said.

Antonius set his eyes to the skies and in the distance behind Gammon he saw Peter and Josiah being pursued by Elana. Peter and Josiah were still having a hard time against her. Every time Peter called down lighting, Elana would dodge it or deflect it his way. Josiah dared not fly close to fight her because Peter had warned him that Elana was very skilled in close confrontations.

Antonius turned his attention back to Gammon who was now taking quick steps his

way. He started running towards Antonius.
Antonius could feel the power in him rising. He
kept still and baited Gammon. Antonius did
not want Gammon to be aware that his power
was being restored. The second before Gammon tackled Antonius, Antonius side stepped
him and ran for his sword. Gammon ran head
first into the statue and it came crashing down
on him. After Antonius collected his sword he
stood ready against Gammon. The hole on his
upper right chest closed and the wound continued healing. He started to regain the feeling
in his right arm. He clenched his sword harder
then released his grip a little to confirm the feeling was returning.

Gammon came back up from the rubble
and growled. Antonius smiled a little when he
saw Gammon rise from the rubble.

"You think this is funny?" Gammon asked.
He stepped forward from the rubble and started charging at Antonius again. Antonius took
his sword in both hands and prepared himself.
Gammon rushed at Antonius and started
swinging his claws. Antonius used his sword to
defend himself against Gammon's claws.
Gammon came with a strike from overhead but
Antonius dodged it, side-stepped Gammon
and slashed at his side. The cut was deep. Antonius jumped back and took his stance. Gammon held onto the wound and fell to one knee.
Immediately Antonius heard Elana scream.
Then he saw lightning shoot across the sky. He

turned his attention back to Gammon who was slowly getting back up. Red blood was flowing from his wound. This was strange to Antonius because he remembered that the last time he caused Gammon's blood to flow it came out black.

Gammon stood up and rushed at him again. Gammon continued to claw and throw punches at Antonius. Antonius used his sword to sway away Gammon's claws and he dodged many of Gammon's punches. But one from above struck him across the face. He was knocked back and fell on his face. He lost his grip of his sword.

"I don't care if Elana will be mad at me for killing you. But at this point I really don't care. This has gone on long enough Antonius. The games end here."

Gammon raised his hand high and with a clenched fist. He wanted to crush Antonius where he lay. Before he could bring down his arm three arrows struck him. Two hit him in the side where Antonius had cut him and one close to his heart. Gammon set his eyes to where the arrows flew and saw Xaria standing at the end of the garden. Gammon was distracted for that moment. Antonius saw this as his chance. He collected his sword. Gammon pulled out the arrow that was close to his heart first but before could go for the other arrows he noticed that Antonius had picked up his sword. Gammon disregarded the other two arrows and charged at Antonius. Antonius dodged his attack. Antonius saw that Gammon in his carelessness had left himself open. He saw the opening and without hesitation drove his sword through Gammon's heart. Gammon stood frozen as the cold steel remained in him. He looked down at it and at Antonius. The sword appeared to glow for a short moment then it returned to its silver shine. Gammon blood ran down the blade, onto the hilt and on Antonius hand's. Antonius was looking up at Gammon and saw his form was changing again. Immediately he heard a scream that shook his heart. It was loud and freighting. It was Elana.

Peter saw his chance now that Gammon had been wounded severely. Elana was hurt as well. He leaped off Josiah and dove fast for Elana who was hovering in the air holding her chest and weeping. Peter used his staff and hit her side. Josiah flew down and caught him. At once Peter called down a blade of lightning which pierced through Elana's heart. She died before her body hit the earth.

Antonius felt a raindrop land on his ear. The shadow of the moon had completely passed over Noble City. But the sky had become overcast and grey. As Gammon's form became more human again, Antonius drew back his sword. He kept his eyes on Gammon's face and as the face continued to change he realized that the face and body taking form was that of Marcus. Gammon was no more. Marcus still had the wounds inflicted on Gammon. And when he came to himself he began to fall back but Antonius caught him and supported his head.

"No, no brother…this cannot be happening. Please." Antonius said his voice breaking with every word.

Marcus's eyes appeared glazed and he looked terrified. He shook as if he was convulsing then he stopped and realized where he was. His chest was bare and the wounds remained. Marcus looked to Antonius and said.

"You did it." His voice was shaky and weak. Xaria realizing what just happened ran over. She knelt by his side and when she saw his wounds her eyes welled up with tears. Marcus looked to his wife and smiled. She apologized to him as she reached for one of the arrows with trembling hands. But Marcus took her hand gently.

"Don't."

He put his hand on her face and said to her as he wiped the first tear that escaped from her eyes.

"I don't have much longer."

He closed his eyes and as a tear escaped his eye, a raindrop landed on his cheek. He looked to Antonius who was still a bit frantic.

"Be still brother." He said then he coughed. "You never left me in the dirt. You never left me lying in the dirt brother." Antonius saw that

Marcus's eyes were set somewhere behind him. He turned and saw that they were close to the tree where his mother found him crying in the garden.

Marcus turned to Xaria whose tears were flowing. He professed to her.

"I love you."

She took a hold his face and kissed him.

"I love you too." She professed with a trembling voice.

Marcus closed his eyes and they saw a smile appear on his face as a tear ran down his cheek. Then in a calm voice he said,

"Yes father I remember, I remember."

Antonius held Marcus closer as his breathing slowed and he went silent. Antonius took off the cross around his neck and threw aside. It landed on the edge of his blade, which was covered in blood and mud. He and Xaria wept as a calm wind blew by them. Not long after the heavens opened up and the earth was drenched in rain.

Epilogue
An Unfortunate Revelation

At the moment Peter struck down Elana, Titus was released from his trance and Jeffery, Julian and Simona were able to subdue him. Before then it had been a great task taking him on. Jeffery wanted to go against him alone but after the spell-bound Titus proved to be stronger than he appeared Julian and Simona fought with Jeffery but they did not make much of a difference. As he was being held down by Jeffery he began shaking violently then he yelled and beat his chest. He broke free from Jeffery's grasp and realized where he was. He appeared very confused. Jeffery helped him up and after he explained what happened to him, Jeffery told him everything that happened from the moment Astra was taken until Antonius joined the battle and he made it possible for them to advance to the palace. Titus asked after Antonius. Jeffery had no response for him so Titus left them and ran in search of his brother.

The rains beat down hard on Noble City as the Twelfth Rising Guardian wept over the body of his fallen brother. But in his heart he felt somehow the wrong he had done could be undone. He hoped that The Great King could restore Marcus's life. Peter and Josiah landed just as Antonius lifted the lifeless body of Marcus. Peter and Josiah were silent as they watched Antonius. Xaria asked where he was going but he did not give her an answer. Peter went to Xaria to console her. Josiah put his wing over them as Peter led her back into the palace and reassured her that he'll keep an eye on Antonius.

Antonius walked with the body of his brother in his arms through the wet dead streets of Noble City. He was heading to the cathedral. When he got to the tall doors of that Mighty structure he looked to the skies and yelled. His powers pulled the doors open and he saw the people of Noble City gathered in the cathedral. Darius was closest to the door and was the first to see Antonius enter. The people began to look his way and saw the king they abandoned carrying the king they felt abandoned them, they felt broken. They could feel his brokenness. Antonius did not set his eyes on the multitude before him but on the altar in the distance at the other end of the cathedral. Darius wanted to speak to Antonius but he judged the situation and knew no words could help. Antonius started taking slow steps towards the altar and as he advanced the crowd made way for him. Half-way he fell to one knee and dropped Marcus's body. He crawled to Marcus's body and as he lifted up the body, Cara, a young female senator helped him. He continued and when he reached the steps of the altar he laid Marcus's body down and let out a loud cry that shook the foundations of the cathedral. He fell over Marcus's body and appeared as if dead.

After Peter had taken Xaria in from the rain, he went outside, found Elana's body and took her to a stream about three miles north. Josiah stayed with Xaria. Peter went and buried Elana's body by the stream and he said a little prayer before he left her. When he returned to Noble City he saw that many people were gathered outside the doors of the cathedral. He was aware that Antonius was in the cathedral. He could sense his spirit and knew that sorrow had greatly overcome Antonius. Peter went into the cathedral and saw Antonius at the feet of the altar and the body of Marcus behind him. He had nothing yet to say to Antonius but he knew it was not right for Marcus's body to lay there. He went to take the body but as he approached he could feel Antonius's sorrow and it weighed heavy on his heart. He felt as though a great stone had been put on his back and he could not walk well. He held his heart and endured it. He picked up Marcus and took him from there to the palace.

When he arrived at the palace with Marcus's body, Jeffery, Julian, and Titus met him at the door. Titus wept when he saw Marcus. He immediately recognized him though he had not seen him in a little over nine years. They took his body to one of the palace chapel and prepared his body for burial there. But they did not bury him yet. Jeffery asked Peter how Antonius was but Peter in response shook his head and responded that Antonius was not doing well.

❖

The Jewel of Konstuliana awoke to see her father standing by her side. Astra was in one of the royal chambers in the palace when she woke up. Mitis gave her a cup of water to drink. David's daughter Hedona and Helena were helping Mitis attend to her needs. There was a knock on the door and after Mitis gave word for the person to come in, the door creak open slowly and Simona walked in. Astra turned to her cousin and though she was weak she smiled and reached out her hand towards Simona. Simona went and sat on her side, took her hand and kissed it. Simona smiled then embraced her. Mitis asked Simona, Helena and Hedona to remain with Astra. As he got up to leave Astra with a weak voice asked about Antonius. Mitis hung his head, turned and urged her not to speak. He urged her to rest. Then he assured her he'll be back. Mitis left them and went in search of Peter. He found Peter with Jeffery, Julian and Titus in the chapel. When he saw a body being prepared for burial he approached slowly. When he came close enough to see that it was Marcus, he covered his mouth with his hand, raised his eyebrows and ran his hands through his hair. The silence in the room spoke magnitudes about the grimness of the situation.

Peter left the chapel and went to check on Xaria. She was in the queen's chamber and Josiah was in the outer part of the chamber watching her.

Peter entered the chamber and met Josiah who had kept his eyes on Xaria as she lay in bed. When Josiah saw Peter he urged Peter to be quiet for he did not want Xaria to know that he had not left yet. Josiah had been feeling something strange about Xaria's spirit. He brought this up with Peter and Peter confirmed he had been feeling something strange about her spirit as well.

"There has been something peculiar about this feeling as well." Peter said as he kept his voice low.

"Yes it is too familiar and troubling."

"It is like two spirits are in her body," Josiah said.

Then it dawned on Peter and he said,

"She is pregnant."

"But…when?" Josiah asked.

"But there is something wrong with this second spirit." Peter said then when he realized who he sensed he clenched his staff. "I can still sense a little of Gammon in her. He is in the spirit of the child."

"She must have conceived the child when Marcus was still cursed. These fallen children always have a way of leaving their spirits to linger in the world of men. If that child is born he will be born cursed."

"Then what shall we do?" Peter said.

"We can't do anything for the child. We don't have that kind of power. Only a small group of people whose existence is questioned

have the power to forever vanquish the presence of lingering spirits in this world."

"The Saints," Peter said.